THE
SECOND COMING

Robert Marshall

A Bright Pen Book

Copyright © Robert Marshall 2014

All rights reserved. No part of this publication may be reproduced, stored in a retrieval system, or transmitted in any form or by any means, electronic, mechanical, photocopy, recording or otherwise, without prior written permission of the copyright owner. Nor can it be circulated in any form of binding or cover other than that in which it is published and without similar condition including this condition being imposed on a subsequent purchaser.

British Library Cataloguing Publication Data.
A catalogue record for this book is available from the British Library

ISBN 978-0-7552-1629-1

Authors OnLine Ltd
19 The Cinques
Gamlingay, Sandy
Bedfordshire SG19 3NU
England

This book is also available in e-book format, details of which are available at www.authorsonline.co.uk

Author's Note

"All truth passes through three stages. First it is ridiculed, second it is violently opposed and third it is accepted as self evident."
Arthur Schopenhaue

This is a fictional work written to entertain and encourage those with curious and open minds to scratch below the surface of what we are taught. It is the result of much contemplation and soul searching which has led me on an amazing personal journey of discovery. If you experience half the pleasure, wonder and eureka moments reading it as I had researching and writing it then I will be very happy.

With their permission, the characters Morgan and Pender are based very loosely indeed upon two real historical researchers, Alan Wilson and Baram Blackett and some of the mighty odd things that have happened to and around them since they discovered, amongst other things, evidence for a real king Arthur in South East Wales. A list of their thought provoking research is listed at the back of this book and I thank them and a host of others for their help and co-operation over a number of years in putting this project together.

Wilson and Blackett also observed that the accurate translation of the most ancient Welsh texts illustrate a very different history to that re-written by Stubbs and Guest to support the Saxon supremacy and Hanoverian line. Our hidden history is far more exciting.

So far as I can ascertain, the historical characters, items and some events mentioned in this book are real and factual. The majority of the living modern day people do not exist and those that do have been given names and persona to protect their identity. Many of the things referred to actually happened, though maybe not exactly as they are written here.

I have seen and photographed both the memorial stone to King Arthur and the metal cross mentioned in this book. They really were discovered at a dig at St Peters Super Montem church in 1990, and, so far as I am aware, they are hidden safely until the time is right for them to emerge.

Science has now confirmed that there was a multiple comet strike in the UK and some of Europe in the 6th century and that amounts of an unknown unique and sought after substance may well have been present at the sites of impact.

It is also true that a film crew captured some of the interviews and footage referred to in this book. A list of the actual clips is included at the back of this work. Some are available online and most are available on DVD. After interest from the BBC and some other broadcasters it is also correct that the documentaries proposed were side-lined, apparently because of the nature of their content.It should not go unnoticed that Sir Isaac Newton was perfectly aware of the situation regarding the original nature of Jesus and the original version of Christianity but that he choose to lock them away rather than risk his reputation and reveal them. As a leading member of the "Enlightenment" however, he was almost certainy instrumental in keeping the truth alive using various hidden codes and messages. A whole book could be written just on them. Over the years various threats have been made to some of those trying to bring this history to light and there appear to have been some very mysterious deaths along the way.

Parts of sky discs referred to in the story have been found in the UK but I have superimposed some of the details from the Nebra Sky disc onto those finds for the purpose of this story. Recent archaeology suggests that these were commonly owned by the ancient elders of many peoples who had an urgent and intimate relationship with the heavens. No-where is this better illustrated than in cup marks in the shapes of stars and constellations on some standing stones in Wales. If you search the internet regarding the constellation Cygnus and the imploded supernova in its vicinity you will find many interesting revelations propounded by those scientists much more eminent than I.

As you well know, dear reader, truth is much stranger than fiction, and so, in the interests of confidentiality and safety I will leave you to sift fact from fantasy.

This story may lead the enlightened to some real historic sites owned and protected by the church and others. Standing at them and absorbing the atmosphere is a most wonderful experience to share, particularly for those with sensitive or "psychic" gifts. Do remember to be very careful. These are sites that many would like to see legally and properly explored and many more would like to see hidden and forgotten. Most are under some sort of surveillance. I'd just like to make it clear that whilst I am passionate about discovering our real history I do not condone the digging for, or removal of, antiquities for commercial or other benefits without proper permission and investigation. If you have a chance please do visit some or all of the locations mentioned in this book but go with an open mind and take only photographs and memories.

In my personal life, despite experiences to the contrary I like to think that there is good in every one, whoever we are, whatever we believe in and wherever we may be, and, that if enough of that sunlight shines the world will be a better place.

In the words of the late Dave Allen, "may your God go with you, whoever he may be."

Robert William Marshall
Inner Temple, London, 2013.

Author's Web Page

www.thesecondcomingblog.com

-1-

The City of Caradoc, Winter AD 580

The cruel wind of change from the north whistled in slicing gusts. It tore relentlessly at Illtyd's gold trimmed, white linen tunic as he stood on top of the ruined tower of St Peter's Church like an eagle preparing for flight. He fought the stinging hailstones, brushed long grey strands of hair from his eyes and pulled animal skins tightly across his shoulders to counteract the early morning's icy blast. At least his mind could escape the elements as it wandered off to fond memories of childhood days in Brittany when he, Arthur, Samson, Gildas and Gennovasius were Breton brothers.

But all things must come to pass and these were troubled times.

He was standing on the holy ground where Joseph of Arimathea, James, Peter and the others had lived in beehive hermitages half a millennia before. This place was a portal and he closed his tired eyes to commune with the Infinite; seeking guidance on what he should do.

The veil between the living and the dead is thinnest just before the dawn. Only now had he discovered how the Great Bear, Arthur, his cousin had died. He was a ruthless giant of a man with long black hair and fiery eyes; he was built like an ox with the strength of a lion and the cunning of a fox. With his power and charisma he had kept the invaders at bay throughout his reign. When he was 67, he met the Saxons head on and delivered them the most bloody of all blows at the Battle of Baedon, just a few miles away. Now he, the defender of Britain, was dead; murdered in a far off land by a native assassin with a bow and poisoned arrows.

Illtyd held on tightly to the metal cross that the alchemist, Merthyn, had made in honour of the great man. It was crafted from gold, silver and an unearthly material found in the craters formed by the ravages of the recent comets. The new amalgam was luminescent in the morning light. He held onto it tightly as if his grip alone could bring Arthur back to life. Hurriedly, he scratched the secret signs on the back of the memorial, hoping that one day they would benefit those who fought the battle for light against darkness.

"One day an infant shall be born and this cross shall lead the way."

In the distance he heard a constant drumming, like a heartbeat. Peering through the morning mist, he could see a procession of torches winding their way from the sea. They were bringing the bodies of Arthur and his wife, Gwynfar, back to the city of Caradoc for the last time.

He recalled Madoc's vivid description of their deaths and he wretched with revulsion. Natives had slit the throats of the guards at the makeshift fort before sneaking into Arthur's tent and shooting him at point blank range. Despite his wounds, he rose to his feet and killed two of them before the poison killed him. They restrained Gwnfar, stripped her naked and slit her open from top to bottom, in the process slicing her unborn child in two. Blood and entrails spilled across the ground. The attackers were caught and boiled alive but that was little comfort to those remaining or to the great British Nation who believed that Arthur was immortal.

Illtyd's hair became a tangled mess in the furious wind. His mind filled with confusion and apprehension. Tears rained from his eyes as he kissed the cross and held it close to his chest. It flashed, sparked and throbbed in unison with the approaching drum beat. Was it the cross or was it just an echo from his yearning heart?

Dark clouds moved across the sky like the arch angel Azael spreading his wings. He stood in meditation, chanting words from a time no one could remember, words handed down in the oral tradition when his forefathers were driven out of Egypt.

Slowly he turned to face the rising sun, now just a diffused ochre glow through the driving hail that poured blood red onto the hills and valleys that Arthur had once called home. From his vantage point he could see the funeral procession meanandering along the old cattle track. One by one the white robed dignitaries appeared through the morning mist and the forests of pine below the mountain top on which stood the city of Caradoc.

A mixture of smells drifted up to him from the settlement. He detected the aroma of meat and vegetables and of Hawthorne and oak. The cleansing scents of sage and wode rose from the fires around the burial chamber which had been cleaved into the hillside outside the city gates. The smoke kept the evil spirits away from the ethereal body until it had completed its journey to the other world.

Once, this place had been much bigger and more important. It had been the great fabled city of Caer Caradoc, a place where King Caradoc, aka, Caractacus, had lived in a stunning castle and from where he had ruled over so much of the country. His reputation for fighting the Romans was legendary but, now, he too was buried nearby, on the highest part of the mountain. Once he was betrayed, captured and taken to Rome to be paraded before baying mobs. The intention was to execute him, but, his eloquence, strength and passion saved him from that fate and secured him a place of reverence amongst the ruling elite. He achieved the impossible; he took Christianity in its purest form to the imperial city and lived to tell the tale. Like Arthur he had become a legend in his own lifetime, but time makes a mockery of us all.

Many places in mid and Western Britain, including the mountain top city of Caradoc had taken the full force of the multiple comet strike around AD 562. The cataclysmic event wiped out thousands of lives through fires, pestilence and sickness heralding a dark age for decades. Sixty years on, people had begun to return and repopulate, regenerating their culture and community from scratch. Only a few of the buildings and a small part of the church had survived. Now it was being rebuilt together with the college and religious dormitories that surrounded it.

The destruction of lives and homes had left most of Britain a barren wasteland. The Saxons, the Irish raiders and others were taking advantage of this weakened state by infiltrating beyond East Anglia into communities which could no longer defend themselves. Only the forces under the command of Arthur and the kingship of his father Meurig had managed to keep them at bay, and now within the year, they were both dead. This crisis had no obvious solution. Arthur's older sons had died fighting the Vandals and the Mercians; only two survived, those from his latest marriage, but they were too young to take control.

Reluctantly, Illtyd had gone along with the plan of the elders to hide the passing of Arthur. Only a precious few knew of his death. That way, they figured, they would be safer from attack. After their humiliating defeat at Baedon, the Saxons wouldn't cause any more trouble so long as they believed Arthur was in charge. Illtyd smiled to himself as he recalled the victory that day. He was proud to have been there, fighting alongside his kith and kin. He wore deep scars to prove it. His heart went out to those that died each one a hero.

So, on this cold winter morning the procession led the "unknown" bodies across the plain, through the Pass of the Soldier to the main gates of the city where the grave cave had been dug into the side of the mountain and a stone erected to the unknown who fell defending their country and their people. This stone formed the last of a circle of twelve stones that honoured the fallen heroes from the time of Caradoc in the first century, including those that had died at the treacherous hands of Hengist and his Saxon thugs at the so called Peace conference held nearby. Now, finally, Arthur and his men and the twelve great battles they had fought to rid the country of the Saxons, the Irish and other raiders, would be remembered for ever. It was the national monument erected to mark the famous victories, the Round Table of Fallen Knights, the place where they could be revered and mourned. This would be the Grave Monument of the Soldiers, (Munwent y Milwar) and part of the mountain would retain the name and their glory forever.

To the locals that gathered in the dawn's early light, these bodies, supposedly of two unknown knights, represented a whole army to be honoured. In keeping with tradition the rest of the dead, in their thousands from all sides, were buried around the ridges of the battlefields on which they fell. If they were suspicious or curious about whom the bodies actually were it was not obvious. The giant Merthyn, man of Carmarthen, also known as Taliesin, made notes for the "Songs of the Graves", the great book of remembrance which recorded for all time the place of the burials of the important and famous, lest, in days to come, they might be forgotten.

From his lofty view point Illtyd could see the procession arriving and gathering around the grave. The carefully embalmed bodies, encased in gold suits of armour and wrapped in deerskins were being placed on tables decorated by white cloth with a red cross in the corners, the emblem of Joseph of Arimathea, the man, who with Simon, Peter, Mary and Jesus himself, had brought true Christianity to these shores. As the oiled protective skins were pulled away, the two knights in golden armour reflected the rising sun, glowing gold, pulsating, glinting with power and energy. Merthyn was standing over the bodies chanting. Some joined in while others offered flowers, prayers, trinkets and bowls of food to assist on their journey to the afterlife.

Illtyd carefully made his way down from the ruined tower of St Peter's Church and into what was once the centre of the old building. The roof was a charred skeleton and the glazed patterned floor tiles showed marks of great burning from the anger of the comet.

Making sure that he was alone, Illtyd carefully lifted two of the floor tiles with an iron bracket that lay in the ruins. He scraped out soil from the compacted earth and took one last look at the sacred cross and the engraving, *Pro Anima Artorius*, (for the soul of Arthur). He held it to his chest then kissed it. As he did, tears fell onto the freshly engraved magical symbols he'd carved on the back.

"We will never forget you, may God forgive us for hiding this secret along with your body and may the tales of your greatness inspire generations to come and empower them to strive for what is right and good. Rest in peace Arthur, our once and future King."

Following the dedication he buried the cross in the earth and replaced the dislodged burnt green glazed tiles, in the process hiding a beacon of light in a world of darkness.

Deep in reflection Illtyd made his way back across the ancient track that led around the derelict walls of the old city. Carefully he picked his way across the loose stones to the gathering where Merthyn stepped forward and embraced him. He could see the hopelessness and apprehension in his eyes; "Be strong my brother Illtyd."

Together they took the service of burial and the rights of passage ceremony. The sun was now golden and the birds sung in the sky. The white frost on the grass and trees, the deep blue sky and the mist created by their breath bathed the scene in magic and mystery. First they made the sign of the five pointed star to each compass point, chanted the words of power and then turned to face the church that Peter had founded in AD 38, some 200 yards away. They held aloft their staffs, drawing the ancient shapes of energy and power as they went, calling to the spirits, the angels and to God in a unique blend of pagan, Old Testament and early Christian ritual. Everyone joined in the chanting and the wailing as the bodies were lowered and stones placed carefully around them. Before the final closing of the cave Merthyn took a long piece of golden cord and made a circle around the bodies, the circle of the sun. As above, so below. Arthur was reunited with the sun of God.

The earth used to fill the grave was damp but very special. It had been dredged from the mystic spring that formed the source of the River Ilid, a few feet away. Everyone knew that the stream which bubbled up and ran along the valley towards Gilfach Goch had been named after Joseph of Arimathea. Suddenly a large white swan broke cover from the magical pool and soared high into the sky. As it did so a feather fell from its wings. Illtyd watched it dropping slowly, so slowly, through the sky.

As the chanting grew louder Illtyd felt himself, like the feather, drifting, floating through time and space. In his hypnotic state he visited a morning long into the future. There were strange carriages with wheels near the church which seemed to be partly covered by a large white tent. Men in odd garments were walking up the ancient roadway towards the site. One man in particular drew his attention, he was waving at Illtyd. Could they really see each other across the centuries? Merthyn instinctively moved one hand to hold the bronze, silver and gold sky disc of time that laid around his neck and which had been passed down to him from Maria Magdalena via a long line of Druid and Egyptian ancestors. He placed his other hand strongly upon Illtyd's shoulder bringing him back to his own world.

"These are strange times brother, I see what you see, the time will come when all will know who Arthur really was, where his body lays and the secrets we have had to hide. On that day justice will be done and the truth shall be known."

-2-

St Peter's Super-Montem Church, Mynnyd Y Gaer, South Wales
2nd October 1990

Overnight, the violent storm had tried its best to wash the archaeological dig off the mountain. As the sun rose the damage could clearly be seen. The giant cream coloured tent that had been erected over some of the church dig site had been partly destroyed. It hung in tatters like banners from the camp of ancient knights before battle. Rain filled the trenches, undoing days of hard work. Those who had stayed overnight had done their best to make repairs by setting up bilge pumps powered by generators. They were exhausted, sheltering in their tiny arctic tents.

The smooth running of this important investigation was quite a feat. The giant tent, fresh water, food, generators and all the equipment had to be brought over difficult terrain to reach the site. Pender had taken great care to account for everything; he knew how vital it was to their research to get this right. Now all his brilliant efforts lay in ruins.

Daniel Everson, the archaeologist in charge of the dig, blessed the fact that his own sown-in ground sheet had held through the restless night. It was a small simple tent but in these conditions that was a distinct advantage. He had just managed to slip into a deep sleep when he was awoken by the sound of a four wheeled drive vehicle struggling to make its way up the narrow muddy track that led from Llanharran towards the site of the ruined Castle of Caradoc and beyond to Gilfach Goch.

After three weeks the excavation was behind schedule and cash was running out. Already there were disputes about the use of short cuts and power tools, conserving and dating finds properly and accurately recording the evidence. The overnight storm had only added to the tense atmosphere.

Until now they had managed to encase much of the church in a protective tent. Workers had even erected a makeshift fence around the site to keep out treasure seekers. They had applied themselves effectively and diligently, excavating layer after layer of soil like turning the pages of a giant history book.

Morgan and Pender had hoped that more local people would have volunteered to help reveal their history. The fact was that they had something of an uneasy relationship with them. Realising its importance to early Christianity, Morgan and Pender had bought the ruins from the Church in 1980 but the extent of the land was limited by the walls and a metre or so outside them. The local authority owned a further small area around the church that made up the burial ground and a farmer owned the land adjacent. A footpath led from the ancient track across the 100 yards or so to the ancient monument.

A large promontory overshadowed the church area and local folklore recounted the tale that St Peter himself had preached from its stony top in the 1st century AD. Folklore and ancient texts alike placed the castle of Caradoc and a large important city in that area. The name of the adjacent village in antiquity, Peterstone, was said to have derived from the fact that St Peter himself had originally founded the church upon an ancient rock held sacred by the early Druids. Some places just store a mysterious power and energy that our distant ancestors instinctively felt. They would mark such powerful energy points with a special stone. Often these huge boulders were brought large distances from other sacred sites bringing with them their own power and life force, such as the great stone upon which the Templars built the magnificent cathedral at Chartres in France. In Wales there was a tradition that churches were named after the person who founded them and this one was St Peter's. The analogy was tempting.

In 1987 a large memorial stone was found face down forming a bridge across a brook to a nearby field. Now rather worn, its face contained an inscribed wheel of life and an inscription in which the name of Peter is just tantalizingly visible. It is still displayed at the Margam Stone Museum, nearby.

Just a few hundred yards from the church is the source of a stream called Cant Ilid (or the stream of St Ilid.) Ilid is the Welsh name for Joseph of Arimathea. Clearly this whole area was once of great significance.

Some places seem to attract momentous events throughout history and this place is one of them. In 1326 Edward II and his favorite Hugh Despenser were forced to flee London, taking with them a vast treasure. There was news that Edward's estranged wife Queen Isabella and her lover Roger de Mortimer had landed in England and were seeking power. Edward had most certainly lost the confidence of his people. He had been involved in wars with his barons and his reliance upon Despenser who was hated and despised by many was deeply unpopular. London was no longer safe for him so he retreated to Wales where Despenser controlled a number of Lordships with heavily fortified castles. On 27th and 28th October, Edward was in Cardiff and on the following day he nominated the massive castle of Caerphilly to be his headquarters. An impressive structure, it had been made to a design conceived by William

Marshall, Earl of Pembroke and the head of the Templar Knights. It was re-fortified by Gilbert de Clare in 1268.

On the 2nd November Edward left a garrison there to protect half his treasure, some £13,000, while he moved on with the other half of his booty to Margam Abbey and then to Neath where Despenser had a castle. The Queen and Mortimer made their headquarters in Hereford and put Henry, Earl of Lancaster in charge of the army, with orders to capture the King and Despenser.

On 16th November the King, his Chancellor Robert de Baldock and Despenser were betrayed by locals and captured in the woods on Mynyd Y Gaer near the site of the archaeological dig. The treasure deposited at Caerphilly was recovered easily but the other half was never found. Legend has it that the treasure was buried before they were captured and that despite interrogation neither the king nor the king's men ever revealed its whereabouts. It hadn't even occurred to Everson that the treasure may have been buried at or near the church.

Having completed his prayers the archaeologist pulled on his boots, stepped out of the tent and into a mud bath. He struggled towards the track to meet the provisions vehicle and the workforce. He stopped for a moment and looked around, trying to visualise things as they once were. The ancient field names indicate that this place once nestled in a large forest clearing on the peak of this mountain range known as Mynydd Y Gaer, or, Fortress Mountain. The name of the old forest was once "The Woods of Heaven" but most of the trees were felled to make pit props for the coal mining industry centuries ago.

Gazing up the mountain towards the place known as the Pass of the Soldier, he thought he saw two men dressed in white, one of them waving at him. Instinctively he raised his hand and waved back, but the figures had already disappeared. He looked again; surely it must have been the early morning mist that was playing tricks with his eyes, which were, he had to admit, not as sharp as they had been when he was younger.

He saw the distant shape of a flying swan disappearing and became aware of a soft white shape brush his face. His hand outstretched instinctively and a white feather landed in it.

A shiver ran down his spine as the cold penetrated his clothing. He gazed over to one side where the green hilly landscape was peppered with rocky outcrops one of which towered over the area of the church. It was easy to imagine the village elders and leaders speaking to the people from this place, even before the church was built. He had seen such places used as Oratories, sometimes even as places of sacrifice, often in connection with astrological markers.

The track up which the vehicle was trying to drag milk, bread and other provisions was once thought to have been the main road from Cardiff but now it lay in disrepair across the naked, rugged peaks and valleys. Behind the truck he could see the diggers, like soldier ants making their way along the narrow pathway that led up the mountain. An eerie silence hung in the mist around the church. No one knew how remarkable this winter's day would become.

The men walking up the pathway looked like steam trains, their breath bellowing smoke behind them in the frosty air. Everson waved and squelched back into his tent, picked up the daily log that Pender had been writing and read through the last few pages. To date, their finds had been interesting and informative. Before the dig the authorities had scheduled the church as 12th century Norman which was always an unlikely scenario for those in the know. There were some places in Wales that the Normans never really penetrated and this was one of them. Before the official dig, Morgan and Pender had discovered an 8th century window in the ruins near the porch. They had tried to get CADW to amend the 12th century claim in their records but without success.

A geophysical survey of the immediate area suggested a random series of buildings were situated around the church but they were outside the area they were allowed to dig. However, there was plenty of evidence of several stages of building within the church and at the very bottom layer before natural earth there appeared to be a beehive style structure. It was obvious by looking at the topography that the church had been built on an earlier raised site, maybe even an early Iron Age enclosure. From the existence of 'puddle pools' littering the immediate landscape it seemed likely, at least to some, that the region had been of major importance in making metal weapons and other goods. Stones with carved indentations were found that appeared to have been used to shape molten metal. One was found along the track en route to the castle of Caradoc. It was too large to move so Morgan and Pender had turned it over to conceal its importance, intending to return for it at a later date.

Most professional land surveyors that specialised in early settlements had to concede that the church occupied a favoured position in a much larger settlement. Had this really been the spot where Ambrosius founded a college and military training camp and at which Simon Peter had set up the first church on the sacred rock just as legend recorded it? After all, Jesus gave his brother Simon the nickname Petrvs which in Greek means "Rock" and is supposed to have said, "On this rock you will build my church." Could this have been referring to Simon Peter in South Wales?

Everson pulled out a tray of finds from under the camp bed. There were highly glazed green roofing tiles and patterned floor tiles indicating a building of some status. There was a small metal axe which Morgan felt could have been used for inscribing early Coelbren, an alphabet once thought to be fake but now proven to have existed as far back as the Chaldeans. There was also a small dagger and a 12 inch circle of sandstone, two inches thick and inlaid with what appeared to be four rusted nails in the shape of an "M" or a "W".

No one knew what this unique find really represented. Some conjectured that it may have represented Cassiopeia, others thought the M was for the Mary Magdalen cult.

Another find that intrigued him was the huge number of skulls and leg and arm bones that had been arranged as skull and cross bones. Oddly they were in every part of the dig and apparently dating back to the very earliest layers. Clearly something relating to skulls was important here. The link to Golgotha, the place of the skulls, and the crucifixion seemed more than a co-incidence. Could this really be the very first church in the UK?

One of the most interesting finds had been under the altar. Its foundations were made of pure white quartz, usually reserved for the most holy. The altar itself was built over a grave and in the grave was found a skeleton of a man some seven foot six inches tall. His arms and legs were tied as if to keep a cloth covering in place that had long since disintegrated. Around his neck there was a metal necklace and a circular disc which could have been gold or bronze. The bones had been carefully placed in a casket and taken by Morgan and Pender for safety together with some of the other finds. Everson hoped that for the integrity of the site, these would be expertly examined, dated, identified and preserved. He had noticed that they had recently become withdrawn and secretive and he hoped upon hope that their intentions were honourable.

His train of thought was rudely derailed as one of the men pushed his way into the tent; "Morning…"

The thick set black haired man did not wait for an answer, "…are we having our morning briefing then, boyo?"

It was a perfectly reasonable question but it jarred his senses. Today he felt fragile and apprehensive. There was something in the air but he couldn't put his finger on it. Everson didn't reply, instead he motioned for the man to leave the tent; he took hold of his own note book and followed him, joining the gaggle of others looking forward to their morning brew. He pulled his parka hood around his head and flicked through the book with his navy blue fingerless gloves, lifting his eyes occasionally to give the plan of action for the day. Simon was to concentrate on the altar area and he had decided to try to get down to the natural surface in the centre of the existing church ruin where the evidence of the beehive shaped building was starting to emerge.

The morning passed with nothing unusual to report, barrow load after barrow load was taken from both the active areas of the dig and sifted and scanned with metal detectors before being dumped onto the growing spoil heap. The wind had freshened considerably but that was nothing new on the exposed mountain side.

Suddenly Simon called to Everson. There, at the side of the altar, the "right hand of God", two large rectangular stones were emerging from the soil.

Walking the few feet from his trench to Simon's, the archaeologist removed his trowel from his back pocket, knelt on the sodden earth and started carefully scrapping and brushing. They were roughly cut stones but fairly smooth, no marks, no writing. At some point in time a floor had been laid over them, perhaps to conceal them?

It looked like a grave. Everson kept scraping and brushing until he had cleared the two stones. They each measured six feet by two and a half feet wide. Tony Ashwell photographed and recorded the find with a grid measuring pole and made the appropriate notes for later study. The other members of the dig gathered around whilst Everson loosened the earth around the sides.

Most of the church had caved in on itself and the main part of the tower, walls and flooring had been robbed to make foundations and walls for the surrounding houses. This made it hard to date the layer in which the large stones were embedded. The archaeologist guessed them to be 13th to 14th century. On the wall opposite the suspected grave was a niche about the same size as the memorial stone which Morgan and Pender had found earlier. The stone bore the inscription;

Rex Artorius fili Mavricus; (The King Arthur, son of Maurice). Morgan and Pender had argued that a similar situation had occurred at the intact Mathern Church where a memorial stone to Tewdrig, believed to be the grandfather of Arthur, was found in the wall adjacent to the altar. They believed that his body was found in the grave there "at the right hand of God." It seemed perfectly logical therefore that Arthur may, perhaps, be buried under the unmarked slabs.

As the earth was moved from around the stones each handful was sifted and checked for any clue to the age. No one noticed how the threatening clouds were gathering on the horizon, like an army preparing to strike. The spirits of the sky were awakening.

With the aid of a crow bar at each end, first one stone and then the other was lifted and moved sideways to reveal compacted sand. Simon felt that the material may have been used to backfill a crypt or chamber. It was a distinct possibility, the iron bar he had sunk into the sand seemed to go down around four feet before there was a solid clunk. Was it a step or maybe a stone coffin? Simon was puzzled; he gazed across to Everson who tried to remain composed, they both knew that there was no sand naturally on this mountain. The chances were that they had stumbled upon something of great importance.

Everson and a young man called David, who was seconded from the Archaeology department at Bournemouth University, started to work clearing the sand from under the slabs. Suddenly Everson realised that in their enthusiasm they were coming perilously close to undermining the church wall foundations. Above ground around five feet of the church wall remained but they had dug down another four feet. The risk was that nine feet of heavy stone wall could fall on the diggers. It wasn't safe to continue without strengthening the wall and the pit. The engineer would have to be called, and that meant yet another delay.

After all the excitement the others returned to work in the centre of the ruined church whilst Everson called the civil engineer. Their trench had passed through four old floor layers and they still hadn't hit natural. There had certainly been several buildings on this site going back in time but dating them was not easy. It looked as if the church had been added to at one end and shortened at the other. The last extension was made around the 12th or 13th century and this seemed to cover the possible crypt which was recently discovered.

What particularly caught their eye about the trench towards the middle of the church ruin was that it seemed to be uncovering evidence of a round or "beehive" type building. The foundation stones were still in place and there were signs of timber posts and a hearth with charcoal in the centre, the usual tell tale sign of a domestic fire. But more than that there was evidence of a fierce inferno which had fused bones and glass to floor tiles. They were extending a trench to try to pinpoint the date of the building.

Deep in thought, alone, beside the altar, Everson was calculating how best to strengthen the wall in preparation for digging out what was almost certainly a crypt. Spaces at 'the right hand of God' were reserved for someone of immense importance. Could this really be the last resting place of the King Arthur of legend as Morgan and Pender had predicted?

Two things were nagging at Everson. If Arthur ever existed he would have lived, died and been buried around the 6th century and this was a 12th or 13th century extension to the church. What could this mean and why lay two slabs of stone with nothing written on them? From their position in the earth layers it looked as if they had always been hidden from view. It seemed as if the approximately 13th century floor had been laid over the top of the slabs as if to conceal them forever. Something told Everson to turn the plain smooth stones over and look on the reverse. He struggled to flip them and puffed heavily after the task. As he dusted the damp sand away he saw that on the first one there was a letter "I" carved towards the top and half way down was a small hole. On the other there was another letter E but nothing else. Hidden beneath the stones was a small tile with indentations. He rubbed at the sandy earth with his jacket sleeve until the letters revealed themselves. Part of the tablet was missing but he could read the word, ROTAS across the top and the same word down the left hand side. The second word down was OPERA and the third TENET. Only part of the fourth word was visible, ARE. He didn't need to see the rest of the missing tablet to know what it meant. It read ROTAS OPERA TENET AREPO SATOR. It was a ROTAS tablet, a kind of magical charm. Backwards in the Roman form of the Greek alphabet it meant something like...."As you sow, so shall you reap"...He kept the tablet but quickly returned the stones without telling the others, his mind was working overtime.

"Oh Christ!" Although the outburst sounded loud to him it seemed as if no one else heard. His agony was taken away on the wind towards the threatening bruised clouds in the sky.

He stood there speechless, motionless, confused. No way, it couldn't be... His attention was captured by another shout, this time from the central trench. Using a metal detector, Colin had discovered something metallic and solid, something apparently buried under the glazed tile flooring of what they thought to be the 6th century part of the church. Armed with a toothbrush and his small trowel Simon was working on the delicate job of trying to reveal the find. Slowly the impacted earth loosened and bit by bit the find emerged. It was a piece of metal around an inch and a half wide. As he brushed he began to make out indented writing; P, R and then an O, PRO. There seemed to be a disc or circle that started at the top of the O. Everson could not resist taking over. Simon seemed relieved rather than jealous. He traced carefully around the outline until he came to another straight piece of metal, and on the other side the same shape. A longer piece of metal ran for around a further six inches and had more writing upon it.

As the damp earth was brushed away it could clearly be assessed. It was a metal cross with a disc behind the part where the horizontal and vertical shapes met. There were murmurs of excitement buzzing around the mountain top. The archaeologist beckoned to one of the team,

"Better try and contact Morgan and Pender, they'll definitely want to see this!"

Once the find area had been gridded and photographs taken the cross was very carefully lifted and placed in a plastic tray encased in cotton wool. The dark clouds were gathering, pulling a curtain across the sky so it was hard to find a spot where the light was good enough to see the fine detail. Everson gently held the cross in his hand and laid it on the grass in a slither of sunlight. Even though it had been in the ground for centuries it managed to shine just a little, as if sending a message to the heavens. Taking the fine bits of dirt from it with a tiny soft brush and using a strong magnifying glass he kept in his pocket for such occasions, he was just able to see a man on horseback wielding a spear or a sword on the disc in the centre of the cross and an inscription that ran the whole length of its ten inches;

PRO ANIMA ARTORIVS
(for the soul of Arthur)

He placed the cross on the ground and looked at his hand. There was a mark or rash where the cross had been and his skin felt slightly sore. As he spoke the words of the inscription again the wind picked up from nowhere and black clouds pulled across the sky bisected by a lone shaft of sunlight that hit the ground around the cross and intensified it like a lighthouse guiding ships to safety. As it started to rain the light was fragmented into a prism, a rainbow in a microcosm, a world within a world, as if it had been released from some ancient slumber.

The sudden clap of thunder overhead startled everybody and they all gazed upwards in awe. The sky darkened further as if someone was drawing the curtains between life and death. The act had begun. The wind freshened into gusts and hailstones started to fall. It was a scene of biblical drama.

The excitement over the finds would have to wait. The clouds were moving quickly, shifting into shapes of all sorts in the bruised and wounded sky. The wind was now gusting and the hail stung as it hit cold skin. They all ran for cover but gusts of wind tugged at the tent stays, pulling and ripping, heaving and cutting. In the maelstrom of lightning and thunder the gusts hit gale force ripping and tugging at what remained of the canvas from the storm of the night before, in the process shredding it in all directions...like a swordsman decimating his foe. It was suddenly pitch black. People were shouting and flashing torches in panic and despair, urgently trying to keep what remained of the tent in place. They failed.

Coming over the ridge was a whilrling funnel of black cloud, darker than the darkest sky, swirling like a giant spining Dervish on speed. Some ran from the site. Some stayed trying to hold down anything of value. The noise and the force of the wind, the frozen hailstones, the lightning and thunder, the feeling of strange deep foreboding, it was like the last few moments on the Titanic. In a crescendo the madly spiralling column of air hit the dig site like a sledge hammer. With one mad ripping sound that rent the air like a crack of lightning the remaining covering was gone, whisked away like a huge ghost into the air and along with it Everson's tent, most of his notes and photographs. People ran one way then another. The paraphernalia of the dig spun into a cauldron and then flung out circling in the sky like kites above the mountain.

In the holocaust Everson was struggling to stay upright by leaning into the whipping wind and slashing hailstones. The torrent of rain and the lashing wind suddenly revealed a small clay pot near to the mysterious slabs he had so recently looked at. In the melee he slipped face down into the mud and water. He clasped it and arose triumphant as if receiving baptism. Realising that everyone else was too busy trying to cope with the onslaught from the heavens, he slipped the pot inside his parka and shovelled earth back over the stone slabs, hoping to hide them once more from prying eyes. Several times he was blown over into the mud and stones, hit by flying debris, forced to his knees like some biblical sinner. He instinctively knew he had to rebury the slabs that had been uncovered, but he didn't know why.

His task was just about complete when the exposed wall started collapsing as he earlier feared it would. In the chaos Everson prayed, it seemed like the only thing a Cistercian monk from Caldey Island could do. The words kept repeated in his brain, "This is a find no one is ever meant to see."

A bolt of lightning scorched through the air, Everson felt the static whisk past him setting his hair on end. A scream cut the dark Armageddon and, after a volley of lightning, he spotted Simon trying to make his way over to help him. The young man was briefly silhouetted against the violent sky. His body contorted, his arms involuntarily stretched towards heaven. There was another crash of thunder like the blast of cannons in the midst of battle just as another part of the church wall tumbled on Simon.

Everson tried to get to him across the slippery earth only to see that he had been burnt badly by the strike, burnt like toast left too long under the grill. Putrid smelling smoke and steam was rising from his scorched flesh. The stones in the wall had crushed what was left of him and his blood ran into the wet earth echoing some primitive sacrifice. In the last throes of life, or maybe in a reflex of death, Simon's arm slapped across the mud, the cross so recently found slipped out of his grasp and into a puddle. Everson reached out and picked it up, slipping it quickly into his inside pocket. It seemed to vibrate with energy, like a wild bear searching for its pray, like a murdered king seeking revenge.

Everson paused for a moment; there was nothing he could do for Simon now.

The others had gathered up as much as they could before retreating from the mountain like a well beaten army. The sound of the wind in the ruins echoed like the ululations at a primitive funeral.

As he struggled away across the field against the mighty power of the elements, frozen in sadness and time, he looked briefly back only to see a huge bolt of lightning illuminate the whole area of the church. Blinded by the light, stabbed by the sharp wind in his ears he had the impression that time was standing still. For a fleeting moment he thought he saw the shape of an angel, but he must have been mistaken...surely this could not be the work of an angel.

"My God", he mouthed to the elements, "what have we done?"

-3-

The Office of CADW, just outside Cardiff, Wales
21st July 2009

Flashing lights lit up the rear view mirror as the constant blast of an impatient horn shattered his thoughts. Instinctively he swerved the car back into the inside lane as the shockwave of the passing black Audi buffeted him sideways. "Phew", he sighed, that was too close. Of course he could not have been expected to recognise the driver, Bryn Evans, the man they called the *Welsh Detective*, but, Evans knew him and had been keeping tabs on his activities for some time.

As a young archaeologist, Dr Roger Felix had made his mark in academia, supplementing his career as an 'expert' on television. In so doing, he had certainly helped to make archaeology much more sexy and popular. Now 54, his receding hairline and slight paunch were signs that he was not as sharp as he was. Recently he had been baffled by a piece of research, it had reached a critical stage and he was at a loss as to what to do next. He didn't like to think that he had a huge ego that had to be fed but he did feel that as head of the renowned dept of Archaeology at Sheffield University he deserved better treatment than he had experienced from CADW, a body tasked with protecting and preserving ancient monuments in Wales, much like English Heritage and the National Trust in England.

Instead of the help and information he usually received from such bodies he had experienced nothing but delay, frustration, intrigue and in some cases damn rudeness for months. All he wanted to do was talk to the correct representative body about re-opening a dig and about what happened at the previous one back in 1990. His reputation and his engaging personality had ensured that in over 25 years he had always worked in a professional and amicable way. Why and how could something so simple come to this, a show down with Sylvia Clarke, the head of CADW? If he hadn't been suspicious before, he most certainly was now.

"Turn left at the next junction and join the A4054."

The honeyed tones of Miss SatNav were reassuring. He contemplated how he had ever managed without her; in fact, he was beginning to imagine what she looked like, what she might wear, could she fancy a Doctor of Archaeology specialising in metal analysis?

"At the roundabout take the third exit and your destination is 400 yards on the left."

He parked his Honda Civic, stepped out clumsily and noticed a tall thin man in a long camel hair coat waiting near the entrance. Walking towards him, Roger was faced by an engaging smile and an outstretched hand; "Robin Bryant."

Roger shook the friendly appendage but instinctively kept his distance. He reminded him of Dr Who.

"Robin Bryant" he repeated, "I have been helping Morgan and Pender for years and they asked that I come to this meeting with you, I trust that's OK?"

Roger vaguely recognised the name but had not expected any gatecrashers at the meeting. He maintained a polite ambience.

"Good to meet you Robin. How did you know about the meeting?"

"Morgan called me yesterday and explained, he wanted me to hear what CADW had to say first hand, as you know he doesn't trust them at all, why don't you call him to make sure it's OK?"

Roger had already decided to do just that, he flipped open his Nokia and dialled Morgan's number; no reply, no answer phone. Returning the phone to his pocket Roger thought for a moment and then gestured to Robin,

"Come on then, I guess it would be good to have a witness to the conversation."

Robin smiled as he covertly pressed the *on* button of the digital recorder in his pocket and adjusted the tie pin microphone before following Roger into the building.

The large reception area was predominantly wood, glass and black plastic; a brave attempt to link the colour and texture of materials with the past. The décor almost worked. The young receptionist, who had been happily chatting on the phone in both Welsh and English, hung up and approached the visitors. "Good morning, I'm Rhianon." She's just been on the customer service training course thought Roger cynically. She ushered them into a large meeting room set out with one long central table surrounded by chairs. She served them coffee with a vivacious smile, "Ms Clarke will be with you shortly."

Roger turned to Robin, "How long have you known Morgan and Pender?"

Robin removed his outer coat and was placing it around the back of his chair. "I first met them when I volunteered to go on the dig at St Peter's in 1990. I was a young trainee journalist hoping for a scoop."

Roger jolted, "Ah, so you were there. Are you still a journalist?"

Robin sensed the apprehension and held up both hands in a motion to surrender, his eyes were staring and confident, "It's OK, trust me, I am on your side".

Roger had no chance to do anything else, the door opened and Sylvia Clarke wafted in on a carpet of confidence and Channel No 5. She looked to be in her early forties, attractive, fit and officious. She sat at the head of the table and placed a large file beside her. A spot light hit the top of her expensively cut, blonde highlighted bob making it shine so loudly, it was almost glaring. She looked across at them without any sign of a smile or weakness; maybe she had nothing to be happy about, certainly she meant business.

Her introduction set the tone, "I am Sylvia Clarke, I am in charge here at CADW, and you have 15 minutes."

Roger felt uneasy, not because Ms Clarke was an intimidating woman, he'd met plenty of them before, not even because the slit in her black pencil skirt was revealing too much muscular thigh. It was her glassy cold stare that tried to pin him to the wall as he stood that he disliked.

"As you know I am here to talk about my application to re-open the dig at St Peter's Super Montem church and ..."

She cut him short; "You don't have to stand, this isn't a court. As I told you on the phone that is quite impossible Dr Felix. We haven't even had a report from the dig in 1990 and it is now 2009. We will not allow another one."

Robin shuffled uncomfortably as Roger pressed on. "I believe you list the ruined church as 12th century Norman?"

She sighed as she checked her open file, "Yes, yes of course, you know that."

Roger was feeling frustrated and annoyed; after all he had travelled miles to meet her face to face. "Well, if you'll permit me to speak..." he said, returning her stare with his own. She crossed her legs, revealing yet more firm flesh.

"Would you say that your inspector who listed the church knew the area and its history well Ms Clarke?" The woman remained in poker faced silence as Roger continued. "I understand that he has had no formal education in Welsh history." It was phrased as a question but Roger knew this to be a fact.

The woman sensed trouble and tried to head it off; "We have every faith in the people we hire, each knows the area they work in, each have their own field of expertise and if needs be, there is plenty of backup."

Roger jumped in; "So why did he visit the church on a bus, wander around lost for two and half hours trying to find a site that he had supposedly been in charge of for 15 years and which is clearly shown on an OS map. Why did he ask the police at the Talbot Green Police Station to take him to the site and then back to the bus stop shortly afterwards without a careful examination of the building? Doesn't this indicate that he had never inspected St Peter's church before, let alone be in a position to list it as 12th century Norman?"

A nervous rash made its way up the woman's neck; "This is preposterous, what are you alleging?"

"I am not alleging anything; this is just what the local police told me when

I enquired. In fact..." continued Roger with increased conviction, "...you may like to look at this photograph of the remains of a window near to the porch." He slid it across the shiny table and it landed in front of her. She picked it up, briefly examined it and then tossed it back down.

"So?"

Roger was curious, "don't you recognise that this is an early English arch lintel near the porch, it's certainly pre 12th century Norman."

Clarke looked supremely unimpressed. "I've no idea; I am the Administrative head of CADW, not an historian or an archaeologist. What is your point Dr Felix?"

"I think you have made my point for me Ms Clarke." He moved quickly on. "If there are clearly 8th century features in the church, then how can you list it as 12th century Norman? And if you are wrong about this should you not, at the very least be interested in my contention that the dig should be re-opened to get to the bottom of its history? Morgan and Pender's chief archaeologist believed that there may be a first century church or building previously on the site, which, of course would make it of international importance."

Robin sensed that an explosion was imminent; he had been listening carefully trying to record every word.

The rash made it up to her cheeks. "As a matter of fact Dr Felix we have interviewed the archaeologist concerned and he has confirmed to us that he never said any such thing. He did say however that it was years before he was paid for his work and that he was never asked to lodge a formal report with us."

Her breasts heaved as she breathed deeply in then out as if to emphasise her points. She continued, "I have already explained Dr Felix, we granted permission for the owners to dig the site in 1990. They appear to have ignored the archaeologist's advice, attacked it like mad men and left the most unholy mess when they left. The Local Council even had to fund a cleanup operation. We have never had a chance to look at the supposed finds and we have never had a written report of the dig, as is required by law. In fact, all we have received from Morgan and Pender since 1990 are rude and abusive letters. All we know about their finds is what we read in the press....and what the aggrieved archaeologist has said...how do you expect me to react?"

Dr Felix faced her across the table, "Logically and professionally. I expect someone in your position to react appropriately." He continued, "You are aware that CADW spent months and months delaying the permission for the dig."

Clarke looked blank as Felix continued. "By the time permission was granted, the weather was terrible. In fact two violent storms blew the whole operation off the mountain."

"That", said the red faced woman "was hardly our fault. If they had complied with requests for information promptly they could have started the dig sooner, it was no excuse to leave a sacred site in such a mess!"

Roger looked curious; "A sacred site? Didn't the church virtually give it away as a pile of stones?"

Clarke chose to ignore the point but Felix continued. "Didn't your representative go to the dig to regularly inspect progress? If they were doing such a bad job wouldn't he have filed a report saying so?"

There was silence, Roger didn't press the point but carried on. "I can do nothing about what happened then, that was almost twenty years ago, but I do have the owner's written permission to re-open the dig, complete the work and make a full report. This is your chance to get an amicable closure to the matter."

Sensing that he may have made up some ground Roger continued; "Are you aware that the earliest records, some of which are contained in the Myvyrian Archaeology, tell us that until 250 years ago, there was a market held at and around the site of the church and that there was a large town nearby? In fact, the Brut Tyssilio, which had to have been written before 684 when we know the writer died, states that the father of King Arthur was buried inside the giant boat shaped burial at the fabled lost city of Caer Caradoc. Recent infra red aerial photography shows many interesting features on Mynnyd y Gaer. There is most likely an early castle, a religious complex, burial mounds and a town. Morgan and Pender believe this really is Caer Caradoc, one of the most important locations in all of ancient British history and the home of King Caradoc 1, son of Arch, who fought the Romans from 42-51AD and who actually took the pure version of Christianity as taught by Jesus to Rome."

Nervously shuffling her papers together and looking across the room at Robin, Clarke took a deep breath and turned to Roger; "Not a shred of evidence Dr Felix, not a shred, no archaeology, no academic support...just more fairy stories, mistranslations and the re-interpretations from those clowns Morgan and Pender, they've set Arthurian research back 50 years."

Roger looked across at Robin. His face showed no emotion. Inside, Felix was fuming. How could a person in this lofty position be allowed to assassinate people without letting them have their say? Surely as a government employee she should at least be open minded? He felt he was on a hiding to nothing.

For very different reasons Clarke was likewise fuming inside. She did a good job of hiding it but the growing pink rash on her neck gave her away.

Roger continued anyway; "When people have spent over 25 years funding research out of their own pocket, turning over every stone, delving into every ancient manuscript, how can you just dismiss their findings with a wave of your hand? Have you seen the research, have you read the books, don't you know that the ancient Welsh records are littered with references to Caer Caradoc and the things that happened there?"

Clarke sat up straighter, thrusting her substantial chest forward; "Ha, the Welsh records, you mean that motley collection of wishful thinking translated by Iolo Morgannwg and the other mad people on Laudanum in order to create allusions of grandeur for Welsh Nationalism."

Roger felt his heart sink as he studied her face now glowing red under her spot-lit bob. Robin was keeping quiet; "I am talking about archaeology and what the evidence tells us, what are you talking about?"

Clarke was trying to regain her composure; "My point is that there may be a load of stories, legends, texts and so on but there is no proof whatsoever for any of it!"

Felix tried to remain calm, seething never did an argument any good; "Well we agree then, the only way we can know about the church for sure is to re-open the dig."

The woman cleared her throat to relax the tension; "We both know that Morgan and Pender think King Arthur is buried at the church and that they didn't finish the dig last time. If they find something they can hang a story on they probably think they'll make millions."

Roger's next line of questioning seemed to bring her back to her senses; "Just what are CADW here for? Isn't it to investigate and preserve history? Just how is your attitude helping in any way, the church at St Peter's? You say it is sacred yet you list it incorrectly as 12th century Norman; your mandate is to protect ancient monuments yet you allow cattle to trample all over the ruins; you stand by and do nothing when the locals steal the remaining stones! Is that how you preserve our heritage? What are you afraid of?"

She looked like she was about to blow her top; "Nobody speaks to me like this, how dare you? You sit here in my office as an historian and archaeologist giving credence to documents and research that have long been shown to be utter rubbish!"

Roger held up his hands, "Hang on, that's just not true, by your own admission you say you have never studied the Welsh Texts and that you rely on your advisors... what if they are wrong? Are you saying that those records starting in the 6th century that are larger than the bible are all fabricated and completely false?"

Clarke looked unimpressed but Roger pressed on, suddenly locking on to her previous comment; "Anyway, what is so bad about finding something that proves King Arthur existed? Don't you think that would be fantastic for Welsh tourism and history?"

The daggers in Clarke's eyes were there for all to see. "So that's what this is all about, trying to prove King Arthur was a real person and not some hopeful legend I suppose that you, Morgan and Pender are all in cahoots seeking your fortunes."

Felix was genuinely taken aback, "For me this is about a fascinating archaeological site that, if properly excavated and recorded, could progress our thinking and knowledge of the darkest part of our historical age. I'd love to know what it is all about for you"

Sensing an awkward hiatus, Robin spoke for the first time, "I wonder what the new Ancient Monuments Board for Wales will have to say to the Welsh Assembly about this matter?"

Recovering, Clarke carefully pushed her hair from her face with her right hand and smiled sarcastically; they could feel a killer punch coming... "From the 1st April 2006 the body to which you refer have technically been in place to advise the Welsh Assembly about all things archaeological and historical, but, what you obviously don't know is that the AMAB has no legal basis, no human resources and no responsibilities or funds of its own. In fact CADW provides all the necessary support. Perhaps, if you were cynical you could say that CADW controls it and since I am effectively CADW, I can tell you exactly what they'll say."

"Which is?" enquired Roger.

"If the finds from the 1990 excavation are lodged with us for examination, which, of course, they will never be, and if we receive a full report of the last dig completed by a qualified archaeologist that was on the dig at the time, which will never happen, we may be able to consider moving forward. Until that time there is nothing further to say...in fact Morgan and Pender have been a thorn in our side for years and I'll be glad to see the back of them."

Seething, Roger moved towards Clarke. "How can you possibly say that without studying their work?"

In haste, the woman stood to leave, no smile, no warmth, just Chanel No 5. Roger stood up and blocked her way, desperate to continue the conversation.

"What do you mean you'll be glad to see the back of them? What's going to happen to them?"

All she returned was a stone cold stare. There was a very brief pause before Roger continued, "Look, I have travelled hours to see you, the least you can do is hear me out."

She paused; "If I were you, I'd be very careful about who I worked with and what I did."

Roger stepped back; "Is that a threat?" He felt her eyes burn into his soul and knew it was time to play his final card, "I have run several tests on the cross that Morgan and Pender found at the dig. The early tests were inconclusive but there has been a giant leap in technology over the last few years."

The woman did not blink; "So what? A fake is a fake whether it was cooked up in 1990 or baked on the wave of Arthurianism in the 13th century."

Again she motioned to leave but Roger placed a hand on her shoulder, he had a bombshell to drop; "But it's neither; it is 6th century, contemporary with Arthur."

Clarke brushed off his hand from her shoulder like a fly from food. "Get your hands off me; do you want me to call the police?"

Roger retreated, stunned in the shockwave of her reaction, something had clearly hit a raw nerve so he pressed the point home; "You were offered the cross and the other items to test at the time of the dig but refused to have anything to do with them or Morgan and Pender... you must be pretty sorry you didn't take them up on their offer now?"

She did not reply as she left the room. The sound of her heels sounded faintly ridiculous as she clip clopped down the corridor.

Roger looked down and noticed a card that had fallen from her file. He quickly pocketed it.

"What was that?" Robin enquired from across the room.

"Nothing, I just dropped my pen."

Bryant didn't press the point but it didn't look much like a pen from where he was standing.

-4-

Norwich, Norfolk
23rd July 2009

After a sad and thoughtful drive William pulled his car into the natural woodland burial ground near Norwich. It was a lovely place, as burial places go, a natural forest complete with wild flowers and a brook. Here he felt the connection between this world and the next.

A blackbird sat on a low branch singing. William empathised. He closed his eyes and hummed one of their favourite tunes, "Hotel California". Slowly he drifted back ten years to when they had been sitting at this very spot agreeing how lovely it was and how they'd want to eventually be buried in such a place, free of religion, at one with nature. In his mind he could almost see her, feel her, smell her scent and hear her voice. We never fully realise what we have until it's gone.

She was buried here four years ago. It had been a simple ceremony conducted by his shaman friend Michael and the wooden plaque he used to mark her grave was still in place. Soon it would decay to dust and be gone. And now Michael, too, was dead. He had been a huge bear of a man, invincible and unshakable, a guardian angel. Where were Michael and Sandra now he wondered, doubting the finality of death. The blackbird repeated its song, over and over.

The sky had been the same shade of blue on the day of the funeral, the fluffy clouds passed over head as they had before, but she was not there. Part of his life had been severed the day she died in the London bombings on the 7th of July, 2005 - the date was indelibly marked on his memory. Now the best he could do was live in two worlds, one of reality and the other in which she still lived. He saw her in every pretty thing and in every beautiful woman. Sometimes he thought he'd glimpsed her but tantalisingly the vision never lingered. She was his soul mate, she wasn't meant to be taken so soon, fate had cheated them both.

The amazing staff at the hospital had done all they could for the victims. Someone had tried to piece together Sandra's body, to reinstall her dignity and grace but he could tell that her soul had departed. Gone, but most certainly never forgotten, at least whilst he had breath left in his body.

William smiled as he remembered them watching the film *Truly, Madly, Deeply*. They promised each other that whoever died first would try to contact the other. She said she would try to 'annoy' him; he was still waiting, still hoping.

Sandra lost her life at 09:47am on the number 30 bus travelling between Marble Arch and Hackney Wick at Upper Woburn Place and Tavistock Square. The Metropolitan Police said that there were four blast sites - three on the underground and one on the bus killing 52 and injuring more than 700. A memorial to the dead was being erected in Hyde Park. 52 people of all nationalities ages and religions. The theme was lovely, a column and inscription for each one.

It was the not knowing that had got to him most of all, who were these people? Why did they want to kill and maim the innocent? There is no reasoning when hate takes over in our hearts, when we pull the curtains and blame everyone but ourselves. Why should individuals have to suffer so much for the decisions and stupidity of politicians and those who seek to control for power and glory. What sort of God would reward such violent and inhumane behavior? Whatever happened to love and tolerance? If a God exists then who made him or her?

Apart from visiting Sandra's grave, the other reason he was here, on the outskirts of the fine old city of Norwich, was to visit his mum. She was 89 years old and had taken a fall but the doctor who had called said she was comfortable and that she would be OK. He wished that he could spend more time with her, funny how life gets in the way of the things we really want to do.

The call shattered his contemplation by the graveside. It was the hospital, his mum had lapsed and was going downhill fast, and the doctor said something about a severe stroke and urged William to come as quickly as possible.

The phone clicked off and there was peace and quiet again in the place of life and death. William swallowed hard. He had been dreading this day for years; another death, so soon. When his mum had gone there would be no one left, he was the last.

William didn't remember driving to the hospital, he could only think of his mother. He never knew his father; his mother never spoke of him and even kept her maiden name. She had been his whole world when he was a child. She used to read him stories of knights and battles. She'd invent armour and shields for him and his friends. His would be half green and half yellow with a bright red lion standing rampant roaring. His best friends shield was red with three silver chevrons. He loved that imaginary world.

He was recalling these stories as he entered the ward and was met by a doctor. "I'm William Marshall, my mother is here, Ellen Royal, am I in time?"

The doctor motioned for him to sit down. "This morning your mother suffered a massive stroke. We've found a weakness in her heart that caused the blood to pool, forming a clot which moved to her brain. We are giving her aspirin to try to thin the blood but we are not very hopeful."

William stared into space, assimilating the news in his mind. "Is there anything more you can do?"

The doctor reached over and rested a kind hand on his shoulder; "Your mother is a strong woman but there is nothing more we can do. I am sorry, come along, let me take you to her."

William's head fell to his chest, his heart pounded as if it would burst and his legs were like jelly as he tried to walk down the long clinical corridor. The lights hanging from the ceiling seemed to swing in and out of focus.The smell etched into his brain.

The doctor led William into a small single bed room and closed the door. Ellen was propped up in bed, an oxygen tube tapped up her nose and a canular in her arm with a drip by her bedside. William stepped in and held her warm hand and the doctor left them in peace. She was motionless but he saw a faint flicker of her eyelids that said, "You made it, thank you" and he felt the faintest of touches as she tried one last time to squeeze his hand. Tears formed at the corner of closed eyes. For a moment her body rose and her mouth slightly quivered as if she was trying to say something but all he could hear was the tell tale rattle on her chest as she laboured to breath.

"Mum, oh mum, thank you for everything…I love you, I'll always love you." He stroked her white hair back from her forehead as he tried to comfort her in her last moments.He hoped upon hope that she could hear him.

"It's ok mum, just try to relax and imagine you are walking along the beach, that's where we can always meet, you know… on the beach… just listen to the sound of the waves, it's the sound of life, it never ends…"

William bowed his head, closed his eyes and prayed, calling upon the angels of goodness and light to guide her to the other side. Mercifully he didn't see her last heave of breath but he was aware of a bursting ball of white and blue light in his mind and when he opened his eyes she had gone….the ball of light still hanging in the air. Suddenly he felt surrounded by overpowering feelings of love and relief. William could hardly see through the waterfalls in his eyes as he sat gently stroking his mother's head.

In an instant the hovering light had gone and there was neither sign of life nor pain on her face, just a smile of love. He sat with her until her hand went cool.

"Be at peace mum, be at peace."

A nurse came and brought William a cup of tea. "I am so sorry." The nurse had a lovely smile, one so often used to soften the blow of bad news.

William nodded, his chin quivering with grief. "She was a lovely lady, your mum." He looked at the nurse and she immediately sensed his pain. Her lips didn't move but he heard her voice and saw her angelic smile.

"It's OK William, I know you are hurting now, but keep your faith. Your mum has passed safely over, she is with the angels and her life's purpose has been fulfilled whereas yours has just begun. Your mum was most insistent I give you this." She handed him an envelope.

William looked at her through blurry eyes, "Thank you."

She leaned over to hold William's hand; "Do you want to talk?"

He moaned; "I've lost my wife, my best friend and now my mother."

The nurse held him compassionately as he sobbed. "They are only in the next room you know, just because you cannot see them does not mean they are not there. You should still talk to them; they want you to do that."

William nodded, "Thank you, you are very kind."

Gently she guided him to a quiet room, "Take as much time as you want, I'll be around if you need me."

William lowered himself into the armchair and leaned back. Exhaustion carried him into a light sleep. He awoke with a start to see the nurse sitting in the chair beside him. "I've finished my shift so I thought I'd just look in on you."

He felt as though he was in a dream and that at any moment he'd wake up. William rubbed his eyes and gazed back at the young nurse; "Thank you for being so kind, you're an angel."

"No, I'm not an angel, your mum was the angel; I am just a trainee!"

There was something special about this girl but he was not sure what it was. He knew that he felt calm when she was there, her face was like porcelain and her ambience was serene and loving. He looked at her name badge: Sister Herbert.

"Thank you" he repeated.

"You are most welcome William, my first name is Bridget, call on me if you want." With that, she smiled and left. That's strange, he thought, he hadn't given her his name, had he?

Alone now, he picked up the envelope and emptied its contents onto a table. There was the watch he'd bought his mum when he was 12, he remembered saving up the money from his paper round. She had always treasured it and wore it every day even after it had stopped working. He looked at the time, it was the exact time that she had died and the date shown was the date of her passing.

There was also a faded birth certificate dated 1966; his birth certificate, there was his name, but this wasn't the birth certificate he'd been using all his life. He read it for the first time; Father: Robert Marshall, Mother: Isobel Marshall. What, where was Ellen's name? He was distracted by some photos. They were of a young family; mother, father, son and daughter on a beach. He looked at the boy's features. They were certainly his but he didn't recognize the other faces.

The last piece of paper was faded and very old; it was part of a family tree, the pedigree of some of the de Spenser and Clare family going back to the 11th century. On one corner was scribbled 'Williams dad now called Everson' what could this possibly have to do with him? Such a mystery and now his mother was gone there was nobody who could explain it to him.

William put everything back into the envelope, left the room and walked back onto the ward, hoping to catch Bridget before she left. Another nurse approached as he entered. "Can I help you? You look lost". Williams eye's were, scanning, searching for the kind smile that had meant so much.

"I, I'm ok thank you"

He wasn't, and the lie was easily detected.

"I was hoping to see Sister Herbert".

It was the turn of the nurse to look white; "You haven't heard then, I thought most of her friends would have heard by now…"

William's eyes met hers but she pulled away unable to maintain contact.

"I am sorry but Sister Herbert died in a car accident two weeks ago".

William's head was spinning, nothing made sense.

-5-

Bishop's Palace, Lambeth, London
24th July 2009

The sun shone brightly, reflecting the river onto the vast glass expanses and aluminium fronted buildings that line London's Southbank. From the helicopter, the heat haze made it look as though the stone mansions along Pall Mall were fluid and rippling. The Thames shone like polished steel snaking around the government heartland of the city. Particularly prominent from above was the Tate Modern and the shining dome of St Paul's Cathedral. The city in summer heaved with tourists, a mass of ants crawling around, indistinguishable from this height. Each one going everywhere but no-where.

The Pope's envoy, Cardinal Valetti arrived securely and anonymously in a church seconded helicopter from Biggin Hill airport where a private jet had landed from Rome less than 60 minutes earlier. Below him, Valetti picked out the MI6 and MI5 buildings as well as the revolving wheel of the London Eye and the Houses of Parliament.

As they landed at the Bishop's Palace he looked at his watch, 30 minutes late, he was going to be the last one to arrive at the Christian World Planning Committee. Accompanied by an assistant and a private body guard he made his way from the helicopter across the courtyard through the Norman-style arched entrance, along the stone corridor to the Great Hall. He left his attendants in the ante room and the entered the Hall with a flurry, his gown following like a faithful dog. At last the meeting could get under way.

The hubbub turned to silence as the Archbishop of Canterbury rose to his feet. The dust of ages and little flecks of gold played in the sunbeams as they peered through the mullioned windows. He looked around at the gathered elite representatives of the Christian Faith and steadied himself by leaning on the giant rectagonal banqueting table that spanned the length of the room.

"Welcome to London, gentlemen and thank you for coming. Before we address the matters arising from our previous meeting, I want to brief you about a serious issue that has come to my attention." The Primate paused and slowly sipped his water.

"Please look at the contents of the folder before you. You should have a list of photographs and text regarding a vital historic document called "The Hereford Mappa Mundi" which is kept at Hereford Cathedral. As you may know, this document is the only surviving complete medieval map of the world. It measures 1.62 meters by 1.35 meters and is made of one sheet of vellum. It has been dated on art, historical, and paleographical grounds to between 1290 and 1310 AD."

He proceeded to explain that on the map there are around 500 illustrations including 420 views or symbols of cities and towns, 15 depictions of biblical events, 33 depictions of plants, animals, birds and fish, 32 pictures of the peoples of the earth and 5 images relating stories from classical mythology. The illustrations on the map are one of its most remarkable features, both in their variety and number.

Outside the boundary of the earth at the top the map, a painting depicts Christ in judgment and has the letters m,o,r,s (spelling 'mors' – Latin for death) around the outside. This reflects the Christian view that all earthly life is subject to death and judgment and that the map is, above all, a depiction of the place of humankind in the eternal, divinely-ordained order.

Other examples of similar maps known to have once existed include the Ebstorf map which was destroyed in 1943, and the Duchy of Cornwall map, which is roughly contemporary with the Hereford Mappa Mundi but of which only a small fragment now survives. It is different from other existing large medieval world maps such as the 1375 'Catalan world map', now in the Bibliothèque Nationale de France, as these are based on 'portolan charts' which depict coastlines more realistically but did not have the spiritual and didactic purpose of the Mappa Mundi. In this respect the Hereford Mappa Mundi is the best surviving graphical representation of the synthesis of classical knowledge with the medieval worldview. The Hereford Mappa Mundi is world renowned and recently this wonderful document has been placed on the world protection register of UNESCO.

"I am sure we are all aware of this wonderful document, how has it become a serious issue, after all these years?" asked Valetti, sarcastically.

The Archbishop looked uncomfortable. "Recently, when the original map was being assessed for preservation purposes, it was scanned using the very latest x ray, infra red and ultra violet techniques. The scans revealed something important, something that we need to address together."

He paused as if wondering whether he should be imparting the news at all. There was complete silence in the Great Hall as he motioned to the door keeper to leave the room. Leaning forward on the table to fully engage their attention he looked around and continued; "The new tests on the vellum reveal that in the distant past, some of the original map was damaged by the removal of certain information and subsequent over painting."

There was a pause; he had the attention of every man in the room. "The figure of Christ had originally appeared over a particular part of the map, not the Holy Lands but… Britain."

Valetti leaned forward, his heavy brow revealed his concerns.

The text read, "Jesus the Christ is buried here."

The murmurs in the room sounded like the babble of a Jewish market as the words sank in.

The American representative was Tom Merryweather, a large portly figure in his early sixties, not known for his insight. "Your grace, if I may, why would anyone have originally added such information, who was responsible for creating the map?"

The Archbishop had to refer to his research notes; "On the lower left hand corner is the name Richard of Haldingham and Lafford, which are places in Lincolnshire but nothing much is known about him."

Merryweather thought for a moment, "I am not questioning you, of course your grace, but it seems inconceivable that we know nothing of a man who created such an important document."

Cardinal Valetti adjusted his glasses and coughed impatiently. "Surely it doesn't matter who created it, shouldn't the question be, who knows about this and how do we keep them quiet? Imagine if someone decides to reveal to the masses that there was even a chance that Jesus lived and died in Britain after the crucifixion. How much would the media pay for that scoop? The paparazzi would be all over the Pontiff making his life hell!"

The Archbishop continued coldly; "The testing and preservation of the vellum was done by Dr Roger Felix, an academic and an expert in the field. I had thought that perhaps we could all just ignore these finds or make them disappear."

Valetti lost his sense of humour; "Who is this Felix character and where is the vellum now?"

The Archbishop moved his arms in a calming gesture; "The Vellum is safe and back in its secure location but alas, Doctor Felix has become very interested in the matter. CADW, the Welsh body responsible for historical sites, say that he has requested to re-investigate the site of St Peter's Church near Cardiff, on the pretext of looking for the legendary King Arthur!"

Valetti looked most surprised; "King Arthur? What on earth has he got to do with it?"

The Archbishop responded; "The hidden portrait of Jesus and the text were not the only things that someone had tried to remove from the map…they had also tried to remove the image of three silver chevrons on a red shield and some text over mid Britain which translates as: Here is the land of Arthur."

Valetti's hard features and severe glasses made him look older than his early 40's. "Well, thinking about it logically I don't really see what all the fuss is about. This map was made in the 13th century when people involved in the Crusades told tales of King Arthur, his knights and the Holy Grail to bolster courage and provide justification. Naturally these stories filtered through into art and fantasy. There are stories that the tomb of God is in France and that the Templars had the head of John the Baptist. Religious secret societies are invented in novels and films for the gullible masses to swallow up. And what has been the effect on the Faith? There are more Christians around the world today than ever."

It may seem surprising to some how unmoved Valetti appeared to be by the idea that Jesus may have lived in Britain after the date of his crucifixion. However, from very early on, some members of the Church have been aware of the stories and legends, no doubt augmented over the centuries, of Jesus and his followers coming to Britain before and crucially after the crucifixion. Traditions link King Arthur to Jesus Christ and the Holy Family. In the 14th century as part of the genocide of the Welsh by the English a monk called Scolan or Scholaticus was tasked by the Church to gather all written evidence of these tales. In the twenty years of his search he found mounds of books and parchments recording various things about Jesus, mostly in ancient Latin and Welsh. Exactly what he found is unclear but we do know that he took the collection to the Tower of London where it was burned as heretical as were some of the people who had been deliberately hiding these texts including Richard of Haldingham who created the Mappa Mundi. After his death the monks at Hereford tried to obliterate the offending information rather than destroy the whole wonderful map that had taken so long to complete.

Gutto'r Glyn a 14th cent bard from "The books of the Cymru (Khumry) and their remains."

"Went to the White Tower where they were hid,
Cursed was Ysgolans (Scolans) act,
In throwing them in heaps into the fire"

In his reports to Henry II Gerald de Windsor identified the things that the Welsh knew as dangerous and even advocated the total extermination of the whole Welsh nation, suggesting that the area should become one vast hunting and game reserve.

Merryweather revealed the speed of his thinking with another question: "This St Peter's Church that Dr Felix is now interested in; how is it related?"

The Archbishop indulged him; "In 1980 the Church in Wales were approached by two historians, Morgan and Pender, who wanted to buy a little known and obscure ruin known as St Peter's Super Montem on a remote mountain in South Wales. To the Senate it was just a pile of rubble they were happy to offload, which they did without consulting the Ecclesiastical History Department or, my office."

He continued; "In 1986 the two historians published a book called *Artorius Rex Discovered*. It turned out to be different to the other nonsense published about Arthur. Their work was based on ancient Welsh documents which they translated. It seemed that Scholasticus had not gathered up every piece of early Christian material, especially that remaining on stones. From their work they hypothesized that King Arthur might be buried at the church. They didn't manage to complete the dig because of terrible weather and a tragic death. However their dig at the church in 1990 did turn up some interesting finds including a very tall 6th century skeleton interred under the altar and a metal cross which, legend tells us, was made by Merlin and which, according to the early saints has ethereal properties. Some say it is marked on the reverse with magical symbols leading to the exact location of the body of Jesus."

Valetti's face showed real interest and concern; "So where are these finds now?"

The Archbishop shrugged his shoulders.

"I am afraid we don't know, but, so far as the cross is concerned we think Morgan and Pender have hidden that somewhere. If it surfaces and if it is genuine then it could present an embarrassing problem. When Doctor Felix went to see our friend Ms Clarke at CADW about a new dig he told her that he had re-tested and dated it to the 6th century so, he must have had it at some point."

Valetti continued his inquisition; "And their book, if that held so much information about the real Arthur then why wasn't it a best seller?"

The Archbishop relented; "We declared the book to be heretical, we didn't want to risk any destabilization of the government or the church. MI5 were tasked with discrediting Morgan and Pender and all their labours, they did a pretty good job."

Valetti smiled; "Nice work, Your Grace, it's a shame you can't get hold of that cross, perhaps I can help? And what about the site, doesn't that need protecting?"

The Archbishop was able to confirm that the St Peter's Church site had recently been put under 24 hour surveillance.

-6-

BBC, White City, London
27th July 2009

Helen Daniels arrived at the BBC very late. She was anchor woman on *Crime Prevention UK* and had missed the morning planning meeting. All day long she had been trying to play catch up. She looked gaunt as her 45 years revealed themselves beyond the Botox. Her weekend had been a disaster and her new pills were obviously way too strong. They made her sleep but they didn't bring any relief from her troubles.

As an investigative journalist, she was familiar with being threatened by those she upset. She'd been sworn at, spat at and was even punched in the face once but these recent threats were much more sinister and calculated. Whoever it was had her personal phone number and kept calling her. British Telecom changed it which put an end to the calls for two days then they started again. She was onto her third mobile and that had just been compromised. She also received letters at the BBC. They were perverted and graphically detailed, explaining what the author wanted to do to her. The invisible stalker syndrome was the diagnosis of the Beeb's shrink. Apparently it was a common hazard that went with a high profile television career. It was one she could do without.

More recently and most worryingly letters had started to arrive at her home address. It had got so bad that she was frightened to go out and had taken to barricading herself in at night with the lights on.

Then the low-tech freak became hi-tech and started sending emails, lots of them. You should never open attachments but these opened automatically, revealing images of corpses, cut up and dumped. The message was always the same: "Drop it or die."

The IT guys at the Beeb tried to make her anonymous but they were up against a twisted and very talented geek.

For a while she didn't know which one of her investigations had triggered this hate campaign but then the communications had become more specific. It was the documentary series about King Arthur, the one that she had been discussing with Dr Felix, Morgan and Pender.

The police had initially been very good, after all she had spent much of her life helping them but even they had admitted there was no more they could do, they certainly didn't have the manpower to guard her 24 hours a day. She felt betrayed and alone.

Mark, in IT, had spent hours working with forensics to try to trace the emails. Mostly they were either nyms or emails that had piggy-backed genuine email accounts; clones of friends carrying the enemy to her. The police had set up a sting clone email account and had been trying to monitor the traffic. The most recent theory was that it was someone inside the BBC who was willingly or unwittingly sending them. Understandably Mark was not amused, as head of IT, it looked bad on him.

It had been a wearisome day. She looked at her watch, 10.30pm. She resolved to hand in her notice in the morning. No investigation was worth all this crap. She knew her father would support her decision, that's why she had just sent him the email. Maybe she should have talked to him sooner, after all he was certainly the right man to talk to, but, she had always been independent. Her father called it stubbornness and he was probably right.

She stood up carefully from the swivel chair brushing a hand through her long blonde hair; well it was just about still blonde, even a girl in her forties needed a little help from a hair colour now and again. She couldn't help feeling a bit dizzy as she stretched her arms above her head in a protracted yawn. "I must get more sleep" she said aloud.

A sudden bang froze her to the spot, but it was only Bob, the Beeb's security guard on the evening shift, he'd been blowing up balloons for a colleague's birthday surprise when one burst. "Are you alright Ms Daniels?"

Helen gathered her composure and sighed with relief. "Yes thank you, Bob, I'm just paranoid."

He helped her on with her coat and she walked out through the doorway, his eyes following her.

"You take care now!"

Helen turned and waved, "You too, good night."

Passing her boss's office, she slipped her resignation letter under the door.

The guard at the front of the building spoke covertly into his pay-as-you-go mobile phone; "She's on her way."

Outside, the curved entrance to the BBC building a stocky man in a light mac stood in the shadows lighting a cigar. Spits of rain wet her face. Even at this hour, the city was buzzing with traffic, like a bee waiting to sting.

Helen pulled the collar of her black coat up around her neck trying to make herself invisible.. Just to her side a man in his 30's, tall and athletic looking had caught up and was walking alongside her, nervously she looked round.

"Are you going to the car park? Can I walk with you?"

Relief! It was Mark from IT. "Sure, that would be brilliant...I didn't fancy the walk on my own in the dark...especially, well, you know after the emails and stuff."

Mark smiled knowingly as she continued; "I was too late in this morning to get into the underground car park."

"Same here, late nights, not enough sleep, it goes with the territory.....it certainly screws up your love life!"

Helen fell silent as they walked along the pedestrian way, into Hockley Road and towards the car park. There was a slight smell of cigar smoke on the wind.

"If you're lucky enough to have one."

"Have what?" asked Helen.

"A love life, I mean."

Helen was happy for the distracting small talk; "And I take it you don't have a love life?"

Mark shook his head; "I'm a divorced IT geek, it doesn't read well on the dating pages. What about you?"

Helen stopped walking and eyeballed him.

"Are you trying to chat me up?"

Mark blushed and there was an awkward pause.

Back in her office the phone was ringing. This time it was a friendly call, her father had just read her email and was desperate to speak to her.

Mark was transfixed by her eyes. He'd fancied her for years but had never thought he was worthy of her attention. She hooked her arm in his, the moment passed and they continued walking in silence, each aware of the other but not knowing what to say.

She looked so alone and vulnerable; "Have I said the wrong thing?"

Helen took time responding, "No, I've just realized what a hold this stalker thing has had over me, I've not even thought about romance for weeks!" Suddenly all the stress and fear brewed up and she burst into tears. He stopped and held her in his arms, stroking her long hair and wiping away her tears. It seemed only natural to hold her tight. He felt her breasts heaving against his chest, a moment he had dreamed of for some time.

Mark looked steadily into her eyes; "I think you should know that I may be on to something. I have traced some of those emails to an ISP in Mexico, it has been hot routed to try to disguise the fact that it has come from a proxy account belonging to Morgan and Pender."

"Shit, they're the two I've been working with on the Arthur project! Why have you only just told me?"

"I only found out this evening, I wanted to be sure of the facts."

A few moments passed until Helen was able to look at the man again. When she did, they both stood in silence gazing into each other's eyes. He held her face in both hands and pulled her towards him. Their lips were trembling, just inches apart. They saw a car go by. A door bang disturbed their intimate moment. He slid an arm around her shoulders and they continued on their way. She didn't object, suddenly she felt butterflies in her stomach, like a first love all over again, God it had been years since she had felt that. Neither was aware of the stocky man following some distance behind.

Tired of the ringing, the security guard entered Helen's office and answered the phone.

"Helen, Helen, is that you…?"

"I'm security, Miss Daniels has just left for the evening. Can I take a message?"

"I'm Helen's father, I need to get hold of her urgently. Her life may be in danger… Christ, can you run after her? Please can you tell her to go to a public place and stay there, tell her to ring me straight away."

The guard remained calm and sympathetic; "Of course sir, I'll see if I can catch her up."

Helen and Mark arrived at the entrance to the car park quicker than either of them really wanted. They stood looking rather awkwardly at each other.

"Look," He said, "I probably shouldn't say this, but, will, umm can I…"

Helen sensed the moment but was in two minds, her heart overruled her head; "Take me out for lunch tomorrow? Yes of course you can." Mark smiled and she reached up to peck him on the cheek. Their happy moment was broken by Helen's mobile phone; the William Tell ringtone identified the caller as her father. She turned the phone off and put it back in her pocket.

Mark was love struck and sought excuses to keep her talking. In truth she was glad of the company and she wasn't looking forward to going home to an empty house.

"Hey, look, we've even parked near to each other!" He knew it sounded rubbish as soon as he said it and they looked playfully into each other's eyes like two teenagers. They opened their respective car doors and waved to each other. "See you tomorrow Helen."

Soon he was gone and she was alone with her thoughts wondering whether she should retract her resignation. She checked her rear view mirror before reversing out of the parking space. She thought she saw a shadow move in her peripheral vision. Instinctively she locked the door and slammed her foot down on the accelerator. The car stalled. Desperately she tried to start it again. Someone in front was waving her down, someone she knew. Then the man with the cigar appeared from nowhere alongside the driver's window. He leveled the silenced Welrod and shot. A single shot before she could say a word. One small piece of lead travelled through Helens head and shattered the glass opposite killing her instantly.

There was a small clean hole in one side of her flesh but on the other side of her head parts of her brain ran down between the fine spray of blood and sticky grey matter mingling with shards of glass on the passenger's seat and door.

The man in the mac slipped the gun inside his coat, removed the cigar from his mouth and crushed it under foot as if it was a beetle. Like the coldness of the night there was no emotion on his face. At that moment he didn't love, he didn't hate, he was just a paid assassin. The other man melted into the shadows, shaking. This was not the way it was meant to be.

-7-

Newcastle
28th July 2009

Rachel sat in the foyer of the Great Northern Hotel, sipping coffee and waiting for the taxi to take her to the interview. Her eyes glazed over, she hadn't slept well and, worryingly, she hadn't been able to get hold of William to tell him what she was up to…well, she had left him a message, that was the least she could do. He wasn't going to be pleased with her, after all, she had promised to go with him to Canterbury for the funeral service of their mutual friend Michael.

As an idea it had always seemed to work pretty well. Rachel's childhood chum, Nicole researched and made television documentaries with Helen Daniels and helped out with some of the research. She was given the inside story in order to write news articles which accompanied and helped promote the films. It was a win/win situation. The production company and the television station secured valuable coverage and Rachel had been able to sell her stories.

Rachel knew that Nicole had been working on a special project for some time but, unusually, she had not been very forthcoming about the subject matter. Yesterday she had received a call from Nicole who said she had arranged an appointment for her with two historians, Morgan and Pender; she explained that she had been researching some of their claims about King Arthur and that the filming was almost complete.

"You'll love this story" she had said confidently…. "you'll need to come up straightaway, it's hot and I think it's all going to kick off." Nicole sounded even more enthusiastic than usual. Rachel flicked her face with her finger, a habit that betrayed concern. She hadn't asked what the urgency was and Nicole hadn't exactly said. Whatever the situation, it was damn inconvenient because it required that she drop everything and drive from London to Newcastle. Although Nicole actually lived in nearby Hexham, she didn't invite Rachel to stay over… maybe there was a new man in her life?

Back in London William was just stirring. He had been feeling increasingly odd recently, almost not really there. Distant, and de-personalised his doctor had called it. The few hours of sleep had been fragmented and haunted with dreams of Michael, only natural as his friend had died in suspicious circumstances and it was his funeral today.

Still half asleep, William managed to find the switch for the coffee machine without wearing his varifocals. Reaching for the fridge door he became aware of the red flashing blur demanding his attention. There was a message on his home phone. It must have arrived when he'd switched it off to avoid the stupid sales, mechanical and silent calls that seemed to have increased lately despite his registration with the Telephone Preference Service.

"William, hi, it's Rachel. Will, I'm really sorry to do this to you; I can't be with you for Michael's funeral, I've got an urgent appointment in Newcastle, don't be angry, see you soon."

William's head found his hands in a kind of automatic grief. Michael's death just before his mother's hadn't really sunk in and he didn't know how he'd face the funeral service alone. He knew he shouldn't rely so much on Rachel emotionally but today he really needed someone.

Rachel took a taxi from the hotel to Morgan and Pender's place which resembled a fortress more than a home. The imposing Victorian rectory was protected by a high stone and flint wall topped with glass and barbed wire. The taxi stopped at the double re-enforced iron and wooden gate which was covered with graffiti. Beyond the video surveillance cameras she could see the rambling old building, its large gothic style windows covered with ornate metal security railings. Rachel paid and exited the taxi. The driver took off quickly, racing to the next job.

She brushed herself down even though she was only wearing jeans and a cotton blouse. Her wavy dark hair was swept back from her face in a plait revealing her youthful complexion and good bone structure. She stepped towards the wooden gates but was stopped in her tracks by the sudden and aggressive barking of two Dobermans. Regaining her composure, she used her mobile.

Pender answered, "Just a minute whilst we sort the dogs out." He had a very aggressive version of the Geordie accent. The sounds of barking were joined by shouting. Bolts clunked and hinges creaked. Eventually the gates opened and Pender appeared. He looked to be in his mid 40's, fair haired and ruggedly handsome but there was no sign of a smile, if anything, his look was one of suspicion.

"You look nothing like your photo" he said, "Don't go near the dogs, they'll bite" he pointed to the two vicious dogs straining at the leash, sniffing and growling. Rachel didn't need telling twice.

Then Morgan appeared at the door, a stocky gentleman in his early seventies, grey thinning hair tied back in a pony tail, again, no smile, no handshake, and no warm welcome, just a look to weigh her up.

The Rectory was a beautiful building with an adjoining coach house set in extensive grounds next to a Gothic graveyard. The grounds were the domain of the dogs, this place was not just a house; it was a castle.

Morgan and Pender ushered Rachel through the hallway which was lined with prints and photographs and into a study that was stacked with old books opened at various pages. Piles of papers, floppy discs and CDs were strewn about. It was clear that their priorities lay in research rather than décor. Morgan studied her, reading her thoughts and motioned her to sit down.

"We are in the middle of researching another book" he said, gesturing in the direction of the piles of material that surrounded them. "That's the thing with old books you either read them or dust them. As you can see, we do the former."

Rachel felt a little uncomfortable but tried not to show it. "It's a lovely house."

Pender replied, "It will be when we've finished the renovations but our research comes first." The only emotion showed was for his work, a lifelong passion, a commitment that may easily have become an obsession.

Morgan and Pender sat down on chairs behind a large desk and Rachel sat in front, feeling like a schoolchild ready for a history lesson. Morgan and Pender started talking simultaneously which frustrated them and confused her. Morgan motioned to Pender, "How about making a cup of tea… I am sure this young lady could do with one." Rachel looked grateful. Pender muttered something under his breath as he left the room, dragging his foot.

Morgan explained that Pender had been in a hit and run accident years ago which left him with a weakness on his chest and a bad leg. As he leaned towards her to explain this, Rachel noticed a spark of wisdom and secrecy in his eyes. She knew she'd never get the whole story from him.

"Are you sure you want to get involved with this? We'll probably never get to the bottom of the threats."

Rachel sat upright, "What do you mean, *threats*?"

Morgan rolled his eyes, "Surely Helen and Nicole told you?"

Rachel's look said it all. Morgan picked up a handful of letters and notes and handed them to Rachel. They were all written on light blue airmail paper and comprised of stick drawing diagrams and descriptions of how the author was going to make Morgan and Pender suffer by crucifying them "in the fire and brimstone of hell. For all that you have done to God."

Rachel was gripped in horror suddenly realising that she was touching the very paper that this nutter had handled. She dropped them onto the table like hot potatoes.

Morgan engaged her, "Charming isn't it? We've endured threats for years but these ones are really sinister."

Rachel was visibly upset, "Why would someone write such vile things, why would someone want to kill you?"

Morgan shrugged his shoulders, gesturing with two open hands; "Clearly we have upset someone, somewhere!"

Rachel looked intently at Morgan, trying to read any clues; "Any ideas?"

Morgan looked thoughtful. Ideas, yes, plenty. If what we have found out about King Arthur is only half true then it could be embarrassing to the church and to the government.

Feeling uncomfortable Rachel adjusted her hair, took out her reporters notebook and poised a sharp pencil over the page; "Care to elaborate Mr Morgan?"

He motioned for her to put away her book; "There are things about this you simply cannot try to print."

She looked deflated. Morgan picked up her disappointment; "It's for your own good."

She put the book down and listened. Morgan chose his words carefully; "Don't think for one moment that the church, and I mean any denomination of the church are cute and cuddly. They run a profitable business offering hope, forgiveness and salvation in return for large sums of money. Then, of course, there is the government. Doesn't matter what colour you support, they are as much interested in power and control as the church. Does that answer your question?"

Rachel looked Morgan directly in the eye; "You mean the church and the government are trying to kill you? You are joking, right?"

Morgan was deadly serious.

There was a large bang from upstairs, Rachel jumped out of her skin.

Morgan smiled; "It's ok BT are here fixing the phone lines."

Rachel sighed, grateful for the light relief. "So, Mr Morgan, is there anything you can tell me that I can print about the story?"

For the briefest moment she thought the older man was going to open up but, just then Pender came back into the room visibly shaking, the tray of tea only just making it to the table.

His face was like thunder because he had overheard some of the conversation; "It's those MI5 bastards, they are in cahoots with the Welsh Police, they never liked us, they want to see us dead..... we know too much to live that's what this is all about....that bastard Robin Bryant, we trusted him but he was just one of them, ridiculing our research and smearing our reputations!" His aggression was deep, almost violent and his body shook. He tensed his hands, making fists as if striking an unseen and unknown enemy.

"And now they've killed Helen Daniels, the bastards."

There was silence as each looked at the other. Rachel was frightened by his behaviour, her voice was slight, "Helen, what do you mean they've killed Helen Daniels?"

Pender was still shaking; "I've just heard it on the news, they've murdered Helen Daniels."

Rachel went white, she didn't know whether to speak or run; "Who, who has killed Helen Daniels..."

"THEY have, THEY have killed her; the only media person that has taken our work seriously in the last few years."

Rachel caught the mood, "Christ, why would anyone want to kill Helen, she was a respected television journalist." She found herself caught up in the emotion of the moment and started crying in shock and disbelief. She had worked with Helen a few times and she always seemed professional and fair.

Morgan and Pender were talking at each other in stereo again but she didn't hear a word, her mind was on other things, she tried phoning Nicole but only got her answer phone. "Nicole, it's Rachel, call me the minute you get this message, it's urgent. I've just heard about Helen."

She was inconsolable, she tried to be composed and make herself heard; "I'm really sorry guys but I'm far too upset to do this now, can I come back later, please?"

Suddenly the shouting stopped and the surreal moment passed. Morgan looked more understanding and sympathetic; "Of course you can, come back this evening when you feel better."

He looked back towards Pender; "Come on, we have things to do anyway."

-8-

Home Secretary's Office, Whitehall, London
28th July 2009

Vanessa Grey, operational head of MI5 was ushered into the Home Secretary's office. She sat when he beckoned and listened as he opened the conversation, "You have seen the Archbishop's briefing document concerning the potentially dangerous revelations uncovered when the Mappa Mundi was recently tested, I take it?"

"The stuff about the land of Arthur and Jesus Christ being buried here; yes, I've read it." She replied impatiently. "So what, the medieval world was full of propaganda and claims; religion is power and control and the church are masters at both, right, so what's new?"

The Home Secretary was slightly taken aback; "Religion and belief are stability Grey, don't ever forget that."

Grey nodded reluctantly; "I know."

The Home Secretary continued, "This archaeologist, Dr Roger Felix, who carried out the new experiments on the Mappa Mundi whilst handling its preservation. Turns out he was also advising Helen Daniels at the BBC about the documentary she was making on Morgan and Pender's Arthurian research. It seems that Felix is also friendly with Morgan and Pender. Chances are he may have shared the information he discovered with them and Helen Daniels. This chap Felix is quite a closet sympathizer of those researchers."

Grey was well briefed, she had seen incompetent political Home Secretary's come and go and hated pretending they knew more than she did; "Yes, I know. Felix has been to see CADW to try to get them to agree that Morgan and Pender's dig at St Peters Church be re-opened. He told Sylvia Clarke that he had re tested the cross found in 1990 and proved it to be 6th century. That would put the cat amongst the pigeons. I am guessing he has also told Daniels and she has told the BBC."

The Home Secretary looked Grey squarely in the eye; "Daniels was murdered last night, a professional hit by the looks of it. Do you know anything about it?"

Grey shook her head and raised her hands; "I know but it wasn't us. We are not happy at all, she was one of our best assets."The Home Secretary looked lost, clearly he had no idea that Helen had been working with MI5. "Our man tells me that people from the Homicide and Serious Crime Command augmented by SO15 are all over it."

Grey looked thoughtful as if she felt more explanation was required.

"It doesn't surprise me that the counter terrorism guys are involved. The government and the Church first approached MI5 about Morgan and Pender and their research in 1985.Quite a bit before our time. They had been re translating the ancient Welsh records and propounding a very different history to that which is taught. Whether they were right or wrong, academics and the church thought that they were getting uncomfortably close to undermining the current monarchy, historical and religious dogma. We have managed to restrict the sales of their self published books and have a code red mandate out against them so that no private broadcasting, publishing or other media can get behind them in a big way. Now they have discovered the power of the internet it is harder but we re-route their net access with a dummy clone front end and we have a dedicated "listener" for them at GCHQ so that we can sanitize any potential problems. I think they must be getting "outside help" though because some of the information they have managed to get on to the internet is volatile and could possibly could stir up nationalists and religious extremists. Our strategies so far in discrediting and harassing them in various ways over the years have kept a lid on their endeavors, we certainly treat them as potential terrorists, especially as they seem to have contacts with groups in Israel. It seems like our friends at SO15 have the same intel."

This was news to the Home secretary, but then everything seemed news to him.

"We're talking MOSSAD?"

Shrugging her shoulders to side step the question she continued, "I believe the problem escalated recently when Daniels started deviating from her agreed course and taking Morgan and Pender's research too seriously. Despite our blackout mandate the BBC looked ready to run with a major documentary series. When we contacted them they banged on about Public Interest and open editorial policies so we reverted to more covert means. We tried calling her in and warning her off, we visited her personally and offered a nice little sum for her to walk away and not to have anything to do with the matter, we even asked the Archbishop of Canterbury's office to give her a call. She was determined that Morgan and Pender were on to something fundamentally important and that they should have a fair hearing."

The Home Secretary's steady accusing look demanded more clarification and Grey obliged; "No, really, we certainly didn't neutralize her, she was our asset but she did seem to be losing her way. We've heard chatter that the CIA via the US National Security Agency have more than just a passing interest in this because of some of the more outlandish religious and historical claims Morgan has made, for example, he suggests that America was "discovered" by king Arthur's brother Madoc in the 6th century."

The Home Secretary spluttered, "You are not serious". She was. Apparently the mineralogist Henry Schoolcraft (born New York State circa 1812) engaged in surveys that took him into Native American country. In the era 1760-1870 the legend that a Welsh Prince had sailed to America in antiquity was known to many. There are 25 reliable accounts from migrating investigative explorers who encountered American Natives who could speak and understand Khumeric (The ancient Welsh language).

Some of these people had been shown ancient books written in a strange alphabet, probably Coelbran, (called bibles) that had been in their possession for centuries. When President Thomas Jefferson heard of such books he demanded that they be located and burned. The Cherokee nation was systematically removed from its homelands (a 'cleansing' called the Trail of Tears) When he was told that this action was illegal and unconstitutional he said, "Who will take the matter to court?"

There was a moment of incredulity.

"Of course there is the little matter of the metal cross that was found at the St Peters dig which Morgan and Pender apparently keep well hidden. If it really is 6th century and mentions King Arthur it is probably the only definitive proof that such a person existed."

The Home Secretary tried to look more informed than he actually was. "But that would be great for tourism wouldn't it?"

Grey tried to explain; "Depends on your point of view, Morgan and Pender argue that they found the cross at St Peter's by following a description in a hitherto undeciphered ancient Welsh manuscript. They argue that if the information is right about that it is also right about other things…"

"Other things? Like what for example?"

Grey stared him down; "Like the fact that JC didn't die on the cross and that he came to the UK and was buried here."

It took a few seconds to sink in; "Christ, like the evidence of over-painted drawings found by Felix on the Mappa Mundi."

Grey nodded; "Exactly, but there is something else."

The Home Secretary was all ears; "It may be nothing, but we managed to get hold of the metal analysis for the cross, it has small parts of gold and silver but Felix has not recorded what the rest is made of."

The man looked puzzled; "An unknown metal?"

Grey shrugged her shoulders as if not having any other information or maybe she was trying to find out how much the Home Secretary really knew.

"Who do you think killed Helen Daniels then, Grey?"

Grey shook her head; "I don't know, but the CIA have asked us to set up a joint operation with them to find out what is going on, I suggest we accept ".

The Home Secretary nodded in agreement. Grey went to leave the room.

The man called after her; "Just make sure you keep Morgan and Pender under close surveillance, but at all costs you must protect the Meurig project… do I make myself clear?"

He had and there was silence.

-9-

London
28th July 2009

The meeting at the agency in St Paul's had gone well. It was great when his business get-togethers were in London, especially when they were only a brisk walk away from his apartment on the South Bank. So, these guys wanted his company to come up with an inter-active game for the Welsh Tourist Board, something that would attract visitors to come and explore the culture and not just drop litter on Mount Snowdon. Natasha would be good at this one. The budget wasn't huge but it was enough. It was a project he was looking forward to getting his teeth into. He wasn't sure how he'd managed to do the deal so easily, the agency just said that he'd come highly recommended; the best way to come, he mused.

At this time of year the tourists were crawling like flies all over London, but he didn't mind that, having people to watch and things to see helped to take his mind off his almost permanent state of grief. Michael used to say that there were two ways to live your life, to walk through the woods without a sigh or run roaring like a lion and that wisdom was in knowing which was appropriate. William had tried to glean wisdom from the old shaman and now, when he really needed something to cling to he could not find it.

Michael's death made no sense on any level. Suicide was certainly not part of the shamanic belief system.

William was 16 years old when he first met the shaman at a psychic fair. He stood six feet five inches tall with a barrel chest, generous features, unrestrained long grey hair and a beard to match. To William, he resembled a friendly grizzly bear. He was warm and good humoured. William felt an affinity as soon as they met. Where others might shake your hand on a first encounter, Michael liberally dispensed huge hugs. Throughout their friendship there was so much that Michael did not reveal, a mysterious character, he practiced Native American rituals, read the tarot and communed with both the living and the dead. William trusted that Michael would always be there for him as a wise friend and protector. "Where are you now Michael" he said out loud. There was no response.

He remembered fondly the time spent with Michael trying to learn about the ancient ways of the earth and its energy but, looking back, William was sure he hadn't made a very good pupil. He got too easily distracted by his poetry writing, football and chess tournaments.

Things changed a lot when Michael lost his heart to Angela who was young, beautiful and interested in esoteric arts. She was also rich, financially, having secured excellent settlements following two previous marriages. She was good company and William enjoyed the odd weekend away with the couple, camping in the forest, drumming, communing with trees and spirits. They often spent time with the Lakota tribe and invited William along one year but that was just a step too far into the wild for him.

Three months ago William and Michael bumped into each other in Covent Garden. Michael had just finished a Tarot reading and was taking a break, indulging his love for ice cream, despite his diabetes. He seemed really upbeat, especially after two scoops of passion fruit and coconut. So when William heard of Michael's death he simply could not believe it. Apparently Angela had been away for a few days and had returned to find his body on the floor, his wrists cut and blood all over the carpet. This most certainly wasn't part of the Shaman's code.

The police found no signs of foul play but the autopsy identified very high amounts of potassium in his blood with nothing to account for it. Following the inquest the verdict was left open and with it the book of Michael's life.

Angela was understandably shaken; she had apparently lost a lot of weight during the ordeal but somehow managed to look even more beautiful. She said that Michael had been feeling down but had no idea why. He had left a will leaving everything to her. There were some debts which Michael had apparently run up and that annoyed her; she was always complaining about his profligate attitude to money but these would be settled from his estate.

His funeral was scheduled for this very afternoon at Canterbury Cathedral, of all places! Michael had often talked about his wishes to be cremated and for his ashes to be scattered to the four winds.

On the way back to his apartment, William crossed the Millennium Bridge towards the Tate Modern. His eyes were drawn to huge figures recently attached to the exterior of the old power station. One was of a man with a gun aimed at people as they walked across the bridge. On closer inspection the gun turned out to be a video camera. All is not what it seems and William pondered on this idea for some time. From the wall his eyes gazed up to the sky where interesting cloud formations created constantly changing, wholly original art forms. He could make out an elephant and a giant bird and then he saw something more familiar, a cloud pattern that resembled Michael's distinctive bearded face. It smiled for an instant before morphing into a new pattern.

He bought a Cappuccino from one of the stands outside the Tate and sat drinking it on the steps leading up to the main entrance. Again, he reflected on his good luck at getting the games contract this morning, it had virtually landed in his lap. At least now, with Natasha on the books as a co-director, he felt confident they could pull it off and make a good profit. She was the one with the programming skills and together with his creativity, they made a good team. William liked Nats, as he tended to call her, very much; she was good company, sharp, level headed and gorgeous. Even when she was being serious, her Russian accent made her endearing. Endearing and formidable; what a combination and what a turn on for William! He particularly liked it when she swore in her native tongue.

Further along the Southbank he stopped at the book stalls in front of the BFI complex. He loved a good rummage through the rows of unloved pages. They were in no particular order so it was like a giant lucky dip. As he began to focus on the books he felt a pain akin to a migraine; he had experienced this several times over the last few days. It started as a sharp stab at his temples and spread across to the back of his head. It was accompanied by flashes of lights and diamonds of reds, yellows and blues which merged into faces and figures. As the moment passed he realised he was holding a book. On the black dust jacket were two men wearing serious expressions and 1980s suits, fashionable in their time. The title intrigued him; *Artorius Rex Discovered*.

"Are you going to buy that mate?"

"Umm, yes, yes, how much is it?" William asked, returning to his senses.

"That one's a fiver."

William paid the money, tucked the book into his briefcase and continued on his way. He felt discombobulated by the sequence of events and was looking forward to getting back to his apartment when the dizziness returned. Sounds distorted, images blurred and his body was growing numb. He managed to sit on a bench outside the National Theatre where a fat woman was eating a greasy beef burger. He clutched his briefcase in one hand and slumped along the bench, his head coming to rest on her shoulder. He was out for the count. The drugs that had been slipped into his coffee at the Tate earlier worked and two fat ladies stole his wallet.

When he came round there was a street artist in his line of sight, a beautiful vision, a tall, slender ballerina in a red dress holding a red apple, poised and statuesque. His head ached and throbbed but in that moment he thought he had died and gone to heaven. Someone dropped a pound coin into the cup at her feet and she came to life, a music box dancer. Recovering a little, William was enchanted by her grace. He retrieved two pound coins from his trouser pocket and slipped them into her cup. The girl smiled and spun into ballet steps once again. She finished by handing William her apple; it must have been the two pound package.

More alert now, he continued on his way. He put the souvenir apple in his jacket pocket. That's when he realised that his wallet was missing. The woman, the drugged coffee, the dizzy spell, it all added up. Fortunately they had only taken his empty decoy wallet, what fool would carry valuables in their pocket in London these days? Thank God they didn't take his briefcase, although that was indeed strapped to his wrist.

-10-

Canterbury Cathedral, Kent
28th July 2009

It was a day like no other. Looking towards heaven masked by the gathering black clouds he was acutely aware of the hairs on the back of his neck prickling like needles to warn him all was not well. The Canterbury skyline was as dark as night as William hurried through the ancient precinct gate, late for the service. He hardly registered the cacophony created by the Japanese tourists pouring into the gift shop to his left. He did however notice two nuns in almost luminescent white with black headdresses gliding along like spirits, deep in conversation. They disappeared through the main doors of the Cathedral reminding him of a painting; who was that by?

In awe, he took a sudden step backwards and immediately felt a bump then heard a screech followed by a thud.

"You clumsy oaf!"

He had knocked over a rotund bag lady who was now lying on her back like a turtle struggling to right herself. The miscellaneous contents of her plastic shopping bags were strewn over the gravel pathway and her huge floral knickers flashed, what a picture! William tried to help her to her feet, averting his gaze from her over exposed parts. She seemed to be more helpless than hurt.

"Sir William Russell Flint," He blurted out.

His automatic and unexpected response caused the woman to rock backwards again this time taking William with her. He was temporarily immersed in grubby clothing, flaccid flesh, body odor and lavender oil. After an embarrassing tussle they both made it to their knees and William gathered some of the items that had fallen out of her bag.

"I am so, so sorry, are you alright?" He apologised.

The woman fixed him in the steady stare of an elderly schoolmarm as she snatched some of the contents of her bag from him.

"Does it look as if I am alright?"

Her chastisement sent him back to his schooldays and triggered memories he thought he'd forgotten.

"Ah, the painting, those nuns reminded me of a painting by Sir William Russell Flint!"

His unpredictable outburst was returned by an equally unpredictable action. The woman took his hand and examined the lines on his palm. Her face turned white as she let the hand go.

"My God it's you...May heaven help us all." She recoiled as if she had seen a ghost.

William picked up a bunch of violets which she had left behind and went to follow her but she had managed to travel a long way in a short time, despite her baggage. He slipped them into his pocket and made his way to the service, pondering on the unusual effect he seemed to have on the woman.

The shafts of sunlight piercing the black clouds picked out the green lead roofing and reflected shards of gold and silver from the Miracle windows. The dressed stone that had once upon a time made its way from the quarries of ancient Normandy stood out as if energized by the foundations beneath the current building. These stones cloaked the earlier Saxon structure which had been destroyed by fire. The Saxons had in their turn built upon the ancient foundations left by St Augustine and before him a most ancient Apostolic Church founded by King Lucius. Layer upon layer upon layer of theological structures were built up from the ruins of their predecessors.

It was raining in the distance and a magnificent rainbow arched over the sky. The pot of gold was a long way off on a day such as this and it seemed that at any moment the bruised sky overhead would open to unleash the anger of God. Finally the clouds did burst, a pathetic fallacy underlining his own internal storm. He was late for his friend's funeral.

Subconsciously he was putting off the moment when he had to enter the cathedral. Michael despised the grandeur and insincerity of the Christian Church and would have never consented to being buried in its 'hallowed' ground. Why did Angela ignore Michael's wishes and betray everything he stood for? Was it for Michael's sake she sought this religious outpouring or as a balm for her own guilty conscience?

What was the mysterious power she'd had over him, what was she after? On balance, William had decided that he would attend the service for Michael's sake.

He entered the cathedral via the Thomas Beckett Porch. Close by was the spot where the martyr had been murdered on 29th December in 1170. Was it just coincidence that this was the very same spot where Vikings had slain Archbishop Aelfheah in 1005.

 No wonder it felt creepy. William sat crumpled on the ledge along the return of the stone wall looking down at his undone bootlace. The sadness of the occasion seeped into his soul just like the rain had seeped into his boots. A pair of wide-fitting beige shoes with velcro fixings and sensible rubber soles came into his vision and stopped in front of him. "Do you have a ticket, sir?" He looked up to see the attendant with her blue rinse, neat hand knitted cardigan and patronising mode of address.

"A ticket?"

"Yes", she replied, "it is £10 to enter."

William stared blankly at her struggling to quell his agitation.

"I need to pay to come to my friend's funeral in the house of God?"

"I am sorry Sir, I didn't realise." She replied sheepishly, deflecting her gaze.

William moved away around the outskirts of the church, dodging the gawkers with the £10 tickets, trying to quell his anger and muster the courage to join the congregation for the service. Reflecting on the ticket price reminded him of Henry VIII. The King's methods and motives might have been dubious but at least he put a stop to the rampant money making of the church in the 16th century. He had very effectively done this at Canterbury by demolishing the Shrine of Thomas Becket during the Reformation. Beckett's shrine was erected as an offering magnet and was popular all over Europe and beyond. Henry once had 26 cart loads of gold, silver and other treasures hauled from their coffers. What the king did with it was quite another story. At least he had kept the filthy lucre from lining the ermine pockets of those using the church as a cover for accumulating wealth whilst the poor suffered.

It was important for him to remember Michael at this time so he tried to put out of his mind the centuries of misinformation that the church had propagated. From a niche near to the tomb of the Black Prince, William could at last see Michael's coffin displayed on an elevated area that once housed the Shrine of St. Thomas. Above, the 13th century windows showed scenes of pilgrims who visited and were healed. Dramatic stained glass windows were the propaganda TV adverts of their time. They had worked a treat.

William turned his attention to the Priest who was absolving Michael for his Paganism and for ignoring religious dogma. The Holy Father was trying to usher Michael into the kingdom of heaven. William wondered how much the ticket price for that attraction was.

The two nuns clasped their hands tightly in prayer in the front row. Thunder clapped and rain crashed like a waterfall against the roof. The one with the red hair and porcelain features was noticeably agitated. She clutched what appeared to be a small leather bag on a thong around her neck and then gazed over at William who caught and held her attention. Recognition washed over him in an instant. He had known her from somewhere before. Just then she tore her face away revealing her soul purpose. She rocked backwards and forwards, backwards and forwards, backwards and forwards; her face looking flushed and feverish; her eyes were wide and wild; her breath was quick and shallow.

The thunder rang out, the rain crashed down; the blow of a gladiator through the tears of a clown. The clocks stopped at 3.30pm in St Thomas's place of miracles where so many had been healed under the stained glass of blessings. William watched as each mourner became aware of the movement of the nun. One after another they raised their faces in judgement and disbelief.

She rocked backwards and forwards, backwards and forwards, backwards and forwards. The Priest's hollow words heightened her agitation. He made the sign of the cross as if that could prevent the mysteries of the world from unfurling before their eyes.

She rocked backwards and forwards, backwards and forwards, rubbing her hands across her breasts and legs, rubbing and rubbing, rocking and rocking, rubbing and rocking until her robes gaped at the knees exposing the soft white flesh of her inner thighs.

The congregation was transfixed as her skin became illuminated by the sheets of lightning from heaven lancing through the eyes of the building. The faithful stood rapt, looking on like abandoned sheep. The Priest's forehead beaded over in perspiration, he fought to continue, powerless to stop her, incapable of ignoring her. Mourners with children grabbed them and bolted ungraciously; some stomped away in disgust but most remained, transfixed.

The other nun spoke in undertones, pleading to her, desperately trying to fend off the unstoppable.

A biblical thunderclap shuddered the entire magnificent building, seconds lasting forever in some bizarre giant cosmic orgasm. Lightning bisected the stained glass windows showering technicolored rays of violet, red, and green across the cathedral, illuminating the nun for an eternity. She rose as if struck from her seat and rushed at the Priest. He cowered, futilely making the sign of the cross and reciting the Lord's Prayer then stumbled backwards clutching his cross, stumbling and clutching, falling and cowering.

The redheaded nun glanced at William in a heartbeat of serenity and smiled, her eyes penetrated his soul making him feel naked in her presence. Extraordinarily composed in the moment, she spoke with the authority of one possessed by an ancient deity.

"Don't become victims, those who can make you believe absurdities can make you commit atrocities. The church is a lie. I have given 15 years of my life to it but I now know the truth and you must also learn it before it is too late. The church has legalised robbery and called it truth, it has burned the books of your true history, conquered belief through torture with its armies of righteousness, invented memories and gospels with the intention of controlling you but you don't see it. I have found the truth and the freedom it brings. I have seen the way, the truth, and the light. I hear the words of the ancients and I hear them laughing at you for your weakness and stupidity, like lambs to the slaughter."

She unfurled her red hair ripping frantically at her garments, freeing herself from bondage. She revealed her glistening body in the presence of the Almighty then sank to her knees, sweat creating rivulets between her breasts, trickling over her stomach and mixing with her bodily fluids on the polished stone floor as she writhed and groaned. A silver flash, she drew a knife blade across one wrist then the other, splashing the crucifix of the Priest who was paralysed by her spell.

Rubbing her bleeding wrists over and between her thighs she moved rhythmically as if in sexual union with some unseen lover. As she arched her back she uprooted the leather pouch from her neck and clasped it in her hand. Her tormented body thrust backwards crashing into Michael's coffin sending it flying to the floor.

The incessant lightning overhead created a strobe-like slowing of time. Fully revealed now in her naked gyrations on the tiled floor it was clear she was pregnant and her expectant body heaved in time with the rumbles that seemed to shake the very foundations. Synchronised with a thunder crack and lightning strike from straight above, the nun shaped her body into a cross and shouted…. "My God, why have you forsaken me?" With a final jolt she was still, white and blue foam oozing from her mouth. Her crucifixion was complete.

Only William and the second nun moved to help her, slipping and sliding across the blood and sweat as they hurried. Most of the remaining congregation fled screaming, but, a handful looked back, paralysed like pillars of salt. William knelt in the blood and the grime beside the naked nun, resting her head on his knee. She was still and cold but there was movement in her belly. Her baby was kicking. He looked carefully for signs of life, barely discerning the shallow rise and fall of her chest. The scent of fresh blood on innocent skin triggered race memories for him. Her life was ebbing away like the retreating seas at full moon; dying like a Templar Knight at Acre. Somewhere he had seen this all before.

Close up her beauty stunned William. He removed his jacket and slipped it over her; as he did so the bunch of violets he'd picked up earlier spilled from a pocket and spread across the girls naked breasts. Kneeling by her side, he pulled off his white shirt and ripped it in half making two tourniquets, one for each wrist. Quickly he tied them tightly, trying to stem the spurting blood.He felt transfixed by her ambience and saddened by the profound tears running down her face. He gathered her in his arms holding and rocking her, lightly, caringly, willing her to live. He held her hand lightly as he gazed into her beautiful face; her eyes were closed but moving as if in a dream. More than once they fluttered open and her lips created the slightest of smiles. Her faint grip clung to his fingers as if her soul might fly in an instant. He bent closer to whisper in her ear;

"Sister Herbert, Bridget, I am here for you, I believe you and I believe in you."

A moment or two passed. It wasn't just his imagination, her eyes did momentarily open and smile through tears of joy or pain, he wasn't sure which. Feebly she pushed her other hand into his, passing him the leather pouch soaked with her blood.

"Do this for him, William" she whispered, drawing William's gaze to the shape that kicked in her womb. "He is your son"

William was totally bemused, his son, how could that be? Perhaps she was delirious, perhaps she had mistaken him for someone else, perhaps they had slipped back in time. He thought he glimpsed figures moving around her. Something made him nod and comfort her. Now he was fighting back the tears and failing. His salty sobs mixed with hers as her eyes closed with a sigh. He had no idea what was happening. She looked like Sister Herbert, the kind nurse at the hospital where his mum had so recently died. Her face felt like an echo from another place and time, one he couldn't see through the gathering mists of his mind. His head ached, oh how the pain shot through from one side of his head to the other and back endlessly, hurtfully.

The other nun knelt next to the Priest cradling his head in her lap and stroking his brow. He was grey, sweaty and lifeless. Cathedral attendants ushered everyone out of the building with clinical efficiency.

The thunder, lightning and torrential downpour had passed leaving the atmosphere eerily calm. Dressed only in a blood-stained white t shirt William crouched, gazing into the roof space. He'd been entirely oblivious to the sirens until four paramedics with stretchers rushed along the Nave to the Quire. Reluctantly he was ushered away from the injured nun. Two paramedics checked his make shift tourniquets and pushed an oxygen mask over her face. The other two tried to restart the Priest's heart with paddles. The noise of the voltage echoed to the heavens, calling out for life to return but his God had collected him.

The paramedics talked to their patient as if everything was normal; death was a daily occurrence for them and in an instant of well choreographed ballet they were on their way, the second nun following close behind.

William's attention was drawn once again to the roof space where he saw a man's face carved into the wood. The face looked like Michael, like a shaman. The Green Man, he mused, what was this pagan symbol doing in a Norman Christian church? Suddenly he was calm, serene, reassured as if the very hand of God had touched him. His soul returned to earth just in time to catch the paramedics wheeling the stretchers down the Quire towards the South exit.

"Where are you taking her?"

"The Kent and Canterbury, Ethelbert Road" replied the last paramedic edging out of the door.

Now feeling completely alone, William reached into his pocket to extract the nuns blood stained, leather pouch. As he lowered his gaze the coffin came into his line of sight. The fall had caused the lid to dislodge. With some trepidation he bent slowly and pushed it to one side. He found only a lump of concrete where Michael's body should have been.

In the far distance there was just the vaguest rumble of thunder, the dragon had come, done its worst and moved on, this time unnoticed. The pain in his brain wouldn't go away. He sunk to the floor head in hands and prayed.

-11-

Newcastle
28th July 2009

Rachel left Morgan and Pender's impressive house to walk the relatively short distance back to the hotel. The breeze was refreshingly cool on her face and neck. She forced herself to take some long deep breaths to try to relax and focus her mind which was spinning like a top. Her heart was pounding; there was an odd feeling in the air, what on earth was this all about? King Arthur, threats, murder. At that moment she was far too upset for any of it to make any sense whatsoever.

To be honest she hadn't ever given any thought to whether King Arthur was real or not. Frankly she didn't really care, but now she was being forced to care. It hadn't even dawned on her that her own life might be in danger.

She couldn't understand what the big deal was. So what if King Arthur had been a real person, why on earth did it matter after all this time?

Deep in thought, she didn't notice the stocky bald man following her or the smell of his cigar smoke.

When she walked up the steps and into the hotel reception Nicole was waiting anxiously, she had obviously received Rachel's message. They hugged warmly which triggered mutual sobbing as they released their pent up emotions. Nicole broke the clinch gently and stood slightly back, her long fair curly hair framed her face and her mascara ran down to her jaw line. Neither of them noticed the man watching them through the glass doors.

Rachel put an arm around her friend, "My God, Nicole, why on earth would anyone want to kill Helen Daniels?"

Nicole regained a little control and whispered; "She had been getting threats ever since she started working on the Arthur documentary."

Nicole carefully wiped her face with a tissue, removing most of the spoilt mascara. Rachel stroked her hair to comfort her; "Morgan and Pender showed me some of the letters they had received... come on, let's go up to my room and have a chat."

There was silence until they were in the hotel bedroom. Nicole looked so forlorn despite her cascading blonde hair, her little ski slope nose and her plump lips. Rachel had not seen her friend for some time and she was looking her up and down.

"Hold me Rachel," Nicole pleaded, "It's been a terrible day."

Rachel drew her close; she could feel her firm breasts pressing through her blouse and into her own bosom. Nicole rested her head on Rachel's shoulder dripping tears onto her bare neck, inhaling what remained of her morning perfume and recalling the time as kids they had spent in exploring and experimenting with each other's bodies in the fields around Carcassonne.

Rachel ran her fingers through Nicole's hair whilst Nicole placed her arms firmly around Rachel, drawing her nearer still. She took Rachel's head in her hands and gazed into her watery eyes. Rachel noticed Nicole's lips quivering in anticipation as she alternated her gaze from eyes to lips and back. Nicole cupped Rachel's head in her hand and pulled it closer to her own, kissing her fully on the lips. This action sent a hundred butterflies from her stomach to her groin. Nicole's hand moved across Rachel's breast squeezing gently, Rachel gasped. At first she acquiesced, lost in the pleasures of their shared past. The drama and tension of the day momentarily slipped away. Suddenly the sound of distant thunder broke the spell and Nicole tore herself away, standing like a naughty schoolgirl. Rachel felt simultaneously relieved and disappointed. From then on they kept a polite distance, Rachel sitting on the bed and Nicole on a chair.

Rachel was first to break the silence, "Fancy a little something from the mini bar? Gin and tonic, maybe?"

Nicole nodded and continued the conversation. "Helen handed in her resignation last night before she was killed." She took the drink from Rachel and sunk it immediately.

"How do you know?"

Nicole steadied herself; "My boss at the Beeb called me about the murder and told me that they are shelving the documentary."

Rachel looked puzzled; "Because of Helen's death?"

Nicole shrugged her shoulders; "They told me my services were no longer required and ordered that I return all the research and copies of any of the footage I had regarding the project." Rachel nearly dropped her drink. "Shit Nicole, that's all a bit sudden?"

Nicole looked sheepish as she went on; "There's something else, they found out about the S&M stuff I do on the web and threatened to use it against me if I didn't tow the official line about why the documentary was pulled."

Rachel's eyes lifted to the ceiling; "The official line being?"

"Basically that the research was crap and that Helen was prefabricating information to make it sensational; you know Helen would never do that Rachel!"

Rachel looked surprised at both pieces of information! "What did you say?"

"I told them to go fuck themselves and that I'd stick it all over the internet."

"Was that a good idea?" There was a pause until Rachel continued. "You kept the S&M stuff quiet."

Nicole was fortified by the alcohol; "Well it's not something you write on your T shirt – actually it probably is these days. Last year I went to a fetish club for a laugh. I loved it, the costumes, the play, the sex. I make sure that the stuff I do for the web stuff is safe. It supplements the dosh I get, or let's say I got from the Beeb's contracts."

"Did Helen know about this?"

Nicole was unsure; "I think she had a rough idea but she was too polite to comment on morality, she was a great person."

Rachel's mind was working overtime; "These threats Helen was getting, it couldn't have been related to your fetish work could it?"

Without hesitation Nicole replied; "No way...although there was one time when Helen and I were at a BBC party. This bouncer-type who chain-smoked cigars said he was a fetish photographer. He had an excellent portfolio and I agreed to do a photo shoot with him at a studio in the West End. He paid me nearly a grand for the shoot, easy money. He didn't seem to have any interest in Helen, or the documentary."

Rachel changed the subject; "I saw Morgan and Pender this morning, as arranged."

Nicole nodded, "What did you make of them?"

Rachel looked thoughtful; "They seemed OK, I wasn't really with them long enough to take a view. Pender heard about Helen's murder on the news whilst making a cup of tea and he went bananas, and, inside, so did I actually. I have arranged to go back to see them this evening although I suppose there's no point now that the documentary has been pulled."

Nicole held out her glass for a top up, Rachel obliged; "I guess that depends on whether you want to get to the bottom of what's going on."

Rachel was confused so Nicole continued; "Helen's dead, Morgan and Pender are getting death threats, doesn't the journalist in you want to know what's behind all this? And besides, whoever it is will surely be aware that we're involved too."

Rachel went as white as a sheet, it was an untimely reminder of her own vulnerabilty; "Oh shit, shit!"

Nicole carried on; "When Helen and I first met Morgan and Pender to discuss the possibility of a series of documentaries, I wasn't sure about them. They are a bit eccentric and obsessive about their research but as I spent more time with them, I began to see that they had a point and had just cause to be frustrated and paranoid. I felt they were holding something back though."

Rachel sipped her drink; "What's really happening Nicole? If you know something I ought to know, now would be a really good time to tell me."

Nicole looked stoic; "Ok, I am not sure what they really know but I'm pretty sure that they are hiding something that is very sensitive and I think that is why Helen was murdered, because they told her...or at least whoever murdered Helen thought they had told her. You have seen how they live in a virtual fortress, they have had attempts on their lives before and I believe that they are genuinely living in fear, it can't be pleasant."

Rachel looked dumfounded; "They showed me some of the threatening letters they've started getting. Have you seen them?"

Nicole; "No, no I haven't...what do they say?"

Rachel hardly liked to repeat them; "Not very pleasant, whoever is writing them is really sick; there was stuff about being tied up and slitting throats. We really should go to the police."

Nicole looked scared; "They are the last people we should go to."

Rachel looked inquisitive.

Reality seemed to dawn on Nicole; "This thing Rachel, this horrid thing, it's far too big for us to handle, I just wish I could disappear, I wish I could tell you."

She picked up her handbag and made for the door.

Tears of worry and fear whelled up in her eyes. Rachel felt deeply for her; "Please, please don't go Nicole, there must be something I can do to help, as you said yourself I'm a journalist and I want to know."

Nicole was now crying and shaking her head "No, no Rachel, you may want to know but you don't want to die.Just do yourself a favour and get as far away from here as you can. Forget the whole thing, I can't get you more involved in this, I just can't ...it wouldn't be fair."

Rachel tried to stop her leaving the room; "What are friends for?"

Nicole was insistent as she moved to leave.

Rachel shouted after her. "Let me drive you; stay, please stay a while."

"No, no thanks, I'll be OK."

Too tersely, Nicole pushed her away; "I'm sorry Rachel, I can't, I, I just can't, I have a date later and I need to get ready. I love you Rachel, don't ever forget that."

Something was badly wrong. "Please, promise me you'll go to the police or someone Nicole, call me, let me help, please let me help."

Nicole was already half way down the corridor; "I shouldn't have called you it was stupid of me. Please go home and forget all about it, I can't expect you to help me out of this mess."

Rachel was beside herself; "Help you out of what? What mess? Nicole, come back."

The lift doors opened and shut in a trice and she was gone. Silence hung in the room in the space where she had been. Rachel knew she should have run after her but she didn't. It was not an option to just go home and forget all about it, what on earth was going on? She just couldn't leave, could she? She gazed at herself in the mirror, she looked like a ghost.

Maybe they had both had a little too much to drink and weren't thinking clearly. Hardly able to keep her eyes open, Rachel curled up on the bed. The thoughts of the day stormed her subconscious tiring her physical body. She thought she heard a long sigh in the room but couldn't be sure, soon she dozed off.

She awoke suddenly. The first thing she saw was Nicole's briefcase under a chair on the other side of the hotel bedroom. She got up and splashed cold water on her face and neck in the bathroom before calling Nicole. She wasn't answering so Rachel left a message.

"Hey, Nicole, look, I don't want to interfere but I'm calling the police. I love you and I'd hate anything to happen to you…are you OK? Call me I want to help…oh…by the way, you've left your briefcase here…I'll drive it over in the morning?" The answer phone clicked off.

Rachel knew Nicole didn't want to involve the police but she didn't know what else to do, she couldn't stand by and do nothing. She looked up the contact for the Newcastle Constabulary; it wasn't as easy as you'd think. They seemed to have so many different numbers and sections and she dared not call 999. With her mobile charging, she tried on the hotel phone but was left on hold for 25 expensive minutes, in the end she decided to try later; a decision which would prove fatal.

-12-

London
28th July 2009

William was exhausted by the time he arrived home from Canterbury. His first job was to strip out of his bloodstained clothing, shower and change. Next he raided the fridge and sat down to reflect on the day's events. He had been offered a commission for a computer game, been drugged and mugged, a girl in a red dress had danced and given him an apple, an almighty storm broke over Canterbury, he'd knocked over and upset a large mysterious lady, Michael's body was not in his coffin, a nun, who resembled the nurse at the hospital, went berserk and slit her wrists and told him she was having his baby. Not your normal day he thought as he scratched his head and ate his strawberries. To get some air, he slid open the patio doors and peered North West across the Thames to the setting sun.

He thought about the nun, remembering the way she had looked at him, her pleading eyes, and her serene pale china face after her own violent turmoil. Did she really say, "Do this for your son?" How could it be his son? Oddly he felt a sort of calmness, the type that hangs in the air almost timelessly after a storm. Nevertheless the vision of her haunted him and he wondered whether she had survived.

Today was one of those unique times when it seemed as if the veil between the living and the dead had been momentarily pulled aside. Such experiences were more common when he was a child. He recalled that when he was around five or six, he would be woken by someone calling his name. Often he would creep to the window and, peeping out, catch a glimpse of a female figure dressed all in black with a black and white cowl. Occasionally she would turn to meet his gaze, a gentle smile surrounded by wild red hair. Suddenly William's body went numb. My God, he thought, that's it; Sister Bridget, the nun in the Cathedral, the woman calling him when he was young. They were all one, weren't they? The link was too strong to ignore however impossible it was.

He swallowed two pills his doctor had prescribed for his depression with a strong mug of tea and studied the apple from the mime artist, the book,

Artorius Rex, with the unfashionable cover and the leather pouch from the nun. Loosening the draw string he noticed how the woman's blood had dried and congealed on the leather, it looked like an item of sacrifice. Inside were thirty pieces of silver. Slowly he examined them, grouping them into patterns on the table. They were all irregular and, like jigsaw puzzle pieces, they were marked on one side only. The marks were small and faint as if they had been scratched crudely onto the metal with a sharp nail or stylus. In the late afternoon light the patina looked ancient, the edges old and worn. William was clueless and curious.

Absentmindedly, he picked up the apple and went to bite it but it was made of hard wax. Feeling stupid, he went back to the jigsaw puzzle pieces, moving them about into different patterns. Finally they fitted together but the letters didn't make a word that he recognized: O U O S V A V V.

He used his portable scanjet to make a copy of the completed puzzle, saved it on his laptop and emailed it to his old friend Roger Felix at Sheffield University. They were best friends at school but life's pressure and occupations kept them apart. They did keep in touch now and again, particularly when William needed some accurate and unbiased archeological and historical advice, which, frankly, was fairly rare.

He double checked the words he'd typed into his email browser…"Hi Roger, long time no see. Hope you are OK. What do you make of this? Keep smiling, Will". William attached the picture and hit 'send'. Looking up he realized there was a message on his phone.

It was Rachel, "Jesus William, where the hell are you? Why don't you ever have your mobile switched on? I've been trying for hours to get you. For God's sake call me, I need to speak to you!"

He fished his mobile phone out of his pocket…bugger, she was right, he'd turned it off at the cathedral and forgotten about it. He picked up the receiver for the landline phone and dialed her mobile number.

He fanasied about a sleep but knew it would have to wait a while.

-13-

Newcastle
28th July 2009

As she woke from her nap she felt disoriented. In the distance she could hear sirens and heavy machinery. She moved slowly towards the window hoping to see the source of the commotion. Great clouds of black smoke billowed like dancers in a ballet choreographed by fire. Somehow it reminded her of a dying swan.

Excited by the drama she pulled on her jeans, white T shirt and red high heels and then grabbed her tote bag containing her camera, mp3 recorder and mobile phone. Her Swan Lake ring tone started, it was William.

"Rachel, hi it's Will, what's up?"

Rachel sighed; "William, where on earth…?"

"You OK, Rachel?" He cut her off.

Rachel was nodding, "Yes, yes I'm OK William but I've had a terrible day up here. Helen Daniels has been murdered, Nicole's being weird and I'm late for an interview which is probably pointless now since the BBC have sacked Nicole and stopped the documentary. And now there are sirens going off and there's a big fire somewhere nearby."

William sensed the fear in her voice but was confused by the onslaught; "Rachel, Rachel, it's OK, just calm down."

Rachel took a moment or two; "I'm scared Will, I'm so scared, I have to do something."

William thought for a moment; "Just stay calm Rachel and lock yourself in the hotel room, do not go out for any reason, do you hear me? Forget about the interview, I'm going to come up."

William looked at his watch, "If I hurry I can get a plane to Newcastle… where are you staying?"

That meant a lot to her. She gave the hotel's address, and thanked him for his thoughtfulness. She didn't agree to lock herself in her room however.

There was a general melee in the reception area as she rushed through, tying her hair back as she went.

The cool air hit her like a slap in the face but it smelt of acrid smoke and the newshound in Rachel was on the scent. Adrenalin replaced her fear with excitement and she broke into a power walk. Another police car zoomed by, blue lights flashing.

Morgan and Pender's place was now nearby and as she turned the corner she saw it. The old building was alight. Flames licked out of the roof timbers like demons repossessing their own. Only hours ago she had been in that building, now it was Dante's inferno. Oh My God! She mouthed.

She started taking photos of the circle of fire trucks, police cars and ambulances. Fumbling in her bag she pulled out her press card and flashed both it and her sassy smile at a policeman holding back what was by now a small crowd.

"What's the score?" she asked.

"There'll be a statement as soon as possible" he hissed… she fluttered her eye lids and pouted. She hated playing the girly card, but it usually worked.

"I am sorry miss, this one is top secret." Rachel looked at him, he bit his lip. He realised he'd already said too much.

She raised her eyebrows as the young constable turned as red as the fire; "Care to elaborate?" she asked as she covertly switched on her mp3 recorder. The policeman shook his head and walked away to join his colleagues.

Inside the burning inferno a man was struggling with the door that led from the cellar to the old coach house, no doubt a route often used by grooms in the olden days. He had rehearsed this scenario so many times in his mind. He put his parcel down on the floor and shoved the door with his shoulder. Time was running out, the smoke was filling his lungs with searing pains. Had his lifetime's work come to this? Had they really won? Would the world ever know the truth?

Rachel was too busy pimping around the fire trucks, the ambulances and the police officials to notice a large black car pull up delivering a tall, well built man in his early sixties.

Around the back of the burning building in the graveyard the smoke billowed in the breeze making visibility difficult. A young female police officer had just radioed that her designated area was secure. She hadn't seen the shadow, darker than the acrid smoke that lingered amongst the headstones. The almost silent footfalls behind her were lost in the din of the fire scene. Without warning one gloved hand covered her mouth and the other grabbed her around the waist. She tried to respond in the way that had been drummed into her during her police training but, in the heat of the moment, she fell to pieces and flayed around like a rag doll. Her attacker let her struggle for a while, enjoying her writhing body against his groin but this was neither the time nor the place. He kneed her inner thigh which sent her to the ground and thrust her face into the earth of a newly dug grave. He applied a hold to her neck pressure points until she passed out. She was lucky, at least she was alive. Her radio blurted, demanding a response but the attacker was gone.

Rachel jumped as the heavy tap on her shoulder demanded her attention. She spun around in an instant to see the man that had arrived in the black Audi. "Bryn Evans, mam" he said in a Welsh accent, flashing his badge.

"I need to ask you a few questions."

She looked at the badge with disbelief "Interpol, why do you want to talk to me?"

The man pulled himself up to his full height. "Because, earlier today you paid a visit to two gentlemen in this house, now it has been set on fire, and, bingo, here you are watching your handy work!"

Rachel backed off. "Hang on, not so fast boyo; do I look like an arsonist?"

Evans grabbed her by the wrist, "They come in all shapes and sizes and it's well known that they like to watch their own handiwork."

Rachel scoffed; "You can't be serious?"

"Come on mam, you'll get your chance to explain…we've been watching you."

Rachel doubted his motives, his credentials and his manner. How did he know of her visit, why did he suspect her, was he really from Interpol? "What do you mean; the house has been deliberately set alight? How could you know that?"

His eyes were dark and steady. She quickly jerked her arm down and away, something she learnt on a self defence class. Her high heels slowed her down as she tried to run. She quickly regretted her vanity. Soon one of the younger policemen caught up with her and rugby tackled her to the ground, his hands all over her in the process. She managed to smack him in the face, "Keep your hands off you bastard!"

He smirked as he spun her around, leaned her against a nearby car and thrust his knee between her legs to stop her struggling. The handcuffs were applied in one slick manoeuvre. Evans caught up, a little out of breath, but obviously in good shape for his age. He flashed his Interpol card to the policeman. "It's OK officer, thank you, I'll deal with this."

The Policeman looked rather disappointed. Rachel looked bedraggled as the detective helped her up and led her away, still wriggling and resisting. "That twat touched me up; I want to lodge a complaint against you bastards."

Evans picked up Rachel's bag and pulled her towards his car, giving the nod to the policeman as he went. "My word she is a feisty one" he said out loud but he whispered to Rachel, "Come on you are in enough trouble already let's get you out of here."

Rachel sensed he was trying to help. They had nearly reached Evans car when the policeman came running over, "Hey, not so fast."

Evans looked back, fearing the worst, his heart sunk.

"You'll need these" the policeman said tossing the handcuff keys to Evans. "Play nicely," he whispered as he helped her into the passenger seat, and fastened her seat belt, I'm on your side!"

-14-

Newcastle
28th July 2009

The mayhem, the flashing lights and the hi-viz jackets of the fire-fighters glowed like fire flies then faded into the distance. Rachel's adrenalin was staving off the feelings of nausea induced by the fire scene and the movement of Evans' car as he drove quickly through the streets.

"So, are you really from Interpol?" She looked at him trying to detect any signs of foul play.

"Yes really", he replied, with something of a smile, "my ID is in my pocket, have a look."

Rachel lifted her handcuffed wrists to indicate that her hands were otherwise engaged. Evans pulled over, took the car out of gear, engaged the handbrake, removed the keys from his pocket and undid the cuffs. Naturally Rachael tried to open the door and run, just as they do in all cop movies. The door didn't budge. She looked across to Evans fearing the worse but the man's whole demeanour was one of calm control.

"The child lock is on." He managed a smile, "Rachel, listen, you have stumbled into an ongoing investigation and that is, very unfortunate for you."

He slipped his hand into his pocket and pulled out his ID card. The picture was a little old and there was more hair on his head but it was unmistakably him. Soon they arrived at Rachel's hotel. She looked surprised. "Hey, how did you know where I was staying?"

Evans stopped the car and looked at her. "We have a live system called I-24/7 which is a global communication network covering 186 member countries via local and central computer bases. The chances are that if you have used your phone, your credit card or sneezed in the last few minutes we'll know where you are!"

Rachel pulled down the passenger seat visor and looked at herself in the vanity mirror. My god she thought to herself, what a mess.

"So, what have I stumbled into?"

Evans looked pensive.

"I wish I could tell you, but I can't. Look, I have to go back to the fire scene, will you promise to go and lock yourself in your room and try to get a good night's sleep. I'll come over and see you the in the morning."

Why were people so obsessed by getting her to stay in her room, maybe he was a friend of William? The thought made her chuckle inwardly so she didn't press the point.

As she studied the man's face she thought she saw a tear in his eyes….. maybe it was the smoke. "Don't be concerned", she said, rather glibly, "I'm a big girl now."

Evans wiped his eye, unable to hide his emotion. "You remind me so much of my daughter, you may be in great danger."

Rachel was taken aback by discovering that the Welsh ex-rugby playing cum Interpol officer would reveal his emotions so easily.

"What do you mean by great danger?"

Evans held her attention; "Look, right now you are a suspect and the local Old Bill will be trying to find you, so don't push your luck and don't leave the area, I'll come and see you in the morning, OK?"

Rachel was upset and shaken; she tried not to let her vulnerability show. She opened the car door and stepped out into the cool night. Evans stayed until she was safely in the building. In fact he was still there when she looked out of the window of her room. She waved and he left.

Despite the hour and her exhaustion, she called the news desk of the local paper; this had to be a scoop. She was devastated when they said they already had someone there covering it and they didn't need her photos. They didn't even care that she may have a back story about Morgan and Pender. Exasperated, she slammed the phone down on the duty editor; "Arsehole."

Tucked behind the chair she saw the briefcase that Nicole had accidently left behind.

She knew that one day her curiosity would get her into big trouble, it might as well be today.

-15-

London
28th July 2009

Angela sat quietly on the balcony of her Victorian Villa overlooking Highgate Cemetery. She loved watching the eerie evening mist hanging over the graves. It was a special house once inhabited by the Rossetti family and there were some faint traces of Dante's sketch work still on some of the plastered walls. Michael loved this house, its link to the past and the cemetery, but now it was hers, all hers. She sipped her ice cold Vodka and tonic. It was a time of celebration, after all, her widowhoods and her benefactors had brought her quite an accumulation of cash, certainly enough to cater to her extravagant tastes. Her power was increasing by the day and she smiled at how well her ambitions were being fulfilled.

Upon her fingers three yellow diamonds sparkled. She examined them with the manicured fingers of her left hand, tapping into the special and imprisoned powers of her shamanic ex husbands, trapped in the diamonds like Merlin in the crystal cave.

This evening's beguiling should be the easiest of all.

It wasn't often that William stopped and gazed aimlessly up and down the shelves of magazines vying for attention but today was different. The internal flight from London City airport to Newcastle had been terribly delayed and he hoped he was going to make it to be with Rachel that evening. On the phone she had sounded quite erratic.

Bored fingers flipped along the rows of cover girls in provocative positions. He became aware of a disturbance at the counter. A man in his late fifties, dressed in a tweed jacket and brown corduroy trousers was gesticulating and walking towards him. His face contorted by involuntary movements. For a moment their eyes met. His hands and arms moved quickly in a kind of semaphore as if he was communicating with an unseen force.

"Beware the Beguiler of Merlin"...he spat at William, "Beware the force of the dark ones, beware the Lady of the Lake."

William stood, mesmerized, staring at the man rolling and weaving on the spot from the waste up, moving his arms and hands in windmill like movements, banging his own chest with his fist and making contortions with his face that were better placed in a horror movie.Suddenly he moved like a flash, placing his eyes inches from William's face.

"Beware the beguiler of Merlin" he repeated.

William jumped back like a startled deer.

Two security guards appeared and manhandled the nutter past William who noted the stench of alcohol on his breath. As he was dragged by, a magazine fell off the shelf and landed on the floor, its pages randomly opened at an article on diamonds. William instinctively picked it up.

The announcement on the speaker system broke the hubbub of disgruntled passengers. The delay was because of a security alert and the evening's flights had been cancelled.

William's phone rang, a plaintiff female voice, it was Angela.

"Don't hang up William, I know you have every right to, the funeral, the concrete in the coffin and everything, it's a long story, I've got to talk to you!"

Her voice broke up and cracked into tears that felt damp and desperate in his ears. William couldn't bear to hear her crying, had he been too harsh about her?

"Angela, where are you?" His enquiry was genuine and concerned.

"I'm alone in this damn house, I don't know which way to turn, I don't know what to do, I've got myself in such a muddle...oh God I have been so stupid!"

"You mean you're at home in Highgate, right?"

There was a soft confirmation from the other end; it seemed like another world away.

"OK, I'll come over and we can talk."

He'd taken the bait.

William was still holding the magazine which, absentmindedly, he slipped it into his brief case without paying for. Thankfully no-one noticed.

At the taxi rank he called Rachel.

"Rachel, hi it's Will..."

"Will, where are you?" Her voice was much calmer than it had been and William felt better immediately.

"I'm still at the airport; all flights have been cancelled so I won't get to Newcastle tonight. Are you OK?"

There was a brief silence.

"Yes, yes, I'm OK Will but Morgan and Pender's house has burnt down."

"Christ, don't tell me you ignored me and went to try to see them anyway!?"

"Don't be angry Will, you are not my Dad! I guess curiosity got the better of me. There was smoke and sounds of emergency vehicles, I just thought I'd get a scoop and earn a few quid. Everything led to Morgan and Pender's house and when I arrived I saw that it was on fire. An Interpol agent escorted me back to the hotel and told me to stay put as I'm a suspect!"

"You? An arsonist?" William laughed and spluttered but Rachel didn't see the funny side. "Hey, you must listen to your wise friends" He was only joking but Rachel was most certainly not in the mood.

"Don't be an arse Will, this is serious."

A taxi pulled up.

"Got to go Rachel, please don't get into any more mischief, OK?"

Rachel had already hung up. No-one told her what to do.

The taxi's window wound down; "Where to guv?"

William climbed into the back seat and gave the address; "Swains Lane, Highgate".

He dragged his briefcase onto his lap, pulled out the magazine and flicked to the article entitled; *Dust to Diamonds*. He gazed at the photograph first; it was of a woman sitting on a grave stone, showing off a large diamond ring. He began to read;

Emily Smythe wanted to honor her husband Ian in a very special way after he died from cancer last July. So, she had his ashes made into a diamond. It took just a few days for the process, uniquely offered by a company in Austria, to be completed.

Trevor Phillips, Funeral and Cremation Services spokesman said. "It's a great idea, we have been inundated with people wishing to turn their loved ones into diamonds, after all they are forever and it's like having the essence of the person with you."

In order to create the ring, eight ounces or more of the cremated remains are heated to extreme temperatures, and then the carbon is subjected to tremendous pressure. The result is a stone identical to diamonds that develop deep within the earth over millions of years. The nitrogen in the air causes the diamonds to be yellow in color. Yellow or champagne diamonds do occur naturally but are very rare. The cost for a quarter carat is about £1,500.00 and goes up to £6000.00 for a full carat. Diamonds can be made into any size.

Asked if she thought that the idea was a bit weird Smythe said;

"It's the most natural thing to do, this is like keeping the soul of the one you love with you at all times, a soul that can be handed down through the family to generation after generation.

William re-read her comment: *"This is like keeping the soul of the one you love with you at all times."*

"Live in Highgate do you, guv?" The driver interrupted William's reading.

"Oh no, just visiting a friend."

The cabby jumped the gun.

"Hope she's worth it, Highgate's a long drive."

William ignored his impertinence; he doubted whether he should be seeing Angela at all.

The Cabby turned into Swains Lane and slowed outside the Victorian Villa. The curtain at the window twitched; Angela had been waiting.

Everything in his body was telling him not to go a step further and yet he felt compelled, almost as if he was not in control of his own destiny. Before he knew it he was at the front door and in an embrace. It was as if she needed to hang on to something solid and never stop. Gently, William pushed her away. She was crying and her mascara ran down her cheeks as if to highlight her emotion. The sight disturbed William; he hated seeing people so upset. They walked through the period hallway into the kitchen.

"Oh William, it's been such a long while since I have seen you properly, so much has happened, I'm in such a muddle and I really need your help."

William sat on one side of the large pine table. Angela sat opposite, poured herself a shot of vodka and downed it in one. She went to pour another but William leaned across and took the bottle.

"That won't help."

"I don't care William, I don't fucking well care" she lashed out as she tried to retrieve the bottle.

"Well I DO care, look; we all used to be really close."

"Yes, I know." Angela was full of drama, her eyes wide and roaming.

William kept her hands held tight to the table and she calmed down a little.

"Just tell me what's going on Angela?" He was losing patience.

Her wrap around dress gaped open as she leant towards him. It was hard to ignore the silicone but he kept his gaze on her face.

"It all started a few months ago when Michael did a reading. The woman was in her forties, blonde, polite, professional. Michael said he recognised her from some crime program on TV but he always respected people's privacy. He saw all sorts but he was surprised at how agitated she seemed. She said she'd been getting threats."

"Do you mean Helen Daniels?" William asked shocked by the co-incidence.

"Yes, I think that was her name."

Again, Angela tried to fill her glass but William stopped her.

"She was murdered last night."

Angela already knew.

"After she had her reading, a man came to see Michael wanting to know what he had picked up about her, he was really persistent."

"Did Michael tell him anything?"

Angela made a poor attempt to cover herself and shrugged her shoulders.

"Michael never said what he had found out, he was very careful about client confidentiality. The man looked like a thug; thick set, bald, South African and he stank of cigars."

Despite his curiosity William steered the conversation back to Michael.

"How did Michael die Angela, what really happened?"

Somehow his question implied that she was involved.

Either she missed the indirect accusation or she was too drunk to pick up on it.

"I went to a Yoga convention for a couple of days and when I came back I found him dead on the floor. The doctor said that it was an insulin overdose. He'd obviously planned it, he left a note." She winced as she recalled the scene.

"But Michael was a shaman; he'd never take his own life?"

Angela started sobbing again but William held back.

"Michael discovered that I was having an affair, it wasn't important to me but you knew Michael, he felt betrayed."

William was silent, his disapproval was obvious.

"Don't think badly of me William, Michael and I thought the world of each other but for many years he hadn't been able to have sex."

"Oh, that's OK then, your husband has the indignity of impotence so you think that's an excuse for you to shag someone else!"

"No, no it wasn't like that William. At the Yoga convention my kundalini was really rising and I was surrounded by some stunning bodies. I never intended to take it any further; it was just a few days of blissful release. Michael found out because I didn't hang up properly after speaking to him on my mobile. He must have heard everything. He mentioned it in his note."

"Oh God, how humiliating! So what exactly happened when you came home from the fucking convention?" He was testing her.

Ignoring his sarcasm, she moved to pour another drink and this time William didn't stop her. She continued.

"When I came home the rear door was unlocked. Michael was always so careful about security. I went into the kitchen but there was no-one about. I called out to him and went into his study. There he was on the floor, dead."

She continued to sob as she recalled the scene.

"He must have gone berserk because the study was a complete mess, his computer, the pictures of us together, papers, books all smashed up and thrown about. Then I found the note and my heart just broke. I'd been so stupid, if only I'd switched off my mobile!"

Her selfish regret drove William to the bottle. He took a glass and poured himself a shot.

"I didn't think you were allowed to drink?"

"We all do things we regret. Do you have the note Michael left?"

She cringed as the words hit home, wringing her hands like Lady Macbeth.

It was then that he noticed the collection of yellow diamond rings she was wearing and he remembered the magazine article;

"This is like keeping the soul of the one you love with you at all times."

Angela gingerly rose from the table and held on to the kitchen fittings to steady herself.

"The police took the original but I have a photocopy."

As she left the room William spotted two pictures of himself under a blue bowl on the table. One was a picture of him with Michael; the other was of Sandra and him. He put the photos back under the bowl just as Angela was coming back in.

"Oh" she said, "you found the photos then."

William blushed.

"It's OK; I found them with the suicide note."

Angela pushed the folded photocopy towards William who turned it the right way up. There were only six lines, it looked like Michael's hand writing but he couldn't be entirely sure. Tears welled up in his eyes as he read.

Can you imagine how I felt when you cheated on me?
Are you ever going to be able to forgive yourself?
Love is something sacred, not something to be buried and forgotten
Dying is not the end it is just the beginning
Even if you believe it is.
You must live with yourself each time you look in the mirror; I die with a broken heart.

"How tragic..."

"I know, I'm sure it is aimed at making me feel guilty for the rest of my life." Angela seemed only capable of thinking about herself. She sat down again, still wringing her hands, trying to wash away the blame but all William could see were the rings glinting in the artificial light.

Had she really transformed her husband's into diamonds; capturing their souls like the enchantress had captured Merlin's...were they trying to escape?

"William, William!"

William had been miles away and Angela's voice had brought him back.

"Michael's computer, Angela, did the police keep it?"

Angela looked guilty.

"Well, umm, they didn't take the computer, they found it smashed into pieces."

This made him suspicious but he didn't let it show.

"So you've still got it then?"

Angela almost managed a smile.

"I salvaged some of it, it's of no use to me but I thought you might want it, you're into computers and things."

Whilst Angela left the room to get the pieces of the broken computer, William called Natasha.

Natasha was a first class computer expert who could program in every language. She could probably hack into the Pentagon except that had already been done.

"William, don't you know what time it is?" she chastised him.

He didn't but checked with his phone, it was 10.30pm. She was curled up with a book but complied with his request to drive up to Highgate and pick him up. The book was pretty boring anyway and she was curious as to what he was getting up to.

Angela came into the room with a bag full of computer bits which William helped her to empty onto the kitchen worktop.

"This is how I found it, all smashed up in Michael's room."

Angela sat down and started drinking again. This time William let her get on with it. He didn't notice her get up and go to the bathroom. When she returned some time later William was standing up leaning over the table muttering. He was too preoccupied with the computer detritus to immediately register the warm breeze on the back of his neck. As he turned he bumped into Angela who thrust her arms around him to steady them both.

William found that he was looking straight into her dark chocolate eyes, still hypnotically attractive despite the years of misuse. Her lips had been freshly glossed. Like a lioness waiting to pounce, she put her hands around his head and neck and kissed him passionately, pinning him against the kitchen cupboards, thrusting her tongue deep into his mouth in time with the movement of her hips. William mumbled and pushed trying to get away, trying to escape being sucked in, swallowed, entrapped, snared and bewitched.

In one move and without parting from the kiss she removed her dress allowing her shapely naked body to press against him. Everything in William was resisting but his arms and hands felt weak as if he had been stung. He felt the uncontrollable bulge in his trousers and soon her fingers were exploring it, grabbing it, moving it. William's head was full of chanting and psychedelic kaleidoscopes; spirals began spinning deep inside him.

Suddenly there was an impatient and persistent knock on the front door followed by the bell and then more knocking. The spell was broken. Angela peeled away and flopped across the table. William came to his senses and breathed a huge sigh of relief. He covered Angela's naked body with her gown, and adjusted himself; she was fast asleep.

On her fingers he saw the yellow diamond rings. He touched them and they seemed to pulsate. Natasha knocked again, more urgently this time. In haste, William gathered up the computer pieces and rushed to the front door. Soon he was in the safety of Nat's car, driving south towards the city centre.

She looked at William and managed a smile; his face was covered with glossy lipstick.

"Nice lipstick William, what have you been up to?"

William was unsettled to say the least. He felt as if he'd been drugged for the second time in two days.

"It's a long story Nat."

She looked at him and smiled, "It's a long drive."

-16-

MI5, London
28th July 2009

Grey seemed disturbed to think that this had happened on British soil.

"I take it you have heard the news, Home Secretary?" the pause on the phone suggested he may not have.

"Morgan and Pender, they've been terminated." She said.

There was a long silent pause.

"Are you sure?"

"There's a black charred steaming ruin where their house once stood, which is a bit of a giveaway, wouldn't you say?"

"Who...how...when...?" The Home Secretary sounded shocked but Grey was not sure if his surprise was feigned or real.

"I'm on to it, Home Secretary. It might be some sort of incendiary attack, can you check clearances your end, please?"

"Yes, yes, thank you. Remember, the Meurig Project is more important than anything else."

Grey thought she heard a woman laughing in the background. She hung up and called her counterparts at MI6 and the CIA.

After so many years Morgan and Pender had finally and terminally upset the wrong people. She needed to know exactly what else was happening and she needed to know quickly.

-17-

Highgate, London
28th July 2009

As Natasha eased the Porsche Boxter along Swains Lane and onto Highgate High Street William wiped the lip gloss from his face and began his explanation. As he did so he realized how little he understood himself. He never did get around to asking Angela why there was a concrete slab in Michael's coffin, or if she actually did have Michael cremated and made into a diamond ring!

"Have you done something wrong, William?" Natasha was alarmed by his mood and the lip gloss.

"No, no I didn't, thanks to you for turning up and saving me." He smiled with genuine gratitude.

Natasha wasn't so convinced and it didn't help matters when she checked her rear view mirror.

"Any idea who might be following us in that black Jaguar with the weird plates?" She asked as she accelerated.

William moved to turn his head but she stopped him.

"Don't alert them to anything; just tell me what's going on." She demanded.

Natasha delivered her interrogator's stare and then applied her attention to losing their pursuers. By the time they reached the A1 the Jag had gone. She turned and smiled, proud of her escape.

"You have done this before, haven't you?" William was impressed.

She was a natural behind the wheel of a sports car but the movement was making William feel sick. However, he managed to describe all the excitement of the day. It sounded like an implausible film script. He finished with his thoughts on Angela's diamond rings.

"It's like the folk story; Morgan le Fey beguiled Merlin and trapped him in crystal so she could use his power. I loved those tales."

"Hey that's right!" William agreed. "This is all so bizarre, the drunk at the airport mentioned something about beguiling and then there was the magazine article...what the hell is going on?"

"Try coincidence." Natasha's weapon of choice was always logic.

"Try flying pigs!" but the cliché was lost on the Russian.

The conversation had momentarily distracted Natasha and only now she realized that their pursuers were back on their tail. Natasha prepared for the challenge as she approached a tight corner. With her right foot slightly on the accelerator and her left foot flat to the floor on the clutch she spun the wheel and applied the handbrake. The car rocked and swung down a side road. Immediately she killed her lights and pulled in to an office forecourt.

"OK slip as far down out of sight as you can get William."

She followed suit and their heads and bodies touched awkwardly in the tight space.

Natasha motioned to William to get out of the car, he did and she followed him. She walked around to the boot where she opened the lid, reached in and pulled out a tartan blanket. From it she produced car number plates. She gave the front one to William with a screw driver. William exchanged it for a disbelieving look.

"We can't do this, it's, well, it's illegal."

"What is this word, illegal?" she asked, feigning mock ignorance.

William did as he was told.

They were soon back on the A1 heading for the A400 towards Regents Park.

"So, tell me, do you change your car number plates often?"

Natasha laughed; "The plates that we put on are actually mine, the others were just a spare set, I like boy scouts, I'm prepared for anything." Interesting phrasing but he got the point.

She continued; "The other plates belong to a car in Shepherds Bush. The driver was very rude to me once and I hate rudeness in a man."

Natasha was laughing now; it helped break the tension, it made William feel warm and safe, the way Sandra used to. He was impressed by Natasha's spunk and skills and was more than happy to accept her offer of going to her place, which was closer than his anyway.

-18-

Cheyne Walk, London
28th July 2009

Natasha opened the complex gates remotely. At the front entrance she looked up at the security camera, flipped a flap and placed her index finger on a pad whilst gazing into the iris identification unit. The outer door parted and they walked inside. The external door shut before the internal opened.

As they entered the lift William couldn't help but be impressed.

"It's like Fort Knox in here Nats." William commented as they entered the lift.

She took his words as a compliment; "Glad you like it, I developed the system and it paid for the Porsche."

Soon they were in her apartment and slumped on a large comfortable red leather sofa with a view of the Thames from the north side. The lights of London were clear and bright, creating a beacon that could be seen from space.

Natasha walked over to the kitchen; "Tea?"

"Please, with buttered crumpets, I'm British you know." He pushed his luck too far, Nat's fridge was almost empty.

"Fraid you'll have to do without the crumpet."

William managed a smile and pulled the broken pieces of Michael's computer out of the bag and placed them on the glass table. Nat returned with tea and sat beside him, looking at the remains of the hard drive without actually touching them although by now they were probably contaminated anyway.

Data can be destroyed by physical damage or logical damage. With physical damage there is almost certainly logical damage as well. Natasha determined that whoever had smashed up the computer did not understand them fully and this increased her chances of being able to recover some of the data. She finished her initial investigation and went to her bedroom.

William held the mug of tea as he'd have liked to have held Natasha, he longed for the warmth of a hug but the drink would have to suffice for now.

Natasha returned with a tatty looking pilot's case and a roll of small tools. She had changed into a long white smock, her head and face covered with a light green mask. She pulled on latex gloves and placed the computer pieces into a large clear plastic bag. The surgeon was about to operate.

She could see that William was interested and she tried to explain what she was doing.

"Open a hard disk outside of a clean room facility and you run the risk of dust getting in which causes damage to the platters and that makes recovery really difficult".

"I hope you've cleaned this place then."

She was not in the mood for jokes. She placed a large freestanding magnifying lens over the table and put her gloved hands and tools inside the large plastic bag with the remains of the computer and asked William to seal her wrists with tape.

Her salvage operation was delicate and slow. The occasional Russian expletive signposted particularly delicate manipulations and, to William, it reminded him of assembling Airfix kits. Finally she removed the damaged printed circuit board and replaced it with a new one, moved the microchip, changed the damaged read assembly head and installed the hard disk platters into a new drive.

"It looks very complicated." William's eyes were glazing over.

"Mmm, if it had just been the platter that got stuck we could have put it in the freezer and spun the drive manually to try to extract the data, but the damage is much worse than that. Hopefully there won't be any logical problems because you need ILook IXimager for that and I'm not the police or a spy."

Williams face dropped.

"Well, legally, anyway." She smiled like a Bond girl.

The next time he looked at his watch it was 5am. He had fallen asleep. Natasha had worked through the night. At 34, she was younger and tougher than him and as she worked he marveled at her striking looks, she had it all and he couldn't understand why a woman with her brains and beauty was working with him in a small computer game company. He was just grateful that she was.

"How did you get on with the hard drive?"

Natasha removed her glasses and rubbed her eyes.

"I managed to rescue quite a lot of the data." She said in a voice that demonstrated her self confidence. "Now I need some strong coffee." With that she disappeared into the kitchen leaving William to look at the laptop on the table. On it was the text for the book Michael had been writing along with loads of emails. William organized these alphabetically which instantly revealed that about a dozen were addressed to Morgan and Pender. They referenced King

Arthur and work Michael had been doing in the States. William knew that Michael regularly visited Lakota elders in the USA but he'd never heard him mention anything about Morgan and Pender or Arthur.

There were also several emails to and from a Chuck Quinn of the Smithsonian Institute. "Hey Nats here's an interesting one."

Dear Michael,

In your recent correspondence you requested a copy of a press release dated 12.12.1999 that you allege the Smithsonian issued. I have searched the archive but can find no trace of any such press release referring to the discovery of a 6th century skeleton in West Virginia with a DNA match to the inhabitants of Wales.

However, I am familiar with the skeleton to which you refer. It was excavated by Mr Robert Pyle, a retired archaeologist who is trying to establish a link between this skeleton and a pre-Columbus exploration of the Americas by Europeans.

Mr Pyle had the bones tested elsewhere before bringing them to us a few years ago. We processed them at a lab that specializes in the recovery and identification of ancient DNA. The results were consistent with Native Americans.

I know you feel that we are withholding information from you but it is not in our interest to do that. You mention further testing of a different skeleton found in the 1800's which you thought might date to the 6th century.

I have only been able to trace that we once held a mandible associated with this site which was uncovered in the 1800's but unfortunately we cannot presently locate it now. Our collections people believe that it is likely to be associated with one of the many skeletons we have from Tennessee.

I also enquired about the Bat Creek Stone for you but no-one here is working on it. I have found some sketchy information about it though.

It seems that the Bat Creek Stone was excavated in 1885 from a burial mound in Eastern Tennessee (Loudon County) by the Smithsonian Mound Exploration Program, directed by Cyrus Thomas. The specimen was described in the 12th Annual Report of the Bureau of American Ethnology in 1894. In that report Dr Thomas identified the inscription as early 19th century Cherokee however upon further examination the inscriptions are;

1) Not Cherokee and 2) They are not genuine Semitic writing, although some characters appear to be Hebraic alphabet.

I hope that this is useful to your own research.

Regards,
Chuck.

"Well! I had no idea he was interested in all this scientific stuff as well as his spiritual work." William was quite overwhelmed at the information he read.

Natasha searched through the emails she had picked out during the night as being significant.

"Take a look at this one too."

Michael

We are fascinated by your email. We certainly can help you with some more information as we have been studying King Arthur and his family for many years now. Please see the attached file.
Yours,
Morgan and Pender

File attachment: Evidence that Arthur voyaged to America

1. The 6th century "Preiddiau Annwn" (Voyage to the otherworld/America) has been partly butchered over the years and retitled as King Richards's voyage to Acre and Joppa. However, it was written by Taliesin ap Henwg (chief bard to Arthur 2) who went to America (Annwn) with Arthur 2. It clearly states that Arthur went to and died in Annwn and was later brought back to Britain.

2. The ancient texts refer to the sixth century voyage of St Brendan who apparently sailed to America because he had "heard of the previous voyages of the Teyrn" (meaning monarch, most likely Arthur)

3. In 1625 the Lord, George Abbott, the Archbishop of Canterbury wrote a "History of the World" which drew upon early documentation in the possession of the church and others. In this he states "King Arthur knew of America and that a Welsh Prince discovered it." He was referring to the ancient and once well known texts of the voyages made by Prince Madoc Morfan in 562, by the Admiral Gwenon in 573 and by Arthur 2 and his brother Madoc, sons of King Meurig, in 574. The popular line taken by academics was to date the Madoc voyages to another Madoc in the 12th century but this is proven to be incorrect.

4. The 16th century cartographer, Gerhard Kremer (known more commonly as Mercator), corresponded with John Dee who was the Court Mathematician and Necromancer for Elizabeth I. In a letter he sent to Dee, Mercator refers directly to King Arthur's voyages into the far northern oceans in the 6th century. In this letter Mercator cites sources showing that some 4000 descendants of survivors of a supposedly lost expedition led by King Arthur still survived in America. The proof, apparently, was that 8 of these survivors

had arrived at the court of the King of Norway in AD 1354, some 138 years before Columbus sailed. This letter is in the British Library-MSS Cottonian Vitelius.C.vii, f264 et seq.

5. The maps drawn by Mercator as early as 1538 show amazing details of the coastlines of North and South America continents.

6. At least one of the 6th century British-Khumric manuscripts records an epic poem which contains a phrase concerning the existence of the Americas and that, in fact that they were known to a more ancient people.

7. This "other world across the seas" was mentioned by St Clement in "The First Epistle of St Clement to the Corinthians" one of the many early Christian writings not to make it into the bible because it was against church dogma to suggest that the entire human race descended from Noah after the flood.

8. On 16th June 1838 at Grave Creek, West Virginia, USA, a small oval limestone disc tablet (The Grave Creek Tablet) was found, 60 feet down. It had three lines of alphabetic inscriptions making it of monumental importance. No Native American people of North America have been identified as possessing an alphabet and using any form of written language.

9. This mound was quite amazing, 60 feet high, even after the ravages of time, surrounded by a moat four feet deep and thirty feet wide and 250 feet in diameter.This mound bears an uncanny resemblance to some of the major ancient tombs of Britain and is virtually a replica of Twyn Tudor tumulus on Mynydd Islwyn in Gwent (Wales). Inside the mound there were box like burial chambers made from logs. No-one really heard about this because of the uproar caused by Joseph Smith who claimed to have found gold tablets on a hill called Cumorah in 1823. He was inspired by these to found the Mormons. The Grave Creek disc was nothing to do with this or the Mormons however it became caught up in the general situation and the orthodox Christians saw it as a threat to their world.

Natasha was on a roll and highlighted an email that Michael hadn't sent to William but which he composed the day he died. It was still sitting in his drafts folder.

> "My dear William, I have a terrible feeling of impending doom and I know that I am being watched.
>
> I suspect it's related to work I've been doing with Black Elk, in America. He took me to visit a tribe who still write with charcoal on sticks using an alphabet called Coelbren. They speak in an ancient tongue, ancient Welsh. Their traditions say that they descended from tall white bearded men 1500 years ago. I also met a retired archaeologist who had spent years trying to establish who had been first to discover America. Sadly and mysteriously, he died after our first conversation. This is dangerous stuff.

I shouldn't be telling you this but I now have evidence that Angela has been unfaithful and it's broken my heart.

I think my days on this planet are up William and I'd love to see you before I have to go, there are things from your past you need to know.

Blessed be
Michael

William was in tears; his sobbing was heartfelt and inconsolable.
"Poor Michael, he didn't deserve that. I'm convinced it was murder, and not suicide, you know."

Natasha put her arm around William and rocked him gently, like the pendulum of a clock, tick tock, tick tock. The time slipped away as did most of the other remaining information on the hard drive. Apart from the email backups, only the last half of another book Michael was writing apparently survived. It was called, *There is no God*. In his notes he calls God the ultimate placebo.

"I did make another discovery last night." Natasha remembered, despite her extreme tiredness. "In his suicide note, each line starts with a capital letter. It reminded me of a poem but then I wondered if it was a simple improvised code. If you take each letter and read downwards it says, CALDEY."

Can you imagine how I felt when you cheated on me?
Are you ever going to be able to forgive yourself?
Love is something sacred, not something to be buried and forgotten
Dying is not the end it is just the beginning
Even if you believe it is.
You must live with yourself each time you look in the mirror; I die with a broken heart.

William was scratching his head which was dizzy with information. There was almost something dreamlike about the situation he found himself in. King Arthur in America, an alphabet called Coelbren, a suicide note that didn't quite ring true. God, the ultimate placebo?

Natasha caught the mode. "I found an explanation of what the Coelbren alphabet is, if that helps at all".

He read the print-out from Natasha's research:

G J Williams alleged that the Coelbren alphabet of South East Wales was made up in around 1800 and therefore it has no historical value. However, there is much evidence to the contrary. Julius Caesar described the Coelbren alphabet in his De Bello Galico in 54 BC. Ammianus Marcellinus also described it. In 1946, Mohammed Ali discovered 14 leather satchels containing 128 books from a Gnostic Christian library buried at Nag Hamadi in Egypt before AD 400. The book of Massanes contains a description of the same alphabet. Welsh poets used the text at least as early as 1367. Several ancient stones dating from circa 600-1200 carry letters of the alphabet. A manuscript in the Bodleian Library in Oxford of circa 1520 also contains the alphabet.

-19-

Newcastle
29th July 2009

There was an impatient knock like an amplified bee at the door.

"Rachel, it's only me, Bryn, Bryn Evans."

Rachel jumped up with a start and rubbed her eyes. She was disoriented and it took a moment to remember that she was in a hotel in Newcastle. She had spent a restless night dozing and going through some of the DVD containing footage taken by Helen, Nicole and her team which she had found in the briefcase Nicole had left in her room after she had departed in such a hurry.

Evans knock was persistent.

"Rachel, Rachel, are you alright?" He sounded concerned.

She pulled her jeans on and ran her fingers quickly through her long thick black hair in an effort to make herself more presentable. A feather from her pillow floated out of her mane and fell slowly, like an angel to the floor.

"Yes, yes, I'm fine, hang on."

There was a blur as she gazed in the mirror and tidied the hair from around her face, smoothing what was left of her lipstick from the night before to almost cover her lips. She rubbed her eyes but the bags remained.

Less than a minute later she opened the door and motioned for Bryn to come in.

"Coffee?" She asked as she filled the kettle in the en-suite bathroom.

"Yes please my lovely." Rachel detected an unexpected sensitivity. She hoped her senses were right.

"What's the time?" She asked as she plugged in the appliance. She was still disoriented and had no idea how long she had been asleep. Bryn didn't need to consult his watch.

"It's 7.30am, I'm an early riser."

He went to light a cigarette but saw the look of disapproval on Rachel's face

"Well you're not the only one!" She felt slightly annoyed with him for the early call.

Evans ignored the subtle rebuke.

"How much do you know about the documentary that Nicole and Helen were working on?"

"Not much at all really. Nicole initially told me it was a big story that came with lots of surprises."

"What sort of surprises? Any idea?" Bryn's ambience changed to police mode.

Rachel shook her head as she moved over to the table to make the coffee.

"I've been looking through the DVD that Nicole accidently left here in her briefcase."

Bryn interrupted her with his raised voice.

"She left her briefcase here and you only just mention it? Why on earth didn't you tell me this last night? Where is it? Do the police know about it?"

Rachel jumped at his aggressive questioning.

"Wooooahhh, I didn't notice it until after you dropped me off last night. Anyway, it sounds like you know more about this than me, care to share?"

In his enthusiasm Bryn realised that he had been too forceful. He side stepped Rachel's question.

"Look, I'm sorry; this means a lot to me...please may I have a look at the briefcase?"

Rachel regained her composure and handed Bryn his coffee. She walked into the bathroom where she had hidden the case in a towel on a shelf. When she returned she noticed that the big man looked a bit tearful. There seemed to be more going on but she didn't pry, she just sipped her coffee as she watched him open the lid and examine its contents.

"Have you taken anything out of here, Rachel?"

"Like what, exactly?" Rachel looked at him quizzically.

"Like anything at all." He had returned to Police mode.

Rachel thought carefully, could she trust this man? She decided to play it safe.

"Only the DVD, it contains some rushes of the documentary they were making about Morgan and Pender... I spent a couple of hours watching it and making notes."

"Why would you bother, the program's been shelved."

"I'm a journalist, I wouldn't walk away from a good story; people don't get sacked, threatened and murdered for no reason. Do you know that Nicole is also being threatened?"

Evans looked blank, suggesting he didn't. Rachel was upset and hid her head in her hands. When she lifted it her eyes met his. Evans had bad news.

"It looks like Morgan and Pender died in the fire last night."

Rachel shook her head in disbelief.

"I was with them only yesterday morning, they invited me to come back in the evening, that's why I was there."

Evans steadied her hands with his and looked her directly in the eyes.

"This may be just a story for you but it's my life! Think Rachel, think, you may have been the last person to see Morgan and Pender alive, did they say anything that might shed some light on all this?"

She chose to ignore his emotional outburst.

"They told me that people had tried to kill them, that's why they were so security conscious. They said they had spent a lifetime researching the King Arthur story and they seemed genuinely upset that Helen Daniels had been murdered. I think they saw her program as their last chance to get proper recognition for their work."

"Was there anything more specific?" He was listening intently.

"They said there was something big in their research that the authorities would not want to come out. They also said that they had discovered that a long term associate of theirs, Robin Bryant, had turned out to be an MI5 stooge planted to report and cover up anything they found out. The last thing Morgan said to me was that if I had any sense I'd walk away from the whole project."

"He was right about that, you should." Evans now sounded fatherly.

"Am I really in danger?" Rachel hadn't really considered this possibility.

"Honestly?"

Rachel nodded and Evans continued; "I'm not sure." He thought for a moment, "the police and the BBC are looking all over for this briefcase and Nicole swears she doesn't have it. I think she left it here with you deliberately."

Rachel was taken aback.

"So what's the big deal with the case, shouldn't we just return it to Nicole?"

Evans was quiet, his eyes were welling up but Rachel continued.

"There's something else not right about all this, I called the local paper last night offering a story about the fire, some pictures of it and a back story about Morgan and Pender but they didn't want to know."

"Christ, I wish you hadn't?" Evans rolled his eyes.

"Well, I am a journalist, that's what I do for a living"

"Someone in government has slapped a D notice on this. Do not contact the media about it, do not contact anyone at all, not even the police, do you understand?" His eyes were wide and fierce but his tone was one of concern.

Rachel meekly nodded feeling thoroughly chastised but she had more to say.

"From the footage on the DVD, I gathered that Morgan and Pender are, ummm, were convinced that the police were out to frame them and destroy their reputation. They give a couple of examples of what has happened over the last few years. Do you think that could be true?"

Evans looked thoughtful; "There is certainly some colourful information held on police files about them. I can't confirm how much, if any of it, is true.

Actually, I shouldn't say this but it wouldn't surprise me if the police and the authorities were actually involved, that's why I am trying to keep them away from you but I now have another problem." He paused to check he had her attention.

"It gets worse Rachel, my boss called this morning to pull me off the case. My best guess is that this goes right to the top. I smell a cover up."

"So, so what do I do?"

"We need to get to Nicole as soon as we can, she is probably in big danger."

Rachel was trying to think things through logically.

"Do you really think that Helen's murder is linked to Morgan and Pender and the documentary, couldn't it be something else?"

Evans sighed and ran his hands over his bald head.

"The police are holding a guy from the BBC's IT department as a suspect but I think that is far too convenient. The night she died Helen sent me an email explaining that she had been getting threats by post, by telephone, text and email. She told me that on two occasions they had mentioned Arthur, she said they had told her to 'leave Arthur alone'. This is the first I had heard about it, God I wish she had told me about this from the start, she may still be alive today." He took a few moments to recover from the thought.

"But why would Helen tell you?"

Evans ignored the comment, he was getting upset.

"... I phoned her but a guard answered her phone and said she had already left the office."

Evans was checking the briefcase, feeling around the inside, trying to avoid Rachel's enquiries. He pushed a hidden button which revealed a small false bottom compartment.

"This is Helen's case. She kept an emergency credit card and £1000 in cash in it and now they're gone."

Rachel pushed both hands through her long thick black hair.

"I don't understand. How could you know that?"

Evans ducked the question; "Did you ever meet Helen Daniels?"

"Yes, I met her a few times on work-related matters; I liked the way she called a spade a spade, you knew exactly where you were with her, or so I thought."

Evans could not hold back the tears.

"Are, are you OK?"

Evans was drained emotionally and he had to let it out.

"No, I'll never be OK again, Helen was my life, she was my daughter!"

There was a deadly silence until the words sunk in, Rachel felt helpless.

The big man was now crying freely. She put her arm around his shoulder and he sobbed like a child.

Evans' mobile rang. He took a few deep breaths before taking the call. The police field co-ordinator had information about the fire. Apparently in addition to discovering two bodies they had some further information.

Rachel couldn't help but overhear the conversation.

Evans seemed almost reluctant to go; "I've got to get over there."

As he got up to leave Rachel placed a hand on his arm.

"I'm so sorry about your daughter."

He looked back at her with sad eyes.

"So am I Rachel, so am I and I am not going to rest while the bastard that killed her is still breathing, please excuse me, I have to go."

Rachel looked scared, first Helen's murder, now it looked like Morgan and Pender had been deliberately toasted. Evans placed a firm hand on her right shoulder and engaged her eyes.

"Lock yourself in this room and don't leave, I'll be back as soon as I can….I'll get you some breakfast and a paper sent up."

With that he left.

This time she fully intended to do what she was told.

-20-

London
29th July 2009

Cardinal Valetti was very pleased that one of his politician friends had found him a quiet place to stay and work for a while. Its secure internet and communications network was from the highest possible authority. Like him, the CIA wanted to eradicate, once and for all, any proof that Jesus may have survived the crucifixion and any link between the Holy family, King Arthur and their supposed descendants. By the same token he was only too aware that MOSSAD would love to prove that JC survived the ordeal on the cross and died a human death, after all, the Jewish people believe that the true messiah is yet to come. If the CIA were right MOSSAD had already got to Morgan and Pender

Without doubt the two researchers had stumbled upon information that was bad for their health, they had resisted all attempts to discredit them, they hadn't heeded the warnings they'd been sent and they seemed hell-bent on blackmailing the Church. There was little choice but to deal with them and their research work. Now there were just loose ends to tie up. Those who knew too much about what they had uncovered had to be silenced. He wasn't totally heartless, just pragmatic, some collateral damage was inevitable.

Then there was also the little matter of the whereabouts of the real metal cross found at St Peter's Church and the supposed treasure of King Edward and the Templars, now that was something that really yanked his cassock.

-21-

Newcastle
29th July 2009

Rachel was pacing around the room like a trapped animal. She had finished the Full English breakfast that Bryn had considerately ordered for her, she had drunk three cups of coffee and a cup of tea and it was still only 10am so she started thumbing through the daily paper as the caffeine whizzed around her body manifesting mild palpitations.

It was so small she had almost missed the few lines on the front page, *Authors Die in Fire at Historic House*. She skimmed the text quickly; there was not very much of it. The gist was that Morgan and Pender had died in a fire after a gas explosion. She wondered what had happened to the D notice; probably the release had been controlled.

Turning the page, another article caught her eye. Evans was telling the truth.

Man Charged with Helen Daniels' Murder

35 year old Mark Flatt appeared at West London Magistrates' Court yesterday charged with the murder of TV's golden girl crime presenter Helen Daniels. He was remanded in custody.

At about 10.30pm on the night of the murder Helen Daniels left the BBC building with Flatt, an IT manager, to walk to the nearby car park where they had both left their cars. She was never seen alive again.

Miss Daniels was shot once in the head at close range with a 9mm gun and died at the scene. Her body was taken to Charing Cross Hospital for forensic examination.

Police revealed that the weapon left four distinctive marks on the cartridge case of the fatal bullet. Experts say it could have been deliberately tampered with to deaden the sound of the gunshot, indicating someone with knowledge of firearms. Flatt was a member of the Chelsea Pistol club from 2007- 2008.

No weapon was found at the scene of the crime. A gun discovered on the banks of the Thames has been ruled out as the murder weapon following examinations by forensic experts. Police believe that someone may have picked the weapon up and urge whoever found it to hand it in to the nearest police station.

Flatt was arrested at the scene. Police believe that the two had a lovers tiff.

> Police also wish to trace a short stocky man in a light coloured Mackintosh who was seen in the area at the time as they believe he may have witnessed the shooting.
>
> Colleagues say that Miss Daniels had been the subject of sustained stalking and threats by email and post for some weeks prior to her death. Police investigating hate mail have traced the source of some of the emails back to the BBC server to which Flatt had access as head of the department. It seems he tried to disguise the source of the messages but computer experts have been able to trace them back to his machine.
>
> Miss Daniels' line manager at the BBC said "We are all in shock; this killing makes no sense whatsoever."
>
> Police have examined CCTV footage from the BBC which confirms that Helen Daniels and Flatt left the building together a few minutes before she was killed.
>
> There is some speculation that Flatt may have been persuaded to kill Ms Daniels in return for a substantial sum of money which a police spokesman said had been transferred to Flatt's bank account the day before her death. It is well known that Miss Daniels had exposed criminals and rogue trading on television but police were adamant that this was just one of the lines of enquiry they are pursuing.

Rachel was beginning to wonder how much of this story was true. Her train of thought was derailed by a loud knock at the door, it was Evans. He needed a shave and his eyes looked tired and strained; "Any chance of a coffee Rachel?"

Evans saw the paper opened at the article about Helen and it was obvious that he wanted to talk.

Rachel lay on the bed and closed her eyes as he launched into a soliloquy. She had to admit to fighting sleep as he told her about how, after a divorce, he and his daughter had drifted apart but that how, fairly recently they had struck up a relationship again. Evans told Rachel that they had planned a get together next month, a time to catch up and be themselves; alas it was not to be.

Rachel broke the uncomfortable silence.

"I guess the police have been all over your daughter's house by now."

Evans agreed, he said he was dreading having to go in and sort things out. Looking slightly refreshed for having unloaded the burden, he turned to Rachel; "Will you come with me and help?"

"But I am one of them, remember, part of the media circus." She replied sarcastically.

Evans felt the slap; "But you're also a woman and you're involved in all this. I'm going to have to trust you, I need your support and you need someone to keep an eye on you!"

Unsure what to do, she reluctantly agreed. Evans was pleased and he turned back to the job in hand.

"Any more info from the DVD, I assume you've had another look?"

"A bit more."

Rachel made herself comfortable on the bed by crossing her legs and resting her head back against the headboard.

"I'll paraphrase as Morgan can run on. He said that the evidence for two real king Arthurs is pretty conclusive. The church, the media and the government do not seem to want to know. Maybe it is that a mystery once solved isn't a mystery anymore... perhaps it is more sinister than that. He said that there is written evidence for the family tree of the Arthurs stored in many places. Some of the descendants of Arthur are alive and known today although they understandably keep this very quiet."

Evans looked thoughtful; "He is talking about two King Arthurs that would make sense wouldn't it?"

The question was lost on Rachel but he continued. "People say that Arthur could not have been real because he fought the Romans and Saxons and therefore would have had to have been of a great age, but having two Arthurs make perfect sense.....it solves the time issue."

Evans looked deep in contemplation before stroking his chin ad continuing.

"If there is so much evidence why are we always told that Arthur was just a myth? I wonder if it's true that there are still relatives living today?"

Rachel shrugged her shoulders; "I've no idea, why would he lie,.. maybe to sell books?"

Evans conceded the possibility.

"I take it there is more?"

"Oh yes, there is more, much more."

His level of interest in the history seemed inconsistent with her perception of the man. Perhaps he just had nerdish tendencies when it comes to British history or perhaps he loved a conspiracy. She continued with what she had learnt from the DVD, reading from her notes as it was obvious he was absorbing every detail.

"Apparently, a guy called Meurig was the father of the second Arthur and Tewdrig his grandfather. It's an historical fact that Tewdrig was mortally wounded at the battle of Tintern Ford and buried at Mathern, which means, 'place of the Monarch'. The church was supposedly built up around him.

In 1609 and again in 1881 Tewdrig's body was found when work was being done to the church. After his death, his wife Govein went to live and work from a small church on the beach, at a place that bears her name, St Govein's Point, (nowadays called St Govan's). In an attempt to deride this history most historians say St Govan was an Irish Monk. In 1980 a small female skeleton was discovered under the ruined altar. So the hard evidence to prove the ancient histories starts stacking up.

The Arthurs were senior descendants of the First Holy Family of King Bran (Bran the Blessed). At that time the kingdom of these kings extended to Cornwall and Devon, into mid England and most of Scotland.

A stone naming King Meurig was found around six miles from Tintagel, so that may be why the place claims to be the main seat of Arthur when in fact it may well have been a summer or occasional residence of the kings of Gwent and Glamorgan. It is much more likely that the seat of Arthur was at or near Caerleon where he was, according to the Historic Bruts of England crowned King of Glamorgan and Gwent."

"Just rewind that bit again, the bit about the Holy Family."

Evans was enthralled.

Rachel turned back the page and re-read it.

"The Arthurs were senior descendants of the First Holy Family of King Bran (Bran the Blessed)."

Evans was shocked.

"Oh my God, I wonder if he means *the* Holy Family. Now there's something the church and government wouldn't be too happy about?"

Evans motioned Rachel to continue.

"Percy Enderbie wrote *Cambria Triumphans* in 1661. It traces Dukes, Earls and other great Lords of Britain from an ancient Khumric king or Prince. Enderbie traces Charles' claim to the throne from Howell Dda (or Howell the good) ap Cadell of Dyfed. This is important because Arthur's family tree is part of this line. Basically the right to the throne is being claimed through Cambrian (Welsh) decent and so from Brutus. The genealogy is contained in a document known as the Harleian 3859 which is still in the British Museum. Enderbie had no hesitation in stating that British origins were from Brutus. In fact all histories up until 1661 quite clearly give the correct histories and include King Arthur and his links to the Holy Family. Arthur 2, son of King Meurig, in turn son of King Tewdrig and so on back to Brutus was a sixth generation direct male line descendant of Arthur 1. Arthur 2 was born at Dunraven Castle in 503 and was killed in the USA in 579."

Evans again pricked up his ears in astonishment.

"Hang on; did you say he was killed in the USA?"

Rachel checked her notes and nodded and Evans sat with his mouth gaping open.

"Now this is getting silly, that cannot possibly be right, can it!"

Rachel waved her hand as if to create a semi colon in the sentence.

"There's more. The ancient records clearly state that in AD 574 Arthur 2 summoned an army and assembled a fleet of 700 ships at Deu Gleddyf (Milford Haven). He sailed for The Other World which the Spanish called The New World and was away for five years until Taliesin and six others returned with his embalmed corpse in a ship in AD 579".

Evans went to make his own coffee this time; he needed the caffeine to concentrate.

"So, if these guys are right, there were two real Arthurs, their history was well recorded but relatively recently consigned to the dust bin. These Arthurs may have been linked to the Holy family and Arthur 2 discovered the USA... interesting. "

Rachel spoke her mind; "OK, let's assume this is true and can be proven. Is it enough to kill people for?"

Evans put his head in his hands desperately trying to compute the impossible.

"I suppose that depends..."

"On what, exactly?"

"Well, you said it yourself really; it depends on how strong the evidence is, who has access to it and what its effect are perceived to be!" He was looking very thoughtful;

"Let's just say there is proof that King Arthur was real, linked to the Holy Family and descendents living today can prove their genealogy back to that Family."

Rachel smiled, "That would make one a hell of an episode of *Who Do You Think You Are?*"

Evans ignored her irreverence and continued;

"It would be OK if you are the current king or queen but what about if you're not?"

"Rebellion, people losing their heads, a change of religion and all that jazz?" Rachel couldn't help playing him up when he was trying to be serious.

Evans sipped his coffee and Rachel took the chance to challenge his theory.

"No, it's too sensational; after all we'd had all this rubbish before with the *Holy Blood and the Holy Grail* and *The Da Vinci Code*. The world didn't end, nothing changed, and no descendent of JC came forward to save us all. This isn't the middle ages."

Evans did see the absurd side of it.

"OK, OK, point taken, but, what if there was a core of Nationalists, a body of people that were militant and just needed something to build nationalism on. What could be better than to rally around the real descendant of King Arthur, the once and future king, the descendant of Jesus, Britain for the Brits and all that?"

"Do you mean the BNP could make something of it?, fuel racism and unsettle the country, I guess that's a remote possibility."

Evans nodded, "Maybe, it's a thought, and if it is all true, maybe we really should be reclaiming our true history and heritage. Morgan and Pender were sitting on some hot stuff, no wonder the powers that be want to play it down and eradicate the problem. Look at the Edward Kelly suicide for example, you know, the guy that said there were no weapons of mass destruction in Iraq. I don't think many people really believe he committed suicide, do you?"

Rachel ducked the issue and looked at her watch.

"Christ, Nicole, what about Nicole, don't we need to get the briefcase back to her and see if she is OK?"

Evans agreed; "Yes of course we do, there are a few things I need to chat to her about...come on, I'll buy you a pizza first, I am starving."

-22-

Newcastle
29th July 2009

It was meant to be a secret, her little naughty secret.

By day Nicole was a relatively successful documentary maker, well known for sniffing out the hard core of a great story. That was, of course until her unceremonious sacking and instant dismissal from her job. The blow was a stab through the heart. She would check to see if she had any legal ground to stand on but she suspected not, it was only a contract job, full time media jobs were almost extinct these days. At least she'd kept hold of Helen's briefcase containing some of the rushes. She hoped that her calculation was right and that by leaving it in Rachel's hotel room that her friend's curiosity would get the better of her.

Now she would have to live off her secondary source of income until another gig came along. Nicole had a penchant for sexual fetishes. A few years ago she indulged her private interest professionally when she got commissioned by a digital channel to put together a series called simply *Fetishes*. It took her all over the country from Swingers in Devon to a Slap'n'Tickle outfit in Maidstone, from a gimp maker in Durham to a group in Norfolk who liked to fuck balloons.

Apart from the perverts and the nutters, she met some very nice people who were having fun and making a very decent income from their work, (especially the gimp mask makers). In the process of putting together the series, Nicole got the opportunity to live out some of her own fantasies. She had the sort of body most women could only dream of, long limbs, pert breasts and a flawless complexion. She was confident, agile and loved the camera. When someone suggested the benefits of internet porn to her, she was in. It was a lucrative job if you could work for yourself and the only contact with clients was via their internet connections.

For this afternoon she had planned a special Japanese treat. Checking her watch she realised that her hired help, a Kinbaku specialist, was late. Kinbaku means erotic bondage and requires a skilled artist who can tie ropes around a woman's body, making it look beautiful and erotic. He came highly recommended but his lateness suggested he wasn't actually Japanese.

The weblink was set up, the props were ready and she drank a glass of sake while she waited. This gave her time to reflect on the events of the day. Rachel's warnings and concerns for her safety sounded over protective and Nicole now realised that she had probably over-reacted; she hadn't meant to leave in such a huff. She'd explain about the briefcase and apologise later.

Ten minutes away Rudy Strink was nervously running through the drill in his mind. He had studied the YouTube clips on Kinbaku and figured he could fall back on his days in the navy if necessary. Rudy had the body of a military man, he was strong and stocky. He had a hard face but fortunately his baby blue eyes hid his aggressive nature. He was also quite good at accents, managing to disguise his Boer roots when necessary. He was going to need all the charm he could muster to convince his target that he could give a shit about an Eastern art form, albeit, a kinky one. His paymasters had prepared his disguise, now the job was over to him.

Nicole heard Strink's car approach down the gravel driveway as she scrutinised her Japanese style red lips with black eye make-up and re-tied her yukaka.

The door bell rang and she saw his face in the video phone.

"Kon nichiwa, Rudy desu."

"Watahsi wa Nicole desu, kon nichiwa."

Their Japanese greeting encouraged her to let her guard down and she opened the door.

"Seku shii na!" Sexy was one of a handful of words he'd prepared for the occasion and as he eyed her up and down he determined that it was most appropriate.

-23-

Newcastle
29th July 2009

Evans looked nervously around, it had been 15 minutes since they'd ordered the pizzas and they had already made short work of the olive entre. His patience was just about up when the large pepperoni with extra chili arrived in front of him. The plate had hardly touched the table before Evans made his move. He was in machismo mood, bragging about how much he loved chili.

Rachel rolled her eyes and ordered another bottle of San Pellegrino.

"So, tell me how this all started Evans…..I mean how did you first become involved in this case?"

Evans was covertly sucking in air to cool his mouth and he struggled to speak.

"This is hot… better than sex… well at my age it is anyway."

"I appreciate that you are taking an interest in my safety but I'm a news hound and if I'm going to have to watch you endure that pizza, I'd like to know a bit about you." She persisted.

Evans gulped down a glass of sparkling water and looked to see who if anyone was within earshot before he responded.

"Interpol only tends to get involved in things when there are conflicts of interest, or the usual channels can't deal with something…." Rachel's eyes told him to continue.

"About eighteen months ago we were getting intelligence regarding police corruption in South Wales, it wasn't the first time it had happened, there was a spate in the 1970's and again in the 1980s and 1990's but this was different."

He took another sip whilst Rachel shuffled to the edge of her seat.

"As is usual in Police corruption cases another force was given the task to investigate but Interpol acted independently. There were a number of crimes going on and certain people were being framed for them, people who could never have been involved. The other force whitewashed the issue but I kept digging. Most of the corruption seemed to lead back to the activities of two men… Morgan and Pender."

Rachel stopped eating.

"A businessman who had helped fund Morgan and Pender's work was found face down in a swimming pool. There were dealings in priceless artifacts from ancient sites, valuable paintings that had been stolen from a church, two protected sacred sites had been vandalized and things taken, there were various arsons, thefts of large sums of money, threatening behavior, intimidation and GBH not to mention fraud and paedophilia and for all these things Morgan and Pender had been put in the frame at one time or another. There was also a trail of false witnesses and incorrect police records...I could go on."

"Are you saying that the police were trying to frame Morgan and Pender?" She was incredulous.

"Looks like it..."

"Do you have any idea as to who is behind all this, and why?"

Evans shook his head; "I arranged to meet the Chief Superintendent of the offending force for a cozy chat but he died of a heart attack the night before the meeting."

"How convenient...this is serious isn't it Bryn?"

The man nodded and took another slice of pizza, leaving half a chili on the side of the plate.

"I went to interview Morgan and Pender myself some time ago. I am sure they didn't tell me the whole story.

Of course, some of their paranoia was valid. They were being tapped into by MI5 and following my meeting with them I recommended that we start listening too. That's how I knew that you had paid them a visit yesterday."

"Then you must know what happened at the house on the night of the fire." She was fundamentally opposed to such infringements on liberty.

Evans evaded the question as Rachel continued.

"I feel like I've landed in a James Bond novel, is it legal to tap into people's lives like that?"

"Well, if you get the necessary permissions from the Home Office it is." He stole a glance in her direction.

"But you didn't get permission did you?"

"You are right, this is an unusual case, and if I had gone through the usual channels I'd have gotten nowhere."

"So how far did you get, just tell me what the fuck is going on!" Rachel was failing to hide her frustration.

Evans took his time in responding. Nothing would detract from his enjoyment of his final slice.

"Morgan had worked in the ship building industry and had played a small part in getting secret plans for the British Government. Pender once owned a Tattoo shop. They have, or rather *had* spent 30 years researching this King Arthur stuff. I know they have links to the British Israel Society, I guess there is just a chance there is a MOSSAD link. As I said, we put the tap on their phone and email but we lined up behind MI5 and, I'm guessing here, MI6 as well."

"Do you think this could this be linked to a sort of terrorism... Maybe the destabilization of the UK government or a breakdown of the legal or religious system, might that be why people are so interested in them?" Rachel had watched every episode of the BBC's spy drama *Spooks*.

Evan's expression suggested as much. For the sake of his company, he stifled a post pizza burp with his serviette.

Slightly embarrassed, Rachel reminded them of their plan; "Come on, we need to get to Nicole. Hexham is about half an hour's drive from here."

Along the way they stopped to refuel the black Audi and that triggered a memory for Rachel. She turned her face towards Evans who was pulling out of the service area onto the busy motorway.

"The news report suggested there had been a gas explosion at their housed which started the fire."

"So?" Evans glanced quickly at her and then back to the road

"They didn't use gas, only electricity; Pender was moaning at the bills but said they couldn't afford to make the conversion."

"Good point," he replied. "I'm waiting for the forensics; they might throw some light on the truth."

"So how does this work exactly, is it just you that is in charge of the investigation or are the local police working with you?"

"The local bizzies do their bit as usual but I get copied in to look at the bigger picture, that's the theory anyway." He explained.

"You don't sound too sure about that."

Evans braked for a pedestrian who had dashed out into the road; he muttered some obscenity before turning his attention back to Rachel.

"I'm not, I'm not sure at all. For a start we weren't the only ones who were using surveillance. Imagine three separate teams watching and looking. What a waste of resources. What a joke! And we're allegedly all on the same side."

"You don't sound convinced."

"It's all a big game really Rachel, a game I am a little fed up with playing to be honest. I see criminals who are still allowed to get away with some serious stuff because they feed info to the authorities to catch bigger fish. I've seen innocent people who have had their lives ruined to further some cause that is flavour of the month and chip wrappings the next. I have spent too much time whitewashing corruption for governments. In the end it's always the same; power, religion and money."

"You must do some good?" She responded, trying to lift his spirits.

"Yeah, maybe I'm just old and cynical. Now they want to pull me off this case altogether, they think I'm too personally involved and that really pisses me off. I have asked them to reconsider, so until I hear for sure I'm going to keep going."

In the barn in Hexham, Nicole and Rudy had been discussing the ropes, the props and the positions. They had both consumed rather a lot of sake although he seemed completely unaffected by it. In contrast she slurred her words as she got herself ready. He moved about the barn, ostensibly preparing his ropes but actually he was keen to locate the briefcase Nicole had taken from Helen that contained the DVD of the programme rushes, it couldn't be far away.

"So how did you get into kinbaku?" Nicole was just about in control of her faculties.

The man thought for a moment, how considerate of Nicole to let him in, ply him with sake and undress so that he could suspend her from the rafters with ropes. Her place was remote and he could not foresee any disturbances. He thought that he'd take his time and play her along a little.

"I studied Japanese martial arts and spent six months in Tokyo so I could become an instructor. While I was there I met a Japanese girl who turned me on to kinbaku."

"I love it," Nicole replied, "It's a hell of a lot more fun that ikebana. Rudy's grasp of Japanese culture didn't extend to flower arrangement so he just smiled and grunted.

"How exactly do you want me?"

He looked at her shapely figure, her soft skin and huge eyes, what a waste, he thought but there again he wasn't paid to think he was paid to kill and a job is a job.

Back in the black car Evans had just disengaged from a hands free phone call from the forensics team.

There was complete silence because Rachel had also heard the conversation. The suggestion was that the fire hadn't been a gas explosion at all but that the house had been taken out by two smart internal burst incendiary bombs, probably set off by a mobile phone strapped to the devices. An alternate, but more unlikely theory was that a smart incendiary had been fired from a high flying drone. The man had told Evans it was code red.

Rachel was shaking but she raised the courage to speak; "What in God's name...?"

Evans cut her short and smashed his fists against the steering wheel. He pulled the car into the side and held his head in his hands. Rachel moved slightly and hugged his head and shoulders. He moved to shake her off although he didn't really want to; "Are you OK... Bryn, are you OK?"

Evans phone went again, it was his boss; "You've had the news?"

Evans affirmed. "You're definitely off the case now, you hear me, off the case! It's code red, it's over to the big boys."

Evans recovered slightly; "But my daughter, I need to find out who killed Helen. Come on Harry, let me carry on low key for a while, I know you hate this sort of thing as much as I do."

The man at the other end showed no sign of compassion; "You're off the case Evans, take a couple of weeks out, you need it….oh and Evans, don't let me get a whisper that you are interfering in this, do you hear me?"

The line went dead.

Evans felt in limbo, his limbs were numb, and his brain was frozen. Rachel tried to be calm and kind.

"Bryn, just what exactly is code red?"

There was a pause before he answered.

"It's a warning off from the government, it ceases to be a police or Interpol matter and it gets dealt with directly from the top by a neat little team that will cover all the cracks and make things look normal."

"Is it even possible it could have been a strike from a drone? can they do that?, didn't anyone see it happen?"

Evans looked at her.

"They can and they do. Stealth high altitude assassins hit with high impact. There are no trace shells; no-one would have seen it strike, the Americans use it all the time against terrorists in hard to access places."

Rachel had another question.

"The Americans? Why would they do that? No chance that anything or anyone could have survived I suppose?"

"So many questions Rachel. How do you expect me to give you all the answers, I don't even know myself!"   We are not even sure if it was a drone hit or a planted bomb. Anyway there's not a chance in hell of anything much surviving, either way everything will have been burnt to a cinder…"

"Christ almighty…but where does that leave us with you off the job and Nicole and I in limbo?"

Evans looked determined.

"I don't give a shit what Harry says, my daughter was murdered and I'm not going to rest until I catch the bastard that did it…plus, there is no way I am leaving you in danger. Let's get to Nicole."

Rudy climbed a ladder and threaded the rope over the hook that had been placed above the bed. Next, he began to tie Nicole up using a special sequence of knots. It was rather fortunate that she was quite drunk as his handiwork was not the most artful. He started by passing the rope between her legs then knotted it at the back, brought it tightly over her hips and produced a further knot near her naval. Her arms were bound and he made a pretence of caring by asking if it wasn't too uncomfortable for her. Shoulders, breast, and back down to crotch. She was now quite turned on and the numb feeling in her hands she put down to the drink. Nicole was giggling with masochistic delight. The rope was biting into her clitoris rubbing it with every pull, giving her indulgent sensations of carnal pleasure.

Macramé complete, he hoisted her on the rope towards the rafters. He was standing on the bed, making the final adjustments when suddenly he pulled the knife from its sheath under his trouser leg. Nicole gasped as he put his mouth to her ear and whispered in a distinctly South African accent, his foul smelling breath engulfed her.

"So where is the briefcase Nicole?"

Realising too late what was happening Nicole's eyes stared in terror. She started to wriggle but she was bound so tightly that any movement now only induced pain. He was menacing as he ran his hand along her skin, over her breasts and body before squeezing her groin. Her earlier sensations of pleasure were replaced with fear and pain.

"I suggest you co-operate, you're in no position to refuse." He spoke softly but menacingly, the smell of sake and cigars wafted up her nose making her gag.

Nicole's skin was covered in goose pimples of finality. She strained not to wet herself as he started drawing the tip of the knife along her skin on the same route that his hand had taken moments earlier.

"Who are you, what do you want, what have I ever done to you?" She stared into his ice cold eyes.

"The briefcase Nicole, just tell me where the briefcase is."

Nicole tried to bargain. "Just untie me and get me down from here it's getting a bit uncomfortable."

He was displeased; he ran the knife along her breast drawing blood and making Nicole scream and wet herself in fear, the urine dripped onto the bed. She caved in.

"Ok, ok, I took Helen's briefcase and left it in a room at the Great Northern Hotel in Newcastle."

"Arr, you left it with your friend Rachel"

The man stood back and smiled.

"There, that wasn't too painful was it, and the DVD of the rushes, I take it you have watched it?"

Nicole affirmed and the man mocked sadness.

"Oh what a shame…wrong answer."

Evans and Rachel were less than a mile away but stuck at road works. Rachel dialled Nicole's number and on the table next to the bed, the mobile rang in a silly tune. He looked at the trembling girl before him. She gazed at the phone then back to him. He hated it when they caught his glance. Nicole was jabbering; "Please, please just cut me down, you can have the bloody briefcase if that's what you want!"

Strink ran his hands across her beautiful body and Nicole sensed the chance of a way out.

"Do you want to fuck me?"

The man stalled but raised the knife in his right hand.

"You were warned to back off from the project but you wouldn't listen, just like Helen Daniels. What is it with women these days?"

In one movement he held her head back and slit her throat. As her life slipped away she heard Rachel leaving a message on her answer phone.

"We're on our way over Nicole, we'll be there in about three minutes, this is heavy stuff, for Christ's sake, be careful."

The blood dripped with the urine as her body gently rocked from the rafters. Everything blurred in her mind. Suddenly she was rushing down a long tunnel towards a bright white light. Somehow she felt a calmness as she slipped away.

Strink wiped the knife and embedded it into the wooded floor. There were days when he hated this job, today was one of them. He left quickly, but even he didn't have the heart to look back at his handiwork. Maybe somehow if he didn't look again he could convince himself he hadn't done anything wrong.

The Black Audi swerved to miss the yellow Lotus sports car as it sped eractically around the sharp corner of a country lane and they ended up in the hedgerow.

For a few moments the world seemed to be spinning.

"Are you OK?"

Yes, think so, did you get his number?"

Evans shook his head; "Too busy trying to avoid him".

After extricating the car and composing themselves they continued the 200 yards or so to Nicole's driveway and approached her house. The mini was there, good, she was at home.

They knocked on the front door but there was no reply. Rachel looked through the kitchen window, nothing. Evans turned the front door knob and pushed slightly, it was open. Gingerly they entered, calling out to Nicole. Rachel detected an unusual smell, unfortunately it was one that Evans knew all too well. He motioned for Rachel to be quiet and get behind him. Together they crept through the lounge and to a door that was shut. Evans kicked it open and rushed in. Suddenly he stopped dead in his tracks trying to halt Rachel's progress, but she was right behind him.

They looked up and saw Nicole naked, tied and bleeding. She gagged at the sight and smell and then threw up. Her mind started spinning and she passed out. Evans caught her and carried her into the lounge where he placed her tenderly on to a large pink sofa. He rushed back into the bedroom, Nicole was still warm but he knew from the wound and the spurting blood that this was a pro job and that her life had passed into the next world. He cut her body free and laid it on the bed. It was then that he noticed the laptop on the dressing table and the dagger embedded in the wooden floor. Rachel came around slowly but she was inconsolable. He grabbed the computer and led her out of the house.

Rachel oscillated between being numb and breaking into hysterical crying fits.

"Sh, shouldn't we tell the police?"

Evans nodded; "Yes, yes we should, but not until we are a long way from here." Evans had a thought, "You mentioned that your friend William was good with computers didn't you?"

The comment was lost, this was no time to talk to her; she was a quivering wreck.

-24-

29th July 2009
Canterbury

Natasha dropped William back at his apartment early in the morning. He should have gone into the office to make a start on the new contract for the Welsh Tourist Board but his mind was elsewhere. Now he found himself driving back to Canterbury. The material on Michael's computer was playing on his mind, not to mention the events at the funeral. He thought he now understood why Michael's body wasn't in his coffin, it had been cremated and the ashes made into a ring that ended up on Angela's finger. However he was still confused about the red haired nun who looked like the nurse that was so kind to him when his mother had died and who had apparently died before he met her!?

The whole thing made no sense to him whatsoever.

He was in such deep thought that he couldn't remember the drive. He only became alert when he turned his ivory coloured Big Healey into the car park of the Kent and Canterbury hospital.

Another snap storm was approaching, he could smell the scent of water on dust and then felt a few spots of rain. He just managed to make it to the main Accident and Emergency entrance before the black clouds burst, drenching the smokers standing near the front entrance and replacing their nicotine stink with the fresh aroma of summer showers.

The lady at the enquiry desk was neat with a soothing voice and a forced smile. In a well rehearsed pentameter she asked if she could help. William edged forward as if to preserve some privacy; "I'm enquiring about a nun and a priest who were brought in here after an incident at Canterbury Cathedral yesterday."

The woman's face took on a less friendly expression as she eyed William up and down.

"And you are?"

"William Marshall, I was there when it all happened. I tried to help the nun I, I am wondering how she is?"

"Just take a seat please sir, I'll be with you in a minute." The woman adjusted her headset, a call was coming in.

William opted for pacing around the reception area, he hated sitting down and waiting at the best of times. The corridors, the café and the shop were all crowded. People formed queues at desks, some happy, some sad, all were waiting for something. That's life, he mused we are always waiting for something.

As he walked aimlessly over to one of the double doors and peered through the top glass squares reinforced with wire mesh, he thought he caught a glimpse of the girl he had come to see at the end of the corridor. As if she sensed him, she turned around. For a moment, time stood still. He knew that angelic smile, that long red hair. She started walking, almost floating towards him along the corridor, he tried the door; it was locked. She glided closer and closer. He was shaking the door hopelessly trying to get in. Her face reached the glass of the door and pressed against it...she was mouthing the words, help me, help me!

He looked away for a second to the receptionist who was calling him and then back again. She was gone.

He rattled the doors over and over, trying to get in, shouting at the receptionist for her to let him in. William was frantic, overcome with grief and emotion; he felt his grip on reality leaving him.

A security guard approached and asked him politely to calm down.

"But you don't understand, the nun, the woman...I saw her, she was there; I just want to speak to her."

The receptionist came from behind the counter and approached William with a kindly smile;

"I am sorry, Mr Marshall, truly sorry, the priest was dead on arrival and the nun, well unfortunately she died during the night."

William refused the proffered arm around the shoulder and stepped back;

"No, no that's impossible! I have just seen her... please, please let me in there."

The receptionist was cold and matter of fact; "I am sorry sir there is no mistake."

"But, at least tell me who she was, I mean I'd like to send some flowers..." William was trembling.

The guard was a thick set older man with cauliflower ears who may well have once seen action in the ring. He moved across to William and put a vice-like arm around his shoulder. William expected to be man handled but was pleasantly surprised as the man spoke softly.

"Come on, ole son, it's OK, come and have a cuppa."

William was reluctant to comply; after all he had just seen her in the corridor, hadn't he? She couldn't be dead, how could he have seen her if she was dead, was he really going mad?

There was a general hubbub in the reception area that William hardly noticed. His mind was miles away just staring into oblivion. Then he realised he hadn't taken his tablets, the ones the doctor had given him to help him combat his stress and grief. He looked up, the guard re-appeared.

"I've bought biscuits as well, hope you like custard creams? The man put the two teas and biscuits down and sat down opposite William."

"I've finished my shift, don't mind if I join you do you?" With that, he emptied four sugar sachets into his own tea.

William was happy for the company and the big guy was gentle and friendly. He couldn't help comparing him to Michael, right down to his sweet tooth.

"Thank you for the cuppa, I need it!"

The man held out a hand and William shook it.

"Tommy Fielding."

He beckoned William to come closer.

"The nun you came to visit, I've seen her this morning as well".

William dropped a biscuit into his tea with a splash and looked across to the man, he seemed deadly serious. Tommy continued; "Twenty five years in the army, never forget a face, especially not such a pretty one, gorgeous long red hair."

At last! William was about to get up and tell the receptionist she was wrong but the man placed his hand over William's arm.

"Not a good idea William, there's something going on here that's not quite right."

William looked at him inquisitively, expecting the man to expand his statement, he wasn't disappointed.

"I came on duty just before 2am last night and walked around the wards as I usually do." the man sipped his tea before continuing; "The nun was in a side room on her own, fairly near to the door, well that usually means their time is just about up, you know."

William did know, he remembered the day so recently that his mother died in just such a hospital room.

"But at least she wasn't alone; there was a nun, a monk and a doctor with her. She was sitting up on the bed, her wrists in bandages. Then she walked around the room talking to them, she seemed quite agitated."

"Could you hear what they were saying?" asked William.

"No, not really, it was something about taking her somewhere safe, somewhere that sounded like Holdey, or Kolkey? I didn't catch it."

William couldn't believe what he was hearing; "So you are saying that this girl was up and about talking and very much alive? What time would that have been?"

The guard thought carefully, "About 3 o'clock...but that's not all, I saw her not more than 15 minutes ago on my last round, she was in her room, reading."

William sat bolt upright; "Jesus wept! So why did the woman on reception tell me she'd died in the night?"

The hefty man shrugged his shoulders.

"Any chance you could just pop back and make sure she is still there? Can you get me in?" William whispered.

Nodding, he replied, "Meet me in the toilet down that corridor in 10 minutes."

Tommy was on very chatty terms with the cooks in the canteen and he knew they were short staffed.

"Hey, how about I do the tea round for you Lucy, would that help you out?"

The large lady with the ruddy complexion and a northern accent came over and hugged him; "You're a teddy bear mi pet, thank you?"

William was waiting in the toilets when Tommy entered carrying a long green coat and a plastic hat.

"Here slip those on and meet me in the corridor."

William did what he was told and ventured out to meet Tommy who started pushing the trolley down the corridor to the ward. The sister let them in.

"Got you doing the tea now have they Tommy? Who is this handsome man?"

Tommy answered before William could; "Temp staff Olive, can't speak a word of English but he's very willing."

William managed an inane nod and smile, they were in.

Apart from a number of male and female patients in various states of dress and undress and in various conditions there were not many nurses to be seen in the emergency assessment unit. Tommy started dishing out tea and William crept away trying to make his way to the room where the girl had been. He looked through the windows of a couple of rooms and came across the one Tommy had described, the curtains were drawn across the glass, he took a deep breath and opened the door. The room was empty, the bed was made, just a single pink rose lay where once the girl had been.

He thought he heard whispers as he closed the door but he couldn't be sure.

-25-

Sheffield University
29th July 2009

Doctor of Archaeology, Roger Felix found himself in a perilous position when he had been asked to examine and preserve the Mappa Mundi for the Trustees of Hereford Cathedral because he discovered that it contained information that underlined Morgan and Pender's claims. He had an excellent reputation and was respected in academic circles. To align himself to Morgan and Pender was not something he chose to shout about. He knew that he could kiss goodbye to his career should his allegiance ever be detected.

He had tried to hide his excitement, OK, maybe he shouldn't have told Morgan and Helen Daniels about it, maybe he had breached confidences but it was a huge part of the jigsaw of reclaiming the real history of Britain. Surely people had a right to know?

Dr Felix had tried to explain to Morgan and Pender that if they were to get anywhere at all, the finds that they had discovered and which some had consigned to the dustbin as fakes, had to be authenticated. That is where he had really been able to to help. They had met and talked to him years ago but only in the last few months had they allowed him to take a slither from the electrum cross they had found at the dig at St Peter's. It had tested as genuine 6th century and this was to have been one of the revelations revealed by the television documentary that Helen and Nicole were working on. This was particularly important as there had been a long and sustained smear campaign on the internet and in the media alleging that Morgan and Pender had faked the cross by boiling up lead and other metals on a kitchen stove. The lab results proved this to be impossible. The cross contained a high quantity of silver, gold, nickel and, perhaps most bizarrely, an apparently unknown, other worldly substance.

Even more unexpected was Morgan and Pender's agreement to allow Dr Felix to re-open the dig at St Peter's and finish the job they had started way back in 1990. They were all certain that the site would reveal more treasures, hence Dr Felix's application to CADW.

The news of their death had come as something of a shock, not least because it was only a few days since he had seen them. He recalled that they seemed even more on edge than usual. Morgan had come to accept that his work would always be ridiculed by the establishment so he had decided to self publish. Pender made it clear he trusted no-one and he was particularly acerbic that day towards Dr Felix despite his genuine interest in their work. They were convinced that someone they knew was actually working for MI5, spying on them and defaming them. They cited the example of a letter supposedly from them to Helen Daniels' boss at the BBC in which they had accused her and Nicole of stealing priceless artefacts from one of the sites they had identified. Morgan and Pender were surprised that the BBC fell for the faked letter which cast doubt on the whole Arthur documentary and, in their paranoia, they even suspected the BBC of having their own hidden agenda. In their view the alleged spy was none other than Robin Bryant, the man who had sat in on Dr Felix's meeting at CADW.

If Morgan and Pender were right about Bryant then it's possible he had also made contact with Channel 4. Previously, Dr Felix had made several very successful programmes about Archaeology for the station but now they told him, in no uncertain terms, that they were not interested in anything to do with Arthur or Morgan and Pender. Dr Felix was angry but he was also curious. All he wanted to do was identify the genuine genealogy and location of King Arthur in Wales. Who, he wondered, was prepared to murder in order to keep this information secret?

He considered phoning Bryant who had given him his mobile number after the CADW meeting. They seemed to get on ok but Dr Felix was sceptical after Morgan's claims that he was a spy. He also pondered on the significance of the email that William, his old school friend, had sent him. It contained a picture of a completed puzzle of silver pieces on which were letters that he could identify. He tried to apply his rational mind to all the recent events but he failed to arrive at a solution.

His fascination for all things Arthurian over the years had led him to many dead ends. Some academics had secured huge grants for Dark Age research and the facts about Arthur as they appeared in the correct translations of the ancient texts were, shall we say, inconvenient so far as the accepted dogma was concerned. He remembered speaking to an ex student of Cardiff University who had wanted to do a PhD on the ancient translations and Arthur in Wales. She had been told from on high that if she wanted a good career she should leave the subject well alone.

He had been cautious about addressing it ever since but his deep personal interest persisted. If anything, the conspiracy surrounding the research fuelled his curiosity. The rebellious side of him would love to find evidence that proved Morgan and Pender's theories were correct.

He had procrastinated long enough. Reaching into his coat pocket he pulled out the business card that Sylvia Clarke dropped from the St Peter's dig file after their meeting at CADW. On it was the name and number of an International Dealer in Antiquities. He called the number and a man with a Russian sounding accent answered.

"State your business."

Dr Felix was anxious. His cowardly side wanted to hang up but he toughed it out.

"I know where there is something you might be interested in." He said, hoping he sounded convincing.

"Who are you?" was the blunt reply.

He didn't say; "Sylvia Clarke at CADW said you may be very interested in what I know…"

There was silence for a few moments.

"Why Clarke give you my number, this private line."

"You interested or not?" The Indiana Jones in him had taken over.

Pause; "You meet me, you bring thing, and you come alone."

"Ok, I'll meet you but it has to be in a public place and I won't bring the thing, I will bring a photo and we can talk."

"You police, you suffer."

"I'm not police." Dr Felix swallowed hard, who was this guy?

There was a rustle of paper.

"This evening, MacDonald's, Liverpool Street Station, 9.00pm, blue umbrella, don't be late."

The phone cut off, Dr Felix looked at his watch, shit, if he left now he could just make it.

-26-

Early evening, London
29th July 2009

Rachel and Evans had driven down to London from Newcastle in separate cars, Evans in his black Audi and Rachel in her pride and joy, her new yellow Fiat 500. So much had happened in the past two days and the solo driving gave them both time to think.

Evans had been worried about letting Rachel drive, especially after she had seen Nicole's body hanging from the rafters, but Rachel had been determined, after all, what was the alternative? Whether she liked it or not (she didn't), she felt as though she was caught within the pages of a Ludlam thriller. If only she could return to her ordinary life.

Quite rightly Evans suggested that she didn't go back to her rented apartment. Instead, he directed her to secure parking at City Airport where she left her car and joined him in his.

"You OK Rachel?"

She was trembling slightly but he was considerate; "I'm so sorry you saw Nicole like that."

The statement released the valve to her tear ducts and soon her face was soaked in salty water made black by mascara. She turned her head towards the window, trying to hide her pain from Evans. It was a miserable rainy day for the middle of summer.

Evans fell silent as he thought about how Nicole and Helen had been assassinated. As he trawled through his years of experience he determined that there was something about the M O of the assassin that rang a bell. Evans checked the back seat just to reassure himself that the laptop he'd taken from Nicole's house was still there, it was.

The car windscreen wipers were waving first one way then the other, like the thoughts in his mind. Had these terrible things happened because of the Arthur documentary or was there something else, something they didn't know about?

Rachel's phone rang and they both jumped; "William!"

Evans gesticulated animatedly at Rachel, shaking his head and making a motion as if to switch off the phone.

"Call you later William" and she ended the call. Evans explained; "Sorry Rachel, should have explained earlier, please turn your phone off and remove the battery."

"But it's my friend William I need to talk to him." She looked hurt and annoyed.

"But you don't need your location flagged up on a GPS if someone is tracking you, and it won't do William any favours either." He tried to sound sympathetic.

Evans held out his hand and Rachel handed the phone over like a naughty schoolgirl. He slipped it into his pocket and after a while pulled over into a bus lay by. He removed his own phone, placed a small dongle on the end and handed it to Rachel.

"Try this one it's encrypted and scrambled but keep your calls short, William's phone may not be secure. Is there a place you both know where you can meet?"

Rachel thought then dialed the number, William answered; "William, don't speak, just listen...Giraffe 9, OK?"

There was a short pause; Rachel could almost hear the cogs turning in William's mind before he responded; "Sure..."

Rachel disconnected before he could say anything more.

It wasn't long before Evans cruised slowly passed his daughter's house and parked towards the north end of the street. He quickly surveyed the area before unlocking the car and stepping out with Nicole's laptop, which he then locked in the boot. It looked clear so he motioned for Rachel to follow him.

Helen's house was a large Georgian fronted terrace on Princelet Street between Brick Lane and Spitalfields. This was the area in which the Huguenots had made their home after persecution in 18th century France. Ever since, this area has been a refuge for new waves of immigrants. Now some of the houses were getting expensive makeovers but at no. 19 there was a building in a semi derelict condition. Its garden had been built over to make one of the first Synagogues in the UK. The rooms now held semi permanent art displays evocatively underlining the plight of displaced people. Helen had been fundraising for this project because she had strong feelings about history and human survival. She was also rather fond of living in such an up and coming part of the city. As he walked around her house, footsteps echoed on the wooden floors as if to underline its emptiness. Her coffee cup was in the sink, her clothes and shoes were scattered about the bedroom. As he walked down the hallway he told Rachel that he could smell the perfume she used to wear and when he closed his eyes he could see her face, feel her presence. He said he thought that at any moment she'd come walking through the door smiling, she didn't.

Rachel watched helplessly as the pained expression grew on his face whilst they wandered around Helen's home. She wanted to comfort him in some way, to tell him everything was going to be OK, but she just couldn't find the words, she knew in the back of her mind nothing would be OK again. At a loss as to what to do, she slipped am arm around his strong shoulders, instinctively he hugged her tightly, making it difficult for her to breath.

"You can't blame yourself Bryn; this had nothing to do with you."

Realizing he was squeezing too hard, Evans let go and stepped back.

"But I was her father Rachel, I wasn't there when she needed me most, I failed her."

Rachel thought she knew a little of what he was feeling.

"My dad died in a car crash when I was young. I don't even remember him. I've never really known what it is like to have a father, if I had I think I would have liked him to be like you." The comment lingered in the air for a while.

"Who would want to kill Helen, Rachel? It's been going around and around in my mind. I know that this chap Mark Flatt that's been charged with her murder isn't the one, he's just a scapegoat."

"They must have some evidence; after all, they couldn't just charge him for nothing." Rachel was trying to take a balanced view.

"Don't be so sure," he grunted, "you don't know the half of what goes on in the police force."

"So it wouldn't come as any surprise to you that someone has been fabricating evidence against Morgan and Pender?"

Evans came back to reality; "As I mentioned before, their record reads like a far-fetched conspiracy novel only it's got more holes in it. Last year, a man with the same name and physical attributes as Morgan ended up dead in a canal in Amsterdam."

Rachel felt a cold chill down the back of her neck; "Co-incidence or did someone get the wrong man?"

Evans shrugged his shoulders as Rachel continued.

"This Mark chap, do we know what evidence they do have?"

Evans stood up; "I really shouldn't be talking to you about this..."

Rachel rolled her eyes.He continued.

"They say that gunpowder on the clothes he was wearing matches that on the bullet. They also say that traces of this powder were found at his home on a pair of trousers."

Rachel thought for a moment; "What about the emails that were meant to have been traced back to him via the BBC server?"

Evans was nodding; "Sure, but Mark is not the only person with access to the server. He had reported a hack from an external source two weeks before the murder, about the time Helen started getting the threatening emails."

Rachel was in her stride.

"And the gun, what about the gun? If Mark killed her, then where is it?"

"Exactly my point, the guy in charge of the investigation for the Met says he thinks someone picked it up and ran off with it or that there was an accomplice."

"And what do you really think?"

Evans thought for a moment; "I think the police have stopped looking and the bastard that killed Helen is still out there."

He paused to wipe his eyes then continued; "The bullet had been tampered with and so had the amount of powder, this gave the effect of muffling the sound even more. It seems the gun was a Webly with a silencer. It is a bit old hat now but these guns were once often used by commandos or the SAS. I'm convinced that it was a professional hit and that it could well be something to do with that documentary."

"An assassin!" Rachel turned white. She now had little trust in the police, Evans had been taken off the case and she suspected that she could be the next target.Welcome to the world of paranoia she thought.

As if he could read her mind, Evans said stoically, "We're on our own and we'll have to trust each other. I won't let you down."

Frankly she had no alternative but to trust him. With this thought she took a deep breath and released the tension in her shoulders and neck.

Evans noticed how she seemed to relax a little. With that, he produced a copy of the email that Helen sent to him the night she died. There was a line in it that didn't make sense to him and he read it to Rachel.

'...I found a photo of Brighton at the market which I've hung in the front room. It reminds me of our summer holidays and it makes me smile.'

Rachel gazed at the very picture on the wall, trying to imagine why Helen had mentioned it in the same email in which she explained the threats she had been receiving. Evans was quicker to pick up on the message and he lifted the framed print from the wall and turned it over. He took it closer to the light of the window so that he could get a better look. He noticed that there was an ink smudge over the sealing tape which continued under the tape itself, suggesting it had been resealed after it was originally framed.

Outside a white van crawled slowly down the road.

Evans moved away from the window and placed the picture on the table slowly peeling off the tape. Rachel tucked one of her long red nails under the cardboard backing and flipped up a corner, it was a tight fit. As she lifted the backing and a layer of blotting paper, she uncovered a secret. Two typed letters had been hidden between the picture and the backing.

Undershaw,
10th March 1905

Dearest W

I write concerning our most enlightening discussion at Chartwell Wednesday of last week.

Our dearest Estelle did indeed grace us with her presence last evening and I have to say it was one of the most interesting sittings I have had the privilege to experience.

Naturally via her I enquired of the other world regarding the matters that had consumed our thoughts over the last few weeks and I am delighted that she was able to communicate with our good friends who gave considerable information appertaining thereto.

I thought you would like to have these notes to refer to soonest and I look forward to seeing you in person as soon as your valuable time permits.

In offering these for your kindest consideration I am reminded of your wonderful words, namely that; Truth is incontrovertible, malice may attack it and ignorance may deride it, but, in the end, there it is.

After singing two hymns, accompanied ably on the piano by dear Janet and as has now become customary Estelle sat quietly for some time. After a while her breathing deepened and she seemed to drift off into a trace like state. I am intrigued that she is working in the new way by using energy rather than straining to exude ectoplasm from her very being.

Shortly an ancient energy came through, you will know who this is if I refer to him solely as S.

Here, my dear W I paraphrase what was said;

Acting as a guide communicator S allowed a man to speak; this man said he was the historian Josephus;

"I was sent by Titus Caesar with Ceralius and a thousand riders to a certain town by the name of Thecoa to find out whether a camp could be set up at this place. On my return I saw many prisoners who had been crucified, and recognized three of them as my former companions. I was inwardly very sad about this and went with tears in my eyes to Titus and told him about them. He at once gave the order that they should be taken down and given the best treatment so they could get better. However two of them died while being attended to by the doctor; the third appeared dead but later recovered."

As you may imagine W we listened to this with some wonder and trepidation for are we not conditioned from birth to associate crucifixion with death? The idea of Jesus dying on the cross is something that is so widely accepted that it's rarely questioned and here we were clearly being told that he may have survived.

He continued

"And now when the evening was come, because it was the preparation, that is, the day before the Sabbath, Joseph of Arimathaea, an honorable counsellor, which also waited for the kingdom of God, came, and went in boldly unto Pilate, and craved the damaged body of Jesus"

We can assume that Pilate would have experienced many Crucifixions in his time and he was surprised how quickly Jesus seemed to die. The usual duration for a crucifixion would be several days and the victims would die from asphyxiation over an extended time. The punishment was designed to be long and drawn out.

The communicator continued;

The legs of Jesus were not broken as he was deemed to have already died.

The centurion pierced his side with the tip of a lance but he made no sound or utterance and he assumed that he was dead. But he had died not, for he was in deep stupor from drinking a potion that tasted like vinegar which had been administered on a cloth raised on a pole whilst he was awake."

"My God, what on earth do you make of all this then?" Rachel asked.

Evans looked thoughtful; "Undershaw, Undershaw, that's where Conan Doyle wrote Hound of the Baskervilles." He was a big fan of Sherlock Holmes.

Rachel looked blank as Evans continued.

"And Dear W at Chartwell, that's where Winston Churchill lived; this is a letter from Sir Arthur Conan Doyle to Winston Churchill!" He declared with confidence. "It sounds like he is describing a spirit voice giving this information at a séance or something."

Rachel picked the comment up straightaway; "A séance? I wonder what Helen was up to, she obviously wanted you to find this so she must have thought it had something to do with the threats she was receiving."

"I am as baffled as you." Evans was shaking his head.
Rachel read on.

> "We asked S if he could find out where Jesus was in his missing years, a few moments later a different voice spoke through Estelle:
> As a young boy Jesus joined a caravan and took the Silk Road to the East, where He lived with both Hindus and Buddhists, he then travelled far to the shores of Britain where he studied at the college of Llanilltyd Fawr before returning to begin his ministry. Later, after he survived the crucifixion he escaped back to Britain with his friends and some of his family where many of his kin were still living"

Rachel's eyes were wide open, her heart was racing, this was heavy stuff. She carried on;

> "There was a break in the communication dear W, Estelle was breathing oddly and we all feared for her safety. But as soon as the aberration started, it stopped and Estelle came forward into the room again. She seemed very tired and we were all much moved.
>
> W, by way of support for this communication I also wanted to tell you of a letter I have found from the Russian writer Nicholas Notovich, he travelled to a remote monastery in Ladakh, high in the Himalayas of India. There he says he found a book which he had translated from the Tibetan tongue. He says that this tells us things about a man called Issa. It tells how this man having been to the great college of the Silures at Llanilltyd Fawr, came to India in the company of merchants where he stayed briefly with the Jains and then to Jagannath in Puri where he studied with the white priests of Brahma. Issa fell out with them because he preached equality not a system of casts. It is recorded that he said; "God, our father, makes no difference between any of his children, all of whom he loves equally."
> He then goes to the Nepalese Himalayas studying Buddhism and ends up in Palestine where he announces that he is the person who left his home and his parents as a child. This

person was indeed the Jesus that we know today. Notovich says the real story of Jesus/Issa is amazing and it will change the way we think about religion forever."

Evans was shaking his head; "I just don't understand... Llanilltyd Fawr, that's in Wales, it's Llantwit Major in English, but Jesus was never in England or Wales ...was he?"

Rachel shrugged her shoulders but tried to be constructive.

"It sounds like this is all about Jesus, who he really was, what he was really teaching and whether or not he died on the cross. What if this is true? Maybe Helen wasn't murdered for what she knew about Arthur but for what she knew about Jesus? What if the documentary was going to suggest that Jesus survived the crucifixion?"

Evans thought about this. "But that wouldn't make sense, why murder Helen, Nicole, and Morgan and Pender? After all it's one thing for a medium at a séance years ago to say Jesus didn't die on the cross and that he was in Wales but it's another thing to have proof."

Evans suddenly realized what he had said and so did Rachel.

"What if there is proof, what about if Morgan and Pender had found it and had told Helen and Nicole?"

Just then there was a screech of brakes and the sound of a revving motorbike engine outside, there was only time to react, not to think. Evans threw himself on top of Rachel and they both hit the floor just as a roar of machine gun fire rattled through the front window and embedded in the wall opposite. The crash and rattle seemed to go on forever stirring up dust and smashing china and glass. Suddenly it stopped and three grey coloured canisters with yellow rings were thrown through the smashed windows and into the room from the outside, landing one after the other on the wooden floor about four feet from where they were laying. In a flash Evans was on his feet dragging Rachel out of the room and screaming for her to run as fast as she could up the stairs. Within five seconds they were half way up and then three loud bangs and flashes were followed by a surge of fireballs that were scorching through the house seeking to burn their tender flesh to a crisp. Breathless they reached the third floor but the house was now well alight and it would only be a matter of minutes before they were fried. The heavy mix of phosphorous and plastic explosive had partly demolished the floors of the house and set it on fire like the burning of the witches in some Cathar conspiracy.

Looking up Evans saw a trap door to the loft and gambled on there being a route to the roof. Standing on a chair he managed to push open the hatch. The flames continued to rise and the stench of smoke and acrid fumes made their throats prickly dry.

Overcome more by his desire to save Rachel than with value for his own life, Evans jumped with all the agility of a hare in the mating season. At first he stumbled banging his wrists and cutting his hand on the rough splinters. The flames licked around the corners of the doors on the landing and up the last few steps. Just in time he leapt, successfully managing to wedge his elbows over the wooden frame of the hatch. He then painfully and laboriously hauled himself into the darkness. He lay, gasping for breath, on the partly boarded attic, his hands dangling through the hatch. Turning and kneeling with his arms stretched down through the opening he was just able to hold onto Rachel's wrists as she jumped from the chair. For a moment his muscles and tendons burned with agony. The chair she was standing on tossed backwards on the flames leaving her swinging. They were engulfed now in thick smoke, their eyes running and sore and their throats felt full of holly leaves. Evans knew it was now or never. If he let go Rachel would perish before his eyes. Somehow, he managed to hold on and heave, trying to lever himself by his feet inch by inch on the sooty rafters.

He pulled and pulled, bit by bit, stretching and lifting Rachel's arms and body into the attic and away from the flames now licking around her feet and legs. Her head was through and she was trying to use her arms to lever herself across the rafters into the roof. Smoke was making its way up passed her and into Evans eyes, she was getting hysterical and panicky but Evans reassured her. It was a now or never moment as Evans gave an almighty heave pulling the rest of Rachel through the hole, suddenly she was on top of him. How ironic that this saving of a life was so much like giving birth. With no time to spare he turned and slammed the hatch into the hole casting them into darkness but knowing it would buy them a few precious moments. Evans' arms were burning, he didn't know if it was from the flames or from the tearing muscles. Rachel's legs were sore and her jeans were black and smoldering at the hems. At least this time they were both alive.

Evans' former SAS experience and automatic reactions helped him to recover quickly and his eyes adjusted to the dark. There were no signs of light above and no apparent way onto the roof. The only light came from the odd flickering of the flames below as they probed the gaps in the ceiling around the loft hatch damaged by their struggle for freedom. Smoke rose through the cracks which were acting like a chimney.

Then the penny dropped. They were in a long old terrace and at least as far as he could see there was no firewall between the properties. Rachel made it to her feet as Evans pointed into the darkness. He led her carefully by the hand across the rafters and she followed. Slowly they crept over the ceilings of four houses in the row. Behind them the flames were inching their way through the trap door trying to find them. Five houses along they came to a firebreak wall.

Their adrenalin was running high, their hearts pumping, searching for survival. The orange light of the flickering flames cast shadows like demons' faces down the terrace but they also illuminated a trap door in a ceiling. Evans pushed but it didn't move. In desperation he stamped on it with his boot, at first it didn't move but on the third frenzied kick it gave way and fell into the immaculately decorated hallway below almost taking him with it. Without thinking he motioned to Rachel and she took up position above the hole where once the trap door had been. Gently Evans lowered her down wincing as his torn arm muscles took her weight. She jumped the rest of the way slightly jarring her ankle. Luckily the luxurious carpet broke her fall. Evans followed.

For a precious moment they stood and surveyed each other. They were grey from the dust and soot, their clothes were torn and their faces wet with tears manifested by the smoke. Evans just managed to speak through his parched throat; "You OK Rachel?"

She nodded as she dusted herself down spreading detritus over the rather swish stair well landing in which they found themselves;

"Yeah, only just, they intended to cremate us like they did poor Morgan and Pender, right?"

Evans nodded; "They must have known we were in there..."

"Do you think they followed us?" Rachel was confused.

"That or they were staking out the place and it was bugged."

Rachel went stiff; "In which case they heard the whole thing about Jesus, about the letter."

"The papers, they're destroyed." Evans' suddenly realized.

Rachel was flicking ash from her hair and shaking from head to toe but she managed to reach into her pocket.

"You mean these?" she said waving them.

Evans leaned over and kissed her on the cheek; it was an unexpected display of emotion and one that made her feel good.

"Do you have any idea who was trying to toast us Bryn?"

Evans looked her straight in the eye; "Well the canisters they threw into the room were standard CIA issue."

"The Americans? Now the CIA are after us?"

"Let's not jump to conclusions." He tried to calm her.

They heard a bang downstairs, someone else was in the house. Evans put a finger to Rachel's lips requesting her silence whilst he took up a position on the landing. He heard feet run up the stairs, there was only one person, at least they stood a chance.

As the shadow came around the top of the stairs Evans moved swiftly, his military training still in evidence. In a second he had the person in an arm lock on their knees.

There was a scream which triggered another from Rachel. Evans blushed as he realized that he had done a wonderful maneuver but on the innocent lady who owned the house.

He waved to Rachel as the woman kept screaming. It was no use talking to her, she was hysterical. He released his grip, apologizing profusely as the two of them ran downstairs and out of the house. This time they had escaped. There was no sign of the white van or the motorbike but a fire engine was heading down the road from Brick Lane, its lights flashing, sirens blazing.

Rachel headed for the car but Evans pulled her the other way.

"Not the car Rachel, it's too dangerous."

"But the briefcase, the DVD and the notes, they're all in the back of your car!"

"We'll have to come back, for now we've got to get out of here."

As they reached the corner of Brick Lane they heard a police car, Evans pushed Rachel into a doorway and kissed her, the speeding car passed and Evans broke away.

"Sorry about that." She wiped the smoky residue from her mouth. He was old enough to be her father.

-27-

Evening, London
29th July 2009

It had been quite a rush but Dr Felix had just managed to catch the 17.45 Transpennine Express from Sheffield and make a connection at Doncaster to take him to Kings Cross, London. He was no stranger to the city, it was vibrant, bustling with life of all sorts and sometimes he liked that. Today however, he was apprehensive, he wasn't sure what he was doing or what he had started, he just felt that he was on to something big historically. It had been a shock when he'd seen the small newspaper article about the death of Morgan and Pender. In the back of his mind he knew that their death was related to their research, but which bit? What nerve had they hit to start such a knee jerk reaction? Was he involved? Was it wise to meet this Russian stranger? Secretly, he enjoyed the intrigue. Life in academia was generally very dull.

19.45pm, the train reached Kings Cross on time and it was just a few minutes to Liverpool Street Station on the Circle Line. The main rush of the evening was over and he headed for the Costa Coffee franchise and ordered a Cappuccino, he needed the caffeine hit. Finding a quiet place in the corner he pulled out copies of the photographs of the St Peter's cross. They were black and white but clear enough to illustrate precisely the nature of the design of the cross and the wording on it. In the same folder he had the test results of the slither he'd been given just a few weeks ago, a slither that had proved the provenance as 6th century. He sipped his coffee and decided to send a text to William.

William's office and double aspect studio was in the restored part of the Spitalfields market complex. One window overlooked the road and the other the large old covered area built in 1893 to enclose the field of the more ancient market which took its name from St. Mary's Spittle Church, priory and hospital which was founded in 1197. The careful and sympathetic renovation had been completed in 2005. King Charles II granted John Balch a Royal Charter that gave him the right to hold a market on Thursdays and Saturdays in or near Spital Square. The success of the enterprise encouraged a flood of displaced and oppressed people to settle in the area from 1685. William should have been getting on with the new commission but instead he was daydreaming, drifting back to earlier times . The beep of his mobile notified him of an incoming text. Natasha looked up from her computer and smiled.

" Do you fancy a coffee, William?"

He underlined his facial expression.

"Is the Pope catholic? I'm flagging."

She smiled at his quirky ways.

It was normal for them to be grafting late into the evenings especially when they had lots of work on. Natasha had been re-evaluating Michael's hard drive trying to squeeze every last byte of data from its damaged memory.

The text was brief and William followed it up with a call.

"What's happening Roger?"

Roger briefly explained his rendezvous with the Russian. William brought his old friend up to date with the events of the past couple of days and he warned Roger to be careful. There was a silence as the warning sunk in.

"Look, why don't we come and make sure you're OK, we're all meeting at Giraffe at 9pm, we'll only be around the corner from you."

"No, no, I promised there'd be no one else with me, I get a feeling that this is not a person to be played with Will."

"OK, OK I hear you but, well, come straight here afterwards hey? You can stay at mine tonight and we can catch up."

Roger agreed.

Natasha came back with the coffees and some biscuits but even these failed to raise a smile on William's face, his mind had wondered off to the nun, the incident at Canterbury Cathedral and the mystery at the hospital.

Natasha noticed his concern immediately and sat by his side as he started to open up to her.

"Do you think I'm going nuts Nat?"

She slipped a kind hand in his.

"Going nuts? What's 'going nuts'?"

Every so often she came across a phrase she'd never heard before. When he explained its meaning she thought that perhaps he was but she didn't like to say. She knew that he was still on medication and not quite with it some days. William felt tears welling up in his eyes as he looked at her.

"I loved mum, Sandra and Michael so much it hurts." His voice broke on 'hurts'.

She was normally quite cold but on this occasion, Natasha hugged him tightly, comforting him as a mother would comfort a son, as a mistress her lover. He couldn't move, more accurately he didn't want to move from her protection and warmth. The steady and strong beating of her heart echoed in his ear. He was disappointed when she moved away.

She looked at him with those big eyes; "You big soft man, where can I find one like you?"

The words floated in the air for a while until William finally caught them. They didn't have many personal conversations.

"You, you never talk about your family Nats."

"You never ask."

William felt slightly selfish, she was right of course. But it wasn't only his fault, she had decided when they met that she would keep her history private. That was before she realized how special Will was.

"When I was a little girl, I'd sit by the river with my father and he'd tell me stories of a land where people were happy, where they had enough food and enough money to pay the bills without having to work like slaves. We could see the water from our wooden house and we'd skate on it in winter."

Natasha paused for a moment as she journeyed down the long dirt roads and across the fields of her childhood memories.

"We were poor but that doesn't matter as a child if you have good parents. I loved mine but it didn't last. When I was five my father disappeared and the soldiers came looking for him. They took their hatred out on my mother and our home. She saw them coming so she hid me in the coal store in the garden. When I heard her screams I ran and kept on running. The sound of her fear still haunts me."

She shuddered as she remembered and William shuffled closer and slipped his left arm around her shoulder, she didn't resist, she just let herself fall backwards in time as she continued;

"I smuggled myself onto a train and found an empty compartment where I eventually fell asleep. When I woke up there was a man sitting opposite who put a blanket over me and hid me every time the guards came round. His name was Ivan, he was a teacher and he sort of adopted me. I was his Lolita. He taught me things, he taught me to read, he taught me some English and French and he taught me how to please men." Abruptly she finished her sentence; there was no emotion on her face for William to read so he continued the conversation of familial histories.

"I, I'm not really sure about who my mum and dad actually were. I know, well, I think my dad died in a road accident when we were on holiday in the South of France when I was very young, I don't really remember him. I was apparently cut from the wreckage. When my mother died recently she left some documents that have just confused me more."

Natasha looked deeply into his eyes,

"So you know how it feels then William, you know that emptiness deep down that cannot ever be resolved."

It was William's turn to squeeze and reassure.

"What happened to you after that?" He asked, gently.

"When I was 15, Ivan 'sold' me to the Secret Service. He no longer needed me and I was bright so the government was interested in me. For years they trained me in all sorts of things. That's how I know so much about computers. I can strip down any weapon in the field, I can run a mile in 4.1 minutes and I can kill a person with a single blow. When my training was completed I started working for the Secret Service. With no permits and no proof of identity except for what they gave me, I was virtually still a slave.

Her face was empty; "But..." she continued pathetically, "I've forgotten what it was to love...and be loved."

William moved around to face her so that their noses where almost touching.

"It's OK Nats, that's all in the past, the future will be so much brighter for you, I can guarantee it." Of course he knew he couldn't but he was at a loss as to what else to say. She looked at him, trying to summon up a sense of feelings long since suppressed.

"Thanks William, you are a good friend."

Roger finished his coffee and headed for the rendezvous point. He didn't notice that he was being tailed by a stocky South African. Self consciously he loitered outside McDonalds near the bronze sculpture of the Jewish children who found asylum in Britain during the war. He heard a forced cough and turned to see a rotund man in an ill-fitting suit, holding a blue umbrella and eating a doughnut. He looked the complete opposite to the type of character Roger was expecting.

"May I join you?" Roger asked but avoided shaking his hand which was sticky with sugar and jam.

The man grunted his affirmation and when he swallowed his mouthful he was able to speak.

"Please sit, Dr Felix."

"You know who I am?" Roger suddenly felt very vulnerable.

"I know who you are, what you do, where you live, but not, I confess exactly why you are here." His heavy Russian accent only increased Roger's concerns and he remembered William's warning.

Almost two hundred yards away behind a stack of rubbish waiting to be cleared a barrel pointed through a gap and was aiming at the two men, the cross hairs were hard to match and at that range the barrel would have to be held dead still to ensure the right result.

Roger placed the photographs and the test results on the table and the man picked them up and looked at them then he looked over his thick glasses at Roger.

"Ah, I see, the St Peter's Cross."

Roger was surprised that he knew about it.

"There can be no doubt about the testing?"

Roger shook his head, "I tested three times to be sure."

The Russian's breathing was labored as he digested the doughnut and considered the photograph of the artifact.

"And, you took the sample from the cross yourself?"

It was a question Roger had not expected.

"Not exactly, but I was with Morgan and Pender in their study when they brought the cross out. They insisted on taking the slither with a scalpel knife themselves."

"Oh dear Dr Felix, I fear that like me you may have been misled."

Roger's head was spinning.

In the shadow of the doorway across the road the sniper was steadying the cold barrel.

"Misled, what are you talking about?"

"We'd heard about the cross after the 1990 dig but it took us quite a while to track it down."

Roger wondered who he meant when he said 'us' but he dared not interrupt.

"We eventually met Morgan and Pender and asked to buy the cross, there are serious collectors out there who'll pay millions for such unique artifacts. If it's genuine it is probably the only relic that conclusively proves King Arthur ever existed, and, of course there is also it's alleged other worldly properties"

Roger sat riveted; he was beginning to get an inkling of where this was going.

"They insisted it was genuine and showed us your analysis. To be certain we asked for a slither to do our own testing. Reluctantly they agreed but insisted that they take the small slither. We arranged a testing and like you, we discovered that it was genuine 6th century and everything about it fitted, right down to the strange metal readings lending credence to the story that Merlin made the cross partly from a substance handed to him by God himself."

Rogers eyebrows lifted; "God himself?"

The man gazed around before answering; "Yes, we think it was a way of saying that this metal with special powers came from a comet, we paid them a lot of money for it."

"So you have already bought the original cross from them?" He hesitated as he was concerned how his next question would go down; "Shouldn't that have been handed in to the authorities?"

The man laughed, "The authorities? My dear Dr Felix I am a dealer not a lawyer, what do I care?"

Roger didn't want to push his luck, this was not a man to mess with and he knew it. There was a mutual silence as the man gazed into Roger's eyes trying to fathom his part in this charade.

"To answer your question Dr Felix we did buy the cross they showed us but when our client had it tested to make doubly sure they discovered that it was a fake."

The Russian recognized the genuine disbelief in Roger's eyes.

"So the slither was genuine but the cross was a fake? How could that be?"

The man was ready to reply; "I was hoping that you might be able to explain that Dr Felix, but by the look on your face, you seem as confused as I am."

"Could your client have been saying it was a fake to discredit you or try to get their money back?"

"If you knew who my client was you might take a different view, but in one way you are right, they are not pleased with me and they do want their money back!"

Roger could only come to one other conclusion; "So, if your client is not double crossing you, the slither must have come from somewhere other than the cross sold to you."

The man sipped his coke leaving a residue of drink and doughnut in his thick moustache; "You are quick Dr Felix." The irony was lost on Roger who was trying desperately to compute the possibilities. Suddenly he put both his hands up as if to push the man and the thought away.

"Wait, you don't think I had anything to do with all this do you?"

The man leaned forward; "How would I know .Just exactly what is your interest Dr Felix, we are aware, of course that you have spent some time with Morgan and Pender and have applied to CADW to re-open the dig at St Peter's."

Roger came clean; "I have spent a lot of time with Morgan and Pender, that's true. I have gone through a small amount of their research with great care. I think that some of their findings are off the mark but they are certainly on to something. I share their view that there may well be something else to find at St Peter's church, that's why I want to dig it again."

The cross hairs on the sophisticated sight lined up perfectly. A finger slipped across the trigger and started to gently squeeze. Suddenly two girls shouting loudly at each other walked in front of the men at the table.

"If the genuine cross was found at the dig, where do you think that might be? Obviously, having paid Morgan and Pender several million pounds, my client would rather like it or their money back."

Roger was candid; "Yes, I do think that the genuine cross really was found, the old dig reports seem to have been well kept and accurate. Until now I have always thought the cross to be genuine. After all, the analysis of the sample I did doesn't just fit age wise it is consistent with silver, gold and trace metals from that particular area of Wales. The Russian brushed crumbs from his face; "Well, the slither was genuine, if the St Peters Cross is also genuine it must have come from it". Felix thought for a moment;

"Just as a matter of interest, did you have a go between on the handover of money for the cross or was it done personally between you and Morgan and Pender?"

The Russian thought for a moment before deciding to tell him; "It was a go between, his name was Bryant. Do you know of him?"

Roger was uncertain if this was a loaded question, he tried to respond cautiously but honestly.

"Bryant?, maybe, I met a guy of that name at a meeting with CADW. He said that he had been working with Morgan and Pender who had asked him to attend the discussion about re-opening the dig at St Peters. Later when I spoke to Pender he said that he thought he was a Littlejohn, a mole that worked for MI5 and that he was giving away all their research and trying to discredit them."

The man breathed heavily and leant forward; "So why allow this man to act as a go between Dr Felix. It makes no sense. I think it's time for me to pay Morgan and Pender another visit."

He was obviously unaware of their demise, so Roger filled him in.

The Russian showed no compassion, only suspicion; "How convenient, maybe we were not the only people they upset... I wonder where my client's three million pounds are. I will be watching you Dr Felix, if you find any information you will tell me. If I don't get that cross or the money back, I am dead."

Roger nodded pathetically, he was stunned and speechless, it wasn't as if it was a request it was an order from some over-weight Russian dealer with traces of doughnut in his beard. He delivered a potent after thought; "Oh, Dr Felix, I'd give up trying to make sense of all this, it may be bad for your health, and, if there is anything left to be found at St Peters I'd rather like to find it myself, clear?"

A finger pulled the trigger and clicked, snapping seven pictures automatically. Natasha slipped the camera with the long lens into her duffle bag and walked down the street, passed McDonald, towards Bishopsgate.

Roger nervously shook the man's giant sticky hand and watched as he made his way down the escalator to the platforms. Once out of sight, Roger walked past the Hyatt Andaz and then towards Bishopsgate. Natasha was about to join him when she noticed a thick set man with black hair, unless she was very much mistaken her training told her that this was a tail and that called for action. She stopped to check the time and her recording. It was nine thirty and the video recorder in her watch had picked up some decent shots of the man following Roger. William answered his phone. Since this afternoon Natasha had set up a temporary scrambling encryption for the signals.

"Will, Roger's OK but he's being tailed, change plan, leave Giraffe, take Rachel and Evans and meet at kitchen ASAP."

William got the clue, he called their office the kitchen because it was where they cooked up their projects.

"OK Nats, need some help?"

Natasha was in stealth mode; "*Niet*, meet you in 20."

Rachel and Evans had just arrived at Giraffe and William spotted them. They had done their best to dust down the ashes and debris from their clothes but they still carried the smell of roasting timber. Rachel ran up, hugged him and introduced Evans. William led them away.

"Change of plan, let's go."

Natasha called Roger's Blackberry. For a moment she thought he wasn't going to answer.

"Roger, it's Natasha I work with William, don't talk just listen. I have been watching out for you at your meeting, now you are being followed, don't look round!" he didn't, Natasha continued.

"Cross the road and go into Tesco."

Roger spotted the Tesco Express where the old fire station used to be and headed for it; "When you get into the store go right to the back near the cold stuff."

Roger was taking everything on trust, he felt like a character in an action film.

Soon he was at the back of the store, Natasha had entered and was half way down the aisle, she could see that the man following had just stepped in and was loitering at the front lobby waiting for Roger to come out. She made sure he didn't see her. There was something about his features that she felt she knew all too well. They sent shivers down her spine. She made her way to the back of the store and saw Roger at the chiller counter next to the clear plastic curtains that led to the rear storage area. She touched his arm on the way passed, he jumped, she dragged him through the curtain and hit the fire alarm panic button she had noticed when curiosity got the better of her once before. Suddenly the store was in uproar, people were screaming and panicking, sprinklers were soaking everyone and alarm bells were forcing customers to put their hands over their ears.

Natasha dragged Roger through the storeroom and out into Rose Alley at the rear. The plan was to circumnavigate the back streets and get to their Spitalfields office via Catherine Wheel Alley, Middlesex Street and Stripe Street. Roger stopped for a moment, brushed himself down then ran both hands through his hair in an attempt to look presentable, Natasha held out her hand; "Welcome to London Dr Felix."

He stood back and looked at his unexpected and very attractive bodyguard.

"So you're Natasha, I can see why William loves you."

No doubt she was pleased by the comment but she did not show it, she was still very much in her professional mode.

Rachel, Evans and William hadn't really had time to catch up but Rachel was insistent they go to Evans car and get her overnight bag with a change of clothing in it. As a result they left Spitalfields, crossed Commercial Road walked down Fournier Street and towards Princelet Street. At the far end of the road two fire engines were at the blaze, their ladders and platforms concentrating on the flames that were licking at the rooftops. Distraught occupants and curious bystanders stood behind a cordon thrown up by the police. Smoke lingered in the air as Evans scouted ahead and kept an eye out whilst William and Rachel opened the boot of the black Audi and removed the bags, Nicoles laptop and other items brought by Evans and Rachel. Almost as an afterthought Evans looked under the car towards the front. An awkward looking package was strapped to the engine housing. He motioned for Rachel and William to move away and hurriedly joined them.

Evans caught up with William and whispered to him: "The ignition's been booby trapped."

William stepped back in amazement.

Sobering thoughts accompanied them back to William's office. Coincidentally they arrived around the same time as Natasha and Roger. Nervously looking around they entered the building which was shrouded in an eerie silence. Something was waiting for them.

-28-

London
29th July 2009

So far as the Church was concerned the safeguards they had put in place years ago to discredit Morgan and Pender and their book, Artorius Rex, had worked like a dream; until now. The recent discovery of the information on the Mappa Mundi had obviously stirred up Dr Felix's curiosity, enough to make it and him a problem. Thanks to their Common Purpose partners they had learned that Dr Felix had recently sought CADW's permission to re-open the dig at St Peter's Church.

CADW's Sylvia Clarke had been liaising closely with Valetti who had been elected Gatekeeper on behalf of the Cross Denomination Group. Valetti knew that the St Peters cross found originally at the dig in 1990 was genuinely 6th century, that's why he commissioned his top antiquities specialist to buy it from Morgan and Pender. His original intention was to 'lose it' in the Vatican archive along with so many other inconvenient truths. That was before he realised the true value of the unique metal it contained from the comet.

Disastrously, Morgan and Pender had taken the churches £3 million in exchange for a fake. Worse still, someone else had beaten him to exacting his revenge. He was desperate to locate the real St Peter's cross. He knew his career depended on it, let alone the reputation of the Church, the chapter and his own bank balance.

What really blew smoke up his cassock was that on the fake cross they had bought from Morgan and Pender there was no sign of the fabled diagram or map which his advisors had told him might lead to the place of the burial of Jesus or clues as to where part of the true crucifixion cross and other Templar treasure were hidden. To be frank he had little or no interest in whether the crucifixion cross was the true cross or a Roman gatepost but all the ancient texts he had seen from the murky depths of the Vatican had clearly said that Helen, the mother of Constantine the Great had found the real wooden crucifixion cross and had it wrapped in gold, silver and jewels of untold wealth, that was the bit he was interested in, the untold wealth. The story went that she brought the encased cross back to Constantinople. The Vatican historians had done a great job of throwing people off the scent. He knew that the ancient British records underlined the fact that Helen was the daughter of a British Chief, King Coel and that her home would have been somewhere in Britain. No-one would ever find the treasure in Istanbul (Constantinople) because it was never taken there. The exact hiding place had been a frustrating lifelong puzzle. He had always chosen to believe in the writings of Taliesin (Merlin) who indicating that the highest ruler was buried in the land of the Druids.There was far too much at stake for him to be fobbed off and sidelined, it just was not going to happen. He knew he was playing a game on a tightrope without a safety net but the benefits far outweighed the risks.

Rachel, William, Evans, Natasha and Roger Felix sat around the large office round table like knights at a summit. The brown envelope that they were all staring at had been pushed by hand into the security letter box. Gingerly, Evans picked it up, slit the cellotape along the top of the flap and removed two photographs. There was a faint smell of ether and Evans recognised it as the sort of black lined marked envelope that is used to send internal communications between government offices, or wards in a hospital.

The images were stills from CCTV camera footage. The first showed a figure of a young woman with long red hair in a hospital corridor. William nearly fell off his chair; she was the girl he had seen in the Cathedral at Canterbury. The picture showed that her wrists were bandaged and that she looked distraught. He looked at the time and date on the shot. She hadn't died over night; he really had seen her when he was there! The other picture showed the girl being led away by two men and a woman, it looked as if the CCTV shot was of them leaving the hospital, again the date and time stamp showed it was just before he had left the place. Christ, the security guard was right and the receptionist had lied to him! William assumed that it could only have been the guard that he shared a cup of tea with that had sent him the photos, but how did he know where to find him?

They each explained the unusual events of the past few days to the assembled group; the nun, the concrete in the coffin, Angela and her soul diamonds and the information on Michael's hard drive. Rachel and Evans recounted their events; murders and fires and the information they found on the DVD. Roger Felix's offering regarding the nasty welcome he'd had at CADW, the meeting with the artefact buyer and being rescued by Natasha seemed quite tame in comparison.

"Thank goodness we've got Interpol on our side." William smiled at Evans.

"I wish that was true William, Code Red means all investigations stop and my boss has taken me off the case, we are on our own." Evans tried to hide his concern.

William winced; "Then we better get on to the police right away."

Rachel took over from Evans, explaining what she had learnt about police corruption and outlining Evan's theory that the CIA had planted smart incendiary bombs at Morgan and Pender's house. In short they could expect no help or support from the so-called authorities.

"If we can't trust the police and we don't know what is going on who can we trust?" William was getting quite distressed.

"Maybe not even each other." Evans explained, he was paying particular attention to Natasha and she was quick to notice; "Your face seems really familiar Miss, miss?"

"Just…Natasha."

"I'm sure I know your face." He was searching his memory.

Natasha laughed as William looked at her; "Perhaps you always remember a pretty face Mr Evans!"

She laughed but he didn't, he was far too busy trying to identify her.

Evans picked up Nicole's laptop from beside his chair and placed it on the table.

"I understand that you are good with these things William. I just wondered if there might be any clues to Nicole's killer on here."

"It's Miss Pretty Face you should be asking." He replied.

Things were starting to come back to Evans, something about a huge computer banking fraud a few years ago, the thought passed as soon as it came and he pushed the laptop towards her. Natasha eyed it carefully before she started. Suddenly her fingers were just a blur.

The others continued to talk, ignoring the occasional Russian expletive from Natasha. After a while she went pale and took a long slow intake of breath.

They all stopped and looked at her expectantly; "You don't want to see this, it's awful."

Evans came to stand by her side and nodded. Natasha was sensitive to the others.

"First you put headphones on Mr Evans." She loaned him her pair.

The film had recorded Nicole's murder in graphic detail. The last shot was of Rachel and Evans rushing in.

Evans turned to the people around the table.

"Natasha is right; you don't want to see this." He felt physically sick.

To change the subject a little from the gruesome content, Natasha explained how the film was recorded.

"The laptop was picking up a hidden wireless camera which recorded to the hard drive before being encoded and uploaded to an internet server where people were paying to watch."

Rachel was too upset to speak but Roger wanted to know why she was recording her own exploits.

Natasha explained; "It looks like she did quite a bit of web porn. I bet she made quite a lot of money from it."

"So the murderer wouldn't have known he was being recorded?" Evans exclaimed.

"Correct, this is totally secret. I am isolating the murderer's face from the film; in the audio she calls him Rudy Strink which is most certainly an alias. She knew more than she was prepared to tell"

Natasha soon printed out a clear image of the man and had shown it to Evans. He didn't seem to recognise the face.

"Do you have a secure 256 encrypted line to the internet from here?" He asked.

"We have much better than that Mr Evans, as a company our codes are vital to protect."

"Of course you would, can I use it to send these images to Interpol's ScreenIt to check for matches?"

Natasha looked at William and he nodded.

"On one condition Mr Evans...that you also send a couple of the images I took of Roger's meeting with the artefact buyer to check as well."

Evans obliged and William led him to a corner where the computer was surrounded by screens and fitted with the latest narrow view monitor which could only be seen by someone head on. He started it up and showed Evans what to do before leaving him to get on with it. Evans hoped his passwords were still valid. William gazed across to Natasha and smiled. He knew as well as she did that the computer was set up to log destinations, code and passwords.

William went back to the table and was looking at the stills from CCTV footage sent by the guard at the hospital. Rachel came up to him;

"Give me a hug William?"

William turned and held her to him, inside Natasha prickled with jealousy.

Evans returned to the group.

"I ran the mug shots from the laptop as well as Natasha's shots of your Russian acquaintance and Roger's tail. The results should be through within the hour."

"Thank you." Said Roger, demurely, he was feeling out of his depth and wished he hadn't acted in such hubris by arranging the meeting in the first place.

Rachel thrust her hand into her pocket and pulled out the crumpled letters that she had rescued from Helen's house. There was one she hadn't yet read so she put it on the table and tried to iron out the creases. As she did so she summarised the contents of the other letters to bring everyone up to date. This last letter was from Morgan to Helen and she read it aloud.

> Dear Ms Daniels
>
> We write further to your visit to discuss a possible documentary regarding the "Real" King Arthur. You asked if we would send a resume of some of the odd things that have happened to us during our research.
>
> We have had three attempts on our lives and it seems to us that if we do not give up on our research and publications it is only a matter of time before they succeed in terminating us. We can give you more details about these attempts when we next meet if you wish.
>
> As we explained to you, all Pender and I have been trying to do is bring the truth about King Arthur to the attention of the world. We never dreamed we would get caught up in something so dangerous.
>
> We can exhibit, as evidence, fifteen independent witnesses, solicitors' letters, barristers' reports and advices, letters from the Police themselves, letters from Council office files (Access to Information Acts of 1986.) Newspaper and other published reports, Bristol Police enquiries, annual Government Grants Reports of Public Funds, N.U.J. correspondence, tape recorded material, individual infiltrators within Police circles who can paradoxically be described as insider outsiders.

Rachel finished reading the letter and put the papers on the table. Evans picked them up to examine them.

"Well I knew from the footage we found on the DVD that various things had supposedly happened but this is heavy stuff..." Evans was confused;

"But why would Helen hide this with the other letter behind the photo?"

William leaned forward to offer a possible answer.

"There must be some connection between it and the others that Helen thought was vital.....and dangerous!"

Evans was scrutinising the letter very carefully. They all looked expectantly at him as if he'd have all the answers. He didn't.

"Could there be some sort of coded message in here, or is it something in what has been said that's so vital?"

William learnt all he knew from his mystery novels.

Natasha acted on the suggestion of the code and began scanning the lines in all directions.

"I can't see anything obvious." She looked to Evans; "Is it OK if I scan this and feed it into my computer?"

"Sure, if you think it might help." He replied.

Natasha went off with the letter whilst Evans checked to see if there had been feedback from the Interpol search.

Roger looked at Rachel; "You must have had a terrible time, are you OK? You must be very worried."

Rachel was not quite sure how to handle the small talk; she guessed Roger was trying to be kind;

"It's a nightmare; I keep thinking that at any moment I'll wake up...." She paused before going on..."worried?"

Roger hoped he hadn't said too much.

"I mean you must be frightened, you were working with Nicole and Helen on the articles and documentaries weren't you?"

Rachel had been trying to forget, as if she ever could.

"And you Mr Felix, you seem to have a major part in all this, do you think this is all about the cross?"

Roger went cold; maybe it had not quite sunk in for him either.

They were both staring into space, speechless, when Evans returned from the computer terminal.

"We've got lucky, there's a match for Nicole's assassin and for the guy who was tailing Roger this evening, it looks like it's the same person. It's 90% likely to be a guy called Bruce Botha, a South African hit man and former member of BOSS."

"BOSS?" Roger was unfamiliar with the acronym.

"It's like a South African SAS; he has a string of aliases." Evans had dealt with BOSS some years ago.

"That's great so can we just get him arrested and sleep safely." William knew as he said it that he sounded naïve.

"Not going to be that easy, I've forwarded the information to my head of unit but as you know, I'm off the case." Evans was careful not to sound patronising.

"We don't know how high this thing goes or even what IT is! If it's something at international government level we may be stuffed."

Rachel's fear turned to anger; "Oh great, so now we know who this guy is, we have a video of him murdering someone, but no-one can do anything about him because there may be some sort of international conspiracy in progress which is more important than bringing murderers to justice."

"Do you think he was the one who killed Helen too?" Asked William.

Evans looked thoughtful; "Maybe, the car park security video would have helped"

Evans agreed, "yes I asked several times for that, there was supposed to have been some sort of malfunction."

"How convenient!" Rachel was still sulking.

"Any info on the man Roger met tonight?" Asked Natasha, she was far more pragmatic than Rachel.

Evans shook his head. Roger looked around the tired faces at the table it was almost 11pm.

"What are we going to do?"

Evans was calm, he knew he had to devise a plan but he was devoid of ideas at this moment.

"Look, everyone's really tired, I suggest we try to get some sleep and come at this fresh in the morning. I have a safe house in a serviced apartment on Bishopsgate which is only 10 minutes' walk away, why don't you all join me."

Rachel and Roger were happy to go for safety in numbers but William and Natasha had other ideas, Natasha pushed her hair back and put a hand on each hip; "I have work to do here, I'm staying."

"Very kind of you but I'll stay with Natasha." William was reluctant to leave her on her own.

"Ok guys, but be careful."

-29-

Evening, London
29th July 2009

William suddenly started to feel ill; he needed to pop back to his apartment to collect his medication. He could easily have called for a taxi, but, however stupid it seemed, he'd been looking forward to a walk, and anyway, Natasha was most insistent that she'd be OK until he returned. In that sort of mood you didn't argue with her. After all the things that had happened to him it felt good to be alone in the streets, the crisp air of darkness gave him a sense of anonymity and safety.

Despite everything that had been discussed during the evening his mind was fixated on Natasha's past and the fact that Evans thought he recognized her. He wouldn't allow himself to linger on the possibility that she might still be working for the Russian Secret Service.

Evans, Roger and Rachel soon reached the 'safe house' apartment on Bishopsgate. It was one of six dotted about the capital. The security guard recognized Evans and the formality of checks went well. Evans had to admit he was slightly surprised. Either fate was shining on him or his boss had decided not to withdraw his operational privileges.

Soon they were in the luxury apartment. It was a standard modern interior design, all white, modern art and shiny appliances. The area had a double secure biometric entry system. The only windows were along the back of the apartment and were barred. The garden was enclosed with a walled and an alarmed fence. This building was also a place of choice for the rich, shady and MI5 alike during their operations in London.

There was ample room for the three of them but only two bedrooms. It wasn't a problem though as there were two sofa beds in the lounge. The fridge was well stocked, there was a huge high definition screen mounted on the living room wall and below that was a smaller screen which was a live feed from the cameras in and around the apartment block. Infra red sensors triggered recordings whenever people were near and there was a permanent protected fast broadband link into main control.

Evans gave Roger and Rachel a quick tour and left them to settle in whilst he sat at a desk and hit a button. Yet another screen popped up. It gave access to an encrypted secure server which Evans logged on to. Rachel came and sat next to him;   "Mind if I join you?"

He didn't, but his attention was on the screen and the results of the further searches he'd made. Some of the things he was discovering were fascinating. There were hundreds of results for Morgan and Pender and even more for King Arthur. One of the most popular sites told of a unique exhibition and conference that was opening the very next day at Caerleon, not far from Cardiff in Wales. The blurb told of exhibits of original manuscripts from medieval times, archaeological finds and lectures from distinguished professors and other academics. In fact it was a two week King Arthur fest! Morgan and Pender were listed as speakers. The website had not been updated following their death but there was something else of interest. Roger was also on the list of special guest speakers.

Roger explained to Rachel and Evans that Morgan and Pender had grown tired of hiding and keeping information that they had discovered and wanted to use this opportunity to reveal the truth of all their research to the world. He wanted to be there to support them and had planned to deliver his paper entitled: 'The Archeology of Arthur.'

Evans looked at him as he joined them at the table, he was sure it was just an oversight that Roger had not mentioned it earlier.

"Were you going to reveal the St Peter's cross and its authenticity?"

Roger nodded. "Yes, the original idea was to release everything once and for all. They knew it was controversial and had agreed to let Helen and her crew film it. I think they came to believe that once the evidence was revealed they'd be safer"

Evans gazed steadily at him, thinking momentarily; "Clearly someone didn't want that to happen."

Roger looked thoughtful; "I can't do it now, can I, not with that Russian watching my every move. It would be suicide."

Evans looked at Rachel and back to Roger, he was formulating a plan. "It's risky but what if we could make whoever is behind this think that the documentary is still going ahead but with different people?"

Rachel was on the same wavelength; "… yes, and you give your talk as planned Roger."

Roger looked worried but Evans warmed to the idea;

"I'm sure it would flush people out of the woodwork."

"Yes, and us down the toilet." Roger didn't like the plan but Rachel was still developing it.

"I am the link in the documentary thing, right?" they both nodded. "What if I act as the presenter and tell the organizers that there has been a change of plan and I am doing the documentary with another TV company."

"It could work; do you know anyone who could help us out?" Evans asked.

"I still have the name of the camera man and his sound guy that were working on the documentary." She looked at Evans, then at Roger,

"We'd just need to make up a production company name and take a chance."

They both nodded reluctantly and she phoned Jack Grimmer, the cameraman.

-30-

Southbank-London
Evening 29th July 2009

William stopped for a moment and bent double with his hands on his knees to catch his breath. He had run as fast as he could but he had no idea if he had managed to shake off the man who was pursuing him. The night was cool but at that moment the sweat dripped from his face and down his neck. His breath was heavy and labored as he tried to listen for any sound of approaching doom. He'd run down to St Paul's and over the pedestrian bridge to the South Bank, his heart beating loudly from fear and exertion. He felt such a coward for running away. He winced as he recalled the zip of gunfire around him and bullets ricocheting from walls and iron railings. Where were the police when you needed them? He was pleased that the guy was a lousy shot... or maybe it was just a warning? He couldn't imagine a professional hit-man missing; that only happens in Bond movies. How stupid he had been to even think that he wouldn't get caught up in the mess Rachel and Evans found themselves in, maybe in some way it was all linked to him and the things he'd been experiencing? How could it be?

Hoping that he had managed to shake off his pursuer, William decided to continue jogging slowly along the South Bank towards home, not a good idea but the area was well lit and there were a few people about. Anyway, there wasn't an alternative. As he ran along the front of the cafes and offices and through an underpass, he became vaguely aware of a small figure, no more than a bundle of rags, beckoning to him from the other end. Was this a trap? In a split second, he decided to trust his instincts. Now he could hear the urgent sound of footfalls not far behind. When he reached the end of the underpass the bundle of rags herded him through an open iron gate at the bottom of the railway bridge arch, the door closed and the bolt was drawn across. The old man lifted his finger up to his mouth demanding William's silence. The footsteps outside eventually faded into the distance.

Inside, the old man lit another candle to join the existing one. The room was small and damp and on the blackened brick walls there were the housings of old electric meters and cables, on the floor were cardboard boxes and blankets. The man poured a drink from a flask and handed it to William before sitting down on a blanket and propping up his back against the wall. Startled and still breathless, William sat down on layers of cardboard opposite. There was a constant drip, drip of water not far away.

In the half light he looked at the scruffy ambience that was once a man;

"Thank you my friend, thank you."

William couldn't really make out any of the man's features except a long beard and a full moustache. Wisps of greasy hair were trapped by a woollen hat that was pulled around his ears and over his forehead. The man took a slurp of his drink and studied William for a moment. William hadn't expected the refined and educated voice that emerged.

"You know, things are changing and the church is panicking..."

There was a pregnant pause, no mention of the chase, what the man had done, what was happening. It was as if the man just knew what was going on.

"...I do know" the man said in confirmation.

William was dumbfounded but his companion continued.

"The spirits talk to me, I know all about it...and all about you."

William thought he recognized something of the man's mannerisms but wasn't sure;

"Take Maria Magdalena for example she's told me all about how the church have tried to make her into a prostitute and a penitent sinner, she knows that one day the truth will come out and she'll yet be proved right, you'll see."

William wondered whether he was in the presence of a guru or a fruitcake but out of politeness to the man that had possibly just saved his life, he sat and listened.

"According to the Gospels Maria Magdalena was the first person to see Jesus after he rose from the dead. She was there when all the rest had deserted him. She was the apostle to the apostles."

William moved a little closer, trying to pick out the man's features in the candle light. He was certain that this was the same crazy guy who had warned him of the beguiling of Merlin at the airport bookstore.

"She was Egyptian you know. Cleopatra married Mark Anthony and they had four children, two girls and two boys. The oldest girl was called Cleopatra after her mother and she married Juba, the king of Numibia. They had two children, Ptolemy who became king of Numibia and Magdalena. She had dark skin, long wavy auburn hair, and a gentle smile. Jesus the Christ and Maria Magdalena,a match made in heaven."

The man started humming to himself as he cupped the hot drink and took another swig. The two of them sat in the half light studying each other.

"You know Jesus survived the crucifixion and that an elaborate plot was cooked up just to ensure his safety. The Qumran Essenes who lived near Jerusalem knew what herbs to use to make someone appear dead."

William didn't know but he nodded away.

"Normally it takes more than a day to die on a cross but Jesus was only there for up to three hours on a Friday. Even Pilate marveled that he had died in such a short time. When he was taken down from the cross and placed in a cave Maria made sure that she kept an eye on him. It was meant to be a ruse to re-establish the best of the old religions in a modern form. Joseph of Arimathea bribed a Roman soldier to confirm to the authorities that Jesus was dead".

William was mesmerized by the candle light and the story. The old man had lapsed into a mellow Irish accent and spoke in hushed tones.

"Christianity didn't just spring out of Jesus, oh no. It's an accumulation of legends and beliefs brought together into one set of texts to the detriment of all others. Religion, power and politics, they are all the same, my ideas are better than yours and you have to follow because I'm the one wearing the funny hat." He laughed and continued. He was obviously used to speaking to an audience.

"It's ironic that Jesus opposed ecclesiastical bureaucracy, laws, inflexibility, authority, idolatry and sectarianism when now he is the idol of the Christian faith himself. All he wanted was to teach people how they can communicate directly with their creator and that they should exercise love and tolerance. What has resulted is a struggle for supremacy of a "true faith" violence, greed and bloodshed".

William was deep in thought as the man continued.

"Faith in something needs no justification and is only as accurate as the person who propounded it in the first place.

Osiris was said to bring believers eternal life in Egyptian Heaven and the sacred rites of Demeter at Eleusis are described as bringing followers everlasting happiness, just like Jesus. Many miracles happened long before Jesus came on the scene. The Greek and Roman gods were excellent at performing them. Dionysus turned water into wine, God rest his soul for that one. Why, even Romulus was called the son of God, born of a mortal woman."

"I, I don't know what to say..." William was not expecting a lecture on esoteric theology on the way back to his apartment.

"Of course you don't but no one thinks for themselves any more do they? Like sheep, they follow fairy tales, did you know that around 4000BC there is the story of Krishna born to a virgin and being a son of God, the king at the time had all male babies killed and he was said to have performed miracles. Dionysus, Alexander the Great and Augustus are also described as the sons of God, born of a mortal woman. Jesus doesn't have the monopoly on that claim to fame."

"Why do we believe the miracles in the Bible when we don't believe the ancient myths? The Church managed to incorporate all the ancient stories into one superhero, Jesus Christ Super Star. It was an easy way to guarantee converts amongst the pagans and it's been a pretty useful means of controlling populations and making fortunes ever since."

William was wondering why the old man was telling him this stuff.

"You're wondering what this has got to do with you, aren't you?"

Before William could answer, the lecture continued.

"At the Shrine of the Book in Jerusalem there are 200 biblical texts, some haven't even been translated."

"So you are saying that we shouldn't always believe what we read? That we should seek beyond the writer and the reason for the writings?" William was learning.

The man snorted and expelled a great ball of snot from his nose.

"It took several centuries to convert Britain to Christianity but in the last forty years it has begun to disappear, like the ice caps. The young now worship Facebook, not Our Father. Churches are in financial crisis because there are too few worshippers to cover running costs. It serves them right. These days people like to call themselves spiritual, not religious, that's something associated with the WI and the Republicans of the USA."

As if to ensure William's attention, he ran his sleeve across his nose which left a trail of slime.

"The collection of writings that make up the Christian Bible has been used and abused. In the past 2,000 years, it has been an object of devotion, a symbol of anarchy, a means of social control, a form of propaganda and a political tool. It has been elitist, educational and un-scientific. It has created jobs and influenced the development of craftsmanship and technology, it has been both a valuable commodity and a forbidden treasure and, thanks to the Gideons, it's the only hardback in your hotel room."

William was fascinated. "Yes, I can see how Christianity has been a controlling force throughout history."

"Close your eyes William, I'm taking you back in time."

William was shocked; "How do you know my name? Who are you?"

The man ignored his questions.

"We're going back to the 4th century; see the streets and walls, the people and their beliefs. This is where we find a man called Eusebius sitting in his study, full of concern. On his desk are four gospels and other texts. At this time there are around thirty eight gospels in various forms circulating in the churches. The gospels that didn't make the final cut into the bible are more interesting and intriguing than the ones that did and even the ones that made it contradict themselves. The infant gospel of Thomas for example has numerous mentions of a mischievous Jesus misusing his magical powers like a naughty fairy, impishly transforming his playmates into goats, turning mud into sparrows or giving his dad a hand with the carpentry by lengthening bits of wood.

Constantine decided that adopting his version of Christianity would be more effective politically than trying to stamp it out as previous Emperors had tried. But like any successful novel or film, the Christian story had to be full of interest, action and drama. It had to be tightly scripted and well edited and it had to suit the needs of the publisher, in this case, Constantine as Head of State. Mandelson would probably get the job if it was advertised today.

"Hieronymus spent fifteen years translating the Old Testament from the Hebrew and arranging the biblical texts in a way we recognize now. In the process he leaves more out than he leaves in, picks the texts that support the way of national and religious power and propaganda and leaves the golden truths in his waste paper bin. The bible is a translation of edited highlights of a collection of stories written some 300 years earlier. Some of the original stories by Maria Magdalena and Philip were only discovered in your lifetime so he didn't even have the full set.

"But there were, and still are those to whom the truth is known. We are now few and hounded, treated as outcasts and lunatics or fruitcakes as you like to put it."

'Shit' thought William, he read my mind again.

"In the 14th century John Wycliffe made an inspired translation of the bible into English, he also translated and read many of the most ancient texts he could find which told us that people were only answerable to God not to the control of the church. They also explained that people could commune directly with God and did not have to go via the church. Very quickly it became illegal to make copies of any of the Wycliffe papers and anyone caught with them would be tried for heresy and executed after a forced confession. Not far from this very spot here in London in 1496 five people were burnt at the stake for seeking the truth. Many other supposed troublemakers met the same fate. All Wycliffe was trying to do was to bring people the truth as known to the Arthurian dynasty and the Templars after them."

William shuffled a bit on the floor; it was cold and uncomfortable; "So this is what it is all about, the true teachings to all mankind going back thousands of years, a truth that has been hijacked and manipulated for the power, wealth and control of others, a truth that must somehow be told again."

The man stood up and unbolted the door.

"That's it exactly my son, now you are ready to go on."

He held his hand out and William took it. He immediately felt a surge of energy like a shock from a badly earthed electric drill.

"But how does all this involve me?" William was at a loss.

The man ignored his question; "Now you must go straight to Caldey Island to see Father Daniel Everson, he will be expecting you and you will know why you are there."

The man opened the door and stepped out, William followed.

"Did you say Caldey?"

William was recalling the word from the 'code' on Michael's suicide note. Everson? The name scribbled on the genealogy handed to him by the nurse after his mother's death. They both paused, gazing at each other in a moment of unspoken communication before William continued;

"But, but you never told me your name."

The man's gaze was full of love.

"I am the Wandering Jew."

With that the man stepped onto the pavement and promptly disappeared.

-31-

Late evening, London
29th July 2009

Roger Felix dozed on the sofa whilst Rachel made hot chocolate in the safe house kitchen. Meanwhile Evans opened the safe which was located in one of the kitchen cupboards. He removed an envelope, counted the wad of cash and slid it into his pocket. He then took one of four black brief cases that were stacked neatly on the bottom shelf, placed it on a shiny white worktop, fiddled with the combination lock and it opened. Rachel dropped a mug onto the worktop when she saw what it contained. The noise woke Roger. Inside the suitcase were two Para Ordnance 18.9 1911 pistols, silencers, four clips of ammunition, three knives and a servicing kit. He inspected the firing mechanisms and ensured the safety switch was on before shouldering a snug low profile holster and inserting one of the guns in it.

"And I thought that's where the blender was kept." Said Rachel.

"Do you know how to use one of those things?" Asked Roger realising, as he said it, how stupid it sounded.

Evans was quite humourless; "10 years in the SAS, I should do!"

It had been an exhausting day. They sat in silence drinking their hot chocolate and soon Rachel and Roger went off to bed. Evans scribbled a note and then left the apartment; he had a bomb to defuse and a car to collect.

Eventually Natasha managed to hack the G Force site for the car park security cameras and she quickly searched the archive, aiming to get out before she left a trace. According to the files, the footage for the night of Helen's murder had been erased. She sent a stealth trawl through the residual memory cache, bingo; although it had been erased it had not been clinically cleaned. She set the code to download the camera and time period she wanted then sent a worm to crawl out and leave her tracks unnoticed. The download began.

At last William made it safely home. Following his instinct he entered the building indirectly via the underground car park. He collected his essential belongings, jumped into his Austin Healey and drove. It was almost midnight.

When Evans reached Princelet Street, the fire at his daughter's house was under control but the houses either side had also been badly damaged. The fire trucks had gone but a police forensics van was stationed outside. Fortunately, there was no one to bother him at the end of the street where his car was parked.

Shaking himself out of his chagrin he retrieved his pocket torch and slid onto his back shinning the light just to the rear of the wheel on the driver's side. The crude box, not much bigger than a cigarette packet, had two wires leading from the top towards the ignition electrics. He had seen the device so many times in Northern Ireland but it still brought beads of sweat to his brow and bad memories of the friends he'd lost there. He bridged the earth to the car and snipped the right wire then the left, it was always the right and then the left. He exhaled the breath he'd been holding during the operation and quickly examined the packet. It was crude but effective; this device was not the work of a professional assassin. He took a moment to admire his skill. Suddenly his phone rang. Instinctively he eased himself into the shadow of a doorway and flipped the switch;

"Evans..."

The detective could see that it was Natasha's number, the encrypted one she had given to him earlier;

"...Make it quick, bit tricky."

She did; "Thought you might like to know that someone hacked the car park computer and found the footage that isn't supposed to exist. I've sent a copy to your encrypted email."

Evans didn't bat an eyelid; "Well done Natasha."

She rang off. If this girl was who he thought she was they were lucky she was on their side, at least he hoped she was.

Natasha sat and looked at the various computers and flashing lights around the room, they seemed to dance in and out of focus; she was tired, very tired. She locked down the security shutters on the doors and windows and curled up on the long black sofa. Quickly she fell into a haunted, restless sleep.

When Evans made it back to the apartment Rachel and Felix were also fast asleep. He tried not to wake them as he logged on to his emails. There, as promised was the clip from Natasha showing Helen's death in the car park. The images would certainly prevent him from any sleep that night. Curiously the video showed Mark Flatt and Helen returning to their cars and Mark leaving but it also showed two men coming out of the shadows, one jumping in front of Helen's car making sure the car stayed roughly where it was whilst the other one shot her.

Natasha had sent a separate file of stills from the CCTV footage which she had enhanced using a forensic fractal technique. It was clearly Bruce Botha, the same man they had identified earlier, but the other man, well that was another matter altogether, surely it couldn't be Mark Flatt; maybe he was involved after all? Rightly or wrongly he sent the file on to his boss.

Roger awoke in the morning feeling surprisingly refreshed. He checked his phone; there were no calls or messages. Rachel was woken by the heavy and rhythmic snoring from Evans' room. She dragged herself into the kitchen and flipped the switch to start the Italian coffee maker. She looked a wreck and needed a shower but Roger thought she was cute in the long white shirt and knickers. She yawned and pushed back her long black hair with both hands, tying it into a loose bun.

"Coffee, Roger?" She asked.

Roger was staring out of the window and took a second to respond.

"Sorry I was miles away, maybe even centuries away. No thanks, I'm going to make a move. I have to get back to Sheffield, I'll grab one at the station."

"OK, be careful and keep in touch." She was still half asleep.

Roger looked at her and smiled nervously as he gathered his things and slipped his shoes on.

"Sure, and you take care as well!"

He left as Rachel slid off to the bathroom to shower. Evans was still snoring like a train.

Clean and more alert, she figured out the coffee machine and prepared two cappuccinos. She took one along the corridor to Evans' bedroom, gently pushed the door ajar and stepped in. Suddenly there was a frenzy of movement. Evans had woken up, grabbed the pistol from under his pillow and aimed it at her. She winced.

"Oh, sorry Rachel, old habits and all that."

"Being held at gun point for a cappuccino isn't as bad as enduring your snoring all night. You could snore for England!"

"Wales, actually. Thanks for the coffee, it's great." He took the mug and wrapped both hands around it for some sort of comfort.

Rachel sat on the end of the bed looking at him. He was topless and for an older guy he was in good shape. His barrel chest was covered with greying hair, his head was less fortunate.

"Sleep well?"

Evans rubbed his eyes with one hand and placed the coffee mug on the bedside table with the other.

"I never sleep well Rachel, not since Northern Ireland."

Rachel couldn't help wondering what this man had seen and experienced and yet he didn't appear to be desensitised, quite the opposite in fact, he was really quite sensitive.

"Want to talk?"

He looked tempted but shook his head.

"Best not to. Where's Roger?"

"He left for Sheffield."

Evans nodded as if he knew.

"I hope that man knows what he's doing. Can you be ready to leave in 20 minutes?"

"Are we leaving?"

Evans nodded.

"We are going to the King Arthur conference at Caerleon, remember? I think we need to know more about this man and what we're involved in."

Rachel checked her phone; there was a text from William; "Rach, I'm going to Caldey Island to see a Father Everson. Will call you later?"

She told Evans.

"Caldey Island?" he said emphatically, "What the …?"

Rachel looked puzzled; "Where is Caldey Island?"

"It's off the Welsh coast by Tenby."

Rachel didn't even try to understand why William was heading for the remote island.

Roger was on the Underground from Liverpool Street to Kings Cross. He was looking suspiciously at everyone and trying to plan what he should do next. He felt that fate had set him on a course and he was just a passenger.

Back at the office, Natasha had been awake since 6am, working on the computers. Last night when Evans was accessing the Interpol computer she had captured the log in information on another computer. This morning she logged in as Bryn Evans and found some fascinating stuff. There was no sign that Will had returned to the office as planned but there was a text explaining he was on his way to Caldey, she immediately recalled the word from Michael's suicide note and was soon tracing his steps via his mobile GPS on Google Maps.

-32-

Caerleon, Wales
30th July 2009

Once Rachel and Evans got out of London and on to the M4 the drive to Caerleon had actually been quite pleasant, it was nice to be away from the threat of fire bombs and guns. Neither of them knew what to expect at the conference but they knew the world's leading authorities on King Arthur would be there (with two notable recently deceased exceptions) and it seemed to be their greatest chance of solving the riddle in which they found themselves.

Rachel couldn't get hold of the crew that had been working on the documentary with Helen. She no longer found this surprising but it did mean she had to source a new crew at short notice in order to keep up the pretence of making the documentary about Morgan and Pender's work.

Cameraman and sound guy, Pete and Shorty, were ex-BBC Bristol staff and were only too happy to pick up a job that the Beeb had rejected. They were first to get to Caerleon so they parked outside the Roman Bath museum, walked across the road and enjoyed a Welsh breakfast at the Ffwrwm Centre, an atmospheric arcade of period shops around an Arthurian Sculpture park which was lovingly constructed by local Arthurian expert Dr Russell Lambert. Rachel and Evans soon arrived and drove out of town to a roomy Victorian terrace house where Evans' ninety year old aunt lived with her carer. Due to the conference, there were very few vacancies in and around Caerleon so they took it as a change in their luck that they could stay with the old lady. Rachel and Evans set about preparing themselves for the first of several interviews they had managed to arrange at short notice.

After a refreshing break Pete set up his tripod and camera at the sculpture park where they had enjoyed such a great meal.. Shorty clipped one end of an XLR lead into his mixer and the other into the camera.

Pete caught Shorty's eye, "Personal or pole?"

"Pole" he replied as he snapped the mike and rycote onto its fixing and the lead into place. Pete inserted a fresh HD cassette into the Sony broadcast camera and laid down some bars and tones.

Shorty nodded, "Ready?"

Pete checked the white balance, "Check, ready."

Like clockwork Evans and Rachel re-appeared in a change of clothing.

Their interviewee, a small man with grey hair and short beard entered the garden and approached them. Rachel held out her hand as he approached her;

"James Mason?" Rachel shook his hand resisting the thought that he looked nothing like his namesake.

"And you must be Rachel."

She smiled demurely, "Thank you so much for meeting us, this is Bryn Evans, he's my producer."

James sent a friendly nod in his direction. "So what did you think of my book?"

Rachel had to wing it, she hadn't even had a chance to aquire a copy.

"It was very interesting indeed."

James was waiting for a little more information, perhaps even a little more specific praise but it was not forthcoming; "So, this documentary you are filming, what is the nub of it?"

Again Rachel floundered slightly but Evans came to the rescue; "The idea is to get experienced and informed comments about Arthur from a selection of the experts at the conference, I guess you could say the thrust has to be whether Arthur really existed or not."

James studied them both intently, they felt uncomfortable, as if they could be unmasked at any moment. They weren't. Evans motioned for Mason to stand next to the evocative metal sculpture of King Arthur fighting another knight.

Pete and Shorty were taking levels on the fly. They had been a very good last minute choice thought Rachel as she positioned herself to the right of the camera to give Mason an eye-line.

"So, James, perhaps you could give us your take on Arthur?"

"King Arthur is one of the most written about subjects in the world. The trouble is that a lot of writers are trying to find him in their own back garden. There is so much evidence placing him in SE Wales that it is amazing that this idea hasn't been accepted by the authorities. Geoffrey of Monmouth who wrote his History of the Kings of Britain based his story on a person who can be identified with Arthrys ap Meurig. This chap was a hereditary king of the Silures. The problem is that even though the same identification was made in the 18th and 19th century by various writers, academic historians of the present day insist that he belongs to the 7th century and not the 6th century which is the real time of the King Arthur of history and legend. We have been able to sort out some of the mistakes and we have been able to put Arthrys ap Meurig in the correct time period and this is the key to sorting out the whole mystery of the identity of King Arthur. If you put him in the right time period and in the right location, the area of his true realm, you can then solve the other riddles about him. Now, Arthrys ap Meurig also bore the name Arthmail, this is not unusual, characters of that period often had several names and what is really fascinating is that the name Arthmail appears on two or three dark age stones that can be found in the Vale of Glamorgan. This evidence substantiates both his existence and his period. One way of pin pointing Arthrys ap Meurig is the fact that his nephew St Sampson of Dol, Bishop of Dol can be positively dated because he signed his name at the Council of Paris in 562AD and this document bearing his signature does still exist".

Rachel was hooked; "But isn't Wales Tourism missing out by not supporting this theory?"

"Yes they are, the story of King Arthur belongs to South East Wales and not Tintagel Castle or Glastonbury Abbey. I want the world to recognise that here is where King Arthur really lived and where he should be celebrated."

Evans was also fascinated; "But there are so many tall stories about Arthur, how can you be sure you have the true one?"

James glanced away to answer him but Pete the camera put his eye line back on track; "I agree but in a sense that is the biggest problem. Most people just treat Arthur as a fairy story and don't think he ever existed. If you try to establish who King Arthur was there is always someone, normally a narrow minded academic, who is going to shoot you down. The general feeling in the academic world is that this is an impossible problem incapable of solution. It is true that there are so few contemporary sources that it is hard to sort out. But it's like a huge jig saw and you have to carefully fit the pieces together."

Rachel was busy writing notes, Evans was standing behind her to preserve the eye line for the camera, he was in detective mode; "So what would you say the main evidence for a real King Arthur is? Are there any written sources?"

"The biggest problem with the Dark Ages is that there are actually so few written sources. There are the manuscripts of Gildas written in the 6th century. He was a contemporary of Arthur but unfortunately he does not mention Arthur at all, some say that he ignored Arthur because he'd had his brother executed for treason. As a result some historians have said that Arthur didn't even exist. However, the manuscript of Nennius about 150 years later features Arthur very strongly. Geoffrey of Monmouth's History of the Kings of Britain made good use of that manuscript and describes Arthur's twelve greatest battles. There are manuscripts, such as the life of St Sampson which maybe the earliest text dealing with the life of a saint and they have proved very useful. You also have the ancient charters of Llandaff, the register of Llandaff Cathedral, which contain a mass of information relating to the Arthurian period. These mention him and some of his family by name making land grants in the area. But there is a problem here because there is a gap of 100 years and some of the charters are missing, possibly even stolen to create the confusion. It is partly as a result of this gap that Arthrys ap Meurig is pushed into the wrong century.

Evans couldn't help himself; "I guess it's the same with every story, there's no mystery without a body."

James smiled; "You sound like a policeman"

Rachel gulped but Mason didn't pick up on the point.

"I guess you are right in a way. The climax to any research about Arthur has to be to find where he was actually buried. We know he disappeared after the battle of Camlann. According to Geoffrey of Monmouth he abdicated after the battle but he didn't actually say that he dies. It has always been assumed that he died and was buried on the Isle of Avalon. My identification of the isle of Avalon is the isle of Bardsey and in my book you may recall that we had Arthur sailing away from Avalon to Brittany and that is where he spent his last years.

He was no longer a soldier, a fighting king but a man of God. Like many others of that time he gave up his war like ways and turned to the church. He founded two or three churches in Brittany and became known to the Bretons as St Armel similar to Arthmail which was one of his names. We discovered that in the church of St Armel south of Rennes is a stone sarcophagus in which Arthur could have been buried. Unfortunately it is now empty because in the 17th century a neighbouring rector recognised the importance of this and had the bones removed and distributed amongst the churches in the area. Above the archway over the tomb are the words, the tomb of St Armel. The church has an old book on sale in French which tells us that St Armel came from Glamorgan in South Wales and was born in 482".

Rachel's arm was getting tired with writing but this was interesting stuff. Evans kept up the momentum;

"So you think that Arthur was a real person and that he ended up in, France, more specifically, Brittany?"

Mason nodded; "Yes I do, and for good reason. At that time people were leaving Britain in droves because of the Saxon invasions and because plague was sweeping the country. So Britanny, which was then called Amorica, was like settling in a new land to start a new life. As a matter of fact when Arthur was a youngster in the Vale of Glamorgan he would have attended St Illtyd's monastic college at Llanilltyd Fawr now called Llantwit Major. Also present at that college at the same time would have been St Pawl, Sampson, and Gildas. They were close in age to Arthmail and they all ended up in Brittany."

Mason finished his monologue and strode across the grass to greet retired one time astro physicist Dr Russell Lambert. They hugged like long lost friends. Rachel and Evans explained to Dr Lambert why they were there and how they hoped he could help. For a man in his 80's his enthusiasm was electric.

Camera Pete suggested that they move to the nearby "Merlin's throne", a charismatic carved seat made from solid wood but Lambert preferred the ornate tiled wall for his backdrop. He spoke eloquently without prompting.

"Out of the mists of time a name appears and that name is Arthur. In the Nennius writings in the Ashmolian museum there are many things said about this hero figure. Only once had he been mentioned before and that was in Welsh, in the poem the Goddodin, "The ravens of the castle walls were glutted but he was not Arthur". This name in the 6th century poem identifies time, place and potential hero. In Nennius there is much talk of Arthur as an heroic figure, a legend in his lifetime. Caerleon is mentioned frequently in the Mabinogion. On one occasion Arthur is mentioned as visiting Caerleon staying seven Easters and being crowned there. The huge importance of this is that it is taken from very early Welsh stories not from the later romances and colourful tales of the Normans. The story of a shadowy Arthur starts in the 5th century and Bardic law now carried stories of Welsh lands and the hero Arthur transnationally. The true stories were taken to the French Female court of Eleanor of Aquitaine and Marie de France. The rough tough warrior Arthur morphed into a wooing romantic suitor filled with godliness and knightliness."

Dr Lambert winked at Rachel as he drew breath and continued;

"The 5th and 6th century Welsh Church loathed the Arthur figure. St Cadoc said Arthur cheated at chess and the church despised Arthur because he was a danger to them. Arthur became sidelined but in the 12th century there was a great need for a hero figure to lead and Arthur was transformed into an icon figure for the Crusades. It seemed that it was OK for the church to use him when it was convenient to them and to discard him when it was not. Now Arthur has had his roots cut off and his masculinity removed. He has become a world icon claimed by England and Scotland, Germany, France and Italy. But, we, the Welsh whose land is the land of Arthur, have shunned and denied him and all I wish is that we claim him back as our once and future king and recognise his identity for the great man he was."

Evans forgot about the camera and spoke directly to Dr Lambert;

"You know, just about everyone who we have spoken to seems to know that King Arthur was real and that he was from South Wales... so why is there such a problem with the Welsh establishment admitting this and benefiting from tourism?"

"We have a problem with the people paid to protect the heritage of Wales. The government set up CADW some years ago. It is staffed by meritorious, well meaning people concerned with the flagstones of Wales without having any sense of the spirit of Wales and the culture that the flagstones represent. So they defend decaying detritus like castles that represent the oppression of Wales with the same fever as they defend ancient houses. They have a disease of myopia built up from hunching over civil service desks, mainly in London and that disease makes them unable to do anything positive. They can only react negatively to everything suggested to them.

Any civil servant that takes an action that is positive puts his head above a parapet and that parapet is his desk. And, if he sits there like a little rabbit and does nothing to upset anyone he'll be able to retire with a pension and feel good. CADW is part of the problem of Wales; CADW is in fact a disease".

This was perhaps the strongest criticism that Rachel had heard. She could empathise with the sentiments even though she could not understand how something so obvious as the proof that Arthur was from South Wales could be denied for so long;

"So, what would you like to see Dr Lambert?"

The elderly academic thought for a moment or two;

"I can see South East Wales relying more and more on the welcoming industry and I don't know if I will live to see it at its best but the Arthurian history is part of it. I would like to see Caerleon an Arthurian Centre with serious academics and romantics being attracted to it which is why I welcome this conference with open arms. I would like to see the pageantry of Arthur exhibited here. We have already had the reconstruction of the first annual coronation of King Arthur by Dubricus, the original taking place one Wit Sunday centuries ago. I would like to see this celebrated annually making this place the home of an international brotherhood honouring decency and good civilized behaviour, as would have happened in the best of the Arthurian stories. Three things could improve our tourism, to use our warm welcome, make use of our beautiful valleys and elaborate the Arthurian cause".

Evans was trying to get the recent history clear in his mind as Dr Lambert continued.

"The Victorians identified Caerleon as being the Arthurian seat. So did Thomas Churchyard who wrote the Mysteries of Wales and he identified Caerleon as the true Camelot stating that King Arthur was surely crowned here. However this was not new information, the fact that Arthur was crowned here was mentioned in the most ancient texts including the Bruts of England. The one thing that Caerleon has that no other pretend place has is the factual existence of a real building which King Arthur used. The Amphitheatre in Caerleon has been sitting in what has for centuries been referred to locally as King Arthur's Round Table field. It was only rediscovered to be an amphitheatre by Sir Mortimer Wheeler in 1927. Before that time the depression in the ground was known as King Arthur's Round table. We know that the amphitheatre existed before Arthur and that if Arthur had need for a round table he could have held court there with his knights. That is the one thing that makes Caerleon entirely unique among the vast mass of anecdotal evidence. Caerleon is well imprinted into the whole Arthurian saga and 12th century places cannot match them. Caerleon was here and vibrant in the 5th and 6th century".

Rachel finished her notes and Pete stopped recording as a woman in a designer suit arrived, smiling;

"Sorry to intrude but the conference starts in 10 minutes."

Rachel did a double take; it was Angela. She recognized that voice and the false long blonde hair immediately. William had introduced her to Michael and Angela a few years ago. What a small world she thought.

Lambert took Evans to one side; "Of course I didn't think it wise to mention the impending CME which is likely to be what the predictions around 2012, give or take a few years, are all about".

Evans looked taken aback and Rachel almost fell forward trying to listen better.

He waited for Angela to go before he looked around and whispered to both of them.

"Corona Mass Ejection"

If it hadn't been so serious the moment would have been very Monty Pyhthonseque.

There was a small one in 1859 and a massive one is well overdue, it has to be what the ancients have been predicting.

He could see from their faces that they did not have the faintest clue about what he was talking about.

Patiently he sat and they moved closer; "The sun, without which we would not live and breath emits solar and corona flares all the time but every few hundred years or so something much more major happens. These massive and rare corona spurts, which contains electrons, protons and all manner of things are ejected into space in all directions and take around 1-4 days to reach the earth. The baby versions of these cause little damage but the rarer stronger ones somehow link the earth fields with that of the sun and the energy uses that link over millions of miles to discharge itself. When a small eruption happened in 1859 the whole of the telegraph system was knocked out. Now that we are far more reliant on electricity there could be total devastation to anything electric and we are not talking about a few hours blackout we are talking total meltdown for years".

Rachel smiled nervously; "But the scientists know all about this and have a cunning plan to make everything ok, right?"

Lambert shook his head; "Some say they do, and let us hope they are right, but I fear we may be heading for another dark age..."

-33-

Caldey Island
30th July 2009

Although William had every intention of returning to the office after collecting his medication and his car, the curious interlude with the Wandering Jew had thrown him completely off course, and, in an impulsive instant, he had driven several hours to Tenby, where he could get a boat to Caldey Island.

Sure he felt guilty about making a snap decision to leave Natasha at the office in London but he convinced himself she was safe there.

Now he was making the thirty minute crossing to the island on a little motor boat; the bracing sea air whipped across his skin, refreshing him after the overnight drive. He felt that he had escaped into another world, a place far away from the weird and wonderful happenings of the past few days. He was meditating on the coded note that Michael had left behind; CALDEY. Suddenly he heard himself speak out aloud;

"Come on Michael if you are around and can hear me help me out here."

There was no reply but something made him think of what the guard at the hospital said when he asked if they had indicated where they were taking the girl,

"It was something about taking her somewhere safe, somewhere that sounded like Holdey, or Kolkey? I didn't catch it."

What if it was Caldey, the very place to which he was heading?

It was a calm sunny summer day. William inhaled the exhilarating salt air on the joyful journey which was marred only by the whinging of two children fighting over a chocolate bar. Their mother seemed totally oblivious to the fact that they were ruining the journey. Also on board was an American woman, overweight, over tanned and over dressed. She stood out from the British day trippers and William wondered why she might be visiting the island. The rhythm of the vessel changed as the engine idled whilst the rugged fisherman allowed the current to drift the boat towards the concrete jetty softened by old car tyres that dangled like earrings on mermaids in the surf. The sparkling sun danced on the water like a thousand diamonds.

Ropes bound the boat to the pontoon and the travellers were helped ashore by the young seaman.

The small group walked along the jetty and the makeshift sea wall towards the tiny township. An old Land Rover with a trailer approached to pick up the provisions for the island's 25 inhabitants, 12 of whom were monks. Its less than skilful driver came carelessly close forcing them to squeeze into the side next to a prickly hawthorn bush. Perhaps he didn't like visitors. The blonde woman snagged a red high heel in a divot and bounced into Williams arms. Her lunge towards him seemed deliberate. Her glossy red lips made larger by plumping gasped in shock like a fish out of water. Her heavy scent reminded him of a duty-free perfume counter, then her breasts fell off their platform bra and out of her tight blouse like something you would see at an awards ceremony. His instinct was to save her from falling, although the impact nearly ensured that both of them ended up on the dusty roadway. Recovering her composure she tossed her head backwards and turned to look him steadily in the eyes, he wasn't quite sure why but a picture of Miss Piggy came to mind.

"Gee, thank you, you saved my life!"

William smiled politely, hoping the Texan wouldn't take their encounter as justification to tour the island together. He was in no mood for such company. She reached in her bag and pulled out a silver tube, undid the top and sprayed the breath freshener in her mouth. Turning to William she asked;

"So, what brings you to Caldey?"

They were still some distance from the small group of buildings that made up the village and William realised there was no escape.

"I, um, er, I've always wanted to come here to have a look around and I had a couple of days to spare so I just, umm, went for it and here I am."

It didn't sound very eloquent or convincing but it was enough, she wasn't really listening anyway. He pulled out his small bottle of water and took a sip before continuing.

"And", continued William, trying to be sociable, "What brings you here?"

"I'm here to contact Mary."

William looked at her inquisitively.

"You're here to contact Mary?"

"You bet I am." She held out her hand, "We haven't introduced ourselves, Jessica Fuller; I'm America's top TV psychic medium and the star of Haunted America, pleased to meet you!"

"How interesting, I'm William Marshall, I design computer games. What do you mean by contacting Mary?" His puzzled look brought an instant reaction as Jessica threw her hands in the air in mock despair.

"It's only the most famous ghost story in the UK, Mary Magdalen and Jesus here together on this island. Don't they teach you guys anything?"

William's blood ran cold.

The small group were just coming to the end of the rough unmade road that led into the village. To their right were the remains of mill ponds, obviously well used in the mists of time, to the left was a lovely café overlooking the green and in the near distance a few white painted cottages. In the foreground was the post office and store and in the distance, on the hill, was the impressive white Cistercian Monastery. William stood for a few moments just soaking up the atmosphere, it was lovely. The woman fell to her knees and kissed the grass.

"Gee, isn't this the most magnificent place?"

Inside his study at the monastery, Father Daniel Everson was sitting in quiet contemplation. Deep inside he always knew that someday it would come to this. The information that had been handed down seemed like a burden rather than a blessing. So many times he had thought of just throwing the stuff away and losing the key, after all what difference would it make in a cynical world where, on the whole people don't even genuinely care about each other let alone about history and the truth of life. To be honest, after the accident he couldn't really recall what the hell he was meant to be doing with his life anyway.

He turned over the stained seven inch vellum folder in his hands trying to determine why he felt so depressed, so doubtful about the information that he was supposed to guard? He had even begun to doubt the existence of God as he reflected on the specialist's recent diagnosis. He had around three months to live. Could they really be so specific? It might be six months or a year or, heaven forbid, a week? He intended to keep his prognosis a secret. There was no need for the other monks to know. He looked fit and healthy as, no doubt he would to the bitter end. Inoperable brain tumours are often not outwardly evident.

As he gazed out to sea he drifted over his time on earth, the parts of it he thought he could remember that is. When he was 20 he married the love of his life and they had two children a boy and a girl. As a rare treat in 1969, he took the family on holiday to the South of France. He hired a car; it was a maroon Vauxhall Victor with silver trim. One moment they were enjoying the pleasures of the picturesque countryside and the next the car was out of control heading for the cliff edge. Desperately, hopelessly, amongst the screams and the panic of his family, he could not prevent disaster. All the brakes had failed and the steering had gone. Try as he may he could never forget that moment when the car shot over the edge; he had relived that agony in slow motion a thousand times. The last words he heard were "I love you" from his wife then there was darkness. Seven years later he awoke from his coma. He had escaped with his life but with little memory of his family or his life.

The road back to health was a long one. He learnt that his wife had died instantly and that his children had since been adopted. No-one would tell him where they went and he had been far too sick to go hunting for them, maybe that was the fairest thing he could ever do, to let them get on with their lives. An old monk named Thomas had befriended him in hospital and later took him into the care of the Monastery at Caldey.

It was to be a full ten years before he began getting major flashbacks. Slowly, some memories returned and with them came a new insight into history and the most terrible nightmares. He didn't know whether his mind was making up memories to fill in his missing chunks or if the pieces of the jigsaw were real. Had those years really been as he imagined? Determined to make something of the rest of his life, and with the help of Father Thomas, he started reading the history of the region. His thirst for knowledge was insatiable. He studied archaeology and secured a doctorate in record time. But his newly acquired knowledge could not replace the gap in his own history. He often struggled with the competing desires to find his children or to leave them to their new lives. After all that he'd been through, now he was suffering from an inoperable brain tumour with maybe weeks to live, no, there was most certainly no God.

With 30 minutes to spare before his appointment with Father Everson William made his way on to the little gravel track that led passed the post office and museum and left towards the church of St David's. The quaint avenue of trees and herbs led along the neatly walled and fenced gardens filled with flowers and roses towards an elevated outcrop overlooking the sea. The little stone church looked resplendent in the sunlight, its tiny graveyard pregnant with souls awaiting rebirth. Some graves had old stones, most had wooden crosses decaying and impregnated by lichen.

William pushed the door, walked into the damp smelling porch and through to the main building. It was a small, plain church with white walls, clear windows and a picture of Mary Magdalene at the foot of the cross. In antiquity this church had been named after her and had only recently be renamed St David's. He sat on one of the pews and closed his eyes. All he could hear was the distant gentle rolling of the sea, the creak of an old tree in the wind and the birds singing. Occasionally the scent of wild herbs and lavender gently found his nose. The peace in his mind and heart was unique and unmistakeable. In that fleeting moment he felt so cut off from all his worries and woes, all the trappings and pressures of life and all the badness of the world. He couldn't recall when he had ever felt such happiness in his heart. Out of squinting eyes he was just aware of a white robe blowing in a breeze in the aisle next to him. He daren't open his eyes for fear that the feeling would vanish. He wanted to hang on to it for as long as he possibly could. As he kept his head bent in meditation, he sensed the figure move, slightly bending over to touch his shoulder and at that moment he felt an electrical charge pass through his body holding him still like the arms of a mother caring for her son. The moment seemed like an eternity, a suspension in animation, a time with no end. He was faintly aware of long shining hair brushing his face, of a kiss on his cheek... that scent, he knew that scent, yes, of course, Canterbury Cathedral the fragrance of the nuns long auburn hair.

Suddenly he was aware of a sharp poke on his shoulder that brought him swiftly back to reality.

"Oh there you are honey; I've been looking all over for you."

William jumped as if he had seen a ghost. The Texan woman towered over him, interrupting his meditation and replacing it with brash nonsense.

"Well I figured that if I was going to chat to Mary Magdalen I'd have to come to the church she was supposed to have first foundered on this little island."

William turned just in time to catch a loving smile from the form floating out of the doorway.

I think you have just missed her." He said quietly.

The woman came closer,

"Sorry, I didn't quite catch that. "

William pushed past and went to leave,

"Nor did I" said William, "Sadly, nor did I."

He quickly made for the graveyard but there was no sign of the woman in white, just a hint of her scent upon the air.

Although Caldey Island is small it had been inhabited for thousands of years. Once much larger, the encroaching sea had taken away swathes of land some 3000 to 4000 years ago making this outcrop an island, just as Britain herself had been cut off from mainland Europe. The first signs of life on Caldey were from the Neolithic age. Humans have lived there ever since. From his research, Father Everson knew why the place was so important. For those sensitive enough to feel it, there was a very special vibration and atmosphere, something he had experienced in few other places and it was the very reason he was proud to call this place home. The actual monastery was an imposing white Italianate style abbey that had been built in 1906 by the Anglian Benedictines to replace an ancient crumbling structure. The Order was taken into the Roman Catholic Church in 1913 but ran into severe financial difficulties in 1925. The current incumbents, the Cistercians, are a much stricter, more contemplative offshoot of the Benedictine Order and they arrived here from Scourmont Abbey in Belgium in 1929.

William checked his watch as he ascended the stairs to the abbey, it was 2.45pm and he was fifteen minutes early for his meeting. As he rang the bell beside the large glass arched door he could see a figure in a long white gown with a black over vestment heading in his direction. The man seemed thick set, of medium height, and quite athletic. His head was almost bald but his eyebrows thick and bushy framing kind and knowing eyes. His beard and moustache was short and grey with the odd ginger fleck. William put him at around 70 as he opened the door and ushered him in. Father Everson rested a powerful hand on William's left shoulder and stretched out the other for William to shake. This man had been fit in his life and still packed a mean iron grip.

"Welcome to Caldey Island Mr Marshall, please follow me, I've made some tea, I hope you like Earl Grey?"

"It's my favourite." William replied.

"Mine too!" said Father Everson as he escorted William upstairs to his study.

The small white room was sparsely furnished with a large polished oak desk and two simple oak chairs. Shelving lined an entire wall overflowing with old leather bound books and files of different colours sporting degrees of fading. Piles of paper and books that didn't fit on the shelves were stacked on the floor.

William looked around as they sat down,

"What a lovely view of the sea."

Father Everson kept one eye on the boiling kettle and one eye on William as he pulled out a notebook.

"Thank you for agreeing to see me at such short notice Father. I'm sorry I called you so late last night."

Father Everson handed William his tea as he continued speaking.

"I am not sure where to begin really, it's about the dig at St Peter's Church, I believe that you were the main archaeologist in charge there."

As Father Everson sat down his face was overcome with sadness and his eyes filled with tears. William couldn't help but notice how quickly the strong man had wilted before him. Instinctively William got up from his seat moved around the table and placed an arm around the man's shoulder as his tears flowed like an overflowing river, the last few days had been too much for him to bear. Between the sobs the old man managed a few words;

"I'm sorry Mr Marshall, it's not a good time, I've had some bad news, I've been trying to bottle it up and I promised myself I wouldn't let it get to me."

His distress made William's eyes mist over and so the two of them stayed connected physically, sharing the same emotion just moments after they had met. Slowly Father Everson started to rally and William handed him his tea encouraging him to take a sip.

"Would you like to talk it about it Father?"

The man looked at him, he wanted to confide but he'd promised himself he wouldn't. His watery eyes held a pleading that was hard to ignore.

"Have you ever wondered if there is a God?"

William realised this was a rhetorical question.

"Do you remember Mother Teresa?"

William nodded, of course he did.

"Do you know that she struggled for much of her life wondering if God exists? She carried on working with the poor in the slums of Kolkata whilst her soul was in turmoil." He picked up her biography from the floor and read: "Where is my Faith? Even deep down there is nothing but darkness - My God, how painful it is, I have no Faith... I call, I cling, I want - and there is no One to answer - no One on whom I can cling - no, No One. - Alone."

William interrupted; "Gosh I never thought someone so saintly would be so troubled by doubt!"

"It is the way a person behaves not what they believe in that sets them apart from others." replied the monk.

William wondered where this was leading but he didn't mind, he could tell that Father Everson needed someone to talk to and they seemed to have bonded very quickly.

"In a way Teresa was right to doubt."

William remained silent, awaiting an explanation.

"You see William, the church of today is a sham, it is built on misinterpretations and mistruths, fear and nonsense and it bears no resemblance to the original teachings. There is only one God; whoever or whatever you perceive that to be. For me it is the energy that creates and links all things, not an ancient guy with a long white beard sitting on a cloud. There was, of course several good men, special men and women, call them prophets if you like whose real message before massaging and manipulation was the same, a wisdom and knowledge that was known thousands of years ago. In short, people create enemies in the name of religion but originally we were all the same and if we could reignite that bonding there would be peace and harmony in our world."

William was unsure why and how the conversation had started but it seemed to be following roughly the same lines as the education he had so recently received from the wandering Jew.

"So all the prophets and holy leaders such as Moses, Mohammed and even Krishna are like different facets of the one precious diamond and if we all accepted this we could all live without the turmoil created through religious conflict."

Father Everson clasped his hands together in celebration;

"That is exactly what I am saying William and you expressed it so eloquently. There would be no need for an organized church, only learning communities like the one at Qumran and Llantwit Major where Jesus studied the ancient wisdom."

" Excuse me for asking but how does this philosophy sit with you being a Cistercian Monk?"

Father Everson unwrapped an ancient looking cloth revealing a fragile vellum book.

"Because of this" he said.

William looked at the fragile skin, once light brown but made dark by age. On the cover there was what looked like a faint face of a bearded man.

Gingerly he moved his hand across to touch the relic, stroking the face gently as he did so. For the second time that day he felt a tingle inside, it was like a lot of electric shocks running down his spine, it could have been in his imagination but he thought he sensed a low chanting sound. Tears actually welled up in his eyes. Father Everson looked across at William covering his hand with his own.

"You feel it to, don't you?"

William nodded, "Yes father, I do."

He paused as the feelings from the ancient image on the vellum cover permeated through his fingers, along his arms and all over his body. He felt lighter and more at peace than he had ever done and at that moment he was blinded by a bright white light. Slowly his vision returned to normal as he placed the book back on the table.

"What is this book?"

Everson looked around as if to make sure no-one was there; "It is the book of life William, a book made up from the banned writings, incantations and diagrams written and drawn by Mary Magdalene, Simon Peter and others."

Williams eyes were transfixed by the image on the skin of the book, he couldn't resist reaching out his hand to run his fingers across the faded but kind eyes, face, beard and as he did so the tingles in his fingers started again;

"The face Father, it looks just like the face on the Turin Shroud, is it the face of Jesus?"

Everson motioned to William to pick it up again and look inside. He did;

"Jesus is always shown in the earliest art without a beard, some say he may have been both male and female. I believe it is the face of the Nazarene ascetic and prophet, John the Baptist, the vellum is thought to be made from his own skin."

William looked reverently at the cover, "wow, that's amazing...John the Baptist, he is said to have baptized Jesus, isn't he?"

Everson felt it was important to make the point that baptism had nothing to do with Jewish culture or cleansing sins, instead it was firmly a Hindu tradition, as it still is today.

William nodded knowingly he didn't feel at all afraid; he opened the book only to see page after page of text written in Greek script. As he ran his fingers across the words they seem to speak to him, the light that came from each image transported him back in time. He could just make out other beings there in the room, beings with large heads and eyes, beings that looked and seemed so kind, beckoning him.....as if it was all too much he snapped the book shut and put it gently down. He quickly came back to the sound of the sea, the room and the smiling face of Father Everson.

"Isn't it wonderful, William?"

"Yes, it's a miracle."

Everson continued; "The existence of such a book had been known for many years, it was referred to by Serapion, Bishop of Antioch in 190AD, by Origen, historian, in 253 A.D.; Eusebius, Bishop of Caesarea in 300 A.D and Theodoret in 455 in his Religious Histories, although its whereabouts and fate were a mystery."

William looked amazed but Everson hadn't finished;

"In 1886 in a monk's grave at Akhmim, Egypt, nine pages copied from this book were found, they became known as part of the lost Gospel of Peter. That of course begged the question as to where was the original book? In the grave was a description of a man we know well, a man who knew both John the Baptist and Jesus the Christ, his name was Joseph of Arimathea."

William was captivated.

"The early Welsh texts tell us that Joseph of Arimathea, whom they called St Ilid the Israelite, took Jesus, his brother Simon Peter, Mary Magdalene, mother Mary and some of the other disciples and friends to Wales to avoid the persecution. This book tells us that Jesus did not die on the cross and that Mary and Jesus were husband and wife."

William's jaw dropped open but there was more.

"Further, the texts tell us that this travelling party took a river route through France as was the custom to avoid violent weather and pirates and across the channel landing at a place called Dinas Head. Jesus and his friends were taken in by the locals of a settlement near to a place called Nevern in Pembrokeshire where Jesus spent time healing from his crucifixion wounds. It seems that Joseph then set about spreading the true Gnostic teachings of Jesus which were very different from the teachings of the modern church. The original message was simple, that the power of God, however you perceive the great creative force to be, is everywhere and in everything. All you have to do is sit quietly and absorb it. Joseph, or Ilid, is said to have set up a place of discussion and "worship" at an area that is still called Llanilid in Welsh which translates to the Holy Estate of Ilid. According to the early Druid traditions Joseph was the confessor of Bran the Blessed the first British convert to Christianity. Bran was the retired king and he lived close by at Trevran or 'The Manor of Bran'. Both locations were close to Mynydd y Gaer where there is the source of a river known as the River of Ilid, very close to St Peter's Church. When I heard that Morgan and Pender were looking for an archaeologist for the dig at St Peter Super Montem, a church said to have been founded by St Peter himself, I jumped at the chance.

"But the book, how did you come by the book?" William asked.

Father Everson sipped some of his cooling tea; this was his time to confess.

"I am afraid that I have not been entirely truthful with Morgan and Pender, you see there was a massive storm that almost blew our camp off the mountain and completely wrecked the dig. That fateful day we discovered two plain stone slabs. Whilst others were distracted, I lifted them and discovered that they had marks on the back which had been concealed for all that time. It put me in mind of a passage on parchment found at Qumran: 'I will bury the secrets of our faith in an unmarked grave in the hills of our fathers until it is time for the once and future king to rise again'."

"Both Jesus and King Arthur have been called the once and future king and Morgan and Pender had deduced, rightly or wrongly that Arthur lay buried at St Peter Super Montem church. In the throes of the thunderstorm no-one saw me excavate the thick pottery container. In it was this book wrapped in layers of linen and fur smeared with animal grease. It was all very dramatic but it did happen like that." The old man took a breath and gently smiled as he relived the moment. There was more:

With the book was a tablet with coded writing, it read; "as you reap, so shall ye sow"…it's quite rare. One was found in Pompei. It's known as a ROSTA tablet, a kind of early Christian lucky charm. If you rearrange the letters it spells Paternosta, or translated, our father. The spare A and O left over mean Alpha and Omega, the beginning and the end"

William was finding it hard to take everything in but Everson had more to add.

"I also rescued the metal cross from the hand of Simon after he had been killed by a lightning strike, oh William it was both the worst and best day of my life. I gave everything back to Morgan and Pender for safe keeping except this book which I value more than life itself."

Williams face suddenly changed; "But you have stolen it from them; they own the church don't they?"

Everson was unrepentant; "I know, but this has a delicate significance not easily understood and is just part of what is happening in the world today. We were never able to dig the rest of the site where the book and tablet came from because the wall collapsed around us. Dr Felix has been trying to get permission but there are forces at work trying to stop him. You see, I am not sure but I think there are other secrets buried up there, there may even be clues to where Jesus the Christ is buried. If we could just find these things then maybe there could be a second coming in our time, a way to heal our world at last."

William applauded the sentiment but detected a kind of misguided hopeful fantasy in the man's eyes.

"But, even if it was true who would ever accept that Jesus survived the cross and died in Wales?"

Everson looked steadily at William; "Of course some people would never want to change the beliefs that have been instilled in them since childhood but there are documents, such as this book, that record him surviving the cross."

"Ok, but this book doesn't look 2000 years old."

Everson smiled; "I think it's a copy of the text but in the original cover. Dr

Felix dated the cover to 2000 years plus or minus 150 years but he dated the text to 12th/13th century."

William looked thoughtful; "You know Dr Felix, and he knows all about this?"

Father Everson smiled; "He is a man of honor. It is a secret William, a secret to be dealt with wisely."

William felt privileged to be let in on the secret by someone he had only just met. This made him feel instantly part of the mystery and it's unraveling.

"Roger Felix was a childhood friend of mine"

Father Everson cupped his head in his hands as he talked to himself; "Of course, of course he was"

William ignored the unsettling interlude; "I wonder who found the original and made the copy?"

Everson had the answer.

"Sir William Marshall, Earl of Pembroke is supposed to have found it in Jerusalem when he was there with the original Temple Knights. It was apparently kept safe by Marshall's wife's family, the de Clares. No-one knows who made the copy but we do know that at some point Richard of Haldingham, the man who painted the Mappa Mundi came across it. How it came to be buried in the 13th/14th century extension to the church of St Peters is unknown but the Marshall family were the Earls of Pembroke and the St Peters area once formed part of their lands. We do know that Richard of Haldingham, whose family had close ties with the De Clares was burned at the stake for declaring its contents were the teachings of Jesus. It was all hushed up of course and I doubt very much if anything he had survived, apart from the wonderful map and this book."

William was very curious to note the co-incidence that his name was the same as the old Earl of Pembroke.

Everson smiled and took a frail looking letter from the front of the book and turned it so that William could read it;

Jerusalem   2nd October 1187

My Dearest Brother

Love and light be with you. I write this in haste to let you know that am safe. I am first to France and if the power of God is guiding me and this message then by the time you read these lines I shall be on the way back to England to meet up with Richard.

I so look forward to the warmth of your bear hugs and the conversations around the fire, the rides on the albino stallions across the Preseli Hills and the luxury of the cooking at your table.

My time here has been torrid and uncertain. I am surrounded by those that would, in the name of religion, cut open and gut those men, women and children least able to defend themselves leaving the streets and courtyards running red with heads, blood and guts.

I know not what sort of mind men have that do this bidding and I chose to have no part in it. I disown those that kill for no reason.

My distaste and disgust of Guy of Jerusalem is without equal. He destroys and defames all that those of the Way have come to know.

Killing innocent people, defiling women, impaling them on iron rods and roasting them with children on spits before eating their flesh and leaving the carcasses in the streets is no work of anyone's God.

My promise to Henry on his deathbed to bring Arthur's cross to the Holy Seplechure at Jerusalem and ask for forgiveness for his slaughter of the monks and the stealing of their treasure and land in France is fulfilled and I shall leave for England to be with Richard at the earliest moment and return the cross and the Book of Life to it's place with God.

My heart goes out to Sibylla, Guys Queen, since September just last year. She is powerful and manipulative but she is naïve and easily led. She staggers from stud to stud much as a legless calve searches for its mother. But, brother, I have to tell you that she is one of the most beautiful and dangerous women I have ever met. I confess and not lightly that I have laid with her and shall ever remember her long red hair as it fell in ringlets down her tanned skin and to her waist. Will I be forgiven for this weakness brother You know how I long for my real love Eleanor and how little I am able to see her let alone know the warmth of her body. God alone knows why Sibylla is so besotted by this cruel man... She even removed the crown from her head and handed it to Guy, permitting him to crown himself, at the Church of the Holy Sepulchre in Jerusalem.

We live in strange times my brother.

There is much unrest in these parts at this time. Guy thinks he is invincible, but no-one with arrogance like his is invincible. I have helped to set the Templars and the Hospitilers on their way by imparting the knowledge of which you and I are the guardians. I am happy that in some way the secrets will live on in them.

I have also to confess to you of an old score well settled.

You will recall that this butcher is the same stock as those that murdered my uncle Earl Patrick of Salisbury in Poitou, took me prisoner and treated me so badly. How glad I was that I was able to hold the men off long enough to allow my beloved Eleanor to ride safely away and how grateful I am to her for her part in getting me set free. My secret I will tell you brother in case something dire should happen to me. It is my belief that Richard our true king is my child.

But, that is not the worst. Hating every moment of the terrible cruelty and slaughter I met with Saladin and plotted the downfall of this wicked man. Saladin set siege to Tiberius and as predicted Guy attempted to relieve it. Guy's army was surrounded and cut off from a supply of water, and on July 4 the army of Jerusalem was completely destroyed at Hattin.

Guy was one of the very few captives spared by the Saracens after the battle, along with his brother Geoffrey, Raynald, and Humphrey.

Come September, Saladin besieged us here in the Holy City, and Sibylla personally led the defence, along with Patriarch Eraclius and Balian of Ibelin, who had survived Hattin.

On this day by the will of God and the Good grace of Saladin who kept his word to me we have been permitted to escape. I have escorted Sibylla, her daughters and some of her family onto a boat for Tripoli where they will be safe. I am about to board the boat for France.

You remain in my thoughts and prayers always.
William Marshall

William looked at the monk; "William Marshall... I have the same name, except of course I am not the Earl of Pembroke! But why tell me this father, why confide in me?"

"Because William, your link to all this might be closer than you know. I am soon to die and I have no-one else to tell."

He responded without hesitation. William was compassionate; "Don't say that Father, none of us know when we will die."

William thought carefully in the silence that hung in the air.

"Is William saying he was the father of Richard the Lionheart from an affair with Eleanor of Aquitane."

Everson nodded. William thought for a second then continued; "I met a man called the Wandering Jew, he told me to come here; he told me you were expecting me."

"You've seen the Wandering Jew?" Everson's eyes welled up.

William noticed fear and wonder in his eyes; "Do you know this man?"

The monk nodded; "Oh yes, I know of him, he is said to be immortal; a man who is destined to walk the earth until the truth about Jesus and his teachings is known."

"An immortal man, you mean like Superman?" William smiled.The quip didn't go down well.

"No, I mean like the physical embodiment of the spirit and energy of God." Everson looked deadly serious.

"He just seemed like a frail old man to me." replied William.

Everson rested his hand on William's arm; "What we see as reality with our hearts is what we create as reality in our minds. We see what we expect to see and not what is really there, nothing more, nothing less."

-34-

Caldey
30th July 2009

Everson led William back down the stairs and into the Cloisters where he noticed small stained glass windows along the top. One showed a head like the cover of the Book of Life and the other a hammer and a pair of pliers. As they entered the Abbots chapel the first thing William saw was a life-sized wooden carving of Christ lying on a bed with his eyes closed. Instinctively he went over to the statue and ran his hands along it.

Everson was watching carefully; "It is meant to be Christ lying on the stone of unction."

William was moved; "But why carve a statue of the dead Christ like this?"

Everson was unsure;

"Maybe to remind us of our mortality, perhaps to represent the burial of Jesus. There are several similar carvings in Brittany."

Everything the monk said seemed to beg another question.

It was a perfect summer afternoon on the island. Most of the visitors had left and now the only soundtrack was provided by the sea and the gentle breeze through the trees. William and Father Everson had been talking for hours and William's mind was swimming with revelations. Now he felt blissful just walking along the beach with the older man.

Father Everson removed his sandals to walk across the wet sand to the water's edge. William joined him and they sat on a rock dangling their feet in the cool water. Seaweed sunbathed in a pool and tiny shrimps darted to and fro.

Side by side they sat enjoying the ebb and flow of the water and staring out to sea. In those precious moments both men were aware of the therapeutic nature of their meditation. The gentle rhythm of the earth's heart-beat pulsated the waves backwards and forwards across their feet and legs taking away old thoughts and wounds, replacing them with new hopes and memories.

Everson was the first to speak.

"Heaven on earth, William?"

"I feel so at peace here."

William looked at the huge orange sun as it was slowly and majestically moving across the sky pulsating diffused light through the large fluffy clouds, its rays shimmering around a burnished gold halo.

"It's easy to see why people used to worship the sun. I spend too many hours in artificial light."

The monk looked straight at William; "Do you believe in God, William?"

It was the second time he had asked the question, this time he searched his mind for a more appropriate answer, it came to him more easily than he had thought it would.

"Like you, father, I believe that there must have been a creative power to make all this. I'd struggle to personify the creator as a person though. Like you I certainly don't subscribe to the old man with a long beard concept. We are told that God is real but that we cannot see feel hear or touch him. We are told that someone thousands of years ago saw and heard a person who may or may not have said he was God and we are all supposed to believe that without question ad infinitum".

The monk smiled; "Well at least you don't think of God as the Zero point as many scientists do! What are your thoughts about Jesus?"

William suspected his questions were loaded and working towards something, not that he minded, it was nice just to have someone, a virtual stranger, to talk to without judgment or expectation.

"Jesus? Like you said earlier, father, I think Jesus was a special man, one of a number of special people that could help and heal people."

The monk smiled openly;

"You believe Jesus was a man then, not the son of God?"

"Is that OK?" William felt like a school child taking a test.

Everson moved a bit closer and put his arm around William's shoulder squeezing it slightly as a father would his son.

"Of course that's OK, there is no historical evidence that Jesus thought he was divine. A man should believe what he feels in his heart, not what he is told."

William looked up into his eyes; he saw a genuine kindness, an oasis of peace.

"May I ask what you really believe? May I ask what else the Book of Life contains?"

Everson had been hoping that this moment would arrive. He had been struggling with himself, his life and his conscience for too long, he just needed permission to speak and William had given him that.

"Of course you can my son. The information in the book seems very advanced but then we have no way of knowing where that information came from. In essence the book is telling us that the universe and everything in it is made of thought, matter and energy. It says that a thought produces what we picture in our minds, if we think in the right way. Jesus said that when you pray for something, believe it is already yours and it shall be so. He also told us that the kingdom of God is within us. It tells us that most people only use a tiny part of their brain and that the majority is hidden but that if we access it we can be complete. It goes on to show how this can be accessed by harnessing a power from the universe. In essence there are many levels of us; that is, we exist on different levels and frequencies and at all times; past, present and future. Some of these theories exist now in Quantum Physics."

It was certainly an interesting philosophy. The tide was turning so William motioned to the monk to move and took his arm as they walked along the beach. Everson took out a white handkerchief and wiped his nose before speaking, little specks of blood marked the white tissue.

"Did you know that before the Council of Nicea in AD325 there were nearly 200 Gospels circulating? The Catholic Church canonized only four: Matthew, Mark, Luke and John. The 66 books that comprised our Bible were declared to be Scripture by a vote of 568 to 563. Imagine if the vote had gone the other way. The Church would be run according to a different philosophy. Of the Gospels that were voted out, some were destroyed, some were consigned to dusty corners and others were banned to the extent that anyone caught reading them were put to death. One such was the Gospel of Barnanbas, written almost contemporaneously with the life of Jesus. It quotes Jesus as saying: 'I am Jesus, son of Mary, of the seed of David, a man that is mortal and fears God, and I seek that to God be given honour and glory.' So according to Barnanbas, Jesus said he was an ordinary man, not the son of God so you can see why that gospel had to go.

William looked curious; the seed of David, "did he mean that literally?"

Everson's face gave nothing away; "Not literally, exactly, if David existed he would have been alive some 1000 years before. Some say that Herod raped Mary who worked in the temple and that is why Mary invented a "virgin birth" to save face.It also explains why he says he is the seed of David because Herod claimed descent from David and why Herod had all the babies murdered. If Jesus truly was of a "virgin birth" then he has no eartly father so he could not say if he was the seed of David or not!!"

William was all ears but this was a lot to take in, Father Everson had not finished;

"In AD170 Iranaeus wrote in support of pure monotheism and opposed Paul (who had replaced Christ's gospel with a gospel about Christ) for injecting into Christianity doctrines of the pagan Roman religion and Platonic philosophy. He had quoted extensively from the Gospel of Barnabas which proves it was in circulation at that time although it was banned after 325. In AD383 the Bishop of Rome secured a copy of the Gospel of Barnabas and kept it in his private library despite the potential consequences. It seems that the earliest traditions and texts humanized God by making him both male and female, the male being Yahweh and the female being his wife called Asherah, who was also described by Jeremiah as the Queen of Heaven which is interesting because it was also a name given by Ptolemy to the constellation Cassiopeia which he says is a sign of the second coming of Christ. In AD478 the remains of Barnabas were actually discovered and on his breast a copy of his own gospel written by his own hand was found. The famous Vulgate Bible appears to be based on this Gospel. In AD496 the Evangelium Barnabe, as they called it was included in a list of forbidden books. Somehow this work survived and in 1713 Cramer presented the manuscript to the famous connoisseur of books, Prince Eugene of Savoy. In 1738 along with the library of the Prince it found its way into Hofbibliothek in Vienna. So far as I know it's still there".

William struggled to assimilate all the dates and names but the major points stood out.

"Wow, God having a wife. Now that is hell of a revelation, where on earth did the notion come from?"

Everson looked thoughtful; "It's a long story but there are carvings within the walls of Jerusalem itself to show that these were early beliefs"

William felt for the older man. Like Mother Teresa his silence was punctuated by little sighs of belief and disbelief.

"Don't Muslims believe that Jesus was a messenger of God; that he was born of a man?

Everson breathed in the sea air as deeply as he could and exhaled slowly;

"Yes, exactly, if Jesus was GOD, then why did he ask for GOD's forgiveness in Luke 23:34 and in so many other passages?"

William stopped walking and shrugged his shoulders; "I think I get your point father, but I cannot say that I have ever thought about it so deeply, and I have to admit that I am plainly ignorant of so much."

"I am so sorry William, like Sir Isaac Newton who discovered all this in his own research I have been keeping this secretly wrapped up inside me for years and at last it is so good to get it out...being the keeper of this wisdom sent him mad you know...I am so disillusioned and alone, just like he was."

His eyes were full of tears and William tried to comfort him whilst he sobbed. Several minutes seemed to pass before Everson disengaged. He placed his hands on William's shoulders as he looked at him through glazed eyes;

"You are a good man William, but you may yet be more than that."

"What are you talking about?" William felt slightly uncomfortable.

Everson ignored his question and carried on talking;

"What I have told you is only part of the story William."

Their walk had led them away from the beach and into a wooded copse. On the left in some trees was what looked like the round stone wall of an old well.

William perched on the top and Everson joined him and gazed into its depths.

"Legend has it that Merlin lived here for a while and sat contemplating at this very well."

William felt the weight of history upon his shoulders and looked sadly towards the earth, it was his turn to feel the power of released emotions that the island seemed to encourage;

"Ahh, Merlin, if only he was here now to explain what should be done."

"Maybe he is here, with us." The monk spoke without thinking as the breeze whipped up briefly through the tree tops making a whispering sound as if to emphasis the possibility.

William wanted to go back to the conversation about Jesus' death and Father Everson was full of theories.

"According to Islam, Jesus never died on the cross nor was he the son of God sent down to earth in a form of a man to die for our sins."

He stole a glance at William who was listening intently.

"The end of the life of Jesus on earth is as much involved in mystery as his birth. The crucial part of the Orthodox-Christian Churches doctrine is that his life was taken on the Cross, that he died and was buried, that on the third day he rose in the body with his wounds intact and walked about, talked with others and ate with his disciples, and was then afterwards taken up bodily to heaven. But some of the early Christian sects did not believe that Christ was killed on the cross. The Basilidans believed that someone else was substituted for him. The Docetate held that Christ never had a real physical or natural body, but only an apparition or phantom body, and that his crucifixion was only apparent, not real. The Marcionite Gospel (about AD 138) denied that Jesus was born at all, and merely said that he appeared in human form. The Gospel of St. Barnabas supported the theory of substitution on the Cross. The Qumranic teaching is that Christ was not crucified nor killed by the Jews."

William shuffled a bit trying to stay comfortable on the stone wall.

"The Turin Shroud father, do you think that really was the cloth that Jesus was wrapped in after he was brought down from the cross?"

Everson looked thoughtful.

"I am not sure, much has been published about it but the things that haven't been are much more interesting. There have been rumours amongst the church fathers that a false sample of the shroud was given up for testing and in another test sindonologists say that whoever was wrapped in the cloth was still bleeding and that could only happen if the person wrapped was still alive, an inconvenient truth for the church if it was the shroud of Jesus. Who knows where the truth lies?"

William was immersed;

"And I am guessing that the glut of Dan Brown type pulp fiction doesn't help."

Father Everson stroked his chin;

"That's true, you could say that the "Da Vinci Code" is modern fiction whereas the Bible is ancient fiction. However, you could look at it in a much more positive way, at least nowadays people are trying to discover what is true and it is in that course of discovery that pleasure lays for some, just as some people like the planning of a holiday more than the holiday itself."

"Or the travelling but not the arriving." William interjected.

"Of course. I don't think that there is anyone who is not curious about Mary Magdalen, especially as we learn a lot about her from The Gospel of Philip, another one that didn't make the Nicea list and was therefore sidelined from history. Philip spoke a lot about marriage as a sacred mystery and two passages directly refer to Mary Magdalene and her close relationship with Jesus. It stated: 'there were three who always walked with the Lord: Mary, his mother, and her sister, and Magdalene, the one who was called his companion'. Unfortunately the other passage referring to Mary Magdalene is incomplete because of damage to the original manuscript. Several words are missing but the passage appears to describe Jesus kissing Magdalene on the lips and using a parable to explain to the disciples why he loved her more than he loved them."

William's concentration was waning.

"You have done so much research and please do not think me rude, but what is the point of all this knowledge?"

"You are right William; I know a truth that the Church covered up 1700 years ago but so what? It was Jesus who said 'the truth will set you free' and I do think people have a right to know, if they choose to."

William bent down and picked up a handful of sandy earth letting it fall between his fingers like a timer. There was silence as both men reflected on their conversation. The grit that had accumulated on William's legs and feet had more or less dried and he brushed it off with one hand, crossing his left leg over his right to give the same treatment to his other foot. Just then Father Everson noticed that William had a red mark on the sole of his left foot, he tried not to stare, but it was obvious. The monk pulled the top part of his habit around his shoulders.

"Shall we go and get something to eat William, I am getting the shivers."

"Sparrow hopped over your grave?" William smiled.

Everson was not smiling; "Something like that William. Come on, I have something you must see before we eat."

The well trodden earthen path snaked prettily between the trees and then broke out into a clearing. The first thing William saw was the amazing leaning spire of St Illtyds 6th century chapel and monastery which had stood unused since the dissolution but was thought to have been built over the remains of a much earlier religious and military settlement. William was impressed. It was semi derelict but to see such early remains, some clearly dating back to the 6th century was absolutely amazing.

Everson urged him to continue walking until they reached the little church.

The ancient door creaked open. There was an immediate musty smell of damp and disrepair. The wooden roof trusses, partly restored by a local history group looked dangerously unstable. It looked like a structure standing only by the will of God. The wind whistled through the rafters like angels calling some long lost congregation with no hope of salvation. The dark smoked and weathered plaster on the walls was blowing and saturated with mould and green slime. The uneven flagstones merged into an earthen floor where large grave memorial stones had been removed. Lying against one of the walls was one such stone. It had become known as the Illtyd Stone with an ancient inscription in his memory. William ran his hand across the surface. The writing was fading into the past as he looked at it.

Everson elucidated; "Down the side it says, MAGL DUBR, or the tonsured servant of Dubricius, also known as Dyfrig, he was the guy that the Bruts of England say crowned Arthur King at Caerleon."

William was hooked as the monk continued;

"The Stones latin inscription says, SIHGNO CRUCIS IH(U) ILTUTUTI FINGSI, with the sign of the cross, I Illtyd, have fashioned this monument and this seems to refer to St Illtyd who some say was a cousin of King Arthur."

William raised his eyebrows as Everson continued;

"Illtyd was a fascinating man, William, he was known as the original King Maker, he came to this island in the 6th century to continue an earlier small religious and educational establishment."

William was curious; "Why here...?"

"Because the ancient texts, even well before Illtyd, tell us that this place was a stopping off point for Jesus, Mary Magdalen and some of the members of the Holy family that came to this land after the crucifixion. Mary Magdalen is supposed to have lived here for a while after the death of Jesus and after spending much time teaching in the South of France. The little church that you first see when you come into the village was once called St Mary by the Sea, until it was relatively recently renamed St David's. The stained glass shows mother Mary with Jesus and Mary Magdalen and King David with a sceptre."

William nodded; "So that's where the woman got the story of the ghost of Mary Magdalen from."

Everson cocked his head looking for clarification.

"Oh, I met a rather brash American woman on the boat over here; she said she was a Psychic on television who had come to see if she could contact Mary Magdalen".

"How tasteless." Everson replied.

William agreed but was nonetheless curious; "Have you seen her, have you seen Mary?"

Everson looked uncomfortable but didn't reply, instead he led William to a part of the church wall upon which there were a series of ancient but crude paintings some of which could just be seen.

"Have a good look at these William; can you see what they are saying?"

William looked closely whilst retrieving his compact digital camera from its case. The paintings had indeed faded but some were still visible and William snapped away in excitement.

"So, what is it they are saying father?

Everson neatly sidestepped the question, he was thumbing through the stack of requests for prayers and healings that had been left that day by visitors;

"They come from all over the world, even now asking for cures, just like they have for almost 2000 years. People always think of Lourdes or Walsingham but this place has the most ancient shrine of all, Mary Magdalen's shrine."

William looked amazed; "Why don't we ever here about this? "

"I think that is clear William, if this place was in Rome or France or maybe just about anywhere else there would be a huge industry around it but if you mention that Jesus and Mary Magdalen or even that mother Mary were here in the UK you have massive problems, you see it doesn't fit in with accepted dogma!"

William nodded; "Yes, of course, why would the church let facts get in the way of a good story?"

"That's what religion is all about William, good stories and there has been lots of plagiarism over the centuries. Christianity has borrowed heavily from other religions and represents an amalgam of the best bits. The Persian Mithras cult was Egyptianized and then Hellenized. When Rome annexed Egypt in 30 BC, the kingdom faced religious turmoil. The first Greek pharaoh wanted a single god to bring together his diverse subjects. In a 'classic' example of the process of syncretism, the character and characteristics of several earlier gods were rolled into one, the god Serapis. In the 3rd century BC, the worship of Serapis became a State sponsored cult throughout Egypt. After the Roman conquest, the cult spread throughout the Empire. The new god embodied aspects of many earlier deities including the Egyptian *Osiris* and *Apis* and the Greek *Dionysus* and *Hades.* The Ptolemy's intended that the new god should have universal appeal in an increasingly cosmopolitan country. In consequence, Serapis had more than 200 localised names, including Christ!

"A new wave of Jewish migrants and slaves arrived in Egypt after the war in Palestine of AD 135. Into the religious void moved the ideas and agents of diverse cults and 'mystery religions', competing for membership and stealing each other's ideas. The most successful cult of all was Christianity."

William was trying to keep up but theology wasn't his strongpoint.

"So, where does all this leave us then?"

Everson leaned forward, as if he was about to share a big secret.

"OK, I believe that although Jesus was a real man and a great teacher of men, his real story is all about the knowledge he had acquired as a young scholar. There is plenty of evidence that he studied in Egypt, India and Wales. Actually, his wisdom is all about the sun as creator, healer and giver of life and about the energy of earth and the universe. In essence, that's what the bible and the Book of Life is about. The real story of Jesus is the story of the Sun passing through the Zodiac during the year, about the movement of the planets and stars and how they affect us and how we could, if we knew how, tap into these energies and all be gods ourselves creating an abundance of all that we need. Maybe that's why the number twelve is so important in the Christian story."

Everson rested against the little table before proceeding.

"The sun goes on a journey through the zodiac during the year. The journey of the sun matches up with the journey Jesus takes during his ministry. Jesus's ministry is said to last a year. The sun completes its circuit of the zodiac in a year. Jesus is said to have twelve disciples. The year has twelve months. The zodiac is divided into twelve houses representing the twelve divisions of the year; Capricorn, Aquarius, etc. There are twelve cycles of the moon in a year. The Jewish calendar is actually a lunar calendar, with twelve months following the twelve cycles of the moon (Nisan, Iyyar, Sivan, Tammuz, Ab, Elul, Tishri, Cheshvan, Kislev, Tebeth, Shebat, and Adar). The story of Jesus is circular. He originally was said to have been born in a cave and he is placed in a cave when he dies, to be resurrected three days later. The year is circular. A new year begins immediately after the old year ends. We celebrate Jesus's birthday on December 25, three days after the Winter Solstice of December 22. The sun 'dies' on December 22, the Winter Solstice, the shortest day of the Year."

To William this all seemed quite logical.

"The stories, the parables the information it is all an allegory, a way of remembering the movement of the sun, the times of the year and the months for sowing and reaping. In fact the whole thing is a code for living, a handbook of the way of life on all levels, mental, physical and spiritual."

William wondered about King Arthur.

"Do you think that King Arthur is this just another continuation, another way of looking at the movements in the heavens and their affects on earth? The twelve knights, the round table the heavenly king being the sun at the centre?"

Everson smiled. "William I think you understand, just as in the Welsh Mabinogion wisdom and knowledge are passed down in stories and are marked on the landscape to reflect the sky as is the case with Stonehenge and Avebury."

William had an epiphany; "Of course, the Australian Aborigines have their songlines, the Druids had poetry and song, the native Americans chant, in fact I bet everywhere in the world had its own simple way of passing down knowledge."

Everson gave him a hug and whispered;

"And as St Illytd, the man who built this place and lived and taught here was a cousin to King Arthur. You could be fairly confident in saying 'Arthur was here'."

William looked around and unlocked his imagination. He could almost detect the smoky smell of the candles, the sound of the wind and sea outside on a stormy night, the chanting of the holy words and Arthur in communion with his knights and advisors.

Everson removed his shoes and knelt to meditate. William joined him. In this impromptu quiet time they both let their minds wander. William was thinking about the things Everson had told him earlier in the day, they seemed incredible and yet in some way it all started to make sense.

Eventually William opened his eyes and saw the monk kneeling beside him, on his foot he noticed a red mark, the very same mark he had on his own foot. The curiosity passed as Everson sensed his conscious presence;

"I'd like to come and help you sort out whatever is going on, William, I know a lot about Arthur and I might just be of some use after all."

William looked genuinely worried; "I can't expect you to do that father; it may be very dangerous indeed."

"Dangerous, I am already dying William, how much more dangerous can it get?" He was so pleased that he had confided in William earlier in the day, even though he had not told him everything. "Why have I acquired this knowledge if not to use it?"

"If you are sure."

Indeed he was. "I have a couple of things to look after here, but how about if I meet you in Caerleon tomorrow?"

William nodded and on Everson's recommendation, he headed for the jetty where the last boat was about to leave. He hadn't had a chance to talk about the long red headed girl, the meaning of the drawings in the ancient church or why Eversons surname appeared on the genealogical note from his mother passed to him on her death bed. How easily we are distracted from the things we really wanted to learn.

-35-

Late afternoon, St Govan's, Pembrokeshire
30th July 2009

In contrast to the turmoil in his mind the boat trip back to Tenby had been quiet, beautiful and uneventful. There was no sign of the brash American TV psychic, the screaming children or anyone to ruin the reddening ball of sun or the sea spray in his hair. He looked up from the harbour at the array of colourful houses that curved around the bay. He considered staying the evening but there was one place he just had to visit before the sun went down, a place that Father Everson told him all about.

His journey was taken up with playing and replaying the events of the past few days. Every so often fate or serendipity, call it what you will, seems to make itself ever present in ones' life, as if you are on predestined tracks and are being pushed along by a power beyond your own. This is how William was thinking as he evaluated the jigsaw pieces from, Rachel, Michael, the Wandering Jew, the nun, the nursing sister and now Father Everson.

Soon he arrived at the 13th century church of St Michael and All Angels at Bosherston. From this point a public footpath leads down to the world famous lily ponds. William walked across to a well worn oak seat which was thoughtfully placed in the churchyard, sat down and opened the old guide book that Father Everson had loaned to him. He could just about make out the faded text. Apparently present-day Bosherston is very different. The creek, once part of the inlet from the sea, has now been dammed to form the Lily Ponds. Today these are a protected National Nature Reserve. The sea itself meanwhile has receded to form the extensive Broadhaven Beach. Nearly one quarter of the Parish was bought in 1938 to form part of the RAC Firing Range for the then War Department. A small part of this range is still used. Access to certain areas is restricted on some days for the safety of visitors.

After a few moments William made his way along the well trodden winding pathway between the trees. He could smell the sea air in the near distance. It helped to clear his head and he enjoyed this time alone. He would have to return to reality and his commitments soon enough.

After about 10 minutes he rounded a corner in the path and the scene opened out bathed in a surreal golden light. Suddenly he became aware of an almost secret still lake topped with wonderful beautiful pink and white pond lilies. Across the water he could see mute swans gliding gracefully along, their reflections of white perfection a charming contrast to the black coots and ducks sharing their world. Off to the right a heron was carefully picking its way along the shallows near the bank. This place felt like nirvana.

He came to a fork in the path, one way looked clear and obvious, the other less trodden and overgrown. He took the overgrown route. After a while he started to feel quite strange, almost as if he was falling into a dream. A nagging inner-voice reminded him he hadn't taken his medication and that he hadn't eaten for hours. The old dry stone wall covered with green moss overlooking the still water was too inviting to miss. He sat and removed his shoes feeling an instant relief from the heat.

He grabbed his leg and pulled his foot around to look at the red mark that had always been there, how odd that Father Everson should have one just the same. Reaching into his pocket and pulling out a bar made from oats and chocolate chips he wondered how many people over the ages had sat at this very spot enjoying this very scene. Soon the snack and the rest of his water were gone. He pulled his compact camera from his pocket and started scrolling through the pictures of the internal walls of the 6th century church he had taken that very afternoon.

The paintings were very faint and worn but he could make out a young figure with the sun behind his head, a boat and some other marks that looked like a chalice. Snapping back to the present he once again consulted the little guide book on his immediate environs.

> *This place is the South Welsh candidate for the watery home of the Lady of the Lake, from where King Arthur obtained his magical sword, Excalibur. It was back to this lake that Bedwyr supposedly returned the sword soon after the fateful Battle of Camlann. In its favour is the fact that Caldey Island is not far away. This may possibly have been the original Isle of Avalon to which the wounded King Arthur was taken after the battle. The area is also associated with a number of Knights of the Round Table and other famous Dark Age characters. Sir Gawain is said to have retired to a tiny hermitage at St Govan's Head a mile to the south while St Pedrog (apparently one of the survivors of Camlann) founded the the church of St. Petrox, just to the north. Stackpole Elidor, at the tip of the eastern lake arm, has even been identified by some as the site of St Sampson's otherwise unlocated foundation in the area. The hamlet of Sampson sits just to the west.*

There was something about the reference to Gawain that appealed to William. He had always felt an affinity for the knight, even from early childhood.

He flipped back to the reference section in the little book and read the notes;

> Gawain, or Gwalltafwyn, King of Gododdin (Born c.AD 491)
> (Welsh: Gwalchmai; Latin: Walganus; English: Gavin)
>
> Gawain was the eldest son of King Lot Luwddoc (of the Host) of Gododdin and his wife Anna. He appears in early Welsh literature as Gwalchmai, the Hawk of May, and a very handsome young man who acquired for himself the epithet of Gwalltafwyn meaning "hair like rain". He is, of course, world famous as one of the stars of Arthurian Literature: one of the bravest Knights of the Round Table.
> From King Arthur's court, Gawain is said to have undergone many adventures. In later years, Gawain is said, by some, to have abdicated in order to lead a saintly life on the Pembrokeshire Coast. Irish pirates once pursued him along the shore here until he managed to hide in a cleft in the rock. The fissure closed up to conceal Gawain and, in thanks, he established his small hermitage on the spot still known at St. Govan's head. Nearby is Huntsman's Leap, a deep chasm between the cliffs. The Devil is said to have told a man, who had sold him his soul, that he would forgo payment if the fellow could ride across this impossible jump. The canny debtor persuaded St. Govan/Gawain to bless his horse and thus made it clean across the divide!
> When Gawain died, he is said to have been buried under the altar in his little chapel. He was succeeded in Gododdin by his son, Cawrdaf, though little is known of his descendants. They appear to have continued to rule the kingdom for a number of generations, probably until the Northumbrian conquest of AD 638.

Everson had added a hand written note;

> As the church appear to hate anything to do with King Arthur they would have us believe that the little Chapel at what is now known as St Govan's Point was the hermitage of a man called Gobhan or Gobban (later called Govan by the church!) who was born of the Hy Cinnselach clan who lived in County Wexford in Ireland. Historic records tell us though that he was a disciple of St. Senan at the monastery of Inniscathy.
> Tradition says that Gawain lies buried under the altar in the chapel. An old friend of mine, now sadly departed told me that he worked on a dig at the chapel, funded by the church in 1992. They found the body of a man over six feet five inches tall under the altar area and a small lady. The man's body was dated to the last part of the sixth century and the lady to the latter part of the 5th century. It shows at the very least that there was a church building or hermitage on that spot at an early time. The lady just might have been Govein who was the widow of Tewdrig, the grandfather of King Arthur who was killed defending the Ford against the Saxons at Tintern and whose body is buried at Mathern.

There was a cutting describing the chapel itself stuck into the new few pages:

> To enter this picturesque little building it is necessary to descend a long flight of steps, which, legend asserts, cannot be accurately counted by a mortal being. It is very strange that when a group of people are told to count the steps their answers always vary. It may have something to do with the fact that the steps are most irregular, with many half steps. Depending on where a person places his foot the count could vary considerably. The number of steps is approximately 74. The Chapel is simply constructed, having just a Nave (main body) which measures approximately 17' 6" by 12' 6". At the East end is a stone altar, and steps leading to the small cell formed in the rock. The South wall contains a piscina, a small aperture and the main window. The North wall is plain, except for the entrance and a small recess or shelf. The West wall has a circle in the rough plastering high up and to the right of centre. Within the circle there was an inscription, but all that is now visible are what look like the letters A and O. Experts say that these are the only genuinely original marks on the walls. There are sadly a number of modern graffiti marks. The West wall also has a small window and a doorway leading out to the rocks below and to a roughly built well.
>
> In the floor near the main entrance there used to be a well, the water from which could only be procured in a limpet shell or small spoon, drop by drop. It was said to be a cure for eye complaints, skin diseases, and rheumatic tendencies. The rough built well outside the Chapel (which is also dry now) has a double legend of being a wishing well and a healing well.
>
> In August 1902 the Chapel was visited by King Edward VII and Queen Alexandra, who expressed their delight at all that they saw.
>
> Historical Note: Experts, including representatives of H.M. Office of Works, agree that the building is at least as old as the 11th century and may well be as old as the 6th century.

Squinting at the small text made his eyes blurry. He rubbed them gaining instant relief from tiredness. Out of the corner of his eye he caught the glimpse of the reflection of a beautiful girl. Her long, white gown shimmered in the water. Her curled red hair dancing in the breeze. His eyes slowly cleared. With a frantic beating of wings the swan tread water and took off, neck outstretched, towards the bay. He looked around but in the same heartbeat the girl was gone.

Fascinated he looked at his watch and at the falling sun. This little chapel was less than a mile away. If he hurried he could be there before dark.

William hurried back to his Austin Healey and drove along the coast road, through the firing range and down to the cliff edge. There was only one other vehicle at the car park, an old green land rover. In the front seat two honey coloured Labradors were sitting close to each other gazing out to sea, panting. There was no sign of their owner.

William walked across to the sign that was mounted next to the footpath on the edge of the car park; 'Welcome to the Pembrokeshire Coastal Path'. He followed the arrow on the sign and looked downwards. The very steep steps led directly and exclusively to the door of the chapel. He could see that the building itself was in good repair, no doubt thanks to the National Park. It looked like a tiny stone rectangle with a tile roof nestled right into the foot of the steep cliff, like a child clinging to its mother, like a lost soul searching for faith. Just beyond the church William could see the steep cliff faces on each side and the rocks falling away into the sea.

Across the bay he saw a white swan flying and watched as it landed on a rock beside the shore. The gentle ebb and flow of the sea was like a lullaby to William who suddenly realized how tired he was and how little sleep he'd had over the last few days. The steps ended at the chapel doorway. The entrance was just a stone archway leading into the building.

Gingerly he stepped inside, pausing whilst his eyes adjusted to the semi darkness lit only by the fingers of light from the sunset through a small window opening opposite. The place smelled of damp and urine and there was graffiti on the walls. The sacred well near the door was capped to avoid further damage and the basic stone altar had been marked with paint and chalk. At first William thought that this was just more graffiti scratched and painted by those with no regard for the sanctity of history but he was wrong. Sure there was some mindless scribbling but as his eyes adjusted he saw other markings, some of which he recognized. To the left of the altar was a doorway which lead directly into the nearby cliff face and behind him was another door that led out onto the rocky terrain, the small beach and the sea.

William lit a match as he bent down to examine the front of the stone altar. It had a circle gouged into it which was divided into eight triangles like a wheel with spokes. He had seen this drawing at Ephesus, in Turkey and had made a note of its meaning in his notebook. The diagram forms the synthesis of five religious symbols. *I* for Jesus, *X* for Christ, a horizontal line across a circle for son of, *Y* for God and an *M* on end for saviour. To the right of the altar stone were faintly discernible letters, the same ones in fact as those revealed on the 30 pieces of silver given to him by the nun.

He blew out the last match and explored the doorway that led to the cliff face. It was a small enclosure made by falling rocks that had lodged against the church on that side presumably in antiquity. Legend suggests that if one hides in the secret place, turns around and makes a wish it will come true. William couldn't resist.

Moving back into the nave, he felt an urge to look outside. He stepped across to the small window to the right of the altar overlooking the sea. The sun had almost reached the water and the rocks were bathed in a mixture of silhouette and warm orange light. He became very aware of the pounding of the sea mirroring his heart….."Mum, is that you?" his mind went back to the oh so recent words he had spoken to his mother as she was dying;

"It's ok mum, just try to relax and imagine you are walking along the beach, that's where we can always meet, you know… on the beach… just listen to the sound of the waves, it's the sound of life, it never ends… mum?"

Very slowly his attention was drawn to a shadow seemingly blowing in the wind standing overlooking the sea. It was the shapely figure of a woman staring out across the water. Carefully he made his way along the rocky pathway towards where she was standing, stopping briefly at the remains of the well he had read about in the guide book. Once famous for its healing properties, it was now dry.

For a moment he could imagine Gawain, a seasoned knight who had fought alongside Arthur before hanging up his sword and becoming a holy man and a healer in his old age. In the distance the feminine silhouette was still there, her hair and garments animated by the sea breeze.

Bit by bit the moon was replacing the sun. In it's essence he saw the goddess turn towards him illuminated and glowing, beckoning; pulling him towards her, like a boy to his mother, like a man to his lover. She was the truth and the light, the female trinity, the mother, the daughter and the Holy Spirit.

-36-

Earlier that day, Home Secretary's Office, London
30th July 2009

The imposing Georgian interior of polished oak panels, red carpets and embossed ceilings was the very epitome of royalty, security and secrecy. The traditional room had been painstakingly reconstructed after the demolition of the ancient structure at 2 Marsham Street, Westminster. Underneath the ancient façade was a fully functioning panic room seven stories down that could sustain life for two years.

Lunch on the run was venison sandwiches and Assam tea. The meeting was long overdue but vital. It was classified and coded Cobra red. The Home Secretary, Sir Philip Greenaway, had summonsed Vanessa Grey, Head of MI5, the Head of MI6, Brad O'Brien of CIA operations in London and the Archbishop of Canterbury.

Greenaway pulled no punches; "Would anyone like to explain what the hell is going on with all this King Arthur bullshit? So far I've got it in the neck for authorising the termination of two guys called Morgan and Pender in Newcastle, which I didn't actually authorise, the assassination of a BBC producer and presenter, Helen Daniels, which I know nothing about and an attack on a house in Princelet Street of which I don't have the faintest clue."

Nobody spoke.

"Well come on, for Christ sake, some-one talk to me, some one knows something."

"Why don't you ask MI5, they seem to know everything?" said O'Brien.

Greenaway gazed at O'Brien suspiciously;

"Two spent CIA issue incendiary cannisters were found in the burnt out shell of the Princelet Street House belonging to Helen Daniels, care to explain?"

O'Brien struggled his shoulders. There was an uncomfortable silence.

The man from 6 said nothing. Greenaway looked at Grey and she finally spoke;

"OK, OK, we know something about this; we think that the murder of Helen Daniels was a professional hit. The CCTV footage of the incident had conveniently disappeared but we found a "ghost" of it on a hard drive belonging to the company. We think the assassin is ex-South African BOSS, Bruce Botha. By the way someone else is on to this, the ghost images had already been accessed"

Greenaway looked at her expecting more information, it didn't arrive; "and the other people investigating are?"

Grey said she didn't know; "Someone professional. There was nothing we could trace back."

Greenaway breathed something of a sigh of relief;

"Are you telling me that we didn't take her out?"

Grey looked intense, fixing her eyes on O'Brien;

"No, we didn't, I've told you that before."

Greenaway tried to choose his words more carefully;

"Do you know who did and why?"

Grey remained calm. She looked across to Obrien;

"Who, no, not yet, why?, maybe because she learned something highly sensitive from Morgan and Pender. They had shared a lot of their information with her."

O'Brien chipped in; "We have had our sights on Morgan and Pender for some time. They caused quite a stink during their lectures in the US when they alleged that King Arthur and his brother Madoc discovered America in the 6th century and that Arthur was murdered by Indians before being brought back to the UK!"

Greenaway looked dumfounded; "Sounds like a load of bollocks to me."

"Actually it's not such a stupid idea. They brought up quite a few things that are, shall we say, inconvenient, so we banned them from visiting the USA again." O'Brien looked slightly embarrassed.

"They discovered that some bone fragments found in the 19th century in Kentucky date to the 6th century. These were buried with carvings in stone which matched those found in Wales in the 6th century. They were of the Coelbren alphabet. These carvings, if true, blow away the accepted history of early America. Of course we had to speak quietly to the Smithsonian where they were kept and they, well, shall we say, disappeared."

Greenaway thought for a moment; "It sounds like Morgan and Pender were accidental masters at pissing people off."

O'Brien looked serious; "I can't say we're devastated that they're dead."

Grey had been observing intently; "Someone gave the authority to terminate them, our forensic guys tell us it's a hit made to look like a fire."

Grey looked at Greenaway who was fuming; "Or a fire made to look like a hit... Our intel is that the authority came from the PM, presumably after consulting you."

Greenaway was speechless; he looked like a child who'd just been grounded.

Why would the Prime Minister go over his head on something like this?

Grey turned to O'Brien; "There must be plenty of loose ends for you to tidy up. I presume you eavesdropped on their calls and emails?"

O'Brien nodded; "Yes, as have you. Some of their stuff was dangerous to you guys as well as to us, not to mention the Church."

Greenaway looked to the Archbishop of Canterbury who tried to elucidate;

"Forgive me if I go over old ground. In the 1980's we became aware that Morgan and Pender were digging into various records that the church had flagged as 'sensitive'. They had discovered that the Charters of Llandaff Cathedral which date back to the 4th century actually do mention King Arthur and his family by name. They don't actually call him Arthur but by cross referencing the names with other contemporary documents and stones it is possible to make a solid case that there was a real King Arthur who was a king of Glamorgan and Gwent in the 6th century. Many people had spotted this over the last three hundred years but no-one had done what Morgan and Pender did and that was apply industrial research analysis techniques to their studies, narrow down the place where he may have been buried and find some real archaeology".

The room was silent as the Archbishop was urged to continue;

"Also, presumably as the result of their research; in the mid 1980s they bought a ruined church called St Peter's Super Montem on a remote hill top in South Wales. The local church and owners thought it to be just a pile of stone, just another derelict church that had fallen and decayed, but they were wrong. Morgan and Pender published a book setting out their research which they felt proved the importance of the church in both religious and Arthurian history. They were certainly on to something so, with the help of the government we tried to limit the books impact and to ensure that no publisher or media would touch it. We couldn't stop them publishing it themselves though but we did the best we could to undermine the distribution and promotion of the book and to tarnish both their research and their reputations."

He looked only mildly ashamed of the Church's actions and went on to explain how Morgan and Pender found the St Peter's cross at the dig and how the text on the cross may indicate the ancient lineage of Arthur going back to relatives of Jesus Christ and maybe even to Jesus himself. Morgan and Pender argued that if the texts were right about the cross then they could be right about Jesus not dying on the cross and his lineage down to King Arthur. If this was real and descendants could be traced then those descendants were directly related to the Holy family. The Church deemed this information too unsettling for the Christian population and the situation became even more intolerable when two genealogical experts were employed to trace the ancestry using the ancient texts.

The Archbishop felt obliged to reveal the big story;

"The main line comes down to the Spencers. Therefore Diana Spencer, Princess of Wales and her offspring are potentially lineal descendents of King Arthur and via him they possibly go back to the Holy family. I think the family knew about this link and that is why Diana gave William a middle name of Arthur and called herself the Queen of Hearts, a direct reference to Mary Magdalen, because, in a sense, she may have been related to her."

Greenaway looked flabbergasted; "But there is no proof, right?"

His Grace continued; "If Morgan and Pender had been allowed to finish their research and excavations, if they found the body of Arthur and, heaven forbid, Jesus Christ and if the DNA could be matched to Prince William, then God alone knows what might have happened!"

Greenaway felt isolated; "So, did the Prime Minister know all about this?"

The Archbishop nodded; "Yes, he asked me for a private briefing, I think he felt that it was too secret to share."

Grey looked at Greenaway, she couldn't decide whether he was truly in the dark about this or whether he was just acting. Greenaway felt just the same about her.

"How convenient then that Diana was killed in a road crash when she may have been pregnant, or is there something else we ought to know since we're all in confession mode?"

The Archbishop felt he had to come clean;

"We heard that Diana was going to include the story and the possible link as the USP for her new biography. You will understand, of course, why that could never be allowed to see the light of day."

"So why have I been in the dark about this for so long?" Greenaway appeared genuinely exasperated.

"Maybe your predecessor hid the file in the back of a drawer hoping it would go away! Maybe the PM has decided to act alone on this." Replied Grey.

Greenaway gazed intently at O'Brien; "You knew about this?"

"Yes, the former Archbishop explained the problem to me some time ago."

The Archbishop concurred; "He also briefed me fully, I am not proud of the way the church and MI5 worked together to discredit Morgan and Pender. They were made to look like bungling fools and criminals so that no one would ever take them seriously. We accused them of forging the St Peter's cross and fabricating evidence. We thought it was all over until we heard that Helen Daniels had been digging too deeply. The last straw came when Dr Roger Felix went to CADW to ask for permission to re-open the dig. He'd tested a sample of the cross using the latest technology and it apparently proved to be 6th century. We knew we had to stop this information from being made public. Imagine the embarrassment to the church, the government and the Royal family, watching a programme on Horizon alleging Diana was related to King

Arthur and Jesus Christ! It would heap logs on the fire of conspiracy theories, we'd never hear the end of it."

"And did you tell anyone else, anyone at all?" asked Greenaway.

The Archbishop rang his hands together before responding, trying to rid himself of any evil.

"We had an interfaith meeting with Cardinal Valetti on behalf of the Pope and various other church members that's all. I can assure you, my conscience is clear."

"It wouldn't be the first time in history that the Church has murdered others to retain its power and control." Greenaway couldn't hide his cynicism towards the Church.

"Or indeed the first time that the state has murdered people inconvenient to its cause."

The response from the Archbishop cut deep.

They all knew that in their different ways over hundreds of years innocent people had been sacrificed to sustain the old lies.

"That still leaves the question, who did 'pull the trigger' on Morgan and Pender, Daniels and her side kick. Obrien kept very quiet, in fact, they all did. The hiatus passed awkwardly.

Grey offered only what she was prepared to.

"When we were investigating the cock up with the car park CCTV footage, we couldn't get anywhere with the security company. The BBC record all their calls. The security guard on duty that night took a call in Helen Daniels office from a cell phone traced to her father, Bryn Evans, an Interpol officer. In the call Evans told the guard that he thought Helen was in great danger. The guard promised he'd go after her and warn her but it appears he never did. That guard is an agency temp and he also works for the security firm who looks after the car park where Helen was murdered, he has since disappeared."

"So he probably knows something, I'm guessing." Greenaway was good at the blindingly obvious.

"We're onto it." Grey tried to hide her impatience. "We're also watching Evans. I leaned on Interpol and had him removed from the investigation, that was pretty easy to do, but, of course, he's doing a Dirty Harry and we are watching to see what he turns up."

"Have you told the police that they're holding an innocent man?" asked Greenaway.

Grey shook her head; "The ghost footage from the Car Park security computer seems to show Mark Flatt waving down Daniel's car whilst the other man shot her."

Greenaway was confused; "So the man they are holding is one of the murderers?"

"It's not as simple as that, we think that someone at Police HQ may have doctored the footage to get a quick arrest; you know that the Chief Commissioner is being investigated."

O'Brien smiled; "Hey, Greenaway, I can't believe you don't know what's going on with your own PM and security, what do Home Secretary's do here in Britain?"

The two of them starred at each other for a moment longer than was comfortable before the Archbishop broke the tension.

"We need to find the real St Peter's cross. What is supposed to be written on the back could be absolute dynamite."

The others encouraged him to continue.

"Legend has it that there is a diagram or text telling where the true crucifixion cross, as brought back to Britain by Constantines's mother, Helen, was hidden. It may also even indicate where Jesus Christ himself was buried."

The religious leader became the voice of God, and lo the others listened.

"Whatever it takes, if Jesus Christ is buried in our land then we must find the body before anyone else and we must get the original St Peter's cross, whatever it takes, do we all agree?"

Greenaway needed further clarification so the Archbishop laid it on the line.

"If it can be proved that JC did not die on the cross and that his body is buried somewhere then he did not ascend to heaven after the crucifixion and the whole basis of Christianity is undermined but worse still, as you know, the Jews believe that the Saviour has not yet come and this only fuels their cause, in fact it also plays right into the arms of Islam. We must win; whatever it takes we must win."

Swept along in religious fervour like the gathering for yet another Crusade, the people of power lost themselves in the importance of their worlds and themselves.

"Whatever it takes!" They shouted in unison as if the result of a Holy War itself rested upon it. When the din died down they eyed each other again with distrust. You could have heard a pin drop. The last crusade was in their own back yard.

Only Greenaway had worked out that all may not be what it seemed. He couldn't help wondering if Princess Diana had been murdered or if the whole thing really was an accident. His briefings on the subject, he mused, had been oddly limited.

-37-

Caerleon, Wales
30th July 2009

It had been an extremely interesting two hours. No-one had seemed to mind them filming at the conference, in fact there were several crews milling about unchallenged. Everything seemed so open and above board. Maybe they had got this Arthur thing wrong. This didn't seem like the setting for a spiritual Armageddon. People seemed more interested in contemporary gossip, especially about the deaths of Morgan and Pender.

Angela kept gazing over at Rachel, no doubt trying to place where she had seen her. That was it, she recalled, William had taken her to one of Michael's parties.

Rachel was looking carefully at the many exhibits. Everything from Romance to "claimed" reality was covered here. Inevitably many people had chosen this worldwide event to launch their new books, DVDs and merchandise. There wasn't a shortage of Arthur theories. If you wanted to, here you could be convinced that Arthur was a comet, an alien from another planet, the second coming of Jesus Christ or the survivor of some ancient master race that planned to take over the world.

A tall man in his late thirties stepped up behind her and was looking over her shoulder.

"Some people believe anything." He said with conviction.

Rachel turned to look at him with a start, but she was quick to respond; "And some people believe in nothing!"

The well dressed toff held out his hand; "Touché, Robin Bryant."

Rachel returned the compliment, trying not to let on she knew very well who he really was. His smile was contagious.

"What's your take on Arthur?"

"I'm here making a documentary about who the real King Arthur was."

The man stayed poker faced; "Another fairy story documentary then. Of course no-one really knows if he ever existed or not, who are you making it for?"

Rachel was mildly irritated, perhaps she was meant to be; "You can't be aware of the work of Morgan and Pender then, they have unearthed some pretty strong proof."

"You don't believe anything they said do you?" Bryant was laughing.

Rachel kept calm; "You know something I don't?"

She found the man arrogant. "I know lots of things you don't, c'mon I'll buy you a drink."

Rachel was in two minds, she couldn't see Pete, Shorty or Evans but she didn't want to miss the chance of potentially vital information, particularly as this man's name had come up at the meeting at William's office in Spitalfields as well as being mentioned by Morgan and Pender themselves.

"Thanks but I can't be too long."

Bryant motioned for her to follow him and she did.

Soon they were sitting at the bar of the White Hart, an historic pub built over the site of a much older building. On the wall a note about its history explained that the site had once housed the meeting place of the local Friendly Society and that it was famed for having a brewery that brewed ale as strong as brandy which was carried from Caerleon to Ireland during the reign of Elizabeth I.

Rachel placed her order and went to the toilet. Robin made sure no-one was looking and turned the watch on his wrist upside down over the lemonade and lime pressing a button in one smooth movement. The slug of valium and sodium pentothal would be undetected in the drink and he hoped it would make her more inclined to supply him with reliable information before she dozed off. By the time she had returned and placed her petite shapely figure onto the bar stool the chemical had completely dissolved.

"Cheers Robin, thanks for the drink." She took a sip and picked up the conversation from where they left off. She was curious to know his take on Arthurian history but he steered the conversation the way he wanted.

"I was hoping you would tell me what you know Rachel, after all you were working with Helen and Nicole weren't you?"

"How'd you know about them you arrogant little man? Do you know that you've got lovely eyes?"

The drug was starting to take effect too quickly and Bryant knew he didn't have long to pump her for information. Rachel leaned over to him as if she was drunk, her lips red, open and trembling.

"Will you kiss me?"

He obliged. She sighed and propped her head up on her hands.

"Do you want to show me where you are staying?"

He kept focused on his plan.

"Ok, but tell me who are you working for Rachel and what are you after?"

"Working for? I'm working for the boss. What am I after? I'm after you, I love MI5 agents.

Rachel almost threw herself at him; the drug hadn't worked as he had intended.

How did she know of his MI5 connections? Knocked sideways he looked around struggling to keep her upright. This was not going as planned.

"Rachel, Rachel, where's the cross Rachel, where did Morgan and Pender hide the cross?"

Evans entered the bar and saw Rachel in Bryant' arms.

"Rachel!"

He rushed across but Bryant was quick to respond.

"I think she's had too much to drink."

Evans looked at Bryant and then at Rachel, her eyes were blurry and her voice very slurred, she moved her arms and threw them around Evans' shoulders.

"Ahhh Bryn, I love you Bryn, you have the nicest bum I have ever seen; you have to make love to me, now!"

Evans looked at Bryant who was backing away like a nervous lion.

"I was just trying to help, seems like you two know each other, I'll leave her to you."

Shocked, embarrassed and secretly flattered, Evans held Rachel tightly. She was warm and sleepy but there was no trace of alcohol on her breath.

Bryant left the bar like a snake disappearing into the grass.

-38-

Caerleon, Wales
30th July 2009

Evans kept an eye on Rachel whilst he made some calls and researched on his laptop. Natasha was still in London but she was helping him, she was almost too helpful he thought.

After being violently sick Rachel made a swift recovery and was feeling hungry so, when Pete and Shorty suggested the historic Hanbury Arms on the banks of the Usk for their evening meal, she eagerly agreed.

As they pulled into the car park they saw Dr Lambert talking to another man. He noticed them and waited whilst they parked. After the usual greetings he beckoned them over to the wall near the river and pointed upstream.

"Just up there is the site of the original wooden bridge which spanned the river even in Roman times. The water is shallow at that point. It's the place of the ancient ford and fishery mentioned from the 13th century onwards."

All four showed polite interest as he turned to the outside of the building.

"Great place, hey? It was built by the Morgan family and used as their town house until 1593. It's been a storehouse, magistrates' court and jail, though for the last two centuries it has been the Hanbury Arms."

His arm was waving generally towards the building on the side nearest the river. It must have been the educator in him, he couldn't stop issuing information.

"Observe the Tudor windows and the thick walls. Fixed to the wall on the town side is a stone head, locally said to be Roman, but believed by many to be medieval, perhaps coming from the castle."

They looked carefully but couldn't make it out. Rachel's stomach rumbled as they headed for the entrance. On the left was a wonderful paneled room from where Dr Lambert continued his impromptu guided tour inside.

"Tennyson stayed here; in fact the room he slept in remains unchanged. He sat in this very room to write the Idyllys of the King in 1856; 'The Usk murmurs by the windows and I sit like King Arthur at Caerleon.' He loved this area and you can get a sense of it in his poem "The Lady of Sharlott". The model he used for his Idyllys was Malory's 'Le Morte d'Arthur' and he follows some of Malory's plots quite closely. The character of the stories and their very atmosphere change from a narrative with a medieval outlook to a lyrical, idealistic, symbolic form of poetry."

This was an unexpected history lesson but Rachel was far too hungry so she went off to get some menus whilst the Lambert lecture continued with a reading from Geoffrey of Monmouth's *History of the Kings of Britain* in which the famous author mentions Caerleon, the City of the Legions, and identifies it as one of King Arthur's Plenary Courts.

> *Situated as it is in Glamorganshire, on the River Usk, not far from the Severn Sea, in a most pleasant position, and being richer in material wealth than other townships, this city was eminently suitable for such a ceremony (Crowing of King Arthur). The river which I have named flowed by it on one side, and up this the kings and princes who were to come from across the sea could be carried in a fleet of ships. On the other side, which was flanked by meadows and wooded groves, they had adorned the city with royal palaces, and by the gold painted gables of its roofs, it was a match for Rome. What is more, it was famous for its two churches. One of these, built in honour of the martyr Julius, was graced by a choir of most lovely virgins dedicated to God. The second, founded in the name of the blessed Aaron, the companion of Julius, was served by a monastery of canons, and counted as the third metropolitan see of Britain. The city also contained a college of two hundred learned men who were skilled in astronomy and the other arts, and who watched with great attention the courses of the stars and so by their careful computations prophesied for King Arthur any prodigies due at that time. This city, famous for such a wealth of pleasant things, was made ready for the feast. Messengers were sent to the different kingdoms and invitations were delivered to all those who were due to come to the court from the various parts of Gaul and from the near-by Islands in the Sea.*

Rachel returned and sat down to study the menu but Evans was absorbed in the lecture.

"Two hundred men, skilled in astronomy? Why was that?"

This was Dr Lambert's favorite subject.

"Well it is thought that the Silures tribe who had been big in the area for many centuries had their roots in Chaldea and its surrounds. They were experts in navigation and predicting the movement of the heavenly bodies. This had a practical use when travelling by sea and sowing crops but it had a far more esoteric application too. Traditionally, sacred places had been identified and located by reference to the heavens, so for argument's sake, let's take the well known example of the three main pyramids in Egypt being set out on the ground to mirror the Orion Belt. There are plenty of examples in Wales where sacred sites mirror certain maps in the heavens and by using these maps that have been around for over 3000 years in Wales, we can find some very interesting places."

"Is that why magicians say 'as above so below'?"

"Magicians?" Lambert smiled, "That's what the church called the men of science and wisdom in an attempt to write them out of history. We wouldn't call predicting the phases of the Moon magic nowadays would we?"

Evans rubbed his hand over his bald head as if to help the thinking process.

"So, would Geoffrey of Monmouth have known about all this?"

"It's unlikely he would have known more than anecdotal tales. After the Norman invasion the church in its bastardised power-seeking and controlling form really pushed the older beliefs underground although it couldn't kill them off altogether. To get the population to go to church the clergy arranged for carvings of the green man, the three faced goddess and other more ancient indigenous images to be carved into the fabric of some buildings."

Pete and Shorty had excused themselves and went for a pint at the bar. Rachel wanted to order but Lambert was on a roll.

"So do you think that Geoffrey of Monmouth made up the contents of his book?"

Lambert's response was emphatic; "Not everything written by Geoffrey of Monmouth was accurate but, on the whole, he tells us that he presents his 'History' as a serious piece of work and explains that it is only a translation into Latin of an older British work. Actually not much is known about him. He was writing around about 1136 and there's a reference to his book in January 1139, when Henry of Huntingdon, an English chronicler, was shown it during his visit at the Abbey of Bec in Normandy. He had never seen it before and called it 'The Big Book of Geoffrey Artur'. Geoffrey probably called himself Artur because the name was in his family. He was almost certainly of Breton origin, and the name was common in Brittany, whereas it was rare in Wales. He also called himself 'Monemutensis' (a Monmouthian). This is a riddle, because the records concerning him are all from Oxford, where he seems to have lived for about thirty years (c. 1129 to 1155). He mentions Caerleon thirteen times in his 'History' so he may well have spent his childhood in the area riding from Monmouth to Caerleon along the old Roman road that skirts along the river Usk. Writing some time after Geoffrey, Giraldus Cambrensis slated Geoffrey's writings and this may be the root cause why many people think that Geoffrey's work is flawed. Some of the Welsh legends themselves were translated into English by Lady Charlotte Guest and published in the years 1838-1849. These may well have been from very early documents not influenced by the Norman or Breton romances. It's the tale of Gereint, son of Erbin that gives us the clearest picture of Caerleon. 'Caer Llion was the most accessible place in Arthur's dominions, by sea and by land and he gathered about him to that place nine crowned kings who were vassals of his, and along with them earls and barons for those would be his guests at every high festival unless sore straits prevented them. And when he was at Caer Llion holding court, thirteen churches would be occupied with his Masses'. In his 'Le Morte d'Arthur', Malory mentions Caerleon many times but it seems fairly certain he did not actually know the place. Curiously John Leland writing in the late 16th century refers to some archaeological finds with 'certen paintinges on Stonis' and 'a strange disc of the heavens'. Both he, and Thomas Churchyard who published 'The Worthiness of Wales', give a long description of Caerleon which he calls famous but "now of little worth". Clearly there had been a rise and fall in its fortunes. He repeats the well-known tale of the crowning of King Arthur and Guinevere and it's clear that Churchyard firmly believed Geoffrey's tale about King Arthur's court in Caerleon. Actually it was believed by almost everyone at that time."

Meanwhile, Rachel had gone and placed orders for steak and chips. Some days she was a vegetarian and some days she wasn't; today, she wasn't.

Evans thanked her following her return to the table, he could see she was distracted but he wanted to learn more.

"This, 'strange disc of the heavens' what was that all about?"

Dr Lambert motioned for them to draw a little closer, like a story teller getting to the punch line.

"Funny you should pick up on that. It seems from local history that it was found but re-hidden. I think I've worked out where it might be."

Rachel looked at Bryn in an attempt to catch up on the story but Evans just indicated that she should listen.

"Just down the road from here are the remains of an old Castle. This was built on an ancient mound on which once stood the legendary Giants Tower referred to by many very early writers as the place to which Arthur withdrew after his Coronation with his Knights to discuss an answer to a demand from Rome for the customary tribute. In a snub to rival that of the later Henry VIII the tribute was withheld. This also appears to be the very tower that Tennyson tells us was 'Filled with eyes to behold the jousts held in the flat field by the shore of Usk'."

This place has always been an object of special interest to archeologists. By 1839 it had obviously fallen into decay and apparently resembled a gigantic plum pudding surrounded by a moat and topped with trees. Legend had it that the mound was accessed by a huge iron door. The owner at that time searched diligently for years and eventually located an iron door and frame around six feet up from floor level. After much effort the rotted door was removed. The tunnel that was revealed had mostly caved in but they managed to clear a way through. Then it all gets a little odd. Apparently the owner found another door and a stone ossuary in that room. In the ossuary they found a disc, perhaps the very one that Leland had mentioned in his 16th century writings.

"So where is the disc now?" Rachel asked.

"I don't know but tradition tells us that the man who picked the disc up had a fit and went mad. His friend dragged him out of the tunnel leaving the disc and everything else behind. My hunch is that it is still there."

The food finally arrived and the conversation changed to more mundane topics.

Meanwhile, Robin Bryant waited outside the house where Evans and Rachel were staying. He knew they were still at the Hanbury Arms, but the old lady was home. For a professional, he had been careless with Rachel; he wouldn't let that happen again. He nudged the American next to him and they both slipped out of the car and walked to the rear of the house.

"We need a diversion."

"You got it bud, give me ten minutes then go for it."

The steak and chips were delicious and it was a while before Dr Lambert spoke again.

"Damm shame about Morgan and Pender dying in that gas explosion."

"Gas explosion?" Rachel was about to correct him but Evans kicked her ankle under the table and she quickly moved on.

"Guess everyone was looking forward to them coming to the conference?"

"Some will be sad, some will be pleased." Responded Dr Lambert.

"And you?" Evans was intrigued.

Lambert looked directly at Evans.

"Much of their work was great. Of course the huge question everyone wanted answered was whether or not the Cross they found at the dig at St Peter's was genuine and dated to the 6th century. That's why most people have come to the conference and, of course, to see if there was any truth in the ancient rumour that it contained an inscription on the rear which told of the whereabouts of Christ's crucifixion cross and body."

Rachel asked Dr Lambert if he had known Morgan and Pender personally.

"I met them once; they tended to keep themselves to themselves."

Evans took the bull by the horns.

"Do you know anyone who would like to see them dead?"

Lambert looked thoughtful. "Well they upset quite a lot of people with court cases and accusations. They didn't do themselves any favours, you know."

Dr Lambert went back to the earlier conversation.

"I've often wondered if the 'disc of the sky' is still in the mound."

"That would be a great visual for the programme" said Pete and everyone agreed.

"Wow, imagine if we found the disc!" Rachel got carried away with the idea.

Evans wasn't so sure but Dr Lambert was more optimistic. "You guys want a scoop?"

Rachel leaned forward.

"We can get into the mound and probably into the tunnel; they have just started to re-open that dig to co-incide with the conference. Are you guys up for it?"

Evans raised his hands; "Hang on, isn't this illegal, don't we need permission? And we haven't got any equipment."

Lambert downed his whisky; "You saw me talking to a guy when you arrived, right?"

They nodded and he continued; "He is a colleague, Dr David Johnson, he has a van full of gear, we'd planned this little, um, impromptu exploration some time ago but someone got permission before us!"

Rachel looked at Pete and Shorty. Pete smiled; "The camera's in the car, I'm up for it."

Shorty nodded; "Me too."

The American knocked at the front door of the house and awaited a response. Bryant prepared himself to hop over the rear wall and into the back garden. The door opened and an elderly man stood looking at him, Brad smiled; "Good evening sir, it's your lucky day."

He put his foot in the door as the man went to shut it.

"Your wife enquired about a quote for a conservatory last week, and I was in the area so I thought I'd pop and see if it was OK to do the measurements and offer you a price you couldn't refuse."

The man scowled, "She is not my wife; I help to take care of her".

Bryant lept over the wall and into the garden. He could see that the upstairs bathroom window was ajar. He had already noticed that he could reach it from the pitched roof of the kitchen so he took the large grey wheelie bin to the end of the gable and mounted it. Using a down pipe as a lever he was onto the roof and straddling the ridge in no time at all.

Having overheard the conversation the lady of the house had come through to the hallway; "I am sorry I think there has been some mistake, I didn't ask for a quote for a conservatory."

The American looked down at his pad; "This is Camelot isn't it?"

The woman shook her head; "No love, Camelot is a bit further down the road; it's the one with the red roof tiles and round tower on the side."

Brad slapped himself on the head with his open hand;

"I am so sorry, I've been driving around all day I must be tired."

The man went to shepherd him out of the door but the woman was more sympathetic. "That's alright, don't worry. I bet you could do with a cuppa?"

Brad nodded, the ruse had worked.

At the rear of the house Bryant had levered himself through the bathroom window and was tip toeing along the landing.

Dr Lambert, Dr Johnson, Rachel, Evans, Pete and Shorty were tooled up and walking down the High Street. On their left they saw Caerleon House, a large property with imposing sash windows. The courtyard to the rear was the Ffwrwm Arts and Craft Centre where they had been interviewing earlier in the day. It was now quiet and dark. Dr Lambert stopped and motioned towards a gate in the wall on the opposite side of the road. There was no one around as he pushed the heavy old door. It opened with a loud squeak and they all filed through before closing it.

To their right was Mynde House, originally named Castle Villa, a stone house that was built in 1820 by John Jenkins, Tin Plate Master of Ponthir Works and part-owner of Caerleon Works, 1814-1830. It was he who built the very high walls and the battlemented turrets around the four acres of the Motte and Bailey and all that remained of the Castle. It is said he did this to protect himself and his family from possible attack by members of the Chartist movement who had been campaigning throughout the country for the reform of Parliament and the achievement of certain democratic rights.

In the fading light of summer evening they became aware of the tall mound known locally as the Mynde. Soon after the conquest the Norman Lords built a wooden fort on the mound where once a great stone tower had stood. Battles between Welsh and Normans destroyed the Castle on numerous occasions and Brut y Tywysogion, the old Welsh Chronicles, tell that in the year 1171 Iorwerth ab Owain and his two sons destroyed the town of Caerleon and burned the Castle. In 1217 William Marshall, Earl of Pembroke, took Caerleon but it was not until the end of that century, during the lordship of the de Clares, that the town seems to have had a more secure period.

The grounds were quiet. No-one was guarding the archaeological works that were under way. Upturned wheelbarrows and little earth hillocks were strewn all around. There were locks on the metal cages containing tools and on the wooden building that had been erected as a makeshift office.

Gingerly the five of them followed Dr Lambert. They discovered that the current dig had unearthed the old iron door, or more accurately what remained of it. It had been broken down in the earlier exploration. It didn't take Pete and Shorty a moment to move the temporary metal and wooden barrier and soon Dr Lambert and his friend had high power torches blazing down the tunnel illuminating centuries of cobwebs and debris. Pete fired up his camera, mounted a powerful basher light on top and started filming. Shorty kept near with the shotgun microphone on a pole.

There had been nothing much of interest to Bryant amongst the personal effects he found in the rooms of Rachel and Evans. It had, however, been a great chance to plant a couple of microphones with radio transmitters. He left as carefully as he came almost at the same time as Brad was saying his goodbyes downstairs.

In the tunnel the explorers were being careful. They had respect for history, not to mention their own safety. Around twenty six feet into the tunnel amongst the dust, smells and souls of those that had gone before, they found a smattering of pottery, bricks and tiles. Dr Lambert picked them up one by one and shared the finds with Dr Johnson. They looked at each other and nodded.

There was Samian ware from a beaker and some of the tiles had the inscription "Leg II - Aug" impressed upon them linking in to the Roman Legion stationed at Caerleon. Peering ahead they suddenly became aware of another door, one with symbols and embossed carvings on it. Evans made sure his footing was safe before helping Rachel over a pool of water for a closer look. The two professors shone their torches on the intricate designs and Pete and Shorty recorded every detail. Dr Johnson tried to dust off green and orange crustations from the door in the process trying to read an inscription. They could just make out a design of a large female head, around it a mass of embossed lines in the shape of a tree. In the half light only Dr Lambert recognized the figure, it was Asherah, the wife of God!.

Pete asked Lambert to say a few words for the camera and he willingly obliged.

"We are in the heart of the Mystical Mynde, a mysterious mound that stands in the grounds of Mynde House at Caerleon. There have been many stories attached to this place over the centuries mainly connected with the Arthurian Legends. In early times this place may have been a sacred spring or well and used as a meeting place for the famed and secretive Druids. Later it was clearly built over and served as a look out and fortification. In Arthur's time, the 6th century, there was a great tower on this mound which was used as a royal court and later, after the Norman conquest, the Normans erected fortifications here. It was in the ownership of the Morgan family but fell into disrepair in the 14th century. We are standing outside a secret fabled chamber guarded by an ornate bronze door. Folklore tells us that the secret of time itself is kept within. However the secret may well be more down to earth" His pause built tension in the best Hollywood tradition;

"It may well be much more to do with the repression by the church of the fact that God was once thought to have a wife, Asherah. In 1975 a tablet was found in Syria confirming the standing of these mother and father gods and although a photograph exists the tablet itself has long since disappeared"

Evans put his shoulder against the door and heaved, the solid metal didn't budge. Dr Lambert looked at the array of letters around the border, they were written in a strange script. He ran his fingers backwards along the worn text using the torchlight at an angle to get a 3D image.

"It's Coelbren" he said triumphantly.

"Coelbren, isn't that the alphabet Morgan and Pender talked about, is it real?" Rachel asked.

Dr Lambert cleared his throat and Pete swung the camera in his direction, sensing that something important was coming.

"It's real alright and most certainly not a fake as many academics would have us believe. That nonsense all started when G J Williams alleged that the Coelbren alphabet of South East Wales was forged around AD 1800. Actually, Julius Caesar described the alphabet in his De Bello Galico in 54 BC. And Ammianus Marcellinus also described it. But it gets better than that, much better. In 1946 Mohammed Ali discovered 128 books in 14 leather satchels at Nag Hamadi in Egypt, probably buried before AD 400. One of the books, The book of Massanes contains a description of the same alphabet. Welsh poets writing pre AD 1367, 1425, 1450, 1470, 1580, and so on, all speak of the alphabet - allegedly forged in 1800! Several ancient stones dating from circa 600-1200 carry letters of the alphabet. I could go on but I think you get the point."

They did.

Evans was now joined by Shorty and Rachel who were trying to push the door open. Dr Lambert motioned for them to back off. He was running his torch backwards and forwards around the coelbren letters. After contemplating for a few moments he stood up to the door and pressed six of the letters. For a moment nothing happened and then there was a great rumbling and creaking sound accompanied by years of dust and grime. In this Indiana Jones moment the door opened very, very slowly as if some ancient mechanism had been sprung. They all looked at him wondering how he had managed it. Lambert obliged.

"Asherah is not traditionally thought of as a Christian figure but the early original Christians saw her as representing 'sovereign female wisdom'. In Sanskrit she is *Majahabe*, in Greek *Metis*, and in Egyptian *Met* or *Maat*. The inscription around the door says, 'by the name of God you shall enter'. I looked for the name of God which was in those days likely to have been known to the ancient Druid priests as Eli Ner. I just identified the correct Coelbren letters and pressed them".

Pete was smiling from behind the eyepiece of his camera, this was a real scoop. They all looked on in surprise but were even more impressed as they entered the chamber.

In the torch lights they saw the faded red painted walls with green and gold borders. Across the room huge pillars could be seen holding up arched ornate brickwork ceilings. As their eyes became more accustomed to the light they moved slowly around, gazing upwards as they went. Across the domed flaking ceiling they could make out stars and constellations. The remains of paintings of large flying swans seem to surround them. The whole space looked like an area for bathing and purification. In marble plunge pools, now dry, were giant bronze drainage lids each with the head of Asherah upon them. On the walls were paintings of beautiful women bathing and sitting together, some with children at their breasts, some sitting with swans. Dr Johnson identified Isis and Apis. Evans' blood ran cold when he looked at a very large painting of a beautiful woman with two babies, one at each breast. Her skin looked fair and her hair was long and golden like the sunset. Behind her appeared a country scene with two mounds and a large swan in flight. Around her neck was a pendant. At her feet he could make out the name but not what the rest of the inscription said. Pete was filming. Dr Lambert nodded to Dr Johnson who spoke apprehensively.

"This chamber appears to be dedicated to female energy as the source of wisdom and knowledge and the mother of its continuance in the world. There are wonderful paintings of goddesses and a magnificent painting of Maria Magdalena, a person we know better as Mary Magdalen. At each breast she feeds a baby and below reads the inscription, Maria Magdalena, whose earthly body lies buried at this place. The swan is important because it symbolizes the ability of the self-realized master to separate truth from the insubstantiality of fiction. Paramahamsa in Sanskrit means supreme swan, an enlightened being, in this context maybe Maria herself."

Rachel spluttered and Evans nearly choked.

"Jesus Christ, you are joking?"

Dr Johnson was shaking, but definitely not joking.

Rachel recovered her nerve and went over to Dr Lambert.

"Is this the place where that chap you told us about found the Disc of the Heavens?"

Dr Lambert nodded.

They all glanced around the room, Pete filming as he went. Towards the back of the chamber there was a pile of smashed pots. There were rectagonal stone boxes and round containers, some with writing on but all in fragments;

"I have a feeling that if Mary Magdalen's bones were ever here they have long since been robbed together with everything else of any value." Dr Johnson sighed.

Just then Evans spotted a glint on the floor; in fact they all seemed to see it at once. It appeared to have its own glow, it's own light... maybe it was just a reflection? Carefully they surrounded it and looked down. It was a pendant on a chain about four inches across, in the torch light it looked bronze, gold and silver. The bronze had gone a dark greeney blue resembling the night sky and the gold and silver shapes seemed to represent the stars, the sun and the moon.

"It's the Sky Disc, it must be." Exclaimed Dr Lambert, barely containing his excitement.

Johnson went to pick it up but Lambert stopped him.

"Remember the story of the chap who died instantly when he tried to take it?"

Rachel squatted down to take a closer look. She took a pen from her pocket and slipped it under the disc, flipping it over with a flick of her wrist. She looked up at the painting of Mary Magdalen. It was the same disc as she was wearing, had this belonged to Mary? The excitement was too much for her, she reached out and picked it up. They all tried to stop her but it was too late. As she held it she felt a sudden shock through her body. For a moment she was elsewhere in time, she was looking into a pool of water, the disc around her neck reflecting in the water. The vision only lasted a moment. No one else had noticed but they all breathed a sigh of relief as she turned to them.

"See, it was an old wives tale about the disc bringing bad luck!"

Suddenly there were footsteps in the corridor. Powerful flashlights criss crossed the chamber, shouting echoed like thunder. Evans grabbed hold of Rachel and pulled her behind a large pillar and then into a dark crevice.

"Police, you are under arrest."

Some jostling followed.

"I, I can explain...I am a delegate at the conference." Dr Lambert stuttered.

The rather large policeman in charge and his men roughly gathered up Drs Lambert and Johnson, camera Pete and Shorty and led them away.

"I am sure you can explain sir, you'll have plenty of time to do that."

Rachel and Evans peeped around the pillars just in time to watch the torchlights fading down the tunnel and to hear the protestations grow softer and softer. Soon they were left in the dark. At least they hadn't shut the solid bronze door on the way out.

- 39 -

St Govans Point, Pembrokeshire
31st July 2009

William awoke with a start. He looked at his watch; it was 7am. The sun was bright but the cool of morning and the occasional splash from the sea spray made him shiver. As his eyes adjusted to the light he saw a large white swan tread water from the beach and take off into the pink dawn. He moved to stand up but he faltered slightly. There were two or three white feathers on the ground next to him and the warmth of the swan's body lingered on his chest. The bump on his head ached mercilessly. He must have slipped and fallen onto the rocks the night before? He certainly didn't remember that, in fact he couldn't remember much at all.

Gingerly he made his way down to the shoreline where he had seen the woman the night before. A little gust and the incoming tide forced a wave to crash nearby making him turn his head. When he turned back a white swan's feather fell from the sky and landed in his hand. He examined it carefully and stroked it lovingly. Part of him wanted to stay and try to recall the events of the evening before, maybe even the life before, but hunger and thirst got the better of him. He pulled himself together before making his way back up the path, through the church and to his car.

A military police patrol car was parked nearby. As he opened his car door two officers approached him. His heart was pounding, what now, he thought?

"Good morning sir, I am afraid we'll have the ask you to leave the area, we'll be using the firing range for manoeuvers soon."

William breathed a sigh of relief and slid in the car.

"Just a moment, sir."

William jumped.

"Are you OK?"

The policeman was looking at the rather nasty bump on Williams head.

"Oh, yes, yes thank you, I, I just fell and banged my head."

The officers assumed wrongly that William had drunk too much the night before and had slept rough. They smiled knowingly as William drove off, waving.

Back in the village the little green wooden tea house was securely locked. The St Govan's pub looked asleep and he swore he could hear snoring from the nearby cottages. He was ravenously hungry and his throbbing headache made it hard for him to concentrate. As he eased the old car around a bend on the way out of the village he saw an elderly man slumped beside the road. He stopped the car and rushed over to help him. It was hard to see the man properly under a long navy duffle coat three sizes too big for him. He looked at his graying stubble and gnarled face. There was something familiar about the eyes. He knelt down beside the man and removed his hood. He could tell from the strong smell of alcohol on this breath that he was still breathing.

William held the man's hand and squeezed lightly. The man coughed and stared at him with those eyes, those clear blue eyes. William took out a tissue from his trouser pocket and wiped the man's dribble from the corner of his slightly trembling pale pink mouth.

"Are you OK my friend?" He whispered.

The man gripped William's hand and pulled himself up to sit on the grass bank, trying to gather his senses.

"I love sleeping out under the stars; it makes me feel closer to home."

The man looked at William knowingly, he recovered very quickly, almost as if he had been waiting;

"You took your time, do you fancy joining me for a fry-up?"

William was taken aback but the offer of breakfast was impossible to resist.

"You must be a mind reader!" He held out his hand; "Hi, I'm William."

The man laughed;

"Yes, yes, of course you are, now damn well help me up if you want to eat!"

The eccentric man was hauled to his feet obviously none the worse for his ordeal. He started walking along a little track way that appeared from the hedgerow adjacent to the road. He paused to look back;

"Well come on then William, my place is this way!"

Uncertain about what to make of his situation, William decided to go with it. He locked the car and followed the man down the narrow track towards an isolated old stone cottage covered in ivy. An old Land Rover sat in front of a tumble down barn. Two dogs sat in the front seats watching. How hadn't he noticed the house in the trees earlier?

The front door was unlocked, the man pushed it inwards and made straight for the wood burning stove where a kettle was waiting for the heat. He turned and looked at William.

"I've always got the kettle ready."

William smiled as he looked for evidence of modernity. From the flag stone floor to the oak beams, he could find no evidence that the twentieth century had arrived. The man washed his hands in the deep white butler sink with cold water poured from a jug. He then took several thick slices of bacon out of a mesh fronted wooden cabinet and placed them on the griddle alongside some great hunks of bread. The armoma of bacon on the griddle was enough to make a vegetarian salivate.

"My God that smells good."

The elderly man ignored the comment; he had other things on his mind.

"Did you see her?"

"See her?" William was taken aback.

"Gwenhwyfar….did you see her?"

The man asked again as he turned the bacon.

William looked puzzled.

"According to the ancient Welsh *Mabinogion* (called *Culhwch and Olwen*) she's often seen down there…. her name means White Spirit or White Lady".

"Down where?" William wasn't quite with it.

The man handed him a mass of bacon wrapped in chunks of toasted bread on a willow patterned plate.

"Down by the Chapel, where you spent the night?"

William snatched the food, he hadn't meant to but he was so hungry, he bit into the sandwich and savored the texture, the taste the smell.

"Oh, that's just wonderful, thank you."

The man nodded;

"I'll leave your tea on the side, there's a potion of feverfew in it to ease your headache."

William watched the man place the white enamel mug on the table, the food was starting to work its magic on William's blood sugar levels. How did he know where he had spent the night and all about his headache?

"I'm not sure, I did have rather a strange thing happen though."

The man pulled up a rush-seated elmwood chair towards the oak table and motioned William to do the same.

"What did you see lad, what did you see?"

William felt discombobulated. He was being interrogated about White Spirits as he ate breakfast in an ancient cottage belonging to an old man who he had found sleeping by the side of the road.

"I went down to the church for a look around and a bit of peace. Looking out to sea I saw a figure in silhouette, I went out of the church towards the beach to get a better look. I couldn't see her clearly but it was certainly a woman, with gorgeous long hair. At one point, she turned towards me, she was beautiful. I felt this pull like a magnet; it was irresistible. In the half light it looked and felt as if we were literally floating towards each other. Slowly I became aware that she was glistening white, a brilliant white glow like a tunnel that leads to heaven. Together we seemed to move across time. Silly really, I hadn't even been drinking."

The man smiled;

"There's no doubt about it lad, you've seen her all right, I knew there was something a bit special about you when I first saw you."

Again William didn't put two and two together, how could he have known that this man, a man who can change his look like a chameleon to suit his environment was the Wandering Jew that had saved him in London.

"Gwenhwyfar, that sounds like Guinevere."

"Are you into the Arthurian stuff lad?"

"Ever since I can remember." William replied.

"And probably well before." The old man mumbled, too low for William to catch. He seemed to know a lot about Guinevere and explained how she was important in her own right, not just as King Arthur's Queen.

"I suppose our perceptions of Guinevere come from Alfred Tennyson, who created her as a symbol of queenly purity and goodness".

The man thought for a moment, wiping a slither of bacon from his chin;

"The early legends speak of a much more complex character. Guinevere supposedly lived as a ward at the court of Duke Cador of Cornwall. She came from a noble family and was a sort of lady-in-waiting when she met the young King Arthur. In the ancient Welsh Mabinogion tale called Culhwch and Olwen, Guinevere is called 'Gwenhwyfar' or 'Gwenhwyvar' which means White Phantom. It states that she was the daughter of Gogrfan, Gogrvan or Ocvran and she had a sister, named Gwenhwyach".

William was fascinated by the story but also by the fact that this scruffy old man knew so much about old legends. The man was looking steadily at William, sensing his feelings and reactions. William felt uncomfortable under the scrutiny and tried not to look him in the eye as he continued:

"In the poem known as the Welsh Triad, King Arthur has three queens; all named Guinevere or Gwenhwyfar. The first was the daughter of Gwent (Cywryd), the second was the daughter of Gwythyr son of Greidiawl, and the third was the daughter of Gogfran or Gogrvan the Giant".

Suddenly it seemed as if someone had turned on a light bulb in William's mind;

"Three wives all called Gwenhwyfar, that's just too much of a co-incidence, unless…"

The man looked expectantly at William; he knew that he had worked it out for himself;

"…unless Gwenhwyfar was a title given to the queen."

The old man knew that William was nearly there, he just needed a little more help.

"Some ancient legends suggest that Arthur's three wives formed a sort of female trinity, far more than simply a queen, she was also a goddess with triple attributes, a female mirror image of the father son and Holy Ghost. For Arthur to become King of Britain, maybe he had to wed or embrace the concept of the female trinity to ensure a balanced peace, prosperity and abundance for the Kingdom."

"That sounds very pagan, wasn't Arthur a strong Christian?"

"Since when have you believed everything you read William? The old man scorned. "We are talking of the 6th Century, a time when there was great turmoil in religion. Arthur would have been much more familiar with the old ways and the true Christianity brought to this little island in AD 37. The new 6th century teachings of St Augustine or St Patrick were certainly a Paulite bastardisation of the truth. Chances are that he would have been taking the good from both the old Druid lore and the original early teachings."

"You mean hedging his bets?"

William understood. "That would make perfect sense. It crossed my mind last night when I saw the woman on the rock at the beach, to me it felt as if she was the mother, the lover, the daughter and the Holy Spirit, but, but…"

The old man was stroking his stubble encouraging William to continue but William doubted himself and his own intuition.

"But that was just an hallucination, a dream brought on by thirst and hunger, a fever or something."

"Was it William, how can you be so sure, what is reality?"

William placed his head in his hands and rested them upon his knee;

"I can't be sure, what IS reality?"

The man rested a warm hand on William's bowed head sending a tingle of comfort and realization down his spine.

"Sometimes reality is whatever we want it to be. Another cuppa lad?"

William nodded approvingly and pulled out the white swan's feather from his pocket, the one that had fallen into his lap on the beach. The man saw it and froze. It was glowing with an ethereal white light which grew ever stronger, illuminating the room in a luminous fog. William was speechless as he gazed between the feather and the man.

"May I?" asked the old fellow, his frail hand trembled.

As William handed him the feather, the man's body started to shake and he had to sit down. He gripped it tightly and stared wide-eyed at the bright blue and white lights that were now emanating from its tips like sparks of static electricity. William watched transfixed as the man's body convulsed, slowly at first and then faster and faster until his head, limbs and arms were just a blur.

Now the room seemed filled with ethereal whisps of light. William thought he heard the beating of a swan's wings coming in to land across water. As the man shook he unconsciously traced out shapes with the quill. Firstly he formed the shape of a swan that seemed almost to materialize. This then morphed into the shape of a woman; her long white robes and titian hair gently blowing in a psychic breeze. The vision lasted a matter of moments, like a projected hologram of esoteric reality.

Far from feeling afraid William was calm and serene. She was the most beautiful woman that he had ever seen. She glided closer to him until he could smell lavender and lilies, roses and daffodils, the sea and the rain. In her ambience there was everything and everywhere. He was entrapped in the breeze that brought her there. When she spoke, her voice was the sweetest sound. She read William's thoughts;

"Yes, William I am Gwynfar, I am Asherah, I am Hypatia, I am Bridget, I am Artemis and Aphrodite, I am Mary, I am Isis, I am the mother, I am the daughter, I am the holy spirit, I am the lover, I am the sacred feminine of everyone and everything that has ever lived, I am the wisdom you are setting free."

William fell to his knees, humbled by her presence. She placed her hands on his head as the old man had done shortly before and the energy rushed through him. It was as if he had been connected to the creative source of all things. With his eyes closed he was transported to the very point of creation. He swirled with mists and lights in the darkness of space and time, he was on mountains and in valleys, on lakes and in forests among animals and peoples. He was in heaven and Babylon, in Jerusalem and Avalon, flying with swans from the mists of days passed through to the vibrations of this moment.

It seemed as if he was within her, surrounded by her as they travelled through time. Her hair curled around him holding him safe from harm. They were rushing over hills and woodlands, along streams and under bridges, along secret footpaths and alleyways. Then, suddenly they were standing before a large flat faced rock. It was around twenty feet high. Looking left and right William could see an overgrown pathway amongst some trees. As he observed the rock face, part of it looked as if it was man-made. This was a cave that had been walled up. On the front of the cave, about nine feet from the ground there was the embossed relief of a cross, at the bottom were two stepping stones. In his mind he saw a monk walking down the pathway, stopping before the cross, standing on the steps and reaching up to touch it then withdrawing to kneel in front of the cave to pray.

In an instant the scene and the woman had evaporated and William was left dazed. He looked bewilderedly around. He was sitting holding his thumping head in what was left of the cottage. The property had obviously been derelict for many years. What remained of the walls looked like jaggered teeth. He could hear the birds singing in the early morning air and in the distance he heard the heartbeat roll of the waves upon the shore.

Where was the white lady, the old man, more than that, where was the house!

At his feet he saw a fragment of a willow patterned plate. It looked like the plate from which he had just eaten breakfast. He smacked his lips and the taste of the bacon and tea was most certainly still lingering. William searched for a rational explanation but there wasn't one. Maybe this was what 'going mad' really felt like?

He had to get back to the others, this sojourn to be alone had confused him more than being with them and he was now convinced he was ill.

He checked his watch, it was still 7am; time had stood still. He checked his pulse, it was racing, sweat poured from his brow and was trickling down behind his glasses even though he felt ice cold. The pain in his head and stomach were excruciating. He hadn't taken his medication for at least 24 hours, had he?

-40-

Caerleon area, Wales
31ˢᵗ July 2009

Pete, Shorty, Dr Lambert and Dr Johnson had spent an extremely uncomfortable night at the Police station on Cardiff Road. Each had their own cell and each had time to reflect on the night before. There was no denying what they had seen but Pete's broadcast tape had been confiscated despite his verbose and aggressive attempts to retrieve it.

The rather large sergeant entered his cell and deliberately dropped Pete's cheese roll on the floor so that it splattered all over the gritty dirty remains that lingered there. He also dropped the film cassette in front of Pete and stamped on it with his size 12 heavy duty Dr Martens until the contents were in tatters and the plastic cassette shattered.

"Whoops a daisy boyo." he said thrusting a mug of tea in the cameraman's face so that most of it splashed down his shirt.

Pete grunted and tried to restrain himself. He knew that the pictures from the tunnel and the chamber were lost, depriving the world of a vital part of the jigsaw of life. Ignorance, as he had witnessed first hand was alive and well and living in this part of Her Majesty's police force.

Rachel and Evans had suffered a restless haunted night. Evans had spent most of it smoking near the window watching Rachel toss and turn on her bed. Breakfast was a sombre affair and they ate in silence looking out over the back garden. Evan's aunt had spoilt them with a full Welsh breakfast including lava bread. She wanted to chat but could see that this wasn't the time so she picked up the remote and switched on the local news. Rachel cringed, feeling sure there'd be something about the incident last night. Fortunately she was wrong and Evans went back to eating his sausages and beans.

The phone rang, it was the police.

"Evans, these bits of crap are ready for the toilet, you can come and get them before we flush them out… oh, and don't even think of shitting down here on our patch again, you hear?"

Evans looked at Rachel who had heard the aggressive voice on the other end of the phone; "Charming, friends of yours?"

Evans didn't answer but his face went pale.

"I'll go and pick the guys up, it's the least I can do."

-40-

Haverfordwest, Wales
31ˢᵗ July 2009

William had no idea why he was in a bed at Withybush General Hospital in Haverfordwest or how he had got there. The last thing he remembered was getting into his car and setting off for Caerleon to meet up with Rachel and Evans. He shivered from head to toe as he drifted in and out of consciousness. He felt so cold yet his brow was on fire and his head ached so badly that he was sure he was going to die. He tasted the tell tale iron of blood on his lips.

Natasha sat on the side of the bed holding his hand and constantly placing and replacing a cold flannel over his troubled brow. The police called her at 7.30am and she had driven the 241 miles from central London in record time, arriving at the hospital in exactly four hours and forty seven minutes.

The doctor arrived, pulled the curtain around the bed and asked Natasha if she was William's next of kin. She said she was, well, she might as well have been, there was no one else. "What's wrong with him?"

The doctor was checking his pulse as he watched a monitor to which William was attached.

"An eye witness said he swerved to avoid a swan and ended up in a ditch. He doesn't appear to have any serious injuries but his mind is racing." He felt William's stomach and then flashed a light into his eyes to check for a response, his eyes didn't seem co-ordinated.

"Does he take drugs?"

"Absolutely not" Natasha was emphatic, "He hates what drugs do to people."

The doctor looked apologetic;

"Widely dilated pupils under semi shut tight lids, chronic headache and pain, shivering and a high temperature; my best guess is that he has been poisoned."

"Poisoned! I thought he'd had a road accident!"

"Yes he did, the paramedics pulled him out of a ditch near St Govans but there is something else going on in his system."

Natasha looked thoughtful; "He, he told me he was on some sort of medication."

The Doctor looked carefully at Natasha, before responding. "We found some mild sedatives in his pocket".

"Sedatives? Do you mean there's nothing really wrong with him, nothing to make him see apparitions?"

This attracted the doctors attention; "Does he believe he sees and hears spirits?"

Natasha nodded; "Sometimes he says he does, especially lately."

The doctor picked up his communicator and dialed a number. "Yes, it's urgent, I need a brain scan, top priority."

"A brain scan, why?"

The doctor hunched his shoulders and avoided giving her information that would only concern her. He suggested she go and get a drink whilst he carried out the tests.

Natasha looked at William, his eyes were rolling, half asleep as if he was dreaming heavily, his limbs twitched involuntarily. A nurse and a porter arrived and wheeled him down the corridor and out of sight.

On Caldey, Father Everson had just finished hiding a few of his most treasured possessions, leaving instructions for the brothers and packing his bag to leave for the rendezvous with William in Caerleon as promised. It would be lovely to catch a few days of the Arthurian Conference and equally good to meet up with William again. Something about him felt close, like the bond between father and son.

Natasha went to have a cup of tea amongst the visitors and the walking wounded. She picked up the local paper and read about how people caught sickness, diarrhea, MRSA and other viruses from hospital wards. The article was called 'Hospital Lottery' and she shuddered at the thought. Just maybe, though, a creaking unhealthy health system was better than none at all, at least with a lottery there are some winners which is more than some countries have.

She made her way back to the ward in time to see William being wheeled back into position and made comfortable. He had been quicker than anticipated. The doctor approached her and she steeled herself for the worst.

"There is a slight shadow on the X-ray we are concerned about but I am waiting for the CT scan to be analysed. I don't think it's anything too major at the moment but it will depend exactly how it is sitting. We are also looking at the possibility of Charles Bonnet Syndrome."

Natasha expected more of an explanation, he didn't dissappoint;

"It's macular degeneration; it makes some people think they are seeing things."

Natasha asked what she could do and was advised to just sit and talk with him even though he wasn't responding. The doctor's beeper went and he left in a hurry.

William was hallucinating and talking gibberish, the voice didn't sound at all like his.

"William, come on William, stop messing about, I need you." Natasha whispered.

There was genuine feeling in her voice. What was she saying? She hadn't ever really needed anyone before. A tear formed in her eye which she quickly wiped away. William stopped shaking for a moment as if part of him had heard her but his eyes were still mostly closed and moving rapidly as he spoke.

"Mute swans are monogamous; their pair-bond lasts for life. The males establish a territory in spring and vigorously defend it against intruders. In it the pair makes a large nest out of reeds, sticks, roots and aquatic plants, lined with down. In April or May the female lays 4-7 greenish-grey eggs. They are incubated mainly by the female, during 34-38 days. The chicks are born with feathers and with their eyes open, they start following their parents after only a day. The parents will sometimes 'give them a ride' on their backs or under their wings. The young are able to fly at 100-120 days of age, but they will stay with their parents until winter. During the entire breeding period, the adult swans are very aggressive and may attack even humans or dogs that come to close to the nest or the young. They can be found in most of Europe, parts of Turkey, Russia, Kazakhstan, Siberia and China. They have also been introduced into many parts of the world, like North America and New Zealand. The Mute swan is one of the largest birds still capable of flight, reaching a length of 140-160 cm, including tail and neck, a wing span of 200-240 cm and a weight of 8-12 kg. The young usually have a dull grey brown colour at birth and a dark grey bill, but later they become completely white, and their bill becomes orange with a black knob".

He rattled off these obscure facts as if he was reading from Wikipedia and Natasha became increasingly upset by his bizarre behavior. Just as he fell silent a nurse came to check the machine. She offered Natasha a comforting smile and reassured her that William was going to recover. She leant over to put a drip into his canular and Natasha noticed her name tag.

"Thanks, Sister Herbert, I was quite worried."

"You love this man don't you Natasha, he is very special."

The nurse seemed to know her feelings better than Natasha knew her own and she nodded, almost afraid to admit it.

"When we hide our love, love hides from us."

It was a profound thing to say. How did she know Natasha's name?

"A minute ago he was talking about swans. Why would he do that, do you think?"

"I don't think HE is." She replied and held Natasha's gaze.

"I think someone else is speaking through him."

"What?" Natasha shuddered; "The doctors are worried there's something wrong with his brain, are you suggesting he's possessed?"

Sister Herbert placed one hand on William's head and one on his solar plexus and he stopped shaking.

"No, no, not possessed in the way you think, but someone is trying to give us information through William, if you like he is being used a channel. Come and hold his hand again Natasha."

The nurse closed her eyes to concentrate as if she was praying, after a few moments she spoke;

"You are welcome my friend, please realise where you are and do not harm this good man through whom you speak."

There was a short silence before the voice continued through William;

"Because of its pure white colour, the swan is a symbol of light in many parts of the world. Though in some regions it was considered a feminine symbol of the moon, in most it was a masculine symbol of the sun. In ancient Greece the swan was linked to Apollo, the god of the Sun. The god Zeus took the shape of a swan to get close to Leda, with whom he had fallen in love. And in Celtic myth, a pair of swans steered the Sunboat across Cygnus to heaven. As a feminine symbol, the swan represents intuition and gracefulness, this man is a gatekeeper of the destiny of mankind and his child will be the special one."

Natasha looked around her, there was a mist rising from the floor, the nurse seemed to be enveloped in it. Natasha had read about such happenings amongst the Shamans of the forest where she grew up, she plucked up the courage to ask; "Who are you my friend?"

The request was ignored as the voice resumed with a slow distinct rhythmic breathing. Now the voice from William was almost the same as the voice of the nurse, their lips were moving in time.

"The very first images of Jesus Christ showed him as both male and female in the image of the Sun god Apollo....

Apollo was the god of the Sun and Jesus Christ was the god of the Sun. Apollo was shown as having a golden halo of the sun and Jesus Christ was shown as having a golden halo of the sun. Under the Vatican there is a mosaic well hidden showing Jesus with a halo riding a chariot out of the sun.... As a symbol in alchemy, the swan was neither masculine nor feminine, but rather symbolized the hermaphrodite or 'the marriage of the opposites', fire and water. It was an emblem of mercury, as it was white and very mobile, because of its wings. In Celtic and Siberian culture, stories exist of swans taking off their plumage and turning into maidens. As a dream symbol, the swan can signify self transformation, intuition, sensitivity, and even the soul, the 'higher Self' within each person. The Swan totem is associated with love, inspiration, intuition, self-transformation, gracefulness and beauty, and also with travelling to the Otherworld. As a water bird, it is also connected with emotions. Swans can help you with seeing the inner beauty in yourself and others, developing your intuition, accepting transformations and balancing your emotions providing the male and female energy in harmony wherever it is needed."

Natasha was dumb-struck but Sister Herbert wasn't phased at all. It was as if this sort of thing happened in NHS hospitals every day.

"Thank you for this wisdom and knowledge my friend, I ask in the name of the force that created us all, who are you?"

William's breathing began to ease slightly and a calmness descended.

"You will know me as the Wandering Jew, your own father now in heaven."

Sister Herbert ran her hands across William's brow straightening stray wisps of his hair. He sighed deeply. The nurse stepped back and smiled at Natasha who gently squeezed William's hand. There was a smell of ether as the sister seemed to glide closer to William, lean over him and whisper what looked like blue smoke into his ear,

"Time to wake up William"

There was a pause as if time stood still. Sister Herbert turned to Natasha, smiled then walked off. William sat up, coughing and spluttering. Natasha nearly fainted.

"Hey, Nats, what are you doing here? Come to that, where am I? Christ the girl, is she alright?"

Natasha threw her arms around him.

"Oh William, William, you are alright!"

William looked around him, at the canular in his arm and the connection to the heart monitor which had resumed a regular plodding beat.

"Don't you ever, ever do that again William, do you hear?" Her anger sprang from her genuine worry and concern.

The doctor came back and was shocked to see William sitting upright.

"How are you feeling?"

William looked at him and then Natasha;

"Great, I feel great, lovely dreams, but what about the girl, is she OK? I tried to swerve out of the way, did I miss her?"

The doctor placed a hand on his shoulder;

"It's OK William, there was no girl, you must have been mistaken; a witness said you swerved to avoid a swan that had flown in front of your car."

"A swan?"

Natasha took his hand.

"It's OK Will; it's going to be OK."

The doctor looked at Natasha; "What happened, did he just come round?"

"Yes," she nodded, "sister Herbert attached a drip to his canular and rested her hands on his forehead and stomach and then he just woke up." Natasha thought it best to miss out the psychic bit in case the doctor thought she too should be admitted.

The doctor looked at her in disbelief, not least because there was no nursing sister of that name on duty at the time. William coughed to attract the doctor's attention.

"Is there any hope for me doctor?" He was joking but the doctor's response was quite serious.

"We think you have a gliomas growing. They tend to develop from the glial cells in the brainstem. We need to ascertain how quickly it is growing and we can only do that by looking at the cells under a microscope. It is likely to be malignant but some are much slower growing than others."

William looked at Natasha, they were both stunned and Natasha was becoming tearful.

"If you have been having hallucinations or hearing things, feeling a bit dizzy or sick then the chances are it's affecting your senses and the sooner we do an operation the more chance you might have of pulling through."

William looked at him and then at Natasha.

"Come on Nats, we can't sit around here all day, we have to help Rachel and Evans."

Natasha opened her mouth to speak but William pre-empted her;

"I might as well try and do something useful with my life, or what may be left of it!"

Natasha smiled; she had always admired William's care for others over himself. To her he was a knight in shining armour, someone she could look up to and trust and that was very rare indeed.

Of course, neither of them could possibly know that this shadow on the brain was exactly the same as the problem that was also growing in the mind of Father Everson.

The doctor was speechless.

-41-

Caerleon, Wales
31st July 2009

Reluctantly, Evans left Rachel alone at his aunt's house whilst he went to collect Camera Pete, and the others from the constabulary. They complained to him about their treatment at the hands of the police but Evans was less than sympathetic. He wanted to get back to Rachel as soon as possible. They had been released without charge but the brush with the law had definitely left them shaken. Evans was curious about why the sergeant had destroyed the tape but left the broadcast camera untouched. Who, he wondered was pulling his strings?

"Someone's obviously very tetchy about this mound dig and what is being uncovered." said Pete.

"It's because it doesn't conform with what the manufactured history tells us." Johnson was familiar with multiple historical conspiracies.

Dr Lambert accused him of sounding like Morgan and Pender but he just shrugged his shoulders;

"Well maybe they knew something we don't!"

Evans had to agree;

"You didn't tell the police that Rachel and I were there with you did you?"

They hadn't but Evans was puzzled.

"I'm just wondering how the hell they knew of our connection, where to ring or that I'd be there."

It suddenly dawned on Evans that someone must have been watching or bugging the house, someone in cahoots with the local police.

"We've got to go, Rachel may be in danger, I knew I shouldn't have left her there"

In Sheffield, Roger Felix had loaded an overnight bag into his blue Honda Civic, picked some CDs for the journey and was setting off to give his reluctant lecture to the conference at Caerleon. He had decided to include much of what he knew Morgan and Pender had wanted to cover. Sure, it was a risk but then so is crossing the road. He called Rachel earlier to let her know he was on his way. The journey would take him around four hours with a coffee break.

Back where Rachel was staying there was a friendly knock on the door. Thinking it was the old lady, she quickly went to answer. In a flash a man twisted her arm around her back and pushed her face down on to the bed. She hadn't even had a chance to catch a glimpse of him but she could smell body odour and bad breath. The man was fat but strong, his accent eastern European, possibly Russian.

"Where's the St Peter's cross and the disc?"

Rachel feigned innocence;

"What do you mean?"

The man pulled her arm further up her back;

"I can easily break this arm in four places, is that what you want?"

Rachel considered screaming but thought the man might panic. It was hard enough gagging for breath with her face pushed into the duvet.

"Of course it isn't what I want you bastard, let me go."

The man held her with one hand and removed a hood from his pocket with the other. With minimal effort he slipped it over her head as she tried to struggle. He noticed that her dressing gown had ridden up over her thighs as her legs threshed over the bed. Surely someone would hear the commotion. The man ran his free hand up the back of her thighs, between her legs and into the soft moist space between her hips. He grabbed her tight and squeezed, she jumped and moaned in pain but the noise was muffled by the hood and covers. Rachel struggled but the more she did the more the man squeezed.

"Ready to co-operate yet Ms Abel...or do you like it this rough?"

"How do you know my name you moron?" She responded with vigour through the dark mask.

He squeezed and twisted forcing his fingers inside her. She felt hot, faint, and helpless."

"Alright, alright, it's over there, the damn thing is over there under my jeans on the chair, just leave me alone."

The man removed his hand and sniffed his fingers;

"Umm sweet, there, that wasn't so hard was it?"

She still felt his weight upon her and the pressure on her shoulder was making her arm go numb. He forced her face further into the bedclothes. She heard the zip of his trouser fly and felt a knee between her thighs forcing her legs apart.

"It's a real pleasure meeting you Rachel, at least it will be. You can struggle more if you want, I like it when you struggle."

She was suffocating but kept up the fight. Mercifully, she heard Evans call up the stairs, she tried to shout back but it was impossible. Her attacker was totally pissed off, he hadn't had his pleasure and neither did he have what he had really come for. Rezipping his fly he rushed to the chair.

Relieved, Rachel turned over, knelt upright, pulled off the mask and saw her attacker. He looked as monstrous as he behaved.

"Bad move, now I have to kill you."

Rachel could hear Evans' footsteps rushing up the stairs, the man levelled his silenced gun at her and eased his finger on the trigger. Evans stormed into the room. The door caught the man's arm and the shot embedded in the wall opposite.

The momentum threw both men to the floor. Evans' hand was like a vice around the man's wrist as he struggled to point the gun away from Rachel. Their flaying over the bedroom floor was like a Catherine wheel firework going off with no pivotal point to revolve around. Rachel dived behind the bed for cover, screaming for help as shots rang out.

Evans managed to smash the man's hand over the arm of a wooden chair and he grimaced showing a mouth of rotten teeth. The gun flew across the floor but the attacker raised his knee and caught Evans squarely in the testicles knocking the wind out of him. As they both scrambled to their feet Evans took a powerful right hand across the face and a kick to the stomach which winded him, forcing him to bend in two;

"You're dead old man" he pulled a knife from his sock.

Although Evans was doubled in pain he recovered enough to dodge the first blow but the man immediately turned the knife in his hand and slashed the other way in one slick movement. A trickle of blood ran across Evan's hand. As the policeman swung and missed the man nutted him on the top of the head making him stagger and his vision blurred. The attacker grinned as he moved to thrust the knife in a killing blow. Suddenly everything stood still. The whole room froze. No one had heard the crack from the gun. Rachel was shaking, she dropped the weapon and it hit the floor at the same time as the dead man.

Recovering quickly Evans managed a very painful grimace; "Bloody good shot Rachel!" Evan's was grateful but the girl was clearly in shock.

This was certainly not Botha, but who was it?

Rachel couldn't look but Evans rolled the man onto his back and observed his features carefully. Unless he was very much mistaken this was the antiquities dealer, the very same man that Roger had met at Liverpool Street station.

Camera Pete, Shorty, Lambert and Johnson had no idea what was going on. Evans had dropped them at a cafe hoping that a 'full Welsh breakfast' would to bolster their spirits. When he left them they were moaning like old women and he half expected Pete and Shorty to give up on the project. After all, they had spent the night in the cells, they had lost the footage and the pay was rubbish.

-43-

Caerleon, Wales
31st July 2009

Rachel and Evans parked next to the new sports pavilion. It was surrounded, as was most of Caerleon village with interesting and evocative sculptures and carvings reflecting scenes from Arthurian times. Everything in the area spoke of a quiet wisdom and knowledge of those early links with the kings and princes of the Silures people.

They made their way across the road and into the enclosure of the amphitheatre. Evans looked at Rachel, he could detect that she was still trembling a little, the discomfort of the bruising in her crotch was worse when she walked.

"Are you OK?"

His voice carried genuine concern.

"Do I have a choice?" Rachel reached out and squeezed his hand.

Evans stopped walking and looked steadily into her eyes;

"Of course you have a choice Rachel, you can go as far away from here as you can and never look back."

Rachel shook her head;

"No, you know as well as I do that there is no escape from all this... anyway, I want to help catch the bastard that killed Nicole and Helen and find out what the hell Morgan and Pender were on to. I'm not someone who gives up, I just killed a man."

Evans sighed; he knew she was strong minded. Now he felt indebted to her for saving his life. He just couldn't get the attack out of his mind.

Rachel looked thoughtful: "He knew exactly where we were and apparently what was going on! He was definitely after the St Peter's cross and the Sky Disc so he must have been watching and somehow privy to what we know"

Evans nodded; "He must have known that your aunt and her helper left to go to the doctors leaving you on your own".

Evans nodded; "He has to have been well connected to get so much information, have bugs everywhere, or just got lucky"

Rachel mananged a half smile;"He wasn't exactly lucky was he?!"

Rachel cocked her head waiting for more information. "The gun was an old Beretta M1951, a Helwan. They were made under licence in Egypt for the Egyptian army; it's more of an antique than the choice for a modern assassin."

"Effective though."

She felt a sensation which was a cross between disgust and excitement.

"But an air gun would probably have killed him at that range."

Rachel's head fell as the words sunk in. She had killed a man, she, Rachel Abel, had shot a man dead. They had wrapped the body in the carpet from the bathroom and tossed it into the River Usk.

Evans face looked miles away;

"I'm so sorry Rachel, I'm not as sharp as I was, I should have been more careful. Maybe I could have saved you all that distress".

Rachel hugged him;

"Don't blame yourself Bryn, its ok"

After the attack Evans had done an electronic sweep of the room. He found three bugs which he left in place, hopefully they could be used to some advantage. There was no way of knowing though, who had planted them and who was listening.

Clearly someone somewhere would be missing the man at the bottom of the river.

Rachel's face went as white as a sheet;

"I've just had a horrible thought, whoever was listening in to the bugs would have heard exactly what happened".

Evans held her tightly;

"It's ok Rachel, I think that's the least of our worries".

Just then in the distance Rachel saw an older man in a monks habit waving to her; it must be Father Everson, she thought. When she'd heard from Natasha that William had been waylaid in Pembrokeshire she agreed to phone Father Everson and make the rendezvous.

Poor William, she hoped he was going to be OK. His health scare made her realise just how much she missed him and what a good man he was.

As she walked through the wooden "devils gate" and into the field compound that once housed one of the finest Roman Amphitheatres in Britain she could almost visualise the atmosphere, the pomp and circumstance of the music, the might and majesty of Rome and the expectation of Gladiators sparring. She could see laid out before her a vast circle of stone. The walls were around 23-30 feet high and arranged in segments like a sliced cake with gaps. She was happy to take her mind off things by escaping into an earlier time. As she passed between two banks of seating and into the centre of the arena she could see the monk much better. She held out both arms and he hugged her.

"Father, it's lovely to meet you, William has told me a bit about you."

Everson returned the greeting holding her very gently as if sensing her emotional fraility. Somewhere at the back of his mind her face sparked a memory, like a piece of gold held just out of reach from a beggar;

"Lovely to meet you too Rachel, I have heard much about you. How is William, I hope he's OK?"

"I'm sure he'll be fine father, he's pretty tough."

Evans caught the man's eye and held out his hand;

"Bryn Evans."

"Ahh, the man from Interpol, I was so sorry to hear about your daughter's death."

His eyes were taken to the bruise that was coming out across the top of Evans nose.

"Nasty bruise you've got there."

Evans tried to make light of it; "You should see the other chap!"

Everson laughed nervously although he probably wouldn't have if he had known the truth.

Rachel pivoted around in the middle of the arena.

"What a fascinating place, Father."

He enthusiastically agreed; "It's one of my favourite places. You know, over the years even though this site has been robbed for building materials it was shown as a sizable circle on the ancient maps. It was excavated in 1909 and again in 1926 by Sir Mortimer Wheeler who was funded by the Daily Mail and a mysterious organisation called the Loyal Knights of the Round Table."

Rachels imagination was running away;

"Who on earth were/are the Loyal Knights of the Round Table?"

The question fell on stoney ground.

Evans was in a daydream looking at Rachel's perfect slim figure and her very long black curly hair blowing serenely in the wind, Everson must have noticed and coughed again.

"I am really concerned for William do they know what, exactly is wrong with him?"

Rachel noticed Evans stare and ran her hand up and down in front of his eyes. He snapped back to life; Rachel turned back to Everson.

"Natasha just said that he'd been in a road accident but that he is alright"

Evans felt ashamed of himself for being caught eyeing Rachel's perfect body, maybe she hadn't really noticed. Had he taken her and her friendship for granted? Now he was seeing her through very different eyes but surely she couldn't feel the same, after all, as she had already pointed out he was old enough to be her father. To distract himself he read the adjacent National Trust sign about the ruins.

"It is thought that the amphitheatre was built around 90 AD and that it underwent considerable renovation and remodeling in 125AD and 212AD. It is actually oval in shape being 56m on its longer axis and 41.5m on its shorter axis. There was seating for 6000 spectators which was enough room for the legion that was garrisoned just across the road from here, plus visitors."

Everson rubbed his upper thigh; it always ached when he stood for any length of time.

"Do you mind if we go and sit down?"

Both Evans and Rachel were relieved as they were also suffering the wounds of strife. Rachel moved towards Everson and slotted her arm through his to help support him on his way. Evans moved to the other side and did the same;

Everson smiled and accepted their kindness with humility. As they walked he talked about Wheeler, the eccentric archaeologist.

"Mortimer was a fascinating chap. Publically he towed the conventional academic line but he secretly wanted to find evidence for a real King Arthur. In 1924 he was appointed Director of the National Museum in Wales but when he made his hopes about finding Arthur known he was moved on to head the London Museum at Lancaster House in 1926. You see my dears, it seems that no-one in authority, even back then wanted to find Arthur in Wales which is crazy since Winston Churchill wrote that King Arthur was from South Wales in his Histories. He wasn't the only one writing about him. Between 1760 and 1910 some 140 books by Welsh scholars claimed that he was King Arthur, son of King Meurig, who was son of King Tewdrig."

"Did you ever meet Sir Mortimer?"

"No, I don't think so, I lost my memory in a car crash many years ago and I am not really sure what happened before then."

"You poor thing." Rachel placed her free hand on his arm.

Everson placed his over hers;

"Such is life my dear, I hope my time since has not been wasted." Something in Father Everson's eyes said he hadn't that long to live but Rachel passed over the moment, quickly changing the subject back to one of his specialist subjects, Caerleon.

He went on to explain that the ancient name for the first settlement at Caerleon was Caer Wysg meaning 'fortress on the Usk'. It was a centre of trade used by the Britons, long before the Romans arrived. But when the legions, led by Julius Frontinus, came in 75 AD they abolished the old British name and called their fort Isca after the Celtic word for water. This was one of three legionary fortresses established in Roman Britain and their chief city in Wales. The name Caerleon is a Welsh rendering of Castra Legionum.

The Amphitheatre is one of several places identified as the site of King Arthur's Round Table. It would certainly have been impressive and available after the Romans left. As the centuries passed, it became a grass covered bowl-like depression in the ground and at one time it was even marked on the map as 'King Arthur's Round Table'. Large numbers of people used to visit Caerleon just to see the site of this magic place. It was once firmly believed that the cup-shaped hollow was the scene of the Arthurian tournaments and jousting described by Sir Thomas Malory and Alfred Lord Tennyson.

It was Geoffrey of Monmouth's description of Arthur holding court at Caerleon which probably inspired the romantic idea of Camelot being the capital of Arthur's kingdom. Geoffrey tells us that after his first Gallic campaign, Arthur held a plenary court at Caerleon. This was attended by the Earls and Barons of the kingdoms, the vassal kings of Wales, Scotland, Cornwall, Brittany, the conquered islands and European provinces.

During the 1926 dig at Caerleon, three strange lead tablets were found. The first is known as the Caerleon Curse. It was 10 cm square and pierced with two nail holes for attachment. The inscription reads:

DONNA NII MIISIS DO TI BI PALLIIVM IIT GALLICVLAS QVI TVLIT NON REDIMAT N** ***** SANGVINII SVA

This translates as: *'Lady Nemesis, I give thee a cloak and a pair of boots; let him who took them not redeem them (unless) with his own blood.'*

Perhaps it belonged to a gladiator or a soldier who left it on the shrine to Nemesis, the Goddess of Punishment, which was just outside the main entrance to the amphitheatre.

The second lead plate read;

Upon pain of damnation let no man disturb the body of the sun of god that lays on the cross at the Mount of Angels in the heart of the land of Helena the Swan.

And the third:

By this oath made upon our families and their children and in the presence of Arthur upon his crowning this day we knights of Arthur and of the Gods swear to keep hidden and safe forever the fruits of the loins of Mary the goddess of the moon and Iesus the god of the sun.

These finds suggest that Arthur was both pagan and linked to early Christianity. Armed with this knowledge, Evans and Rachel felt honoured to be sitting at the place where not only the Roman gladiators fought but also where Arthur and the Knights of the Round Table sat some fifteen hundred years earlier.

Evans asked Father Everson for clarification on the second tablet that mentioned the Mount of Angels, the land of Helen the Swan and the body of the son of God. Everson handed over the notes of the inscription to Evans for closer inspection; he observed right away that the body of the sun god was spelt with a U not an O.

Everson summarised it; "It's effectively telling us that there is a body of a sun god at that place. This was meant to be a big enough threat to keep people away. Well, it probably was then but now I don't think anyone is too bothered by Nemesis although we still speak her name."

"So who was the sun god?" Rachel asked.

Everson winced a little; "Arh, that's a slight problem, from our knowledge we think of the sun god as Ra but the sun has been worshipped for thousands of years."

Evans was on to it; "What if it was a code for the son of God? Is it correct that Ner was once the word for God?"

"Yes, in the ancient translation from Coelbren Welsh 'Ner, Eli Ner' means 'God, son of the Lord God', how did you know?"

Rachel and Evans looked at each other recalling the night before in the chamber at the end of the tunnel. Rachel spoke first; "It's a long story, we'll explain later. What about the third tablet, the one about Knights, oaths and stuff?"

Everson found the right page in his notebook and read the translation; "By this oath made upon our families and their children and in the presence of Arthur upon his crowning this day we knights of Arthur and of the Gods swear to keep hidden and safe forever the fruits of the loins of Mary the goddess of the moon and Jesus the god of the sun."

"Well they don't touch on that one at Sunday School." Evans was impressed.

Fortunately, despite his research, or maybe even because of it, Father Everson remained a very open minded man of the cloth.

"I have thought about this long and hard over the years. Firstly you'll notice that it refers to an Arthur being crowned, I presume here at Caerleon. That fits exactly with the Bruts of England and with Geoffrey of Monmouth's story, but, Mary a Goddess and Jesus a God? That's harder; the best I could come up with was that they were seen as Egyptian deities or humans that had some of the power of the Gods."

"And for them to be known in these parts they would have to have survived the crucifixion and made it over to Britain."

"Maybe" Everson nodded.

Rachel joined in:

"Fruits of the loins means offspring, doesn't it? Offspring of Mary the Goddess and Jesus the god who lived in the sun?" Rachel was terribly confused. "But why were they making this oath? And why at the time of Arthur's crowning?"

Evans slapped his thigh making them all jump.

"Hey, if Arthur was in fact related to Jesus and Mary in some way wouldn't it make sense to protect the line of kings?"

Rachel became animated;

"Yes and what if this was a secret known only to the closest knights of Arthur? But why call them a god and a goddess?"

Everson steadied himself;

"We do have to ask ourselves if these tablets are genuine. It might be possible that because we are talking about a time when paganism was still around and Christianity was in its infancy that such an oath from Arthur's knights might have been a stronger way of securing allegiance. But then we also know that in this part of the world at this time those who were Christians were the true apostolic Christians and they didn't follow the Paulite word of Augustine. Their form of Christianity would have been the pure form from the very ancient texts that existed prior to the codified change in religion adopted at the Council of Nicea in Byzantium in 324AD at the behest of Constantine who suppressed the Arian "heresy" by having all the work of Arius of Alexandria burned. It is well known amongst the enlightened that there was an original Gospel known as the Q or source Gospel"

"It was just as if they had received the word from the god who lives in the sun himself."

The three of them huddled really closely together as if they had the secret of the world in their palms.

Father Everson continued; "Of course, early Christianity would have been the original teachings; lift a stone and I am there...think of me and I will be with you... These early sayings were borrowed from what people now think of as a pagan time."

Rachel brought everyone down to earth with a bump; "Where are these tablets now? Have they been tested, I mean, do we even know how old they are?"

Everson shook his head; "Thereby lays the rub Rachel, this is anecdotal. I have been trying to find them for years. The nearest I came was by talking to one of Mortimer's friends who has since passed away. He actually showed me a sketch that had been done by Wheeler's wife at the time of the dig, but I don't know about the original tablets."

Rachel's investigative instincts were rising; "But the dig was done in 1926 right? Funded by the Daily Mail and that other organisation you mentioned."

Everson nodded an affirmation as Rachel continued;

"So In 1924 Sir Mortimer was appointed Director of the National Museum, Wales, however, in 1926 immediately after the Caerleon dig he was moved on to head the London Museum at Lancaster House. It's a bit odd isn't it? You find what you think is proof of Arthur being crowned at Caerleon. You presumably bring this to the attention of the Museum of Wales and the next thing that happens is that you get moved to London."

"Oh yes, something fishy was going on. Sir Mortimer also said he found the real site of the Battle of Baedon, not far from Maesteg. If you want my opinion he made some finds that proved something no-one in authority really wanted to know and he was asked to keep quiet and enjoy alternative lucrative work. Of course that's just my opinion."

"This reminds me of what happened to Morgan and Pender." Rachel declared.

"I mean the metal cross that you found at St Peters Church."

The old man suddenly looked drawn and pale; he was finding it difficult to swallow and was wheezing slightly. He took out an inhaler and sprayed it into his mouth and throat. A few seconds later he was looking a little better but there were tears in his eyes.

"It hurts to remember that day at St Peters, it seems like an eternity away now. I wish I'd never seen the place but Morgan and Pender needed an archaeologist and there I was. I wanted to be involved. In some ways you could say it was my destiny. I was working near the altar when one of my colleagues shouted to say that he'd found something in the trench. I went across and took over the fine trowelling and brushing and, as you know, the metal cross emerged. I held onto it for a few days to study it then gave it to Morgan and Pender."

"Did you keep a photo of the cross?" Evans asked.

Pre-empting the question, Everson retrieved a photo from his pocket. It was an A4 printed sheet with the front of the cross on one half and the back on the other. The back contained several marks in different shapes.

"Can I hold on to this for a couple of days, father?"

"Please do."

-44-

Hanbury Arms, Caerleon, Wales
31st July 2009

William had been quiet but philosophical in Natasha's Porsche on the way back to Caerleon. Maybe the news about the shadow on his brain and the diagnosis of possible macular degeneration hadn't really sunk in. Could it really explain all the weird and wonderful things he was seeing? Was he becoming detached from reality because of a disease that was attacking the central part of his retina? Maybe he longed to be once again with Sandra, the love of his life who he missed so much, maybe there was not that much to hold him to this earthly place anyway, even if he kidded himself there was.

The car purred to a rest.

As agreed Roger was waiting to meet them in the car park. Natasha smiled at William, made polite noises and left them to chat whilst she headed for the ladies room.

"It's so lovely to see you again Roger."

William's mind had drifted back to their school days when their leisure time had been filled with table footy and cricket. Pretty tame pursuits compared to computers today he mused. God, suddenly he felt very old indeed.

Roger slipped back easily enough into nostalgia;

"You were brilliant at football; I really thought you'd play professionally!"

William looked wistful; "I wish, remember your famous banana shots?"

Roger did and chuckled; "I never did get the hang of kicking a ball straight. Remember when we went ghost hunting on the beach trying to find that spectral white woman, 'Crazy Mary' I think her name was, she was looking for her husband who was lost at sea?"

William did; "We used to have fun, those great summer nights just passing time gazing up at the stars hoping to see UFO's. Really miss those days"

Roger smiled; "Yeah, that hooked me on astronomy you know, I studied that as well as archaeology. It's fascinating how the two link."

They walked for a while, Roger clearly had something on his mind; "I'll always remember your mum, William, she was so kind to me when I came to stay with you in the holidays, she used to say you and I were two old knights stuck out of time."

Williams's eyes welled up; "Never did quite figure that one out, I can't believe she's gone."

The moment lingered sadly until William felt able to speak; "Roger, I know we haven't kept in touch much for years but I still know when you have something on your mind."

He didn't respond but William persisted; "Do you know more about this thing we all seem to be caught up in than you are letting on?"

He stopped walking and looked William in the eyes; "The girl and the swans you keep seeing, do you have any idea what that is all about?"

William shook his head; "Not really, wishful thinking maybe?"

They both laughed. "You were always very psychic Will."

He shrugged his shoulders; "If I'd have been psychic I'd be a millionaire by now."

Roger was being serious; "I think it's all about women and religion."

William chuckled; "It usually is."

But Roger wasn't unbalanced by the comment; "In the city of Catalhoyuk in Turkey the archaeologist James Mellarch found female figs all over the place dating back 7000 years together with small shrines.Women were clearly the big Goddesses in control of life and death throughout time until the church managed to get the wrong end of Christianity. Recently the Pope has reiterated that women cannot be ordained because it says so in the bible….begs the question, who wrote the bible!"

William was concentrating; "Surely there is nothing unusual about sacred women. Millions of people follow Hinduism, which is built all around Derva, the female shining one."

Roger nodded; "Yes and drawings in the catacombs of St Priscilla under the streets of Rome show examples of women in ordained vestments preaching. It's clear that the Church has tried to cover up the role women played in religion. Even to the extent of changing mosaics, for example, Theodora to Theodor. Clement of Alexandria said women destroyed god's image and the 4th century Augustine, who was obsessed by women and sex, invented the concept of "original sin" in which he said we are all born as sinners following Eve's seduction of Adam. Of course history was re written in AD325 when women's involvement in the church was outlawed at the Council of Nicea. The Holy Trinity of Father, Son and Holy Ghost was invented and all female involvement rubbed out in one swipe.

By 394AD all pagan worship was outlawed by the church. The age of the priestess had gone".

William smiled; "It's all such a long time ago, are you sure this is relevant today?"

"Bear with me, William, you know about the Egyptian book of the Dead, don't you?"

William nodded; "A bit."

"Well think back further still, think back over 12000 years to a place also in Turkey called *Göbekli Tepe*, a place where a group of people built an observatory three times the size of a football pitch. On a central pillar is the figure of a goddess giving birth or being penetrated depending on how you interpretate it! The question is why?"

William was waiting in anticipation "With the help of computer simulation I discovered that the giant stone columns were aligned to track and predict the location of Deneb, which was then the North Star and the brightest in the sky. Today we know it's a star in Cygnus which never sets below the horizon at the latitude of *Göbekli Tepe*. In fact on its north-south zenith it crosses from left to right just above the northern horizon. I believe that the early Neolithic world associated Deneb and the stars of Cygnus with cosmic life and death, it forms an elongated cross shape in the sky which I am sure they linked to the four seasons."

William felt that there should have been a drum roll, a great ta daa, but Roger could see that the penny hadn't quite dropped; "Ok William, here's the clincher, I set about studying various other ancient monuments like, Avebury and Stonehenge in Wiltshire, Newgrange in Ireland, the pyramids in Egypt, and in South America, not to mention the markers of the native Americans and many others... guess what?"

William heard the clang and cottoned on; "They are aligned to and track Deneb and Cygnus."

Roger smiled; "You are smarter than you look, which is just as well!"

William smiled and started walking again deep in thought; "And the link with the girl and the swan is?"

Roger wanted to make his reply count, he couldn't tell William exactly what was going on, it was more than his life was worth, but in one way he wanted his old friend to know. He looked around fearful that someone somewhere may hear; "Ok, brace yourself; you are probably going to think I am mad... I believe that psychically you are tapping into the shape shifting spirit of a female deity linked to the constellation Cygnus, her name is Asherah or Brigid, also known as, Cybele, Isis, Mary Magdalen, Minerva and many others. Her cult, the cult of the swan lingered until Romano-British times, most notably as the divine patron of the Brigantes. Some say that the cult has never gone away entirely. Her feast day is 1-2 February when the geese traditionally fly north taking the souls of the departed with them. In July her followers celebrate the major annual meteor shower called *the Alpha Cygnids*, where meteors are seen to come from Deneb in Cygnus symbolising soul rebirth.

Following the arrival of male dominated *Christianity* Asherah and the female ascendant goddesses were swept aside, relegated to minor saints or spirits who took the form of white swans or white spirits. Her mark is that of the swan's foot, also known by the Welsh as the Alwen sign, which, incidently is said to have been mirrored on the shield of Arthur as silver chevrons on a red background."

William didn't quite know what to say, he knew he bore such a mark on the sole of his foot, as did father Everson; "Are you suggesting that the things I am seeing and hearing are ghosts and spirits that are haunting me?"

"Can you think of a better suggestion?"

"How about steak and chips, I'm starving!"

As they walked into the public house Natasha was snaking her hips, legs and feet provocatively across the stone floor, she stopped and placed three glasses on the table and lowered herself into the maroon leather armchair. She sipped from her own long tall glass of iced mineral water with two slices of lime and rested the glass on the table. William saw Rachel look dismissively in her direction. Natasha glanced at Rachel and smiled before slowly and deliberately crossing her legs before she spoke.

"I still don't understand the big problem with this King Arthur, chap, I mean, how hard can it be, he either existed or he didn't, right?" She paused as the eyes from the gathering came to rest on her. "Is it even important WHO he was, and frankly does anyone really care?"

Rachel took exception; "Someone cares Natasha, let's not forget that at least four people have died researching him."

"We don't know they died because of that exactly." Natasha enjoyed provoking her.

"Well, they were all working on the same thing at the same time and it would be one hell of a co-incidence if there wasn't a connection!"

Natasha sensed Rachel's stress and waved her hands and arms in a calming motion; "It's OK Rachel, I'm playing devil's advocate, someone has to be cool about it."

Rachel bit back; "There's cool and there's ice cold, don't you have any feelings?"

William attempted to diffuse the tension. "It's fair to say, I think, that there are so many stories and possibilities that not even modern day historians and archaeologists can agree, so how can WE expect to get to the bottom of this?"

"That's very true William" added Dr Felix. "The problem is clearly exacerbated by some academics and institutions who feel the need to perpetuate the myths to the detriment of the truth. Maybe they believe that once the truth is out, there will be no easy grant money for PhDs and other research. I've seen that sort of mentality in universities all my life!"

"That's a bit cynical." Said Rachel. "But true."

Natasha wasn't letting up on her and William watched as the daggers flew between them. He couldn't understand the problem; they had usually been so friendly with each other.

"Come on you two, let's pull together on this. If there is so much doubt are we being a bit harsh, I mean, isn't everyone entitled to have a view? You have to admit that the romantic tales of Arthur and his knights beat the gristle guts and bone stories of a ruthless army commander".

Father Everson joined in: "Normally I would agree William, but you are forgetting one thing. There is actually a ton of evidence that not only was Arthur a real person and a real king but that he was indeed the son of Meurig who was in turn the son of Tewdrig, two people we can place and prove existed. However, academics just won't see it because they insist on interpreting the early Welsh genealogies in the wrong century; we do have to ask ourselves why that is the case."

Evans had been observing carefully.

"Can we identify where this all went so wrong and why there is so much confusion?"

Father Everson tried to gather the facts;

"It was Professor Hector Munro Chadwick who constructed his genealogy of the dynasty of Gwent by basing it upon the Bonedd y Saint, which means Pedigrees of the Saints and the Liber Landavensis, which is the ancient register of the cathedral church of Llandaff in Cardiff. However, in doing that he misplaced Meurig the son of Tewdrig, King of Glamorgan and Gwent. Careless I agree, but this created an anomaly which post dated his son Athrwys by more than a hundred years, disassociating him from the events of the 6th century when the real King Arthur flourished.

He had the undivided attention of the gathered band. Rachel and Evans recalled Lambert saying the same thing.

"John Morris confused things further when he placed Arthrwys' son Morgan Mwynfawr, after whom Glamorgan is named, fighting at the second battle of Mount Baedon in AD665. However the same author states that the most important leader of the 6th century was Arthmael but that little is known about him. Arthmael is the same person as Arthrwys, or Arthur, both names are titles, Arthmael meaning the Bear Prince, or Iron Bear and Arthrwys means the bear exalted and we can be pretty sure that in this context they are one and the same."

Evans' detective mind was working overtime, he knew only concrete proof would help to solve anything.

"I don't suppose there is any real proof that Arthrwys and Arthmael are one and the same, I mean that would be too much right?"

"Wrong, there is proof," said Father Everson. "The Vita Cadoci, compiled around 1073-1085 by Lifricus who was the son of Bishop Herewald of Llandaff and master of St Cadoc in Llancarfan, precedes Geofrey of Monmouth's Historia Regnum Britanniae by two generations. It shows Arthur as ruling in South East Wales and as being the prominent king of the time. It also mentions a grant of land known as Cadox-juxta-Neath to St Cadoc by a King Arthmael. According to the genealogy contained in the Llandaff Charters themselves the king reigning over Morganannwg and Gwent at this time was Arthrwys, son of Meurig and grandson of Tewdrig so, therefore Arthrwys and Arthmael must be one and the same."

Roger Felix referred to some research notes which were relevant to this line of discussion.

"OK, so here's a brief resume taken from the research I did about Arthur some years ago. Let's say that Arthur was born around AD 503 at Boverton or Dunraven, it seems from the most ancient texts that his birth was heralded by a dragon shaped star which was in reality fragmented multiple comets that would strike parts of Britain and Europe later that century causing plague and pestilence. It's pretty clear that an Arthur, whoever he was at the time was seen as special from an early age and people linked his birth and life to that of Jesus Christ because both were heralded by bright lights in the sky. We are told that he went to study with his cousins Samson, Illtyd and Gildas at the college at Llantwit Major."

Father Everson was nodding and was able to supplement the story;

"Arthur and his family had strong historic links to Brittany and he spent much time over there helping to defend their territory from invaders.

"Thank you Father, I agree, if I may continue…"

Everson apologised for butting in and Felix continued;

"He comes back to the UK and fights the Saxons in some great battles but is wounded at Camlan and is then taken to Bardsey Island which is thought to be the real Avalon where he is healed by the seven virgins who were actually very clever Druidesses versed in the arts of healing with light, herbs and compounds of all sorts.

When he recovers he retires and goes to Brittany and sets up a monastery.

Nothing unusual in that. As Father Everson says he had ancient family links there and his cousins St Samson and St Gildas had done the same thing. He becomes known as St Armel there. He comes out of retirement and helps to protect Brittany from invaders. Short on adventure he travels with his brother Madoc on a voyage of exploration to the USA where he is killed. He is initially brought back to Brittany and given a burial but later taken in secret by his family back to Britain to be buried at Caer Caradoc near to his father Meurig, and the great Caradoc, the brother of Avrigagus who may also be buried there."

"So Morgan and Pender were right about him living in South East Wales" asserted Rachel.

"I discovered that Cardiff City Council claimed Arthur for their own in 1914, in fact they published a paper about the subject. They must have had great reasons then, so what changed? Now they let Cornwall, Scotland and just about everywhere else claim him but keep quiet themselves."

Evans didn't think it made sense.

Dr Felix threw his hands in the air; "It can only be that the council became aware of a reason not to blow their trumpet as planned. I have to admit that whenever I have tried to do anything really factual in Wales about Arthur I have been stone walled and actively discouraged."

Rachel recalled her recent interviews with Chris Barber and Dr Lambert;

"The Caerleon area seems fascinating, lots of interesting archaeology I assume?"

Rachel was fishing for input from Dr Felix and he didn't disappoint;

"Yes and although the Romans fortified it there was obviously an older city here and an Iron Age hill fort on Lodge Hill nearby. Recent excavation shows that like so many of the old forts it was re fortified and strengthened in the 6th century, Arthur's time, I doubt it's a co-incidence."

"I still don't really understand what all the fuss is about?"

Natasha's flippant attitude disguised her true interest.

Father Everson tried to inspire her;

"The area of the old Silurian Tribes covered what we now know as Glamorgan, Gwent, Herefordshire and well into the Forest of Dean. Everything points to Arthur being a Silurian king and it makes perfect sense that he be crowned at Caerleon deep in the land of the Silures. This was in effect a military town and it also makes sense that Arthur's court may have been at Venta Silurium now known as Caerwent. Geoffrey of Monmouth says that Arthur's Camelot is at Caer Wynt which is now Winchester and you'll recall that the huge wooden round table hangs in the cathedral there. However this is a 14th century reproduction and actually I think Geoffrey muddled up Caer Wynt with Caer Went (now Chepstow). It would have made no sense for Arthur's court to have been at what we know as Winchester because in Arthur's time Winchester was occupied by his enemies the Gewissei who were a fierce Irish tribe. There is a really strong tradition that King Caradog Freichfras which means Strong-Arm of Gwent's main court was originally at Caer-Guent (Caerwent), but he gave the city to St. Tathyw, who founded a monastery to the Holy Trinity. He lived there many years with his followers and when he died he was buried under the floor of his abbey church. At the same time, Sir Thomas Malory tells us in his "Le Morte D'Arthur" that twelve of Arthur's defeated enemies "were buried in the Church of St. Stephen's in Camelot" and that Arthur, the King, was wedded at Camelot unto Dame Guenever in the Church of St. Stephen's, with great solemnity. Caxton, Malory's publisher, clearly states in the book's introduction that Camelot was in Wales.

"Chrétien De Troyes, probably the man to first coin the phrase Camelot, relates, in his tale of Lancelot, how Arthur held court there having recently moved on from Caerleon, thus implying the proximity of the two. So the term Camelot could easily be a generic name for a place of governance and could be wherever the king is holding court at the time. Major excavations throughout Caerwent have revealed many impressive buildings and everyday objects from the Roman Venta Silurum. Some finds such as Theodosian coin hoards may have been deposited in the ground as late as 425".

Dr Felix was getting excited;

"Yes, yes, the Silures tribe were in the region from a very early time perhaps most famously they were led by King Caratacus, whose Welsh name was Caradoc and one of his main bases was almost certainly Caer Wysg which translates as Fortress on the Usk. The Romans called it Isca Silurum, Isca after the River Usk and Silurum after the Silures. It was the chief Roman town in S Wales, now of course called Caerleon."

He paused to sip his locally brewed beer and sighed as if it had given him strength before he continued;

"I have been looking through the Archaeology files for Carwent and discovered that Metalwork, including elaborate pennannular brooches and fastening pins, have been dated to the 5th/6th and 7th centuries. One had a depiction of a man on horseback with a sword or spear raised and this was very similar to the figure shown on the Cross that was found by Father Everson at St Peters in 1990"

Father Everson's ears pricked up as he continued;

"The main Dark Age finds, however, were a large number of burials discovered in two cemeteries. 148 east-west orientated Christian graves, dating from between the 4th and 9th centuries, were discovered around the town's East Gate in 1910 and 1973. The area was a sophisticated burial ground with sections for both adults and the young, and some graves were stone-lined. The second cemetery was around the present Parish Church of St. Stephen. This consisted of 150 graves, some early enough to respect the old Roman street plan. The 6th century burials surrounding it probably included Malory's twelve rebellious Kings. Geoffrey of Monmouth may have been wrong about lots of things but it seems he was spot on with this."

William was trawling his memory;

"Didn't the monk Nennius, include a place called Caer Camelion in his list of important cities in Britain?"

Dr Felix nodded;

"I'll make an archaeologist out of you yet! Today it's called Llanmelin which is a Silurian Hill Fort near to Caerwent so; I guess that sort of fits Geoffrey of Monmouth."

Rachel flipped her note pad;

"OK, but Morgan and Pender say that Camelot was the principal residence of the Glamorgan Kings and was at Caer Melyn in the Cantref y Breiniol -the Privileged Cantref, or Cantref y Brenin -The King's Cantref. They say the Norman French Ca'Melot may mirror Caer Melyn, meaning, the Yellow Fort. As Cardiff is in this ancient Cantref and the site of the Caer Melyn castle is visible from the upper floors of the University Archaeology Department, there is obviously some embarrassment amongst the English & Scots who dominate the research there particularly as they applied for and received massive funding some years ago to 'dig Camelot' at Cadbury in Somerset. Maybe the real Camelot was just under their noses, a castle was still standing and lived in there as late as 1453 when a wedding is recorded as being held."

Dr Felix was developing another theory;

"That's possible but I like the idea that Camelot may have been a generic name for where Arthur held court from time to time so it's possible that there may be more than one in the same way that any ancient round monument may have given rise to the stories of a round table."

Evans looked a little confused:

"But what about Cadbury Castle, in Somerset, are we sure that wasn't Camelot?"

Father Everson was stroking his beard;

"That's a valid point Bryn, but, you have to remember that the first time we hear about Camelot is from the French writer Chretien de Troyes. It is just possible he made it up but it is also possible, as has been proposed that it was once a generic name for an administrative or legal court. Don't forget that in those early times Camulos was a god of war and a lot of place names have Cam in them. It's not hard to see how Camulous or Camelot could be a War Court or a place of justice wherever the king was from time to time.

"It was John Leland, antiquary to Henry VIII who first identified Cadbury castle as Camelot from the names given to the river Cam or Camel at the foot of the fort and the villages of Queens Camel and West Camel nearby. To embellish his story he told Henry VIII that local people had told him that they called the fort 'Arthur's Palace' but the later antiquary William Stukely could find no trace of that name locally."

Dr Felix picked up the story from an archaeological perspective;

"Despite conjecture a dig took place on the summit of the Cadbury fort during the years of 1966-70. They found post holes indicating the presence of a great hall 21 metres long and 11 metres wide. They found evidence of a massive stone wall in the 5th and 6th century which was some 7 metres thick. It was absolutely the right sort of structure that a king would have been happy to have had as a stronghold and as we have noted it was not uncommon in this period to see older hill top forts re structured, re fortified and brought back into use. It is more than likely that in Arthur's time though there would have been a system of forts laid out in a circle with a great fort in the middle. We know that this defence system was in place in the 6th century and worked well as the forts were almost always on a hill top allowing signalling to the other forts and the main central fort. In short, it is highly likely that Arthur would have been there at some point. For security and to keep his troops motivated Arthur would have moved from fort to fort and so it is only natural that many will be associated with him. Don't forget that Arthur's skill was in maintaining an elite horse mounted fighting force. This enabled him to cover large distances quickly and use the horses as part of the war machine."

William shuffled a bit on his seat;

"This is great, why don't people know more about it?"

Dr Felix laughed; "I suspect it's because some of us have spent 20 years trying to figure this out and on the whole people don't have the stamina to ascertain what is right and what is wrong. It's not easy, not easy at all. We know, for example, that there was another great chieftain in the area at the time, a man called Cadwy so there is also a chance that the fort and town were named after him, eg Cadwys Town or Cadwys Fort."

Everson continued the double act; "We also know from ancient records that Cadbury Castle was around in the first century. There is a record of a first century British King who the Romans called Arviragus, possibly the brother of Caradoc (King Caractacus) who, after abandoning Portus Lemanis (Lympne) to the landing Roman re-enforcements retreated to re gather his army at Cadbury. Some say that he was the original St George, known to the Welsh as Gyreys.He led the resistance against Vespasian from there. Later Vespasian laid siege to Cadbury Castle and captured it, at the same time he captured a Royal Crown and a wonderful sword which he used for the rest of his life. Some scholars think that Arviragus is a title, 'King of the Lowlands' and that his real name was different and significant."

Natasha couldn't resist interrupting; "You are not going to tell me that this sword turns out to be Excalibur?"

Everson ignored the comment and continued;

"After they captured the fort, the Romans erected two stones at Cadbury Castle, one for the victory and the other for the Emperor Claudius."

"So we presume that the Romans hang around Cadbury for a while?" Rachel asked.

"Hang on, Caradoc, is that as in Caer Caradoc?"

Everson had to rewind a little to pick up her comment;

"Yes my dear the very same, odd how it keeps popping up, isn't it. For nine years King Caradoc and his brother Arviragus fought against the Romans. The Roman Emperor Claudius offered his daughter Gennisa to Arvirgaus to try to make peace and in AD45 they married in Rome. Six months of peace later when back in Britain they decided that the terms were not good enough and the war continued for another seven years. Some people think that Gennisa was not a name but a description of one who was directly related to the Holy Family. Caradoc was eventually defeated probably at Caer Caradoc hill fort but his brother kept on fighting and inflicted a massive defeat on the Roman army led by Ostorius Scapula in AD53 at a place called Caervelin."

"Umm, does this sound like Caermelin; do we have another contender for Camelot?" Natasha asked.

Everson wasn't so sure.

"Maybe, anyway, we do know that Nero accepted the resignation of his defeated general and he was replaced by Aulus Didius who founded Caer Dydd, which is the castle of Didius, now Cardiff, by the way."

Rachel was indeed fascinated;

"So that's how Cardiff got its name, don't you just love how history dovetales itself in to everything? So what happened to the brothers then?"

Everson continued the story;

"Arvigarus was undefeated; he was a giant of a man with a military genius mind. The Romans called him The Black Bull and he was the Pendragon, head leader of Gwent, pen being Welsh for head and dragon being a leader. Of course he was also given the worthy title of Arthwyr and this adds confusion to those on the trail of a King Arthur."

Rachel was following but was a little confused;

"But it seems like this chap was exactly what we always think of Arthur as being, a strong passionate invincible leader. What about the sword you mentioned? If his title was Arthur, and he lost such a fantastic sword at Cadbury aren't we missing something? Isn't this precisely the Arthur of legend?"

Dr Felix was sympathetic;

"Hey, you know, maybe you're right. There is something in this business about Arthur being a title rather than a real name."

They all looked interested as he continued.

"If we look much further back into the mists of time we find a Gaulish deity, widely worshipped by the continental 'Celts' whose name is known from an inscription found at Beaucroissant, Isère, France where he is invoked as *Mercury Artaius*. The similarities in name between Artaius and the insular 'Arthur' have led some scholars to postulate that they originated as one and the same deity, a god if you like. Artos, the alternative name of this deity is preserved in the place names Arto-briga, near modern-day Weltenburg in Germany and Arto-dunum (fortress of the Bear, modern Arthun) in the Loire. Artaius has a female counterpart, Artio."

William tried to recall his early studies.

"I seem to recall that Andarta was a warrior goddess worshipped in southern Gaul. Inscriptions to her have been found in Bern, Switzerland as well as in southern France and Luxemburg. Like Artio, she was associated with the bear; in fact she was the Bear goddess. OK, so there is something going on with bears here, Morgan and Pender said that Arthmael meant Iron Bear. I don't think they mentioned anything about a Bear God though."

Natasha's ears pricked up.

"Yes, of course, people used to worship bears, it was common in Russia. Why do you seem so surprised, we are talking about ancient peoples here, people that observed and identified with things they saw and experienced. The sun, the moon, animals, each had a characteristic, the bear was big, fit and strong and maybe these are characteristics they wanted for themselves?" She really couldn't see what all the fuss was about.

William agreed and Natasha smiled at him knowingly, Rachel spotted the closeness and wasn't impressed, she looked at William, what were their chances of getting together? Had he fallen for Natasha? She looked at one then the other lost in a little world of intrigue and disappointment, before listening to what William was saying;

"I remember reading about Bear worship in North American and North Eurasian ethnic circumpolar religions. Did you know that before Christian influences the Finns believed the bear to have come from the sky and have the ability to reincarnate? A celebration called karhunpeijaiset, literally meaning 'celebration of bear', was arranged to honor the bear, which was then sacrificed for a banquet."

"Some celebration, poor bear." Rachel couldn't help herself.

Everyone ignored the terse quip as William went on:

"The belief in the bear ceremony and sacrifice was to convince the bear's soul that it was greatly respected. The people presiding over the ceremony tried to make the bears soul happy so that it would want to reincarnate back into the forest. The sacrifice was meant to continue the bear's existence in the woods. Bear meat was eaten and the bones were buried. However the skull, which was believed to contain the bear's soul, was placed high on a venerated old pine tree. This tree, kallohonka, was probably a symbol of a world tree and placing a bear skull on it meant sending the bear's soul back to the sky, from whence it had originated. One day the bear would reincarnate to walk the earth with them again."

Rachel was displeased; she was a token vegetarian and an animal lover so the whole thing was distasteful for her;

"Sounds like hell of a way to treat something you love. I wonder what they did to things they didn't like."

Natasha raised her eyebrows at Rachel's obvious displeasure.

"Let's not forget the Greek goddess, Artemis; she had a link with bears didn't she?"

Father Everson seemed to know all about her;

"Yes, that's right; the Greeks linked the bear in with the heavens. She was supposed to have transformed Callisto, one of her maidens who had angered her, into a bear and then assigned her to the heavens as the constellation Ursa Major."

Evans, who had been quiet for some time could see where this was going;

"So, this thing about the bear seems to be deep in the psyche in many countries from an early time. I saw something in a magazine; it may have been National Geographic where Archaeologists claimed that the bear is the oldest European deity. They base this assertion on the fact that skulls of bears have been found arranged with reverential care in ancient caves across Europe.

Everson seemed to have read the same article;

"Yes, the bear was big with the Ainu in Japan, the Nivkhs in Russia, the Haida of North America, and many peoples of central Asia regard the Bear Mother as their ancestress. The Great She Bear, Ursa Major, watches over us from the sky."

They all looked skyward, it was some light relief in a deep discussion but Everson wanted to add something.

"Ursa is one of the few star groups mentioned in the Bible (Job 9:9; 38:32; Amos 5:8) Orion and the Pleiades being others. Ursa Major was pictured as a bear by both the Jewish people and most North American peoples".

Evans seemed happy with the erudite discourse;

"So are we agreeing that for some reason the bear played a major part in the psyche of ancient folk and that art, or Arthwyr could have been a name with a root from those times meaning big strong leader?"

They all nodded and William voiced the consensus;

"And one that could reincarnate and be a future king? It would certainly explain the fact that there seem to be lots of different Arthurs over a long period of time."

Everson looked thoughtful but had to agree;

"Well, yes, there are other "Arthurs", ie other great leaders. Ambrosius, Arvigarus, Arthwys and actually, later a person called Arthur. So it's possible that this memory of the name from ancient and pagan belief systems was firstly a God and or Goddess that was worshipped, then a name given to a great leader, and, as time went on the name lived on as an actual persons name, like for instance King Arthur of the 6th century who was king of Glamorgan and Gwent".

"I'm happy with that," Dr Felix smiled, "I have never heard that put forward as a concept and explanation before but it does make sense, particularly if we are also saying that Camelot is a name of a legal, administrative or battle court that is given to a place wherever the king dispenses justice or debates laws and powers."

Evans looked as if he felt some real headway had been made but still couldn't work out why at least four people had been killed trying to investigate it. William thought that everyone looked quite tired;

"Who'd like a drink? We all deserve one."

William took the orders and made for the bar, Rachel followed him closely;

"What's all this with Natasha and you then William? have you finally fallen for her charms, I mean, let's face it, you can see most of them from here."

William was a little taken aback;

"No need to be bitchy Rachel, I'm not your boyfriend you know!"

William looked at Rachel and wished he hadn't said what he had, she looked visibly deflated as if a sudden realisation swept over her. She looked William in the eye; he thought he detected a tear.

Evans walked up sensing something but not knowing what, old police habits die hard;

"Can I help you with the drinks?"

He noticed a tear in Rachel's eye; after all he had got to know her reasonably well over the previous few days.

"You OK, Rachel?"

"Something in my eye Bryn"

He disappeared with two drinks knowing that the pain was more in her heart than her eye.

The incident at the bar had not escaped Natasha. Nothing escaped Natasha but she took the drink from Evans and smiled, she grabbed the attention of Everson and Roger;

"Rewinding a bit, what happened to Caradoc?, he seemed like a fierce chap, was he an Arthwyr as well then?"

Everson looked thoughtful, he usually did;

"Not sure. We do know that after Caradoc was captured he was taken to Rome. The idea was to parade and execute him. However he apparently spoke so eloquently in their own tongue that he was pardoned and his family spared. Caradoc's daughter, Gwladys married the Roman Senator Rufus Pudens. When Caradoc died he was buried in a mound now called Twyn Caradoc on the highest point of Mynnyd Y Gaer near to his castle, Caer Caradoc."

Natasha had learned fast;

"You mean the place where St Peter's Church ruins are, where the metal cross and the memorial stone to Arthur were found."

Everson confirmed but Natasha hadn't finished;

"Why does everything seem to centre around there for Gods sake?"

Everson smiled;

"You may be exactly right Natasha, maybe it was for God's sake, after all, the area around St Peter's church was special. We know that Joseph of Arimathea once lived in a beehive hermitage there and gave his name to a rising sacred spring and river. We also know that in the immediate vicinity there was the city of Caradoc, the castle of Caradoc, the monastery of Ambrosius, the National grave monument of the soldiers, the grave mound of Caradoc and probably that of Arthurs father Meurig and of his great grandfather Teithfelt as well as the graves of Avrigagus and maybe Ambrosius."

Dr Felix just needed clarification;

"Ambrosius, he is the same guy known to the Welsh as Emrys Wledig, eldest son of Constantine the Blessed and grandson of Magnus Maximus, right?"

Everson nodded;

"Right, it's worth noting that we need to be aware of how the same person can appear to have three different names depending on who you read. They can be in Welsh, in Latin or in so called Norman English."

Rachel was more and more curious;

"Why Constantine the Blessed, what's with the blessed bit."

Everson took a huge intake of breath;

"Arh, now there's another story."

William was hooked; he felt that somehow he instinctively knew the answer;

"Maybe there were links to the Holy Family?"

Everson smiled at William but didn't think the time was right to open such a debate so he went on to clarify his former statement;

"Let me just go back to Ambrosius for a moment, as he got older his thoughts turned to retiring and holy ways, as they did with many soldiers who had previously trained as monks. He set up a monastery which Geoffrey of Monmouth places at Amesbury, to the East of Salisbury Plain. However this is another mistake as Ambrosius didn't have links with that part of the country. He was however taught at Llanilltyd Fawr, now known as Llantwit Major monastic training centre, where there had been a college since early times."

Dr Felix latched on to something Everson had said;

"Just a minute, let me just take this in, you are saying that there was a monastic training centre from the 1st century at Llantwitt Major where monks would learn?"

"Yes, most definitely and probably a seat of learning long before. Not only would they learn about apostolic Christianity they would be taught languages, how to fight and the ancient strategies of battles."

Dr Felix was confused;

"But how could that be the case? How could the message of Christianity have arrived so quickly?"

Everson wasn't quite sure how deep to take the conversation;

"The Roman historian Baronius says that Christianity was in Britain in 37AD."

Evans whistled through his teeth whilst William made a point;

"Hang on a minute, we are talking about men who were taught Christianity and to fight and to plan and win battles, warrior monks, this sounds very much like the Templars, doesn't it."

Everson nodded;

"Exactly William, this is exactly how they began."

Rachel had to ask the obvious;

"But weren't the Templars meant to have come about in the 12th century when they protected pilgrimages to the Holy Land?"

Everson stroked his chin;

"Yes, 1118 actually but let's just say there is real history and there is history we are taught."

Evans had to ask;

"So, if the Christian word came to the UK in 37AD who brought it?"

Everson smiled;

"That's easy; it was brought here by Jesus himself travelling with Mary and some of the disciples with Joseph of Arimathea."

Evans looked shocked;

"But Jesus died on the cross!"

Everson shook his head;

"Did he? I think not, not according to the earliest writings and not according to the tales of the Druids of Wales. They say that there was a volcanic eruption with a violent storm and in the panic Jesus was rescued."

There was a pause as the information sunk in, Evans and Rachel recalled the letters found hidden behind the picture at Helen's house. He continued;

"Jesus and some of his followers clearly survived and brought the original message here. That version was taught at the early colleges and monasteries, in essence the message was simple, there is a universal force of creation both male and female, that force is sometimes called nature, it relies on the sun, the moon and the seasons. That force also affects how we feel physically and mentally and can with meditation be harnessed for good or bad and it is everywhere and in everyone, it was a simple message."

Suddenly the pieces were falling into place and Dr Felix had an epiphany;

"So, if this power was natural and freely available there were no deities, or energies other than the power that created us, or created life if you like.

There was no need for the church as such, because the force could be accessed directly......wow, there would be no need for any religion and the church would be redundant!"

Evans' mind was working overtime;

"So, are we saying that the "Uthers or Arthurs" the generic term for great leader, certainly the ones after the 1st century, knew of this 'new religion' and it was this that they were striving to maintain?"

Everson looked thoughtful;

"Yes, there is no doubt in my mind that an elite force of knights was trained in both fighting and the true message as handed down from Jesus the Christ himself. Their aim, of course, was to keep this wisdom and knowledge for all who came after them. Make no mistake, these 1st century hero figures were the original Knights of the Temple."

William thumbed through the notes he had made, typically he couldn't read some of them.

"Wow, so this is how the Templars really started! You don't ever hear about that. But, how can we be sure that the Arthur of legend, you know, the one that was supposedly crowned at Caerleon or somewhere near, was kicking about in the 6th century, after all as we have said there are all these other Arthurs or leaders or whatever they were."

William knew he was getting tired because he couldn't find the right words at the right time and part of him was distracted by the way Rachel seemed so upset. Father Everson had picked up on the tension but put it to one side as he tried to explain further;

"Most people see the Arthur legend as a whole but it is made up of several heroic 'Uther or Arthur' figures over centuries. The Book of Llandaff is a vital ancient record because it lists land grants and important genealogies of the time. Any serious Arthurian sleuth has to read these to get a grip on dating. The clincher for the approximate dating of the 6th century Arthur comes from an oblique source. We know that St Samson of Dol was consecrated as Bishop by St Dyfrig in AD 521, and it was Dyfrig who crowned King Arthur. We also know that St Samson was a cousin of Arthur because his mother and father were Amwn Ddu and Anna. Anna was the daughter of Meurig and the sister of Arthur. Samson was known to have attended the Council of Paris in 557AD where his signature quite clearly appears. We know he died in AD 565 so this places Arthur in the frame in the right part of the 6th century to fall in with the other records."

Natasha was quite matter of fact;

"So you are saying that there is absolutely no doubt that the King Arthur of legend was real?"

Father Everson rubbed his hands together;

"Well, it's certainly true that many Arthurs or great leaders have been rolled into one and that in the 6th century there really was a man called Arthur as opposed to having that as just a title, and, that after him there was at least one other king called Arthur."

There was a long pause; there had been quite enough revelations for one day.

The pull of sleep was too much for all of them and they adjourned to their temporary abodes.

-45-

Caerleon, Wales
1st August 2009

Despite the fact that no-one had made it into bed before midnight they all managed to get to the early breakfast meeting that Evans had called. A plan of campaign had to be agreed.

William felt that he had to go to Glastonbury to see Gabriel, an old friend and psychic. Natasha volunteered to take him. Rachel was none too pleased but realized that she had to keep up the pretence of filming the documentary. Father Everson, who was feeling very tired decided to spend a little time meditating. Roger Felix was determined to still give his talk to the conference so opted to spend some time fine tuning it in the light of Morgan and Pender's untimely demise. Evans would stay in Caerleon with Rachel and try to speak to other conference members. They'd also try to find Dr Lambert and Dr Johnson who were conspicuous by their absence, as were camera Pete and Shorty.

It was early afternoon by the time William and Natasha drove across the Summerland Meadows which form part of the great Somerset levels. In the mist they saw the ruined church tower on the five hundred foot teardrop-shaped Tor at Glastonbury.

The church of St Michaels, named after the legendary warrior saint famed for fighting all things evil had been built over the remains of a 5th century fort but was mostly and bizarrely destroyed by an earthquake on 11th September 1275. The quake was so severe it was felt in London, Canterbury and Wales. It was rebuilt smaller in 1323 and then lasted until the death of the Abbey at Henry VIII's hands in 1539 when the church was quarried for its stone.

Once surrounded by water, Glastonbury Tor rises like a tall island from the surrounding flatlands and is now a peninsula washed on three sides by the River Brue.

William had often wondered how the huge earthworks had come about. They didn't fit with the usual iron age defensive pattern of mounds and ditches and the very small flat area on top made it very unlikely as a place of residence other than for hermits who he knew lived there from time to time during history. There had been inconclusive archaeological digs and the whole place seemed to be something of a mystery. He preferred the theory that the terraces around the Tor may have been set up as a labyrinth for some sacred purpose. He could just imagine the ancient Druids in procession moving slowly up the spiral, spouting incantations as they came closer and closer to the top of the tor in order to make an offering to the deities. Today, at some times of the year a few people still followed in the footsteps of their forefathers, walking the route so many had before, three thousand years, or more, ago. When they had visited in the past he and Sandra had often seen gatherings of men and women in flowing white robes high up on the impressive mound.

Ah, Sandra, this place held very special memories for William, it was here, on the very top of the Tor in a raging gale one September long ago that he had proposed to her and she had accepted. He still remembered how she ran around the tower, her waist long red hair flowing and mingling with her green velvet dress. He could see her smile, feel her breath. How happy they had been, how he had loved her, how he had missed her these last few years. If there was a God her death would not have happened, thus, he concluded that there was none.

It seemed strange coming to Glastonbury with another woman, perhaps his guilt was exacerbated by the fact that he was having feelings for Natasha which he didn't expect. He drifted off into another world, a world in which Sandra was sitting where Natasha was, a time in which they were visiting the sacred water well and gardens that were a haven of the very purest kind, a place to meditate and to be at one with everything. In a moment of weakness he turned to Natasha and spoke;

"I love you Sandra." Immediately he realized and bit his lip.

Natasha pretended not to hear, she didn't deal well with emotional stuff, however soft she might be inside.

"God, I need a pee!"

Her sudden outburst brought William completely back to the physical present. He lifted his glasses with his left hand and rubbed his watering eyes with the knuckles of his right.

"Are you OK William?" Natasha glanced at him;

William coughed to clear his throat; he was back in the world, a world he didn't like too much;

"Yes, yes, I'm fine Nats, we're nearly there, hey, that's the place just there on the right."

The turn into the small car park of the Chalice Well Garden was tight and littered with cars, there was just one space, their space, a space for 'friends' of the trust that owned and ran the well and the retreat centre, a space that William and Sandra used when they visited before.

One of the trustees of the Chalice Well came out to meet them, it was

Gabriel, a lovely man, if anyone was an angel it was him.

"William, how lovely to see you." he hugged him in the way that his old shamanic friend Michael had, a genuine hug full of warmth and love.

William returned the greeting and introduced Natasha. She wasn't sure what to make of the welcome but before she realized she too was being hugged. It felt as if a golden energy of wellbeing was travelling through her;

"Great to meet you Gabriel, but any chance I could use the loo please, I am bursting."

There was something in the way she was bouncing up and down from the knees saying please that underlined an urgent visit was necessary.

Gabriel smiled; "Sure, come on in, help yourself to the bathroom, the kitchen, anything... what is ours is yours."

Natasha disappeared quickly into the house. Gabriel looked William steadily in the eyes; "How are you really William, you don't seem yourself."

He could read the sadness in William's eyes but there was more. William found it hard to return his glance; "There's something going on Gabriel, I'm not sure what it is but it's serious and it maybe dangerous."

Gabriel thought for a moment trying to pick up some sort of psychic connection; "You'll find some peace here William, I'm always here for you if you need to talk."

"I really appreciate you being able to put us up at the last moment." replied William.

"You are welcome my friend, just one snag though, it's a room for two."

"That's OK, no problem."

William pulled him to him and held him tightly, it was as if he needed something to hang on to, something to be certain, something to be normal. He didn't want to let go.

After what seemed like an eternity Gabriel broke off gently. William's eyes were full with tears.

"Don't forget I am here if you need to talk, William, don't ever forget that."

William managed a half smile as Gabriel continued;

"I got hold of the old druid Samuel Soames yesterday as you requested. He's coming over this evening. It will be quiet when the gardens close so you'll be able to find a nice peaceful spot for a chat."

"Thank you Gabriel, you are an angel." William smiled.

-46-

Home Secretary's Office, London
1st August 2009

The Home Secretary whisked into the room on a surrogate zephyr of Chanel No 5, his liaison had been enjoyable but all too brief. It was always the same when he and the head of CADW got together.

Flustered and a little red he gazed across the room at Vanessa Grey;

"This better be good, it's interrupting my weekend."

Grey had little sympathy;

"Your carnal passions are legendary, Greenaway, you need to be more careful."

Greenaway didn't quite know how to take her so he opted for a veiled threat.

"How do you like your job as head of MI5, Ms Grey?"

There was an uneasy silence before Grey continued;

"I just thought you'd like to know that it's all going according to plan. Evans and Rachel seemed to have formed a team as do William and Natasha. Dr Felix is captured hook, line and sinker and the conversations we are listening in on at Caerleon are fascinating."

Greenaway stood up and shuffled; he wanted to scratch a private area but controlled himself;

"So, do you think they'll crack the codes and lead us to the St Peter's cross, JC and the treasure?"

Grey gave him a long suffering look which dissected the simplicity of his question;

"You do know that some of the locations they are talking about are around the sensitive area of the Meurig project?"

Greenaway nodded; "Your people must tread a fine line to keep these players safe until they deliver what we need."

Grey was aware of that;

"The Americans disagree, they think we should irradicate all threats after getting all the info needed".

Greenaway was aware;

"I know, I still can't believe that the PM was persuaded by them to fire bomb Morgan and Pender's house, this must be some special relationship with the US I wonder what we get in return?."

"Mmm, or what they have over us….we're their puppets, as usual. Oh and there's chatter that MOSSAD are joining the party."

"MOSSAD?" Greenaway went white.

Grey affirmed.

"Logical if you think about it, the Israeli guys would be very interested if there was evidence that JC didn't die on the cross and he is buried here, it underlines what the Jews believe about the Messiah who's yet to come."

Greenaway got the point;

"Any idea of who we are looking at for the MOSSAD involvement?"

Grey's face gave nothing much away;

"Not clear yet, but we are pretty sure they got to Morgan and Pender and we think Dr Felix could be involved, we have traced a large sum of cash to an offshore account in his name."

"Felix, are you sure?" Greenaway nearly fell off his chair.

"We're not entirely certain yet."

Greenaway demanded more answers;

"What about the others, Marshall, Evans and the two women, is it all a co-incidence they are together?"

Grey tried to lay the cards on the table; "Ok, here's what we know, Marshall is an odd fish, he could be almost anyone. His birth records seem to have been tampered with when he was a young boy. We know he runs a computer games company with Natasha. She's a bit shady. She could be Erin Svatlana, a top Russian agent and IT expert who disappeared off the radar years ago. Evans' reputation at Interpol is fierce but he's never had a daughter and it seems that he's using the father and daughter story as a cover. Helen was, apparently a co-Interpol operative, shock to us as she was also an M15 asset! Rachel's a journalist who has been friends with William for some time but her birth records were also changed when she was young, most odd. We don't seem to have anything on her or Marshall in the files though."

Greenaway was deep in thought;

"Has to be more than a co-incidence that these three are mystery people doesn't it?"

Grey didn't seem over bothered, nothing much ever seemed to ruffle her feathers. Greenaway tried another tack.

"What about the church?"

Grey thought for a moment. "We know that Cardinal Valetti has something of a reputation for volunteering his services and getting his own way. I suspect the church is deeply involved in all this as the very basis of religion could be at stake."

Greenaway nodded; "Makes sense, do you think that the church and the PM are acting together?" Grey shrugged her shoulders like a French woman accused of something she didn't do.

Greenaway looked Grey squarely in the eye; "Do you think the church employed the hit man?"

Grey looked away and he didn't labour the point.

"Make sure you keep these people alive long enough to deliver us the answers we need."

"Indeed."

Greenaway suddenly remembered that Sylvia Clarke, the head of CADW, was in a nearby room waiting for another serving and he showed Grey the door.

Had she swallowed his innocence? Had he really seen through her at last?

-47-

Chalice Well gardens, Glastonbury
1st August 2009

Natasha wandered through the Chalice Well gardens enjoying the fragrance and colours that surrounded her. A little peace in a stormy world. William strolled along another path to the top of the garden for a view of the Tor. He sat on a garden swing seat and closed his eyes, soaking up the wonderful aromas of the early warm evening. This place truly deserves its status as a World Peace Garden.

As he fell deeper into its ambience he was aware of a very particular scent and a friendly feeling around him. He didn't have to open his eyes, he knew it was Michael. This was his favourite place when he had been alive, why should it be any different now he mused to himself. Maybe dying just means we go through a veil to another room. What had happened to his body? Maybe he wasn't really dead?

Natasha was busy exploring an area labelled as King Arthur's Courtyard. The leaflet she had found in the house explained that it has long been a place of healing and that the bathing pool, now shallow, was once deep enough to allow for total immersion. She removed her shoes and paddled in the shady pool. The water was cool and clear and it took her straight back to her childhood when she used to splash in the puddles near her house.

Drawn by the overwhelming vortex of energy created by the rushing of water below the ground, William made his way to the well head. He closed his eyes and his mind gently drifted open. He was now sitting directly over the spot where three underground water courses met and rushed together and he could feel the physical and mental vibration of their power. Suddenly his mind was filled with bright white and golden light and a part of him rushed off with the water to another place and time, down a long tunnel and into the light. Deep in meditation, he was unaware of the tall, stick thin old man who came to sit beside him until he spoke aloud.

"According to legend, the Chalice Well is believed to have sprung from the ground at this spot when Joseph of Arimathea hid the Holy Chalice which captured the blood of Christ as he hung on the cross."

It took William a few moments to return to reality.

"Samuel Soames?" he enquired.

"And you must be William Marshall."

William nodded as he asked Soames whether he believed the legend.

"No, of course not, do you?" Soames laughed.

William shook his head. From the little wall on which they were both sitting they could see the round well head, less than three feet away. It was circular and slightly raised from the ground. It had a criss cross iron grill for safety and ivy and ferns grew all around. Open on a hinge was a large round wooden lid with an intricate design.

"Isn't it wonderful?" William turned to look at him as he continued;

"The design I mean. It's the *vesica pisces,* a sacred geometrical symbol in which the circumference of one circle passes through the centre of another identical circle. The bit in the middle is the *vesica*. Geometrically, this is the basis for establishing the sacred proportions of what has become known as the Golden Mean. If you extend one end of the *vesica* you get a fish, a symbol in Roman times that you were a Christian. The top half of the *vesica* made the Gothic arch used in medieval church-building. Many ancient stone circles in Britain were laid out using exactly the same mathematical principle. The lid was designed by Frederick Bligh Bond, resident archaeologist of Glastonbury Abbey around 1910. It was given by friends of the well as a thank you and an offering for peace in 1919, at the end of World War One. It is said to symbolise the union of the male and female, the light and dark."

Natasha headed up the steps from the mini grove towards the Lion's Head where water gushed from the well and flowed into a gulley towards the pool from which she had just bathed her feet. Over the years thousands had followed this practice, hoping for cures and miracles.

She picked up the drinking glass that had been thoughtfully left there. It was tinged orange and red from the deposits in the ground that were carried in the water. She filled it and drank. It tasted strongly of iron and she felt a kind of flush of light as the water permeated her body. She wondered if it was just the chill of the liquid or if she was really picking up the vibes from the Michael and Mary major ley lines crossing below her feet. For a moment she felt a tingling in her lower body and groin almost as if the mother earth, her own womb and sexuality were one. From where she was standing now she could see the 2000 year old Yew tree, one of several that must have surrounded the original well in a Druids grove in the mists of time. In some ways time had moved on but in others, it had stood still. She wondered if was possible to be in several times at once.

Whilst she sat, she read the leaflet about the wondrous place she found herself in. The text explained that according to legend, Joseph of Arimathea brought a thorn tree to Glastonbury during his crusade to bring Christianity to the country. The Glastonbury Thorn, as it was called, was said to have sprung from his staff after he stuck it in the ground and left it there. Numerous cuttings of the same tree have been taken and grown on various sites around the town. A curious anomaly of the Glastonbury Holy Thorn tree is that it flowers twice a year - once at Christmas and again at Easter. The Christmas flowers from the thorn tree in Glastonbury Abbey are sent every year to the Queen to decorate her tables. Thorn trees in Britain normally only flower at Easter, but the Glastonbury Holy Thorn seems to have held a genetic memory of its original Middle Eastern flowering time. It is said that trees grafted from cuttings of the Glastonbury Holy Thorn lose this memory when grown outside of Glastonbury.

When Natasha found one of the trees she felt moved to hug it.

Back at the well Soames shared his knowledge of the area and its history with William. It was remarkable how what he said brought clarity to the events of the previous few days as if pieces of a giant jigsaw were slowly moving into position.

Soames had a mild stutter but seemed fine if William averted his gaze whilst he spoke.

"Like you, I don't believe that this place is connected to the Holy Grail but, nevertheless, it is a magical and wonderful place, William. The well itself was built around an ancient spring maybe as old as seven thousand years. This whole area would have been an island then and we know from the archaeology that there was a village skirting the island shores from the earliest of times. At that time salt water would have surrounded the island which was directly connected to the sea. For there to be a fresh water spring that never dried up, even in drought would have been a magical thing in its own right. There would almost certainly have been a rivulet and waterlogged area next to the pool. We know from elsewhere that such places are the focus of worship of all kinds. A dig at this well has shown that the Romans rebuilt a well head and pool and it would be quite typical for Christianity to try to claim power by superimposing itself and planting its own stories over the top of older ones, like the grail legend for instance. So, over time the most ancient sacred spot becomes transformed into a place where the grail was placed and the waters suddenly take on the flavour of the blood of Christ from the iron of the nails of the cross.

"From an historical and geological point of view it is obvious that this spring has been in existence probably before man ever lived in the region. The area is criss crossed with springs, actually there is this spring with its red iron tasting water from one region far below the earth and then there is the pure white water from the other well across the road which is quite a different taste. It is easy to see why ancient man placed so much importance on this spot at the bottom of the tor.

"In pre-Christian times, wells, springs, lakes and bogs were seen as the bridge to eternal life and that is why many offerings are found there. You only have to look around you at the well today to see that people still leave tokens and small offerings for various reasons. Memories that are engraved deeply in our souls never change."

What Samuel said made perfect sense. Here was a man in his 90's that had lived in Glastonbury all his life and who knew the history and legends of the place inside out. He was a treasure in his own right and the reason why William had asked Gabriel to set up a meeting with him. How he wished they had met up years ago.

The old man's eyes had almost glazed over, as if he wasn't really present. William dismissed the thought as Soames continued.

"The Abbey is fascinating. Some academics relegate the area to wasteland before the 10th century but that really is not the case. One of the strongest pieces of evidence for pre-Christian worship is St Joseph's well in the Lady Chapel. This is accessed from a small flight of stairs leading down from the crypt to a small chamber outside the Southern border of the chapel where the well sits in an arched recess. Clearly this well is an early feature, and it has been suggested that it may even date back to Pre Roman times. But there is a strong possibility that this, like the well in this lovely garden, is the site of a much more ancient and significant place. It may even have been the very reason that the Abbey was placed where it was originally. The use of wells as ritual centers in pre history is well known and documented, and a tradition of veneration at this site would indicate its spiritual antiquity. Often they are associated with female energy. You know, of course that the Christian St Bridget morphed out of the earlier fertility goddess Bridget otherwise known as Ashera."

"In support of the idea that the area around the Chalice Well and the Abbey nearby was a sacred place at least 4000 years ago is the oral tradition of standing stones that were once to be seen along the lane now known as 'Stone Down'. Older Ordnance Survey maps allegedly show standing stones in this area as well as on Windmill Hill.

"There is very little physical evidence of large standing stones today but notably there are two boulders that mark the entrance to the Tor maze. These are behind a bench near to the start of the lower footpath to the Tor leading from the old Chalice Well Gate opposite the White Well. Local tradition tells us that the two bolders were once one large megalith, the top half of which broke away leaving the two stones we see today. They are referred to locally as the 'Druid's Stones' or the 'Living Rock'. There are many theories but if we look at places built at the same time, places like Avebury, Stonehenge and Carnac in France we see stones line routes between two sacred places. In Avebury for example megaliths line the way from Silbury Hill to the circle and it is my belief that stones marked the way from the well to the Tor. The name of an ancient trackway called Stonedown is evocative of this.

"Two great oaks still survive near one end of Stone Down and they may well be all that remains of the ancient druid grove. We do know that more oaks existed before they were hacked down for timber in the early part of the 20th Century. The very early maps show about 30 'standing stones' but there is not much to show that these were Megalithic. A line of 5 stones is shown passing through a point on the National Grid at an azimuth of about 298 degrees. The alignments are to the Sun at May Day and Lammas, two important days in the Megalithic calendar.

"Supporters of the Somerset Glastonbury claim that the ancient records place the earliest church there, but this is by no means clear cut. Records tell how one of the earliest Christian kings, King Lucius, sent an emissary to Rome in 167AD requesting missionaries be sent to Britain. William of Malmesbury refers to those that arrived as Phagan and Deruvian. He reports how Phagan and Deruvian discovered at Glastonbury an 'old Church built by the disciples of Christ', namely Joseph of Arimathea and his twelve followers. If this is right then it pushes back the date to AD35 -70 and, if, as some texts say that the church was built by the hands of Jesus himself then that could be much earlier. The Roman Historian Baronius says that Christianity came to Britain in AD35, or more accurately he says in the last year of the reign of Tiberius which we know to be AD35. There is no proof that this 'holiest earth of England' was found in Glastonbury in Somerset but it's a great story and one Glastonbury abbey had once used to make it the second most important and richest in all England. There are other contenders for an ancient Glastonbury that no-one hears about.

"From those early shaky roots follows more confusion. It seems that the monks of Glastonbury had a habit of trying to big up their history and it is almost certain that in the 13th century they forged a document called the "Charter of St Patrick" apparently dated 433AD but this forgery doesn't even mention Joseph of Arimathea or the early church said to have been built there. However it does have Patrick in the area and one of the first Abbots. The thing we know for sure about the Abbey in the Somerset Glastonbury is that it was built around the site of a very ancient well and that from carbon dating we can be sure that in the 7th century the area was already surrounded by a Vallum Monasterii being an earthwork or wall that denoted the symbolic boundary of the religious precinct.

"In 625AD, St Paulinus is reputed to have visited Glastonbury, and in 633AD he allegedly arranged for an 'old church' to be preserved by encasement in wood and lead. However, again there is nothing to prove that the records were talking about a Glastonbury in Somerset but we do know that King Ine of Wessex established a stone church here in 712AD. We can't speculate on any earlier structure though. However, *something* earlier certainly existed as the monks made a shrine of it and established it as a place of pilgrimage.

"King Ine is known to have granted a charter to the Glastonbury community in 704AD, and copies of that charter survive to the present day. His charter granted special privileges to the abbey, including exemption from taxation and virtual autonomy of rule within the 'Twelve Hides', a 'hide' being the amount of land traditionally required to support one man and his extended family. We must consider the probability that the document was fabricated or embellished in later years for the obvious benefit of the monks, particularly as we find another region given the same powers much earlier. The significance of the 'Twelve Hides' was their reputed origin. The assertion of the church was that these lands had been granted to Joseph of Arimathea and his followers in the 1st Century AD by King Arviragus. Tradition holds that the generous exemptions offered by King Ine were made as a sign of respect for the ancient claim of the church to these lands. However, he may just have been embodying in a charter an oral tradition made up by the monks in the first place. Sometimes lost falsehoods become truth over time. Now, we know that Arviragus was the brother of King Caradoc of Wales and that Arviragus was sometimes based at the Iron Age Cadbury Castle.

"Fast forward to the Domesday Survey completed in 1088AD, Glastonbury was the wealthiest monastic institution in the country. Its estates made up an eighth of all the land in Somerset. It also possessed holdings in four other counties, including 258 hides in Wiltshire. The grand total of the abbey's land-holdings amounted to 818 hides. The Domesday Book confirms the existence of the Twelve Hides making up the immediate vicinity around the abbey precinct and their special status but this was probably restating the charter granted by King Ine."

William looked over to Samuel, his hands were shaking slightly and he was making a clicking sound with his mouth, he reached over and placed his left hand over Samuel's, it was cold, ice cold.

"Shall we go inside?"

Samuel was not responding, his eyes were closed and his breathing was shallow. William became increasingly concerned. It seemed as if Samuel had to try to concentrate hard to keep himself alert. William wasn't sure quite what to do, he gently squeezed the man's hand, he didn't flinch, it was clammy and freezing. Suddenly he started to talk, his eyes still shut, his voice somehow deeper and more authoritative, almost as if he was channeling the voice from somewhere else.

"Gabriel said you needed my help."

William nodded but realized that Samuel could not see him;

"Yes Samuel that is very true, some very odd things have happened over the last few days and somehow it seems to revolve around Arthur and religion."

Samuel showed no sign of emotion as he continued.

"William, sit a little nearer to me and hold my hands, I need to use your energy to connect to you."

It was an unusual request but it seemed harmless and the old man was very cold.

"William, cast your mind back to the time of the Dissolution of the Monasteries. By the 16th Century, the wealth of Glastonbury was second only to Westminster. It was home to 54 monks and its annual income exceeded £3,000, which was a huge sum in those days. The mysterious Abbot Bere died in 1525. He had been to Italy with a detachment of soldiers and had taken by force various items from the Loretto Chapel there. Folklore would have us believe that by some magic the layout and items of the Lorreto chapel transferred themselves from the dome of the rock in Jerusalem. We still don't know exactly what he took but we do know that he insisted on being buried with a white ball in one hand and a black one in the other clutching a manuscript he had removed from the vaults at the Loretto chapel. When he returned home he had the Loretto chapel reproduced exactly at Glastonbury, he even called it the Loretto Chapel. It had a black marble floor divided into twelve by gold to represent the zodiac; in the middle was a statue of Mary Magdalen pointing to the constellation of Cygnus, the Swan. Bere was succeeded by Richard Whiting - the last abbot of Glastonbury Abbey. To all intents and purposes he was seen as a good man and Cardinal Wolsey described him as an upright and religious monk, a provident and discreet man, and a priest commendable for his life, virtues and learning.

"The death knell for the Catholic Houses sounded when in 1534 Parliament passed the 'Act of Supremacy', declaring Henry VIII the head on earth of the Church in England. Under The 'Treason Act' allegiance to the pope became a criminal offence and contesting the 'Act of Supremacy' became an offence punishable by death.

Publicly the majority of English abbots, including Richard Whiting, became signatories of the act, thereby recognising the King's authority over the temporal church. However, Whiting was not for the Pope or for the King he had access to some far more ancient knowledge and wisdom.

"In 1535, the king's agent Dr. Richard Layton visited Glastonbury Abbey to investigate the allegiance of Whiting although it was more likely a wheeze to try to stitch him up. However he found no evidence of impropriety.

"In 1536, Parliament passed a law seizing the assets of smaller monastic houses. This had the effect of closing 383 institutions with an income of less than £200. Their wealth was forfeit to the Crown.

Things got much worse for the church because this act failed to satisfy Henry's desire for cash and power and the King started looking at the bigger Abbeys. In 1539, Parliament passed a law dissolving the remaining 645 Abbeys thereby transferring their vast wealth to the crown.

"I think it's interesting to note that Henry VIII,as a Tudor with his roots firmly in Wales would have been very aware that the English or British church was where the original Christianity started in AD35 and it wasn't until much later that Rome claimed to be the centre. Like many of his forefathers Henry claimed his link back to King Arthur and it is easy to understand that Henry felt great resentment for the Catholic Church which he saw as an invasion of his lineage.

"Finally in September 1539AD, Layton returned without warning, arresting the abbot at his home in Sharpham. They carried him back to the abbey and spent the night searching his papers for evidence of treason. Not finding any evidence they took him to the Tower of London for interrogation by Cromwell. During the following six weeks the King's officers proceeded to strip the Abbey of anything of worth. Cromwell had predetermined Whiting's immediate future. In November, at the age of 80, Richard Whiting was brought back to Somerset. He was held briefly at Wells where a farce of a trial took place. The next day, Saturday the 15th November, 1539AD, he was taken to Glastonbury. His fate is described in a letter written by one of Cromwell's commissioners:

"Abbot Richard Whiting was hanged from the tower of St Michaels church on the Torre, disemboweled, beheaded, and his body cut into four quarters. These quarters were boiled in pitch and displayed at Wells, Bath, Ilchester and Bridgewater. His elderly head was placed on a spike above the gatehouse of the derelict and abandoned abbey - a building already lying in ruin from where the king's men had stripped its roofs and windows for their precious lead.

"Soon the stone, the wood and glass and anything else useable would be robbed out by the vultures in need of building materials. Like so many others this fine Abbey was wiped from the map.

"Why, you may be thinking was such a brutal thing done to Abbot Whiting when many of the Abbots were paid off and released? A private note from Cromwell to the king suggests that Whiting was hiding details of treasures and manuscripts that despite torture he would not reveal."

William felt a shiver of cold travel down his spine, he knew only too well how the wind howled around the tower and what a dreadful end that must have been for the holy man.

"Even as he was breathing his last Abbot Whiting would have had the satisfaction of seeing a small gathering of his monks escaping over Wearyall Hill. They took with them some of the treasures, manuscripts and relicts of the Abbey. They headed for Strata Florida Abbey, in South Wales, where they hoped to escape from the ravages of Henry VIII's commissioners. All too soon came news that royal officials were on their way to Strata Florida and so the monks fled over the hills to Nanteos House. Here, the old Prior of Glastonbury became chaplain to the local lord, Mr.Powell, and the other monks became servants around the estate. A sense of normality returned but the monks eventually started to die off one by one. On his death-bed, the last monk revealed to Mr. Powell that his little group had brought with them, from Glastonbury, the Holy Grail which had been brought to Britain by their Abbey's founder, St. Joseph of Arimathea. The Powell family took their guardianship of this relict very seriously and it had pride of place at the manor.

"The Nanteos Cup as the supposed Grail became known remained at the Manor, attracting many pilgrims and, apparently performing many miracles until 1952 when the last of the Powells died. The house and the cup were sold to Major Merrilees, who later moved to Herefordshire, taking the Nanteos Cup with him. Nowadays I believe that the cup which measures around 5 inches in diameter and is about 3 inches deep resides in a bank vault somewhere. It is said to be in a very poor state now due to pilgrims' biting large chunks out of it, over the years, in order to aid recovery from their ills."

William had listened carefully and had so many questions for the old man;

"That's fascinating but there are so many claims for the grail, why do you think that this is THE one?"

"William, my friend, I didn't say I believed it was THE grail, although I am sure that it had resided in the vaults at Glastonbury for many hundreds of years and was seen by the monks as something very precious indeed. Don't ask yourself, was that the real grail, ask yourself why did the monks go to South Wales and take the cup there?"

William wasn't allowed to think too long, Samuel caught his breath and continued;

"The Rev. Lionel Smithett Lewis who was a former rector of Glastonbury in his now famous book *St. Joseph of Arimathea at Glastonbury* wrote that 'a plausible explanation of the names Avalon, Glastonbury and the like is set forth by Dr. C.R. Davey Briggs in his *Ictis and Avallon* where he attempts to show that Avalon is also the celebrated Ictis, and he attributes all three names, Ynys Widryn, literally island of glass, Avalon and Glastonbury as derivatives from members of one ruling family'. He derives the name Avallach from King Avallach, otherwise, Apallach, Aballac, Avalloc, of the Grail stories and early histories. It is said that he was a contemporary of Joseph of Arimathea.'"

William marveled at the man's ability to recall quotes from memory.

"Though I disagree with the idea that Glastonbury in Somerset is the place visited and settled by Joseph of Arimathea, much of what Lewis wrote is excellent and fits with the evidence, once one realises that the real 'Avalon' / Glastonbury is on the other side of the River Severn"! There was a pause for the information to sink in.

"The idea that the land of 'Avalon' or 'Avallach' was a little kingdom in its own right is widely entertaining. It is William of Malmesbury the 12th century historian who tells us that King Arviragus made a donation of 12 hides of land, or about 1440 acres, that were to be free of taxes for all time. Since there are

640 acres to the square mile, this is over two square miles. When you realise that at this time in history, most of what is now Glastonbury was under water, with just the Tor and one or two other hills poking above as islands, you would be hard-pressed to find 2 square miles of dry arable land in the area. What land there was would have been highly unsuitable for growing crops. Are we really meant to believe that King Arviragus gave this important dignitary, Joseph of Arimathea, a couple of small islands in the midst of a pestilential bog, cold in winter and swarming with mosquitoes in summer? I don't think so.

"On the other hand, if you cross the Severn in South Wales there is abundant fertile land in the vicinity of either Llanilid or Coity. Llanilid is the Welsh for Holy area of Ilid and Ilid is the Welsh name for Joseph of Arimathea. Not only that, we know that Coity was indeed a tax-free principality with Palatine status, much like Monaco today, right up until about 1400 AD"

Like Samuel, William had his eyes closed trying to tune in with what he was saying.

Natasha was still deep in thought and meditation by the Thorn trees. The four acres of fabulous gardens were quiet and still in the cool evening air.

"So, Samuel, am I right in thinking that you believe that the Arthur and grail story have been transposed from South Wales to Glastonbury in Somerset at a later time?"

There was no answer, William spoke again;

"So what is your take on the real grail story then?"

There was a pause; William was still holding Samuel's ice cold hands. He could hear shallow breathing and felt a cold breeze around his own neck.

Samuel started to speak again; his voice was softer but still audible.

"The story of the Holy Grail forms part of the Arthurian cycle as retold by the 12th century French troubadours. In most renditions of the story the Grail is the cup used by Jesus at the last supper. Some traditions say that it belonged to Joseph of Arimathea, the rich merchant in whose house the Last Supper was held. According to the Gospels, this Joseph was a secret admirer of Jesus. He was allowed by Pontius Pilate to take-down the body of Jesus from the cross and remove it to his own prepared tomb. In the Grail legend Joseph does more; he collects some of the precious blood of Christ, still oozing from his wounds, in a cup. Thereafter the Holy Grail has healing properties and the power to sustain life.

"Joseph subsequently brings the Grail to Britain but unfortunately by Arthur's time no one seems to know where it has gone. As a consequence, in the latter part of his reign, the land is blighted with permanent winter and people are dying through starvation and disease. This is probably not far from the truth. Scientific evidence shows that there was indeed a seven year period between around about AD 552- 563 when trees stopped growing. The suspicion is that during this time there was a 'Cosmic Winter', a cold snap produced by a natural disaster that either involved some sort of asteroidal impact or a major volcanic eruption. Either event would have produced a similar effect. The resulting dust in the atmosphere would have excluded light thereby stopping plants from growing. Famine, disease and pestilence would have followed.

"In the stories the Holy Grail makes its first re-appearance one Whitsunday, at a meeting of King Arthur and his Knights of the Round Table. It hovers above the table and serves each knight with the food he most desires. Then, as miraculously as it first appeared, it vanishes. The knights are given to understand that if they can find the Grail again and bring it back to Arthur's court, then the wasteland will be healed and Britain will be restored. Consequently, they nearly all set out on a quest to find it. This turns out to be more difficult than anticipated and most of them either give up or die in the attempt. A handful including Lancelot get a glimpse of the mysterious cup but only one of them, originally Percival but in later versions of the tale Galahad, is pure enough in body and spirit to be successful.

"Perceval visits a castle called 'Corbenic', where he is invited by Bron, the custodian of the Grail, to stay the night. At dinner Perceval sees the Grail being carried in procession; however, he fails to ask a crucial question, that is, whom does it serve? When he wakes in the morning, the castle is in ruins and there is no sign of either Bron or the Grail. As a result of this disaster, he has to spend many long years of further searching before he once more encounters the Grail and this time asks the correct question. Thereafter he becomes its new guardian and the wasteland is restored.

"There are some key points which are highly relevant from our point of view. Though the original Grail-keeper was Joseph of Arimathea, he is succeeded in this task by Bron, 'the Rich Fisher-king'. In some versions of the story this Bron is Joseph's brother-in-law, being married to his sister 'Enygeus'. We can see clearly the origins of this connection. Bron is clearly the same individual as the historical figure 'Bran the Blessed', the father of Caractacus, who is credited in Welsh records as being the first of the Britons to convert to Christianity. Bran was a king and, in the tradition of St Peter, he was a 'fisher of men', that is he was the first, British missionary. It is also interesting to note that the 2nd son of Caractacus was Linus, the first Bishop of Rome. Of course no bishop of Rome claimed the title of pope before 627AD which was almost 600 years after the crucifixion. The idea that Peter was there and appointing the first pope 2000 years ago is factualy incorrect.

"In the Grail legends Perceval, is a grandson of Bron and Enygeus and is therefore 'of the family' of Joseph. Although there is some confusion here, this is actually quite close to what the Welsh genealogies tell us. In actuality Bran was not the husband but the 'Grandfather' of Eurgain, the real personage behind the 'Enygeus' of the French troubadours. A daughter of Caractacus, she had been exiled with him in Rome. She returned to Britain with Bran and was responsible for setting up the first Christian college known as the Coreurgain. This was at Llantwit Major in South Wales and is said to have been a collection of twelve 'cells' or huts, arranged in a circle around a thirteenth.

"Other legends claim that Joseph of Arimathea was the Virgin Mary's brother or even her husband. Meanwhile genealogies, such as those in the Harleian 3859, tell us that Mary had a 'cousin' called Anna. Descended from her is the 'Avallach' lineage, which later joins up with the Bran lineage. King Athrwys of Glamorgan and Gwent in the 6th century, that is the son of Meurig of South Wales is descended from both lineages, that of Bran and that of Anna. So this Arthur is of the royal holy line.

"Now if we look at the word 'Corbenic' we find that 'Cor' is a Welsh word that means either circle, choir or castle. It can also mean a religious circle or group as in 'Coreurgain', the 'Choir of Eurgain'. Meanwhile 'Benic' is a corruption of the Latin word 'benedictus' or 'blessed'. Thus 'Corbenic' is the 'blessed circle' or 'blessed choir'.

"Looking for a factual basis to the legend of Perceval, there are several potential candidates for the real 'Corbenic' or blessed circle. The first is Llantwit Major itself, where the Coreurgain was said to have been set up, a second is the old castle of Coity but my favourite is Llanilid. In Welsh Llan means Holy Estate of. This is where Joseph of Arimathea, known to the Welsh as St Ilid is said to have lived, so, in Welsh LlanIlid means the holy estate of Joseph of Arimathea, and that's pretty evocative. Trevran nearby is the historical residence of Bran the Blessed. More interesting still is that at Llanilid there is a gigantic earth-circle or 'cor' called 'y gaer gronn' in Welsh, meaning 'the circular fortress'. This appears to be an old Druidic sacred-circle and it is not improbable that it was used by the early Christians. Today it is heavily overgrown with trees but you can still enter it and make out the earth ramparts. In May it has a magical atmosphere as it is filled with bluebells. A large, ancient and very odd stone with undeciphered writing, which is said to have once marked the earth circle, now, stands in Llanilid church

"Turning now to the link between Coity also known as Coychurch and 'Glastonbury', we should consider that the Welsh name for Glastonbury is 'Aberglaston'. Now 'Aber' means the confluence of two rivers and place names at such confluences are usually given that of the smaller tributary. E.g. Abergavenny is the town where the Gavenny River joins the Usk. Thus the town of Aberglaston should lie close to a confluence.

"Historically the town of Glastonbury in Somerset was set in marshland where there was no river. There is a 17th century drainage canal there now but still no confluence. On the other hand in Wales, close to Coychurch, we have the Nantbrynglas joining the much larger Ewenny River. It follows that the name for this confluence should be 'Aberbrynglas'. Bryn means 'Hill' and so, on occasions, does 'Bury'. thus Aberbrynglas means the same as Aberglaston".

"Coychurch, which means 'Church in the Woods' is a very old foundation. Its alternative name is 'Llangrallo', said to mean 'Church of St Crallo'. As I can't find any other reference to this saint, I believe this may be a mistranslation. I believe it means, simply, The Church of the 'Grallo' or Grail. Interestingly there is a dark-age stone in this church with the word 'Ebissar' inscribed on it.

"Upstream from Coychurch is Coity. Here there are the remains of a Norman castle set in another circular earth-work that predates it. The Norman Castle was built by the Turbevilles and is the only one in Glamorgan to hold out against the Owain Glyndwr rebellion. For centuries Coity enjoyed tax-free status, which is something that Norman historians wrongly attributed to Glastonbury in Somerset.

"Next to the castle is St Mary's Church. This too is a Norman construction but it contains an interesting relic, the so-called Coity Chest. Made of oak and about 5 feet high, it has been dated to about 1480, which is from the time of Edward IV and the Welsh revival. It has curiously carved panels on the front of it which are positively 'Rosicrucian'. The themes covered by these are the aftermath of the crucifixion. I believe it to have been a shrine. The question is shrine to what or whom.

"On one of the central panels is a shield with 'arms' of three nails. Other panels show scenes of the empty cross with a ladder leaning on it and other implements, like pliers, that would be used when removing Jesus from the cross. I believe that all this is a coded reference to Joseph of Arimathea, the 'apostle' who removed Jesus's body from the cross. The implication is that the shrine once contained bones believed to be either those of Joseph himself or one of the many saints who claimed descent from the Holy Family. This is by no means an isolated occurrence. The empty cross with the ladder and the spear of Longinus leaning on it are also used on shields in Llandaff Cathedral and elsewhere. One of these is placed prominently over the tomb of St Dubricius, the Bishop who is said to have crowned Arthur at Caerleon. The implication is that this coat-of-arms signifies correctly that he is a saint 'of the lineage of Joseph of Arimathea'.

"The landscape of this part of Glamorgan and the things that are within it are congruent with history and legend. The only explanation for this is that this truly is the mystical land of Avalon. Since Arthur is said to have been buried in Avalon, then it is not so surprising that it is in this vicinity, that his tombstone and other relics have been found."

The information was sending William's mind in overload but it made perfect sense, as always there were so many questions but it seemed as if Samuel was getting tired. William didn't want to overdo it but felt he had to ask;

"Samuel, do I take it then that you don't believe that Arthur was actually buried here at Glastonbury, Somerset in the Abbey?"

Samuel's breathing was almost turning to a wheeze but he managed to speak;

"Ah, William, that old lie and one that has plagued proper Arthurian research for many years, you have to remember that the 12th century was a time when churches and Abbeys were desperate to raise funds and this was, indeed, a great wheeze. If you have the bones and the grave of not just the country's greatest legend but those of his wife you can be sure that rich pilgrims will visit leaving healthy donations.

"This story really started with King Edgar who was born in AD 943. Although he was called Edgar the Peaceable that did not really reflect his life. He was a strong leader who seized the Northumbrian and Mercian kingdoms from his brother Edwy, consolidated the political unity of England and had a fixation, as did later kings with all things Arthurian. With one eye on Scotland and Wales he figured that if he could prove that Arthur was a king of England, Wales and Scotland then he too was justified in claiming such a title. Knowing from the early histories that Arthur was buried somewhere in South Wales he set off on a kind of pilgrimage with an elite force. His band of men moved quickly on horseback as Arthur's armies had done in the 6th century and penetrated South Wales where they captured a minor king and tortured him into telling them where the body of King Arthur was buried. In truth the poor man probably had no idea but he directed them to a mound nearby. He was killed anyway. There could be no witnesses to such a deceit. There the men dug up the occupants; a large boned man and a woman and took them back to Glastonbury in Somerset where they were re-buried. Miraculously the grave was found for the "first time" after Edgar had received a "vision". Later when he was crowned in Bath, six kings in Britain, including the kings of Scotland and of Strathclyde, pledged that they would be the king's liege-men on sea and land. Later chroniclers made the kings into eight. His plan was working. As a point of interest the service, devised by Dunstan and celebrated with a poem in the *Anglo-Saxon Chronicle* forms the basis of the present-day British coronation ceremony. His desire was to be buried near his beloved King Arthur. His wish was granted and when he died on July 8, 975, he was buried in the chapter house by the door of the church at Glastonbury Abbey. He may well have believed at that time that Arthur and his wife were really buried there.

"It is claimed that during the tombs opening in 1052 Edgars body was found to be incorrupt and blood flowed when it was cut. His relics were then interred with those of Saints Apollinaris and Vincent whom he himself had presented to the Abbey in a large gold and silver shrine decorated with ivory images. They were placed on display in the Edgar Chapel at the far eastern end of the Abbey Church. There was no doubt that the abbey was accumulating a succession of relicts and the remains of famous people. This led to it accumulating a massive amount of wealth, no wonder Henry VIII had his eyes on it from an early time.

"Some say that there were no buildings and therefore no church or Abbey on the site at Glastonbury before the Edgar Chapel of the 10th century however this is not quite true as there has been some 7th century material found in the remains of a mound that may have been an enclosure of some kind. There may well have been an earlier building of some sort because we know that St. Guthlac was Abbot of Glastonbury from AD 824 to 851. Unfortunately, the monks who encouraged his cult at Glastonbury were working under the misapprehension that they held the bones of St. Guthlac and set up a shrine to rival that at Crowland Abbey. St. Guthlac of Glastonbury had obviously been long forgotten. It seems that the site has a long history of tailoring relicts and finds to suit the zeitgeist of the day and it is probably not the only Abbey to do so.

"On the 25th May, 1184AD, disaster struck. Most of the Abbey, including the alleged "first church in England" was destroyed by a great fire. The cause of the fire is not recorded.

"Adam of Domerham, writing in his "Historia de Rebus Glastoniensibus", records the sorrow and heartache of the monks. Peter de Marcy who was looking after the Abbey at the time died of unrecorded causes shortly afterwards. An earlier King, Henry 2 appointed his own Chancellor, Ralph FitzStephen, to oversee rebuilding of the abbey, funded largely out of the royal purse. Henry considered himself responsible for the fate of the abbey since the fire took place while it was directly under his care. The new Lady Chapel was said to have been erected directly over the 'Olde Church'.

"Rebuilding had only just begun when their benefactor Henry 2 died in 1190AD and the money dried up. A great plan was hatched to raise funds and secure the interest and funding of the next monarch and the pilgrims.

"In 1191 prompted by the desire to capitalize on their assets, the monks excavated the "grave of Arthur". At a depth of seven feet they found a stone beneath which was a leaden cross with an inscription *His iacet inclitus Arturius in insula Avalonia* - variously interpreted to read 'Here lies King Arthur buried in Avalon'! How convenient. The coffin contained two bodies - a great man and a woman, whose golden hair was still intact, until touched, when it crumbled away. The bodies were explained as Arthur and Guinevere. The wheeze worked like magic. Realising that King Arthur was a powerful symbol as the first monarch of a united England and a popular hero of the ruling classes the new king Richard promised funds for the rebuilding. It would have reflected poorly on Richard to neglect the place of Arthur's burial – especially when his predecessor had been instrumental in locating it.

"The Welsh and Cornish clung to the myth that Arthur had never died, and hoped for his return to liberate them from their Norman overlords. With his corpse discovered, in one coup the rebellious main stay of this myth was diminished.

"Looking back it's obvious to us now that the "discovery" of King Arthur's grave may appear to be little more than a clumsy hoax, but in the context of the times it was a subtle masterstroke.

"A century later in 1278 the bones were placed in caskets and transferred during a state visit by King Edward 1, to a black marble tomb before the High Altar in the great Abbey Church. There they remained until the Abbey was vandalised after the dissolution in 1539. No one has seen, or heard anything of them since. Legend proclaims that after Arthur's body was disturbed, a powerful spirit haunted the ruins of the Abbey, appearing as a black-armoured knight with red glowing eyes and a burning desire to eradicate all records of the ancient Arthurian legends, which is why, it is said, that those seeking to discover the truth, find so few facts available and are plagued by misfortune. The chances were that this was not in fact Arthur's body at all, some of the ancient texts say it was the skeleton of a Shaman who haunts those that disturbed him."

William kept quiet for a while as he tried to make sense of the information the old man was imparting. He still had his eyes closed, it seemed that he could tune in and concentrate better that way.

"That's amazing stuff Samuel, truly amazing but the grail and Arthur and Jesus, it seems that the epicenter for all this is in South Wales but how, why, are they all linked and why doesn't anyone want to seem to want to know the truth?"

Suddenly William jumped out of his skin there was a warm hand on his shoulder, it was Natasha, and Gabriel was at her side. Natasha was smiling;

"It's a nasty habit William."

William looked around genuinely surprised,

"What is?"

"Talking to yourself!"

Samuel had disappeared. William looked confused;

"But, but I was talking to Samuel, he was here just a second or two ago, we've been talking for ages!"

Gabriel looked first towards Natasha and then at William.

"I'm sorry William, I'm afraid Samuel isn't going to make it tonight, I have had a message to say he died in his sleep last night."

William went as white as a sheet and stumbled as he rose to his feet, Gabriel and Natasha both moved to steady him as he held his head looking first at one and then the other and then around the well head, there was no-one else in sight;

"But, but, I've just been talking to him!"

Natasha gave him a concerned sideways look;

"Have you taken your tablets Will?"

He shook his head. Not even Gabriel saw the translucent figure of a knight dressed in black glide effortlessly through the wall.

Gabriel, Natasha and William sat together in the cosy lounge come library of the Georgian cottage that had access directly to the Chalice Well Garden. Gabriel had made them a wonderful cup of hot chocolate, just what they needed after the exploration of the garden. William was feeling really odd, he was sure that he had been talking to Samuel and in his mind was refusing to believe that he had died the night previously.

"Gabriel" he asked, "Have you heard about any comet or asteroid strike on the UK in the 6th century? Samuel told me about it, he said that there had been some sort of natural disaster that led to a wasteland in some parts for a few years."

Natasha interrupted;

"But William, you know Samuel died last night; you couldn't have been talking to him."

Gabriel stepped back, unmoved. "I've never heard that one before William, how about I look in our library index to see what I can find."

"Thank you Gabriel, can I help?"

Gabriel looked across to Natasha and then to William;

"No, it's OK, you relax, it won't take long."

Natasha logged in to her secure mail and looked up at William who was studying her.

"Want a photo?" She said playfully but William was almost looking through her to a picture on the wall. He moved to get a closer look. It was quite an old painting of the abbey ruins. In the foreground was a knight dressed in black armour looking quite foreboding and aggressive. William stood for a moment staring at the picture, something was drawing him beyond the heavy old moulded gold frame and into the scene...suddenly the knight increased in size and lunged at him from the picture. William fell backwards into Natasha's arms and they and the laptop both ended up on the floor just as Gabriel walked into the room.

"Oh, sorry, excuse me." Gabriel moved to leave.

Natasha leapt to her feet straightening her short skirt;

"No, no it's OK, William just fell."

William was on the floor, he looked as white as a sheet;

"The Black knight, he said, the knight in the picture, he went for me!"

Gabriel moved over to the picture, there was no knight, black, white or multicoloured. All he could see was a painting of the Abbey ruins. He helped William to his feet and felt the warm damp blood trickling from a cut in William's hand. Natasha wrapped a handkerchief around the wound;

"You must have caught it when you fell, William."

He wasn't convinced; Samuel had told him about the Black Knight.

William sat down nursing his hand, Gabriel engaged him; "William, I have found some of Samuels old notes in the back of the filing cabinet. He used to come here to the library to work, and for a bit of warmth and company."

William looked at Gabriel; "Notes? About the natural disaster?"

Natasha's attention was secured; Gabriel started reading Samuel's handwriting; "The notion that Britain was filled with small tribes of barbarians at the time of the Romans is false. Britain had approximately 10 million people organised in well defined and governed regions. The thing that allowed England to be invaded, and then only piecemeal, by Saxons and the like was the multiple comet strike of around AD 562. This is well recorded and now recently proven scientifically. The effect was estimated to be the same as 100 atomic bombs. The ancient records tell of a great wasteland for many years giving rise to the Arthurian holocaust stories."

William was looking agast. Gabriel passed the notes to him and Natasha looked over his shoulder as they both read them:

The Prophecies of Eryr

These ancient records confirm the vast destruction of Britain by some heavenly agency. It states that the country is in ruin. It lists the Irish incursions to steal the surviving standing corn. It tells of the flight or removal of the British Army to Brittany and its subsequent return to restore order and destroy invaders. The shattered and lifeless condition of Britain is clearly stated.

The Prophecy of the Eagle of Caer Septon

Another ancient record going back to the astronomical and astrological records which refer to the comet...

"As the dragon often drove off the white, thus is the white driven away. The worst and terrible dragon flees, and with a blast from its mouth burns up the whole island with its fiery flames."

The Prophecies of Merlyn and the Comet

The main point about all these prophecies and records is that they are supportive evidence to a great multiple comet strike, something that nowadays (in the last few years) scientists can confirm.

Merlyn says of the comet;
"A shower of blood will fall and a dire famine will afflict mankind"

"Calamity will next pursue the White One (Lloegres = England) (as opposed to the Red One = Wales). And the buildings in its little garden will be torn down.

"Wales will grieve for what has happened but after an immense effort it will regain its strength" This would be the British recovery under King Meurig the UthyrPendragon (father of Arthur)

As these predictions seem to have come about and it is clear that Merlyn had intimate knowledge of the great floods in 2167 BC (caused by a cycle of comets) it is scary to think that he predicted the next similar catastrophe in around 2015.

> **The Brut of St Tyssilio circa AD 684**
> ".. While these things were happening at Winchester there appeared a star of great magnitude and brilliance, with a single beam shining from it. At the end of this beam was a ball of fire, spread out in the shape of a dragon. From the dragons mouth stretched two rays of light one of which seemed to extend its length beyond the latitude of Gaul, while the second turned towards the Irish Sea and split up into seven smaller shafts of light.
>
> This star appeared three times, and all who saw it were struck with awe and wonder"
>
> Merlyn, standing in the presence of his leader said, "Our loss is irreparable, the people of Britain are orphaned.

William exhaled deeply, the sigh was heartfelt:

"So, I'm not going mad, Samuel was there, I was talking to him, how else could I have known?!"

Then Will remembered that Rachel, Evans and Roger had all mentioned the possibility of a comet strike. Was the grey matter really deteriating so quickly. The black knight though, how could he have known about that?

Natasha didn't comment, she cared far too much about William to make him feel bad.

-48-

Caerleon, Wales
1st August 2009

Roger Felix, Rachel and Evans walked thoughtfully through the streets, past the excavations of Roman military buildings and towards the amphitheatre. The birds were singing and the sky was blue. The warmth of the early sun permeated their souls making them temporarily forget the peril they were in.

"Sleep well Roger?" Rachel asked.

"Not bad" he responded. "I had a text over night from the conference organisers. They want me to postpone my lecture today and wind up the conference with it instead. I'll speak to them about it later."

Changing the subject, Dr Felix was interested to see the disc that Rachel and Evans found in the mound. She knew she could trust him so she retrieved it from her handbag. Dr Felix handled it with the care and respect it deserved and he examined it with a small magnifying glass. On one side was gold with the head of Asherah and on the other were the sky scenes.

"Interesting, very interesting. You say that there was a painting on the wall of Mary Magdalen with this round her neck?"

Rachel nodded but she saw the scepticism in his eyes just before he delivered a disappointing blow.

"This is no older than early Victorian."

Evans and Rachel were naturally deflated especially when they remembered what they went through to keep it out of the hands of her attacker.

"But it isn't that straight forward." Dr Felix continued quickly, noting their disappointment. "An ancient disc almost identical was found around the neck of a large man under the altar at the St Peter's dig in 1990. The skeleton of the man dated to 6th century AD but the disc checked out to be around 2000 years old."

"Was that ever recorded?" asked Evans.

"Well, I don't think it ever made it into the public domain if that's what you mean."

Roger studied the copy more carefully before going on: "It was around the same size as this, made of bronze and inlaid with gold and silver symbols which are thought to represent the Sun, the Moon and the stars. It also featured the star formations of Orion, the Pleiades, Cygnus, Cassiopeia and Ursa Major (the great Bear). The sun is represented by gold, the moon by silver and the stars by a mixture of gold and silver. The aged bronze and copper background makes the whole sky look dark greeny blue. On the reverse is the head of Asherah in silver and gold."

"So where is this disc now?" Evans was intrigued.

"Allegedly it was stolen several years ago from the Museum of Wales." He responded, failing to mask his cynicism.

"Apparently someone tried to sell it on the black market but the police received a tip off and raided the homes of the two suspects. They denied stealing the disc from the museum saying they had found it whilst out with a metal detector. The police found a stash of artifacts buried under the patio of one of the houses and in the cellar of the other. They appeared to be real life Indiana Jones characters."

"What happened to them?" Rachel asked.

"They were given suspended sentences on the basis that they fully co-operated both with the police and archaeologists appointed by the police. The men took the archaeologists to the sites of the various finds and proper controlled digs were undertaken. They claimed that they were only interested in preserving history and that they had intended making a full disclosure in a book that they were working on. They also said that they had tried to make their research work available to others in authority but that no-one in Wales wanted to know. It all ended up as something of a secret, which is a shame given its obvious interest.

"So, how come you know all about it?" asked Evans.

"I examined the Brynna disc for the Museum of Wales when it was first found at the dig and was in their possession and then I was appointed by the police to examine the items found at the two houses."

"These two men, they were Morgan and Pender, weren't they." Evans was fishing.

Dr Felix did not feel he could comment so he ignored the question and went on to explain that the microphotography of the corrosion crystals produced images that could not be reproduced by a faker. He said that he was confident that the Brynna disc he dated for the museum dated back at least to the first century AD because of the radiocarbon dating of an oak bark particle found in an indentation on the back of it. He analyzed the trace elements by x-ray fluorescence and found that the gold was traceable to North Wales, and the silver and bronze to the immediate area around Brynna. The disc that was apparently found by the metal detectorists was a copy, much like the one you found at the Mynde.

Evans looked straight at Roger and repeated his earlier question;

"These men, were they Morgan and Pender?"

"I'd prefer not to answer, if you don't mind". The awkward moment passed as Felix continued;

"Whoever it was I think they were set up. I have heard it on good authority that the original disc is still in the vaults of the Museums of Wales, not that I told you that. I think that the powers that be wanted the disc to disappear and it was convenient to use others as scapegoats. Welsh artifacts have a nasty habit of disappearing, especially if they prove something controversial or inconvenient."

Evans picked up on Dr Felix's implied allegation of corruption at the Welsh museum;

"Do you think someone on the inside is selling antiquities and framing others for it?"

"Your words, not mine. It does seem odd that the card of a shady antiquities dealer fell out of the file on St Peter's church at CADW" replied Roger.

Conspiracies aside, Rachel wanted to know what Dr Felix thought about the Brynna disc.

"My best guess is that it is the sort of disc that would be worn by a priest or a priestess, clearly it is to do with the movement of the heavenly bodies in the skies, and it could certainly be used to predict the seasons and sun and moon movements."

"So the original disc is found on the skeleton of a 6th century man and now two copies turn up, one in a chamber in Caerleon and one by metal detecting enthusiasts in a field. That has to be more than co-incidence doesn't it?" Evans asserted.

"Yes, it is." admitted Dr Felix. "It's just a thought but you said that the chamber in the Mynde at Caerleon featured representations of female goddesses on the walls as well as Mary Magdalen. It could have been a chamber dedicated to a cult which venerated women, a cult that was still going strong in Victorian times."

Evans picked up on another thread;

"If the Brynna disc is original and dates to around the first century as you say, but was found on a 6th century skeleton then someone must have thought it was of great interest even then."

"Yes, it's possible that this disc was thought of as special and magical, maybe something that had been handed down over generations of wise people. Perhaps when it was buried on the 6th century body it signified the end of an era, perhaps it was a message for the future, who knows?" Dr Felix inspected the copy once again and noticed that it differed from the original. He pointed to capital letters that had been scratched along the top on the sun and moon side of the copy disc, NER, ELI NER and the letters on the reverse, **O•U•O•S•V•A•V•V D• M•.**

"ELI NER, the letters that had to be pressed on the chamber door to allow entry." Rachel recalled.

"It means God, son of the Holy Lord God or Jesus." Explained Dr Felix.

"Why would a Christian word be written on a pagan disc?"

Roger ignored Rachel's question, his mind was making another connection.

"The letters O•U•O•S•V•A•V•V D• M• are also really interesting. William faxed the exact same ones the other day, he said a girl had given them to him and he wondered what they meant."

He proceeded to explain that the Morgan family were supposedly descended from Arthur. They were also relations of the Ansons who owned Shugborough Hall. The Morgans knew the Guest family who were responsible for translating the ancient texts of the Songs of the Graves which are meant to be a roadmap of where to find the burial places of the famous people in Britain before the 7th century. At Shugborough Hall there's a sculpture of a Poussin painting in the grounds and these letters feature on it.

Rachel stated the blindingly obvious question;

"So, this Morgan family, are they related to Morgan as in Morgan and Pender?"

There was a vacuum of unknowing but, deep inside, she felt a thrill of excitement and knew that they may be on to something.

"Why don't you and Roger go up there and check it out tomorrow? See if Natasha and William want to join you. When it comes to code breaking they don't come much better than Natasha." Evans didn't explain how he knew.

Once Rachel and Roger had left the amphitheatre, Evans took out his secure mobile phone. Natasha was driving her Porsche on the outskirts of Glastonbury when the phone rang. She looked across to William, he was dozing.

She clicked the security button on her ear piece and answered. Evans kept his voice as quiet as possible;

"Can you talk?"

There was a short pause as the security encryption kicked in;

"Of course."

Evans was direct;

"I guess you recorded my log in with Clone Keystrokes when I logged on to the Interpol computer at your office, right?"

"That depends who wants to know." She remained calm.

"It's OK, I know who you are Natasha, I really need your help."

She looked across to William he was asleep.

"Talk to me."

-49-

Caerleon, Wales
1st August 2009

Roger Felix entered the Georgian House on the high street in Caerleon where the Arthurian Conference was taking place. It was a grand property adjoining the Ffwrwm Centre. Some of the delegates were milling around in the reception area drinking coffee. Roger spotted Angela. He felt drawn across to congratulate her on how well she had organised the conference.

"I'm sorry to have to put your talk off until last but we thought that it would make a great conclusion, especially as Morgan and Pender, um, couldn't be here."

Roger was attracted to her deep, dark eyes;

"That's OK, how are you getting on?" He knew she had been recently widowed.

"It's tough, but, you know..." and with that nod to tragedy, she looked around to make sure no-one was listening then changed the subject.

"Do you know where the real metal cross is Roger, the one Everson found at the St Peter's dig?"

Roger was taken aback by the unexpected interrogation.

"Michael was trying to track that and the Brynna Disc down before he died."

Roger indicated that he was unaware of this.

"Do you know if William is here, I need to see him to sort out issues."

"He was here."

Angela reached across and grabbed Roger's wrist, somehow he felt his strength dissolve.

"I must see him, do you hear, I MUST see him and soon...do you understand?"

Unable to speak, Roger just nodded. The widow planted a lipstick kiss on his cheek and departed. Once gone, Roger slowly regained his strength. She was a powerful energy vampire.

He poured himself a coffee from a large stainless steel urn and grabbed a custard cream biscuit. Just then Rachel came breathlessly through the entrance, spotted him and rushed towards him.

"I've just seen Lambert and Johnson they are trying to get into the dig at the Mynde Mound again...there's a huge argument going on."

He downed his coffee in one gulp and followed her out of the building.

Natasha pulled the Porsche over so that she could concentrate on what Evans was saying.

"This Robin Bryant, Bryn, are you sure he's MI5?"

Evans was pacing up and down the Amphitheatre unaware that Robin Bryant and Brad O'Brien were listening from some way off using a hyper sensitive directional microphone.

"My hunch is that the CIA and MI5 are running a playmate operation."

"Sounds interesting, Bryn, ring off, I'll call you later through a mush box, walls have ears."

The loud shouting in Welsh and English floated over the road and reached the ears of Roger and Rachel long before they arrived. In fact Evans could hear the commotion from where he was and decided to make his way to its source. He passed a tall young man with a pony tail and a fierce looking dog, the man smiled and Evans smiled back.

The conference room was not filling up as fast as Angela had hoped. She closed her eyes and saw Roger and Rachel arriving at the Mound dig. Voices were raised and there was a lot of pushing and shoving going on.

The man in charge of the dig was Thomas Marks. He was an older man with a fine full beard, a huge barrel chest and a swarthy complexion. He waded into the thick of things. Evans headed straight for him and the commotion suddenly subsided. Evans extended a hand;

"Bryn Evans, this is Rachel my assistant, we are trying to make documentary on Arthur."

The man allowed his right hand to slick back a lose strand of greying black hair.

"Ahhh Mr Evans, why didn't you contact me to arrange something earlier, you must have heard about the dig in the tunnel and chamber here."

"Yes, can we have a look at what is going on?" Evans asked.

"Of course you can, but please leave these trouble makers out of your film"

Evans looked at Lambert and Johnson;

"Of course, we don't need any trouble we just want to investigate the story."

Lambert and Johnson fell quiet and left the scene as Evans and Rachel followed Thomas Marks to the tunnel entrance where they had filmed less than 24 hours earlier.

"I understand that there was a little misunderstanding last night and the police destroyed your footage....I am sorry about that."

"I'm sorry as well." replied Rachel. "We really should have made more of an effort to contact someone for permission but we just got carried away, you know what it's like."

Thomas shrugged his shoulders;

"You shouldn't take any notice of what Lambert and Johnson have to say, they just love stirring up trouble, in fact they are nearly as bad as Morgan and Pender."

"You know those two?" asked Evans.

"Unfortunately yes, they've caused me problems for years. They've kept the police pretty busy too."

Evans feigned ignorance; "So what's going on here then?"

"Simple really, the Romans built a bath house here, as they did in many places. The evidence is that it was part of a brothel and gymnasium complex for the soldiers. After the Romans left there was a ditch dug around the area and piled on top. A later look out fortification was built on the mound. In its heyday you could see right down the river to the sea. People who believe in fairy stories like Morgan and Pender and Lambert and Johnson seem to think that King Arthur and his merry men may have used the tower to watch jousting and war game tournaments in the fields around the bottom of it, but that is pure conjecture. The Normans built a wooden fort here that was re fortified and it was eventually taken by William Marshall, Earl of Pembroke."

"William Marshall?" Rachel smiled at the coincidence.

"Have you heard of him? Brilliant knight and the King's right hand man. Anyway, the castle fell into disrepair after it was captured and destroyed during the Welsh rebellions."

They had arrived at the huge bronze door that had opened so dramatically the previous evening. It was still open revealing only a solid back, its ornate face was hidden from view.

"I've got no idea how those clowns opened this door so easily." Said Marks dismissively.

Rachel and Evans immediately noticed that the room had changed. The wall frescoes were gone. In the artificial light only scraped walls could be seen.

"Lambert said these walls were frescoed!" Rachel exclaimed, knowing that she too had seen them.

"In his imagination perhaps, there's no evidence of wall paintings in here."

Evans noticed scrapers, hammers and chisels on the floor but said nothing. Rachel was about to remonstrate further but Evans stopped her.

-50-

Shugborough, Midlands
2nd August 2009

It was a long sultry drive to Shugborough from Glastonbury and Natasha hated the heat. Her hair was tangled from the wind and her white blouse was wet with sweat.

"You look really hot, Nats!"

She smacked him on the thigh; "Ouch!"

"Serves you right." William looked at her face which was slightly flushed from the wind and sun. Her dark glasses couldn't hide her beauty.

They parked the Porsche and bought their entrance tickets and a guide book. It explained that the Shrugborough Estate was bought by the Anson family in the 17th century from Thomas Whitby and is the ancestral home of the Earls of Lichfield. The architect James Stuart enlarged the house in 1750 and created follies and monuments in the grounds. There's the Greek-style 'Tower of Winds', a Chinese-style pagoda a 'Doric Temple' and the Shepherd's Monument. On this monument is an uncracked ciphertext which some believe contains a clue to the location of the Holy Grail.

Roger and Rachel were already waiting by the entrance. Rachel threw herself at William as if she hadn't seen him for years. Natasha thought that the embrace was a little too long. They walked the short distance to where an electric mini bus was waiting to take visitors through the park and down to the main house. A herd of red deer trotted across the horizon and into the trees

Roger was reminded of Natasha's great looks and it caused him to stutter again;

"So, Miss, err...miss..."

"Just Nats, Roger, everyone calls me Nats."

"Don't you ever tell anyone your second name?"

"No, it's impossible to pronounce and I like the mystery."

Well, at least the second half of her statement was true.

The mini bus dropped them off near the café where they bought sandwiches and drinks to take away.

After a quick obligatory tour of the house, they headed for the Shepherds' Monument located in the grounds.

Natasha was unaware of the connection between the monument and their research so Roger thought he'd try and impress her with his knowledge.

"No-one is exactly sure what it means. What we do know is that it's an 18th-century monument commissioned by Admiral George Anson, 1st Baron Anson and it bears an inscription that is thought to be an uncracked ciphertext. It carries a relief showing a woman watching three shepherds pointing to a tomb. See, on the tomb is Latin text, "Et in arcadia ego" which either means 'I am also in Arcadia' or 'I am even in Arcadia'. The relief is based on a painting by Poussin, thought by some to have been a Grandmaster of the Knights Templar. The relief is slightly different from the painting though. For a start, it's reversed horizontally. The letters are also slightly different. In the painting the shepherd is pointing to the letter R in ARCADIA but the finger in the sculpture was pointing to the N in IN, before it was broken. The sculpture also adds an extra sarcophagus to the scene, placed on top of the one with the Latin phrase. Some think it looks Pre-Raphaelite and is a reference to Arthur, the once and future king. Below the relief, there's the mysterious inscription; O•U•O•S•V•A•V•V D• M• People have puzzled over its meaning for centuries."

"So it's a puzzle," The code caught Natasha's interest and she paused for a moment trawling her photographic memory, it didn't take her long to come up with something interesting.."if you separate arca from dia it changes the meaning, it then says something like; "I am also in the holy coffin."

The other members of the band looked at her, stunned by her abilities, but she pressed on as if everyone had been blessed with a classical education.

"With ten letters, you could solve it with complete confidence."

"Funny you should mention that," replied William. "The owners of the hall recently ran a competition to see if anyone could break the code and several decryptions of the inscription have been suggested. For example, a subsequence of the letters apparently matches the first letters forming a phrase in the Latin Bible. Another stronger theory is that it is a coded dedication from Admiral Anson to the late Lady Anson."

William suddenly stopped and gazed intently at the sculpture then at Roger;
"What did you say?"
"What about?"
"Arthur."
Roger repeated the phrase about the 'once and future king.'
Williams mind was working overtime;
"Rachel, was there anything at all in Morgan and Pender's footage about the Poussin paintings?"

She retrieved her laptop from her bag. None of them noticed a rustle in the bushes nearby or the super quick clicks of a Nikon D3 with a telephoto lens.

Whilst Rachel was starting up her laptop, William opened his guidebook and read aloud an excerpt from a 1987 letter from Margaret, Countess of Lichfield, to independent researcher Paul Smith:

> ... outside Rome are seven hills and one of the hills had a shepherdess called Alicia which I think means 'Joy and Happiness'. The beauty of Alicia's character was her utter simplicity devoid of all vanity. She was very beautiful and completely unselfconscious and unaware, for her whole life was dedicated to the care of her sheep and seeing they came to no harm from the roaming wolves.
> One person thought the letters represented a line from the story "Out of your own sweet vale Alicia vanish vanity twixt Deity and Man, thou Shepherdess the way". This person thought that the "U" in OUOSVAVV stands for "your" because one of the "lover codes" in those days when young men scratched with a diamond on the glass of his loved ones window, he scratched "I L U" for I love you.

The guidebook also mentioned another proposed solution. In 2004, Sheila and Oliver Lawn formerly war time code breakers at Bletchley Park were briefed to look for possible solutions. Sheila Lawn proposed an alternative to the Alicia poem, suggesting that the letters stand for the Latin phrase "Optimae Uxori Optimae Sorori Viduus Amantissimus Vovit Virtutibus. She interpreted the message as a declaration of a sect's belief that Jesus Christ was an earthly prophet, not a divinity. The order had to keep its views secret because the Church of England thought it was heretical.

Natasha was interested in the interpretation and Roger thought it held some credence.

"Well actually it's what the Templars believed and it may have been the message that the Rosicrucian's were trying to get through in the 17th century period of Enlightenment. Some think that the inscription holds a clue to the location of the Holy Grail. Following the claims in the book The Holy Blood and the Holy Grail that Poussin was a member of the Priory of Sion and that the painting contains a message about the location of the grail, it has been speculated that the inscription may encode secrets related to the Priory. Oliver Lawn proposed that the letters may encode the phrase "Jesus (As Deity) Defy", a reference to the story of the Jesus bloodline allegedly preserved by the Priory. Both solutions were presented by the Lawns as highly speculative though. The Lawns acknowledged that the message is too short as to guarantee one precise translation."

"Sounds like Dan Brown fiction."

Natasha hated his work.

"What was the point of giving them a flawed task?"

William interjected, he'd found some more information in the guidebook;

"Richard Kemp, from the Shugborough Estate, suggests that the inscription proved another link between the monument and the Holy Grail. Poussin was allegedly a grandmaster of the Knights Templar and they believed that Jesus Christ was human, not a deity. This would suggest that the Ansons were Templars and that they wanted to preserve the knowledge of Jesus as a man, not a celestial prophet."

Natasha replied;

"Well, ok, I can see that they would need to keep such beliefs coded and there is a certain sense about it, in fact it is the message I am getting, that Jesus was human, died and was buried like any other person...but without my own deep analysis I am not sure how you get all that from the sequence of letters?"

"I don't think anyone really knows."

Roger laughed cynically. He knew only too well the relationship between research and grants.

William remembered the dramatic afternoon at Canterbury Cathedral when the nun gave him the bag containing the 30 piece jigsaw of silver. Those pieces formed the inscription along the bottom of the sculpture they were looking at. He also remembered the red wax apple handed to him by the busker on the Southbank. He fished in his pocket and pulled out the piece of fruit. It was quite small, wax with a deep red matt finish.

"May I?"

Roger held out his hand and William passed it to him.

Natasha tried to apply logic to the puzzle;

"There has to be something about the Shepherd and the Shepherdess? A man and a woman and two tombs."

William read from the notes about the work he had managed to research from the internet;

"The first version of Et In Arcadia Ego was painted by Guercino around 1621- 1623. This shows two male shepherds gazing at a skull with a hole in its crown on top of a plinth with the words Et In Arcadia Ego upon it. Poussin's first version which contains the element of drama and surprise on the part of the shepherds that encounter the tomb wasn't painted until around 1630. It has been said that the subject matter was suggested by Pope Clement IX. Poussin's second version of Et In Arcadia Ego was painted around 1640 and this removes the element of drama and surprise on the part of the shepherds replacing it instead with pensive contemplation. Quoting Erwin Panofsky: 'Poussin's Louvre picture no longer shows a dramatic encounter with Death but a contemplative absorption in the idea of mortality". The tomb itself has been transformed from being a decorative design into a rectangular block."

All three were trying to take in the story. Natasha decided to recap, more for her own benefit than anyone else's; "So, this guy Guercino paints

Et In Arcadia Ego in 1621 ish; then Poussin paints two versions both slightly different one in around 1630 and one around 1640. At some point around 1748, Shugborough Hall was enlarged, in 1750 someone decides it's a good idea to make a sculpture version of the painting but do it as a mirror image, changing the text around a bit and adding another tomb."

"That's about it in a nutshell" replied Roger,

"Shakespeare's first folio was published in 1623."

"How do you know all this stuff?" asked Rachel but Roger was in full flow and ignored her.

"1748 is the year that Handel was writing his oratorio Solomon, a biblical subject with a delightful aria about shepherds and shepherdesses sung by a Harlot. Do you remember we saw a picture called Susanna and the Elders dated 1748 hanging in the main hall? That was copied from the original by Guido Reni who originally painted it in around 1620. The blurb tells us that this picture is an illustration from the very same subject; in fact it is remarkably like the first Pouisson painting in that showed two Shepherds looking at a skull with a hole in it. The painting I am talking about shows two shepherds looking at a harlot…. so which came first? The version with the skull, or the version with the harlot?"

"Very good point, skulls represent mortality and harlots, fecundity." William said, recalling the picture.

Natasha's mind was on a slightly different course;

"William, this girl on the Southbank, why did she give you a wax apple?"

"She was just a busker. She had a small basket of apples and was giving one to anyone who gave her a pound. Then she did a little dance and stood absolutely still until someone paid another pound then she did the same thing again."

Natasha kept pursuing the point; "Were all the apples made of wax?"

William thought carefully; "No, no they weren't, I thought it was a bit odd at the time."

Natasha was not sure where this was going but she continued; "And the dance, was it the same every time?"

"Oh, I don't know, I didn't pay much attention I was just walking home."

Natasha urged him to recall.

"Yes, there was something different in the dance she did for me, she was spinning and spinning and then she held out a hand, and looked into my eyes as if she wanted me to follow her. Yes, that's it, she was miming a scene…. leading someone to a spot and then opening both hands and looking as if she had found something…she was looking at me, her eyes asking if I could see it too…then she gracefully moved to her basket, took out the apple and gave it to me."

William fished in his pocket for his compact Fuji camera, here look I took a few pics of her.

Roger, Natasha and Rachel huddled around the screen in the shade to see the images.

Natasha spotted something;

"Look, look, she's wearing a long red dress, the dress of a harlot, as you call them."

William allowed himself to indulge in some free associations;

"Harlot, the Church's view of Mary Magdalen, the Shepherdess...Oh my God!"

"It's staring us in the face," said Roger. "The clues are saying that Jesus did not die on the cross; there are two tombs, one for Mary Magdalen and one for Jesus Christ because he, like us was mortal. No wonder this is dynamite, no wonder I've been getting all those threats."

William looked at Roger; "Threats, you've been getting threats? ...What sorts of threats? You kept that quiet"

Roger tried to brush it off; "You know just the usual ones, back off from wanting to re-open the St Peter's dig or we'll kill you, those sorts of threats."

"You've told the police?"

Roger nodded; "Yes, I've told the police but they aren't taking it seriously."

Natasha was suddenly moody; "You should take these threats seriously Roger, if we are halfway right this is big stuff."

The atmosphere was tense and William tried to diffuse it by returning to the mystery.

"This whole Jesus and Mary Magdalen thing, we have to get it in proportion, it's not really new. There's the theory that Jesus and Mary Magdalene had a child which was then taken to Egypt then on to France and whose blood descendants in later centuries founded the Merovingian dynasty of the early kings of France[*].

Roger placed the wax apple in the sun as he flicked through his own research and continued the discussion.

"I read, the Tomb of God, by Richard Andrews and Paul Schellenberger recently; I must say some of their stuff is thought provoking. It seems to me to be something of an update of the stories that centre on the Rennes-le-Chateau mystery based in the South of France. You know the one where the priest Berenger Sauniere is supposed to have found some sort of secret that made him a rich man".

"One of the many rumours about Sauniere is that he went to the Louvre to get copies made of three paintings, Nicolas Poussin's second version of Les Bergers d'Arcadie, another 17th Century painting St Antony and Saint Paul by David Teniers the Younger and the 16th Century Coronation of Pope Celestine V by artist unknown.

"The authors argue that these share a certain geometry, which Andrews &

---

[*] *The Holy Blood and the Holy Grail by Michael Baigent, Richard Leigh, and Henry Lincoln.*

Schellenberger applied to an old map of the area around Rennes-le-Chateau, leading them to a site, which they identify as Mount Cardou, where they think that whatever made Sauniere rich was/is buried. They claim to have examined many other paintings and only found two other significant examples of the geometry: La Fontaine de Fortune (an illustration from the 15th Century Grail romance Le Cuer d'Amours Espris) and a 13th Century circular map of Jerusalem from the Royal Library at The Hague."

"Let me guess, there's no real evidence, right?" Natasha was losing interest.

"I guess not, but Andrews & Schellenberger believe the site contained/contains the remains of Jesus. On the one hand, they pour cold water on the work of Michael Baigent, Henry Lincoln and Richard Leigh (authors of The Holy Blood and the Holy Grail) and their unproven evidence for a bloodline flowing from Jesus through the Royal families of Europe to Pierre Plantard, the supposed Grand Master of the Prieure de Sion and on the other hand they appear to use The Holy Blood and the Holy Grail as a source for much of their historical information."

Natasha's attention was elsewhere. She had become aware of the faint rustling in the hedges nearby. Rachel was still trawling through the notes she had made about the interviews with Morgan and Pender. William was racking his brains to recall similar quasi factual books he'd read;

"OK, let's not forget Laurence Gardner's book, The Hidden Lineage of Jesus Revealed, he even presents genealogy charts of Jesus as ancestors of all the royal families of European history."

Roger was not so sure.

"It seems to me that despite quite a few differences some salient points emerge: Jesus married Mary and had a child or children; the Church has suppressed the truth about Mary Magdalene and the Jesus bloodline for 2000 years; a secret order protects the knowledge because there may be descendants of Jesus and his wife, Mary Magdalene.

The Roman Catholic Church apparently tried to kill off all remnants of this dynasty and their guardians in order to maintain power through the apostolic succession of Peter instead of the hereditary succession of Mary Magdalene.

William agreed that it was all fascinating but he still didn't know how it affected them. As he sat reflecting on the various theories he noticed that the wax apple was beginning to melt in the sun. Natasha was the first to identify what it revealed.

"Of course, it's a *la wan*!" She peeled away the wax and removed a small piece of white silk.

"The Chinese wrote messages on silk and encased them in balls of wax which were inserted in the anus of those charged with delivering them."

"Yuk, that's gross!" said Rachel.

"No", said Natasha, "That's espionage!"

She picked up the silk and unraveled it. Roger and William gathered around, they were all astonished by the picture printed on it. It was the Mappa Mundi from Hereford Cathedral.

Natasha turned the picture around, then upside down. When she held it to the light she could see a sequence of numbers along the side and over the top, she handed it to Roger and William who studied it carefully.

Natasha sat crouched forward, hitting her forehead repeatedly with the palm of her right hand.

"Are you OK?" asked Roger.

"I know what this is." she said with conviction. "There's a message hidden in the picture, it's a hi-tech code, that's rarely used."

"Can you read it?" William was getting excited.

"It's not that simple, the way this works is that you spread hidden information randomly over a photo using a pseudo-random number generator. Descrambling the photo requires knowing the seed that started the pseudo-random number generation."

William trusted Natasha implicitly, especially in matters IT;

"Nats, isn't this one of the pictures you found on Michael's hard drive?"

"Yes, yes it is. Do you recall the suicide note, the first letter of each line when put together read Caldey. Let's take those letters and give them each the number that numerologists use."

There was silence as Natasha jotted the numbers from 1-9 on a piece of paper and wrote the letters of the alphabet from A-Z along the numerical values.

Roger was intrigued. "That's how numerology works the numbers are then added together to get the lowest figure."

Natasha nodded. Thought for a while then punched the air; "Got it, the seed is 311452. Now all we have to do is apply that to the pixels to read the message". She thought for a moment. "It has to be a co-ordinate"

She reached into her shoulder bag for her laptop but felt something was wrong, the hairs on the back of her neck were standing upright.

-51-

Shugborough Hall
2nd August 2009

Silently, Natasha picked her way through the bushes; her senses alert to every sound. She was now standing very close to where she thought she had heard the unusual disturbance. She could just pick up Roger and William's voices. Moving closer, she spied two men in the undergrowth. One, in camouflage was sitting on a makeshift fishing stool with a camera balanced on a monopod pointing towards Roger and William. The other leant against a tree adjusting a pair of headphones. He held a parabolic microphone which he was pointing directly at Roger and William. He was recording every word. Natasha froze on the spot.

As the men whispered, she reached into her pocket and brought out a mini telescope which gave her a good close up. Suddenly she lost her balance and a cracking twig seemed like a crash of thunder. The two men looked around momentarily but she'd escaped their notice. Judging by their accents, one was British, the other American. By the looks of their equipment, the American was CIA.

Soon Natasha strolled back to her colleagues carrying iced lollies. As she handed them around, she gestured with her eyes towards a note she wanted them to read.

Roger, William and Rachel casually unwrapped their Strawberry splits whilst reading the message.

"Stop talking about the monument, we're being recorded."

Roger slipped the quickly melting lolly into his mouth; "Ummmm, lovely, just what I needed."

William agreed, the conversation must have started to sound stilted. Natasha was uncomfortable with the ensuing silence;

"Hey" she chirped up, "Let's go for a stroll, I'd love to see the rest of the gardens."

They walked for a while and were drawn to the Chinese House. This folly was completed in 1747, making it the first garden building at Shugborough and one of the earliest examples of the eighteenth century fashion for Oriental design.

Natasha pulled out her mobile phone and detached a small black metal end section which she placed at the rear of the room; she then pulled two small antennas from the side and sat it beside her on the bench. She pressed a few buttons and heard a low hum.

"OK, let's talk."

The device she was using set up a feedback field which created a hum over their voices ensuring that the spies would hear nothing but interference.

Roger was impressed with her skills as well as her physical attributes and complimented her in that patronizing way that middle aged single men have a habit of doing. She was used to it.

"You're much more than just a pretty face Nats, where did you learn this stuff?"

"Learn it?- I invented it!"

Confident that the spies could no longer hear them, Natasha offered her theory of choice regarding Jesus Christ. She explained that in the old quarter of Srinagar, Kashmir, there is a tomb for Yuz Asaf. According to the locals, Jesus Christ returned to the city to live out his later life as a Muslim prophet.

"I guess that's possible," Roger acknowledged, "After all, what do we really know about something that happened, or didn't happen two thousand years ago?"

William joined in; "There are also lots of stories about Mary Magdalen, some of the disciples and the family of Jesus travelling to France and then onto Britain after the crucifixion."

"That's a lot of air miles in today's currency."

Rachel was feeling left out.

"Why would they go to places so far away from their homeland?"

"Some make the argument that there were Jews in France and they went to their kinsmen, I'm not convinced." replied Roger.

Back in the undergrowth the spies were more than a little perplexed, the taller of the two, Brad O'Brien, who was on listening post, motioned to Robin Bryant on camera; "I've lost them, I'm just getting interference...I'm trying to switch channels."

Robin had just returned to the bushes after discretely following them to the Chinese House.

Suddenly there was a loud ping and the sound of machine gun fire. Roger jumped out of his skin and William and Rachel looked around in surprise.

Natasha laughed;

"It's OK; it's just my ringtone for incoming email." She picked up her jamming devices and took them out of the rear of the building to where a wooden jetty protruded from the pagoda into the waterway. She sat down and swung her shapely legs over the side until they nearly touched the water. She opened her laptop, attached the encryption and mobile broadband device and proceeded to retrieve the email. It was from Evans, he was checking in to see how they were getting on.

Meanwhile, Rachel had been searching through the notes from the Morgan and Pender DVD that Nicole had left in the briefcase.

"Here it is!" she declared. Morgan and Pender referred to the Shepherds of Arcadia during their interview. "They said that in the painting the three men and one woman are looking at an inscription on a tomb. They said they noticed a gap in the writing in one painting and that two people were pointing, one at a letter and the other to a gap, so they moved the letter to the gap to see what it said. They think the inscription when deciphered from Coelbren to ancient Welsh then English reads;

"I am in the land of Caradoc."

From this they deduced that the person buried in the tomb and where the shepherds of Arcadia had gathered was in the lost city of Caradoc in Wales.

Christianity arrived in Britain between 35 and 37AD with Joseph of Arimathea and others. I guess that means they are suggesting that the painting is a clue to the mystery of where Jesus Christ is buried."

This tied in with what William had learnt from Father Everson. He delivered with confidence;

"Different sources say that Jesus was just a man not a God, that he survived the crucifixion and came to Britain with Mary Magdalen and others where they lived and died. The real Christianity is not that which was fictionalized at the Council of Nicea in the 4th century, it's based on much more ancient, pagan beliefs centering on the male sun and the female moon. And I believe that this is all part of the puzzle as to what Jesus and Mary really stood for and where they were buried."

Suddenly it all seemed to be making sense. Rachel scrolled through the transcripts of the interviews and found more relevant details. Morgan and Pender alleged that the ancient Welsh text, The Songs of the Graves, confirms that Jesus was buried in Wales but they don't give any specific details. They said that they could understand why such incendiary information had been covered up. *(The Songs of the Graves started off as an oral tradition in the 1st Century AD and were written down in the 6th Century by Taliesen, aka Merlin).*

"Morgan said he wasn't too happy about divulging this information in an interview but thought that as he was 77 years old, he couldn't wait much longer, how prophetic."

At last, a real motive for the murders. During their research into King Arthur, Morgan and Pender had stumbled upon information that others had tried to hide for 2000 years. They may have correctly translated the old Coelbren alphabet and the oldest Welsh manuscripts to discover that Jesus survived the crucifixion and lived the rest of his life in Britain. Towards the end of his life, Morgan decided to make his findings public via Helen Daniels and the BBC. Proof, if ever it was needed that there are people still prepared to kill to cover up the past.

It was coming up to 5pm as they said their goodbyes in the car park. Roger opened the door of his Honda Civic as the yellow AA van parked alongside left in a screaming hurry. Nearby Natasha was about to start up the Porsche when suddenly she had a premonition. She waved frantically at Roger and Rachel who by this time were sitting in the car and about to move off. Luckily they saw her and stopped. She walked over to meet them, leaving William near the Porsche.

"Don't start the car Roger."

Arriving by his side she whispered in his ear;

"You didn't call the AA did you?"

The man was indignent;

"No, this is a new Honda!"

The greasy hand print on the door and bonnet that she noticed on the way back to the car had aroused her suspicious mind.

Natasha leaned into the driver's side and tucked her head under the steering column.

"I can't see anything!"

"Looks lovely from where I'm standing." said Roger.

Natasha sprung from the car like a coiled snake and glared at him as she pulled the bonnet release.
Roger kept his distance and felt like a spare part. He knew his history but was as hopeless with cars, as he was with women.

A few Russian explicatives could be heard from below the bonnet and when she emerged their justification was evident. She was triumphantly holding a cigarette packet with wires hanging out either side.

"In this case smoking is most certainly bad for you!"

Roger was shocked and asked her what it was.

She sniffed the packet and the smell affirmed her hunch.

"This, Roger, is C-4, it's enough plastic explosive to blow you and your car to smithereens."

-52-

Caerleon
2nd August 2009

Natasha had been quiet for some time trying to second guess what MI5 and the CIA were up to. In her room near Caerleon she was dismantling Nicole's laptop. The video recording of Nicole's death was horrid but that was not the only reason she was haunted by the hit man's face. Although she hadn't seen him for years she was certain she had known the South African Bruce Botha by another name. No-one else could look that evil. What she couldn't figure out was who his paymasters were for this job. MI5 and the CIA would have been much more clinical than this bodged perversion, wouldn't they?

William had been watching her from across the room.

"Have you figured it out yet Nats?"

She looked at him with her big wide eyes and shook her head.

As she removed the bottom of the laptop she told William that Morgan and Pender had been killed by two deliberately planted smart incendiary devices, adding.

"Evans told me all about it."

William wasn't phased, somehow he seemed to know all about it himself. Someone had already told him, hadn't they? What was Nats up to?

"Nasty, very nasty."

"Yes and there are only a few people who have that sort of cunning and access, the PM, the Home Secretary..."

"What about Helen and Nicole? Did the government employ the South African?" William asked.

Natasha shook her head;

"Niet, I don't think so."

William looked her straight in the eyes and asked her a question he had always wanted to :

"So who do you work for Natasha?"

There was no hesitation.

"For you William, I work for you."

They both smiled.

Minutes later she had removed the black USB memory stick from its hiding place inside Nicole's laptop and inserted it into her own special computer. This triggered an alarm and a flashing message, a level 10 booby trap. The noise made William jump:

"What the hell is that?"

"It's a device that shreds all the contents on the memory stick if you try to open it."

"Why would Nicole hide that in her laptop?"

"We're about to find out." She said as she quickly entered some more key strokes. Within a few seconds most of the files that should have deleted opened on the screen and she worked quickly to back them up.

"If you're quick you can engage software that fools the booby trap into believing it hasn't been opened."

"I am guessing you can't buy that at PC World." He felt right out of his depth.

Once safely backed-up, they started looking at the documents. There were copy emails and letters which showed that Nicole was sending threats to Helen. William sat down, his head in his hands, this was all too much but Natasha hadn't finished, there were more revelations.

"This is strange Will; there are copies of all sorts of things from Helen's computers at home and at the BBC. Nicole must have been hacking them." A series of emails caught Natasha's eye.

"This is interesting. There are loads of emails between Helen to Evans about the Arthur documentary."

"But Evans is not supposed to have seen his daughter for years. Rachel said he made a big thing about it."

"Well, he lied about that and, looking at these emails, I suspect he was lying about being her father too unless he's really perverted." Natasha remained cool as ever.

"You mean Evans was her lover?" he asked.

"How would I know?" she smiled; "but I'm pretty sure this was an Interpol operation to get information from Morgan and Pender."

"Bloody hell, it just gets worse!"

Natasha continued looking through the files.

"Hey, here's something else, a copy of a letter from Morgan and Pender to Helen."

The letter described how Morgan and Pender believed they had found the exact location of the crucifixion cross which they alleged Helen, the mother of the Emperor Constantine brought back from the Holy Lands to Britain.

William was beginning to see how the church might be caught up in this, first Morgan and Pender argue they can prove the Jesus lived and died in Britain and that they know where he is buried and now they allege the crucifixion cross is on Welsh soil too.

It was like Christmas time for the sleuths as Natasha opened another document from Morgan and Pender. This one began:

"There is a strong local custom that Jesus and Mary Magdalen lived in this cave after the crucifixion."

It went on to discuss pre-Christian traditions around the image of a cross as well as astronomical and pagan concepts tied up with local people and culture.

William had to work hard to make sense of it all.

"I can sort of follow it. If what they say is right and the Khumry were descended from one of the "lost" tribes and they did come to Britain and settle in Wales then it would be quite natural for Jesus and his clan to come to Britain to escape persecution. In effect they were coming to their kinsmen and, of course, if Constantine's mum Helen was from the area and was part of the tribe then it makes sense that she should return home as well."

"I feel like we're playing out an Indiana Jones script." said Natasha, she enjoyed the excitement of it all.

"Well, if it's true it certainly undermines the Church and then, of course, there's the treasure element. If its true that the crucifixion cross was encased in silver and gold and encrusted with jewels, and if there is Templar Treasure, it's going to be worth an absolute fortune, quite apart from the historic interest. Thirdly, if Pender is right about the genealogy from Jesus to Arthur and eventually to Princess Diana then that might explain why MI5 are involved. It was bad enough when some people thought she was going to have Al Fayed's baby!"

"So, does this tell us who the hit man was working for?" Natasha asked.

William shrugged his shoulders. "The Church? Monty Python? The Spanish Inquisition?"

Natasha smiled, welcoming the light relief but it was short-lived. Her face turned deadly serious as she read a further batch of emails, there was no mistaking the call sign code spotted.

William knew something was wrong and his eyes demanded and received clarification; "Nicole was a double agent working with the Russians."

William just stared; "Are you sure?"

Natasha nodded.

William thought for a few moments; "Is that why she was killed?"

Natasha had to admit it was possible "This would make one hell of a computer game!"

-53-

Caerleon
3rd August 2009

William was dreaming of flying across the green hills and valleys of Wales. It was a dream that came to him often and the pleasure it brought would linger all day. However this time it was slightly different, he seemed to be vaguely aware of bees gathering around him, swarming close, threatening. Slowly the buzzing grew louder and when he surfaced Natasha was leaning over him, she kissed him gently on the forehead and placed a cup of coffee on the bedside table.

Natasha brought her laptop over and climbed back into bed. William enjoyed this unexpected intimacy and the smell of her damp, freshly washed hair.

"I've found some more stuff on Michael's old hard drive. I managed to take some ghost information and materialize it. There is quite a lot here. It seems Michael had been doing his own serious research too. I haven't got the complete file but there are enough fragments here to make some sense of it."

William leant over to read from the screen. It was notes about aloe and myrrh, medicinal plants used by the Egyptians for healing and embalming. The notes suggested that a formula containing these plants could have been used to heal Jesus after the crucifixion, thus providing further support for the theory that he survived the ordeal.

"Fascinating."

Natasha noticed the time; "Christ, come on, we've got to meet the others in 15 mins."

William looked at her inquisitively, only recalling being tired and curling up on the bed with her. "Did we, umm, you know, did we make love?"

Natasha smiled knowingly "I think you would have remembered if we had, don't you?"

The way she was tapping her nose with her finger added to the confusion. He wasn't sure if he knew anything any more.

-54-

Caerleon, Wales
3rd August 2009

The quaint coffee house in Caerleon was empty until Evans, Rachel, William, Natasha and Roger turned up and ordered breakfast. There was tension in the air, William was wondering whether or not to ask Evans straight out about his relationship with Helen Daniels. He chose to keep this to himself whilst the group shared more of what they had learnt so far.

Roger started off; "The church would have us believe that Jesus was "missing" in his early years but some of the ancient writings tell a different story. From them we know that Jesus the Christ travelled and studied a lot in his youth. He studied the mysteries at the Druid College at Llantwit Major, a place where his uncle, some say father, Joseph of Arimathea set up a church and university. He was a rover known to many people for his healing ability and wisdom. He met up with Mary Magdalena who was an Egyptian Princess related to Queen Cleopatra and Mark Anthony. Together they taught the mysteries, an amalgam of ancient wisdom and knowledge. Jesus fell foul of the traditional Jews and the Romans who planned to crucify him. He and his followers contrived to try to cheat his death and appear to bring him back to life to secure and reiterate the beliefs of the old religion. Being a rich man, Joseph was able to bribe the powers that be to stage the spectacle whilst ensuring that Jesus survived. To avoid persecution Jesus and his family then came to Britain via the South of France and settled with the Khumry, their own people and one of the lost tribes of Egypt. They continued their teachings in Britain and the offspring of Jesus and Mary Magdalen married into the dynasty of Welsh kings which led down to King Arthur in the sixth century and, more than likely, forwards to a member of the Royal family, Diana and thence to Prince William Arthur.

Roger offered more justification for the link with the Spencer family.
"It's a long story"
The room was silent.
Roger explained that the perspective from which history is taught in our

schools, colleges and universities is a very recent fabrication developed in the Hanoverian and Victorian eras. It was created during the turbulent days of the American Civil War and the French Revolution exclusively to bolster England's position at the heart of the British Empire. It exonerates and praises the Anglo Saxons as the bringers of culture to the Isles of Britain, but, in reality nothing could be further from the truth. This newly invented slant on the histories treated everything that happened prior to the Saxons, with the exception of the Roman influence, as myths and legends. There is a long and crafted conspiracy, a web of lies and deceit to negotiate for anyone intent on unearthing this island's true history. Many academics simply give up for the sake of their grant funding.

There is still a place where our real history has been largely preserved. Over time, the custodians of this knowledge have been persecuted both as individuals and as a society. For centuries the Welsh have been the victims of hate and derision, feelings which were born out of jealousy and ignorance. The plan to eradicate our true history and replace it with the Saxon/Hanoverian line is almost complete. However, when you peel back the surface the truth still lays underneath.

Roger's recounting of the less familiar but arguably more accurate history of Britain was fascinating; it was also complex and long. His breakfast of eggs and bacon was congealling on the plate, his tea was cold and his audience was flagging.

William's eyes had glazed over and Natasha was trying not to nod off. Roger took a break and ordered more tea.

"It's really important that you understand this and I think it's the key to what is going on here." Roger chided.

"I can see why all this history stuff could so easily be hidden and rewritten it's so boring." replied Natasha.

Roger looked genuinely hurt. He explained to the group that he had Morgan and Pender to thank for much of the information, which he had been able to verify from the original sources they told him about. He too was scared to go public as he had seen the treatment metered out to them. He knew it would be worse for him since he was also a university academic and part of the establishment. He knew he would kiss good bye to any future grants and work, not to mention his reputation. He wasn't sure what to do for the best, things were moving so rapidly. He'd already escaped death a couple of times within the past week.

Roger looked exhausted but felt so much lighter for confessing all that he knew.

"So this is it then, this is what the murders are all about, Jesus being in Britain and being buried here, leaving a bloodline down to Arthur and forward to Diana and, of course Prince William. I can understand why certain people want this kept quiet. But why would they want to kill off our own history, it doesn't make any sense, I mean, it doesn't make Jesus any less of a great man if he had an earthly body that was found, does it?"

Roger underlined the situation; "Don't forget William, if Jesus survived the crucifixion then dies and his body was buried then he couldn't have done the central thing that Christianity is based on, that is his ascent to Heaven as the son of God. And you also have to consider that in the early 18th century the house of Hanover put forward the strongest case for the nobility with the right religion to take over the British monarchy with the German Georges. British history was re-written, so the stories of Jesus being here in the UK from 37AD and of King Arthur and his links to the Holy family had to go. They would have got away with this if it hadn't been for the fact that Arthur was too big and strong…"

"…and if Morgan and Pender hadn't stirred the whole thing up." William finished the sentence.

Evans cleared his throat and everyone looked at him;

"I think the only chance we have of being safe is to find the body of Jesus and the St Peters cross and let the authorities think they found them first, that way they might just leave us alone, for all we know they might be just letting us get on with it hoping we'd lead them to the right places."

Roger wasn't so sure;

"But if we do that the deaths of people will all be swept under the carpet in some white washed cover up won't they…?"

"At least we'd stay alive. But, even if we find these things what the hell would we do with them?" asked William. "Would we give them to the church and the government who would make them disappear to keep the old lies going, or to, I don't know, someone like the Jews who don't believe the Messiah has come yet, or to an Islamic nation who recognise Jesus for what he was, a great teacher and healer who didn't die on the cross?"

Evans looked at the gathered band. The impact of what William had said sunk in. Whoever ended up with the cross and body of Jesus Christ, if they existed at all, called the religious shots.

Roger looked around, aware of his mortality; "Let's not forget the enlightenment, Sir Isaac Newton and the Rosicrucians, we know that Elizabeth 1, her ambassador Sir Philip Sydney and her court astrologer John Dee were all in favour of the old wisdom and were frequent visitors to St Peters Church on Caer Caradoc"

Rachel looked curious; "The Rosicrucians?"

Roger nodded; "Yes, their symbol was the "Rosy Cross", a device usually drawn as a golden cross sporting either a single, red rose at its crossing or a wreath of roses draped across its upright arm. The cross was also known as the croix fleury. The symbol of the Order of the Garter and also of the House of Tudor was the rose. This makes a link between Queen Elizabeth and the Rosicrucians very tempting.

This link to the Rose Cross fascinated me, I visited the churches of Llantwit Major, Merthyr Mawr and the cathedral at Llandaff where I found several examples of the Rosicross symbols in the form of floriated crosses inscribed on flag stone memorials. At Llandaff I examined the tombs of various members of the Matthews family. On some of these were clearly displayed the arms of Iestyn ap Gwrgan, the last independent king of Glamorgan. In the Herbert's Chapel in the church of St Marys at Abergavenny where the ancestors of Mary Sidney's husband William Herbert Earl of Pembroke lie buried there are ancient floriated crosses on some of the flagstones. On the north side of the church near the high altar is a statue of Jesse, the father of the biblical King David. The statue is large, like an enormous reclining Buddah. Rising from his stomach is the stump of a large tree which had been cut back but was growing again from a side shoot. Clearly this was a reference to the biblical prophecy in Isaiah 1 "There shall come forth a shoot from the stump of Jesse, and a branch shall grow out of his roots." This is a reference to Jesus whose family tree is given in both Matthew and Luke and traces through David to Jesse.

It is not uncommon to find the Tree of Jesse used as church art, and notably in Tewkesbury Abbey, but the sheer size and scale of it in Abergavenny indicated it was more than just passing interest."

"Of course, those few who have studied the subject objectively, but do not dare to say, know that the Tree of Jesse represents Ashera, the wife of God."

Asherah was written out of the history books but continues in collective race memory as the Tree of Life. There was a look of recognition on the faces of those present who realised that the symbol is familiar even today.

A small glint of red light appeared on Roger's forehead. Natasha accurately computed it as a laser gun sight but was powerless to react in time. There was a large cracking sound from the window as the glass shattered and Roger fell forward onto the table. William saw the whole thing in slow motion and smiled at first thinking Roger was playing a joke. Natasha knew instantly that he'd been shot. The bullet had gone through his head and embedded in the wooden panelling behind him. She motioned to everyone to get down as another shot zinged its way through the smashed window and imbedded in the wall, then another and another.

Others now in the tea shop screamed and ran for the rear exit. Natasha headed for the front door and pulled the bolt across to slow up anyone trying to get in. Evans crept to the side window and was trying to see what was happening, his Para Ordnance pistol, cocked and ready.

There was mayhem in the street outside as people ran and cars braked. Shots were still being fired outside but, oddly, not into the shop.

Suddenly it went quiet and a car took off like a mad bull in the mating season.

Natasha was the first out into the street. She committed the car number to memory and spotted a man down on the pavement opposite.

Rachel had an arm around Roger sobbing and shaking him in disbelief.

Outside, Natasha knelt on the pavement by the bleeding man and observed two gunshot wounds to the head and a Government Issue pistol by his side. She frisked the man professionally removing his phone and slipping it into her inside pocket.

Evans and William were by her side quickly, staring at the corpse. Natasha knew enough about firearms to realise that the weapon he was carrying was not accurate or powerful enough to have taken Roger out so clinically. She deduced that he must have tried to take down the assassin but been killed in the process.

Evans joined Natasha and looked quizzically at her; "It's Robin Bryant, the MI5 operative"

Evans nodded, he already knew.

-55-

MI5 HQ, London
3rd August 2009

Grey looked forlorn as she gathered her admin team for the briefing;

"Bryant has been killed in the field. He was working with Brad O'Brien trying to protect a group of people under surveillance in the Meurig Project. His last report said that he'd seen Botha in Caerleon and that he and O'Brien were observing."

David Fennell, Grey's colleague, asked what had happened to the CIA man.

"That's the odd thing Fennell, he seems to have vanished." replied Grey.

"Agents don't just vanish."

"They do if they are double agents or, maybe we are being played. Speaking of which has Evans filed a report?"

Selina from IT Intercept came into the room.

"Someone is downloading from Robin's phone." She said.

"Why wasn't it deactivated when we knew he was dead, you know the protocol, who is doing it?" asked Grey.

"We're trying to trace it, GPS puts it in central Caerleon, it could be Evans".

Grey shook her head;

"Very unlikely, Evans isn't that technical. I am guessing a download from a SIM would be beyond him!"

Grey picked up the phone to Operations;

"I need two armed operatives in Wales and I need them yesterday, I'll brief them by phone."

O'Brien's disappearance had also caused considerable concern within the CIA. He was only in Wales for God sake!

-56-

Caerleon/Cardiff
3rd August 2009

The crazy drive through the streets, hands cuffed behind his back and laid horizontal across the rear seat was making him feel dizzy. Father Everson had most certainly not managed to shake off the ether which still wafted on to his face. He had struggled of course but then everyone does. He must be brave; after all, what did he have to live for? He had already been diagnosed with a terminal brain tumor. Nothing these people could do to him would be worse than the disillusionment he felt for the church.

The car with blacked out windows slowed and came to a stop. There was a brief discussion between the men he couldn't see about whether the way was all clear. With a black cloth over his head he was bundled quickly and unceremoniously from the car through a door with a raised wooden step and along a rough floor.

Even through the Ether he could smell the familiar mustiness, the polish on the wood and the sharp scent of restoration fluid. He had been at this place just a few days ago. Unless he was very much mistaken it was Llandaff Cathedral.

The two men took an arm each and virtually dragged Everson along a walkway to the left of a row of pews through a doorway and down a corridor to an inner hallway. Had Everson been able to see he would have been aware that a series of grotesque old carvings that lined the inner hall, found at a recent archaeological dig, were looking on intently laughing and mocking his plight.

The rough handlers had no respect for people or age as they dragged the still woozy monk down a spiral staircase. At the bottom the stones opened out into an arched cellar illuminated by dangerously flickering old light bulbs. At one end there was a stone throne and around the side a couple of other chairs that had been arranged in a semi circle.

Once tied to a chair he was sat in a place where the minders could see and hear him.

The ropes dug into his arms but he did not make a sound.

A few minutes that seemed like hours passed until a man slid into the room and made his way across to Everson. Holding the rope that kept the black sack over Everson's head he sliced the knot and pulled it off in one movement.

Well, well, Father Everson, thank you so much for coming.

Everson's eyes took a little while to adapt to the half light but there was no mistaking the shape, his malevolent ambience or his satanic voice; "Welcome back to chapter 322."

Everson wriggled, squinting at the man in the half light;

"Cardinal Valetti, so you have a day pass from hell then?"

Valetti was not amused. He immediately stepped forward and brought his gloved hand across the man's face marking it wickedly and drawing a little blood from the corner of his mouth which mingled with his short beard.

"Of course, you know why you are here, don't you, Everson?"

Everson managed a smile; "You want some private tuition in good manners and graceful behavior?"

Valetti grunted but restrained himself from further violence; there would be plenty of time for that later. "Let me just remind you, my old friend..... you are going to tell us where the cross is hidden, the cross that was found at the dig at St Peter's."

At last Everson was putting two and two together.

"Ah, the St Peters cross with "for the soul of Arthur" on it, so, you are still collecting antiquities."

Valetti moved so close to Everson's face that he could smell the foul body oozing from his pores and up his nose. He gagged. "My friends can be very persuasive Father Everson...and we know after you found it you had a convincing copy made which you passed off as the original to Morgan and Pender, they sold it to us for three million pounds but the cross was your fake and so was the report into the age and authenticity that Dr Felix prepared, I take it you and Felix cooked this up between you and that you and he have either sold the original or are hoping to make a further fortune out of it?"

Everson stayed calm; "Oh, and I thought it was you who had all the answers... fancy that, the great Valetti being taken in by a cheap trick, I bet your masters at the Vatican are wondering if it was really you that pulled the stunt, pocketed the money and blamed Morgan and Pender!"

Valetti rushed forward and smacked Everson in the mouth so hard that the chair he was tied to fell over backwards with the force. Everson could feel the blood from his nose running down his cheeks, across his shoulder blade and onto the floor. From the sound that accompanied the strike Everson assumed his nose was broken, it wouldn't have been the first time... as he laid tied to the chair with his knees in the air, his head and shoulders against the cold stone floor his face just started to throb. As the feeling was coming back he saw Valetti upside down, berating himself for losing his temper so badly...then it happened.

The memories started flooding back to him, memories from a time long before the accident.

Everson pretended to faint buying himself a few moments respite. The two minders placed him and the chair upright and Valetti poured a jug of water over his head.

Everson feigned coming to remarkably well "I don't think much of your hospitality Valetti, you could have tried to be civilized and asked nicely. Why don't you tell me what this is all about, I assume you are not going to let me go whatever happens."

Valetti looked thoughtful; "Maybe you are right, maybe we can be a little more civilized about this...as you say you will have a choice, come back to us, to the chapter, give us the real St Peter's cross and help us, or, well, let's say, you die."

Everson's vision was a little blurred, he could feel the blood from his nose running over his lips now and onto his clothing; "Even if I did keep the original cross and had a copy made, why is it so important, important enough to kill for?"

Valetti brought his face down to eye level and gazed intently at Everson; "You don't know do you, after all your research knowledge and skill you really don't know about what Bishop Beere of Glastonbury was buried with do you?"

Everson was trying to recall what he knew about Beere. He knew that he had raided the Holy Land and stolen items from the Loretto Chapel in Italy and that he had made a replica room in Glastonbury Abbey to mirror the Loretto. He knew it had a black shiny floor with a gold circle into which were carved the main constellations inlaid with gold. It was divided into 12 wedges to represent the months, disciples and Knights of the Round Table. Each sement also representing star signs in the sky. A figure of Mary Magdalen stood in the centre pointing at the constellation Cygnus, The Swan.

Valetti interrupted Everson's thought process; "A ball in each hand, one white and one black representing Yahweh and Asherah the male and female in balance. In the white ball was part of an early manuscript said to be in the hand of Taliesin, who some say was the 6th century Merlin or Merthyn. It tells how he and Illtyd melted down two of the nails from the crucifixion brought back to Britain by Helen in the 4th century, some sacred relics brought by traders from Constantinople, some local gold and silver extract and part of a mysterious metal born from the otherworld by a comet. It also tells of how Illtyd made marks on the back of the St Peters cross to act as a map to find the earthly remains of Jesus, he knew that at one time in the future people would want to find the truth….in essence that JC was simply a man. Of course we can never let that information be known so we need to find the real metal cross and the body of Jesus, without the real artifact the legend stays just that, a legend"

Everson was still looking a little puzzled; "So, you haven't found the body of Jesus yet then, my my you are slipping Valetti."

Valetti's eyes widened; "Not exactly, but that's the whole point, when I do they will make me Pope!"

Everson managed to smile; "You can dream of white smoke all you like Valetti but even the church wouldn't allow you to be Pope."

Valetti tried to ignore the rebuff; "We think you and Morgan and Pender have found some strong clues and we are patiently watching and waiting whilst your friends work out the puzzle and lead us to it."

Everson was remembering and not liking much of what he was recalling and hearing. Could he really once have been part of this odd group... yes, yes, it was chapter 322, a well to do cell of the original Illuminati... no, he must have been hallucinating, reading too many novels ... sure there used to be such an organization set up in the 17th century maybe, but that was for enlightenment wasn't it?, not destruction.

Valetti was watching his eyes, "So, how convenient Father Everson, now you are starting to remember, you recall that we have to make sure the information about Jesus and his family stays hidden from everyone to preserve Christianity. You know, don't you, that the real British history can never be told, it is completely incompatible with Roman Catholicism."

Everson was shaking a little; "Yes, yes I had a road accident; I lost my memory... I had to start all over again..."

Valetti was laughing now; "An accident, oh yes that little accident, I believe your wife and two children were killed ... how sad, how very sad... of course it was no accident WE arranged it!"

Everson struggled in his chair in a knee jerk reaction trying to get to Valetti... "You, you murdered them? Why for Christ's sake, why?"

Valetti replied solemnly "Because you wanted to leave our little band of protectors and you and maybe even your wife knew too much, we couldn't let that happen of course"

Everson was in tears; "God, but why the children?"

Valetti kept seeing the funny side of it. "Well, collateral damage I'm afraid, you were all together in the car. Still, there's no justice in the world is there, we can hardly pray to a God that doesn't exist to help us can we?"

Valetti then went on about the accident "We were mainly trying to kill you of course, ironic that you were the only one to survive...you were no threat whilst you had forgotten everything...now, well now that's a whole different matter... you had to go on the dig at St Peters and you had to find that cross didn't you? You were always one for putting your foot in things and stirring up a hornets nest... what an unfortunate day that was for you... anyway, why do you say for Christ's sake, you know as well as I that HE never existed...well, only as a boring but clever man."

Things were oh so slowly coming together in Everson's mind, he wondered how he had known Valetti so well, how and why the place seemed so familiar... was he really once part of some strange group and why, what did they do, what had he done?

Valetti was observing Everson closely, "You really had forgotten all about it hadn't you? You know at one time you were head of this group, of chapter 322; it has in it some of the most powerful people in the world. We all know the truth, we are all enlightened ones; we all know that the supernatural elements of the trinity were made up for power and control by Constantine right from the day of the Council of Nicea in 325 AD.

Our group has been 'protecting' ever since those days. If we control the artificial story of Jesus as a man and a God then we control the gateway to heaven and everything else...people, money, power. That's why when little things come along to cast doubt or threaten to bring true enlightenment to the masses we have to stamp on them from a great height...we can't have the people knowing what we know because there'd be total destabilization of civilization in the west, not to mention a large-scale loss of money, power and respect."

Everson looked genuinely shocked. Valetti brought up a chair and wiped the blood from Everson's nose and mouth. He motioned to his heavies to bring water and the monk took a few sips; "It's not such a big deal...you'll recall father that no contemporary historians mention Jesus at all. Suetonius who lived from 65-135 certainly doesn't. Pliny the Younger only mentions Christians with no comment of Jesus himself. Tacitus mentions a Jesus, but it is likely that after a century of Christian preaching Tacitus was just reacting to rumours. Josephus, a methodical, accurate and dedicated historian of the time records John the Baptist, Herod, Pilate and many aspects of Jewish life but never mentions Jesus. Justus, another Jewish historian who lived in Tiberius near Capernaum, a place Jesus supposedly frequented did not mention Jesus or any of his miracles. Even the gospels themselves do not allude to first-hand historical sources. The four Gospels that eventually made it into the New Testament are all anonymous, written in the third person about Jesus and his companions. None of them contains a first-person narrative. Why then do we call them Matthew, Mark, Luke and John? Because sometime in the second century, when orthodox Christians recognized the need for apostolic authorities, they attributed these books to apostles (Matthew and John) and close companions of apostles for example Mark, the secretary of Peter; and Luke, the travelling companion of Paul. Most scholars today have abandoned these identifications, and recognize that the books were written by otherwise unknown but relatively well-educated Greek-speaking Christians during the second half of the first century."

Everson's memories were flashing back, the research he had done in the past was starting to slot into that which he had more recently concentrated on. "Yes, I remember now, maybe someone who claimed to be a prophet and messiah, of whom there were many in those years is an historical Jesus, in fact just a man. His life story has been intermingled with older pagan myths, and it is very hard for us to see his true life or message. We have little or no information about him, he is effectively without historical basis because any real figure is obscured by a mythical one. God-Man and women myths were very popular and pre-dated the God-Man of Jesus by thousands of years. They all shared a common format which is that the Son of God has 12 disciples, is betrayed and killed by a traitor. Popular myths such as the virgin birth, miracles, curing the blind and ill are also familiar and common aspects of these myths. Such events were also assumed to be true of an historical Jesus. These myths became interwoven amongst the stories of someone who might have been real. Many Jewish sayings became attributed to this character and sayings of John the Baptist too. Stories about the disciples were assumed to be accurate and not simply symbolic stories as the original Gnostic Christians believed. "

Valetti was smiling; perhaps he had after all judged Everson too harshly: "Now Daniel, now that your memory is returning perhaps you'd like to tell us where the St Peter's cross is."

Everson relented, he had a plan but it was a tricky one. Actually, it was the only one he had; "Ok, ok, but you'll need me; the safe has a biometric lock."

Valetti was unsure whether to believe Everson; in the end he gave him the benefit of the doubt: "Untie our guest and clean him up, oh, and bring him a nice strong cup of Lapsang Souchong, your favourite, I recall."

Everson looked gracious, inside he was fuming. He had seen and felt the wonders that the Book of Life had given him, he knew there was a power at work much stronger than any physical human one, even if that was not actually in the form of Jesus.

-57-

Caerleon, Wales
3rd August 2009

Angela had always been cold and calculated. Her acting skills were amazing; she really should have made it big in Hollywood. Instead she loved finding ways of making money that were sometimes less than legal.

She had been brought up as the daughter of a magician, someone who believed he could harness the elements for his own advantage. After his death she had studied her father's papers well. Her strategy of seduction, marriage of those with money and power followed by inheritance had guaranteed her income and an ever growing pot of gold. She looked good for her age, funny how the centuries had passed so quickly. Even so she was not always as wise as she would have liked. Clearly Michael had discovered information that he had not passed on to her and that annoyed her. He had been a hard nut to crack. Could she have underestimated him?

When King Arthur and his family had been alive in the 6th century she had tried the best she could to eradicate them, after all, even though she was the illigitimate daughter of Arthur's magician Taliesin she felt that she should have been queen. Over the centuries she had made it her job to rub out any attempt to prove that her siblings ever existed. Michael had started to take an unhrealty interest in King Arthur. Looking back she believed that he had discovered who she really was, after all, he was a powerful Shaman, but she had defeated better than he.

Although he didn't know it William had worried her from the moment he was born. There was something too powerful surrounding him, a female energy of immense power, even more powerful than hers. Still, he was only human and she was not.

Why was he meddling with the Arthur story anyway? What was his soul purpose? It was most certainly time to rid herself of these niggles.

Then, just as she planned William entered the conference building. She hid, allowing him to be drawn into the web. He walked along the corridor and into the mens toilet.

Angela moved two signs across the hallway to advise people that 'These toilets are being cleaned, please use the alternative facilities on the first floor'

William was just finishing his pee when the door opened. He could see Angela in the mirror entering the room behind him. Quickly zipping his fly he turned to face her.

"Angela, what on earth are you doing in here, this is the men's loo!"

She smiled, unbuttoning her blouse allowing an ample cleavage more room to breath;

"I know, I wanted to talk with you, the last time we met seemed a bit awkward"

For a moment they both stood glancing at each other. William felt the pain in his brain throb and his eyes blur. He felt as if his body was shrinking.

"Why was there concrete in Michael's coffin, Angela? Did you have him cremated and the ashes made into a diamond for your trophy rings?"

The woman looked at her fingers, three rings glinted in a shaft of light that penetrated the room;

"Yes, what a clever boy to have guessed?"

The sarcasm was evident.

"So, have you trapped the souls of your lovers to harness their magic to add to your own?"

The enchantress was gazing steadily into his eyes;

"You know who I am?"

William smiled;

"Of course I know"

The woman moved closer and he stepped back;

"Then you know what I can do"

The enchantress moved her hands in the air and swayed a little;

"I can take all your head pains away Will" she started moving closer. His eyes seemed transfixed on her moving body.William held up two hands to try to halt her advance.

"The hospital tell me I have a brain tumor growing but are not sure how bad it is"

Angela smiled, "I know"..

William placed his head in his hands..

"What do you mean you know.."

Angela was infront of him, beside him, behind him, her arms around him holding him firmly to her.

"Ssshhh, it's ok Will, just relax, let me heal you.."

She held his head in her hands, rubbing gently. He was powerless to move. Her sweet perfume and the soft warmth of her body was permeating him. Slowly her hands started exploring his body, much as they had done when he had visited her recently. His energy was being drained, his head was spinning, his trousers bulging, his kundalini rising. She knew if she could seduce him, if she could get him inside her he'd be lost for ever.

Natasha, Rachel and Evans were looking all over the venue. Natasha felt the hairs on the back of her head stand on end;

"Something's wrong."

Evans nodded; his instinct was the same but for a different reason.

"If you were fanatical and wanted to get rid of people who wanted the truth about King Arthur to come out, what would you do?"

There was a sudden realization that a bomb may have been planted.

Evans looked at them; "Come on, we have to find it, Natasha could you do the ground floor, Rachel, come with me."

Only the power and strength of Angela's body was keeping William standing now. Her deep kisses and probing tounge were reaching his vey soul. His head was spinning wildly as they sank very slowly, oh so slowly to the floor.

In one move Angela was on top of him astride his body, her soft thighs pressing against his hips. She unzipped his jeans, releasing his erect member from its restraint.

Angela took his penis in her hand and moved to lower the softest part of her onto his hardest.

There was a crash and a bang as the door swung open against the wall. Natasha ran in and kneeled at William's side, he was alone, collapsed on the floor.

She cradled his head and shoulders in her arms; "Will, Will, come on Will, don't do this to me now."

Slowly he opened his eyes and jumped back in a start.

Natasha held him tight; "It's ok Will, it's ok, it's me Natasha…"

"Angela, where's Angela, what did she do to me?"

Natasha sat William upright; "Angela's not here Will, no-ones here, just you and I."

With some difficulty she helped him to his feet and over to the sink where he splashed his face with cold water.

"Christ Nats, what the hell happened?"

Upstairs Evans was doing a propfessional job of checking all the usual places someone may plant a bomb.

Angela walked up to him and enquired what he was doing.

"I think there may be a bomb planted here mam"

Evans flashed his Interpol badge; "Oh, so you are not making a documentary, you are snooping around, I'll have to ask you to leave; we don't want to cause a scene or mass panic to spoil this little party do we?"

The woman just didn't look concerned at all;

"And what makes you think that there may be a bomb here, who would want to destroy these lovely people?"

Evans couldn't exactly say it's just a hunch.

"Probably a hoax", he conceded as he motioned to Rachel to withdraw. They would need a plan B.

Angela watched them go without another word.

Downstairs Natasha was helping William out of the building. Rachel fussed around concerned. Natasha waved her away; "It's ok Rachel, he just fainted in the toilet he'll be ok with some air."

The garden of the conference centre 8 minutes later

The explosion felt more like a comet strike than anything else. A huge blast mushroomed from the conference building showering glass and debris across the grounds. The downdraft sucked its way along the walls taking peoples breath away like an untimely divine intervention. Their ears were ringing as they looked along the roadway watching bits of detritus falling in slow motion everywhere. For agonizing moments the darkness lingered making it hard to see and breathe.

There was shouting, screaming and crying everywhere. The first thought was to try to help. Evans, Rachel, William and Natasha ran towards the entrance but the smoke and dust was too hot and dense to combat .

It seemed like an eternity before a police car and ambulance turned up. They arrived at the same time as two local fire engines. A jolly man with a large moustache took control in the smoke filled gloom of oblivion, herding those in shock away from the building which now seemed well on fire. A team of men in their fire fighting suits and masks made their way closer and closer, their hoses spurting like waterfalls. From a new position in the cordoned off street they could see flames and black plumes inside the big Georgian conference centre. There was mayhem; people running, limping and crawling from the wreckage, covering their mouths and eyes, coughing and spluttering coveting the peace that had washed over this tranquil place just minutes earlier. The air was filled with desperation and despair. Trapped souls created grotesque silent silhouettes trying to break windows to escape. Such mayhem, a symphony of sound, a surfeit of suffering. Suddenly, at least to William the scene continued but all sound ceased. For a moment he thought he saw Sandra's face squeezed against a window pain, thought he heard her voice; William, I need you..." For a moment he heard clearly but the voice got softer and softer.

"William, don't leave me here...William I love you..." her hands were sliding down the window pain as her face contorted, slipping away into the dark unknown."

Suddenly he was taken back to that fateful day when his wife Sandra had died in the bus bomb blast. He had berated himself time and again for not being there to help or hold her in her dying moments. He looked down and saw a woman staggering badly burned and injured along the pavement. She looked just like Sandra. She spoke as she collapsed; William just managed to catch her.

"William, help me, I love you."

He knelt and held the bloodstained woman in his arms; she tried to grip him tight. Her burned body and torn limbs formed sad contortions. He could see that she was badly injured, and that part of her body had been blown away. Instinctively he held her.

"It's, it's ok my love, you are going to be ok..."

Even through the smell of blood fire and smoke he detected her perfume, he ran his hand down her face, it was Sandra, how could it be? He kissed her gently on the cheek.

"Bless you William, we will meet again one day but now you must be kind to me and to yourself, please let me go and get on with your life."

The tears ran quickly down his face as the woman's life slipped away.

"Oh Sandra, it hurts so much... I love you."

As he lowered the woman slowly to the ground her face changed. It was no longer Sandra. Two ambulance men almost barged William out of the way as he stood and staggered back into the chaos and confusion.

At the far end of the street Angela was laughing. The timing of the bomb had worked out exactly as she had planned. That part of her job was done, now to nail William.

Another fire engine and an ambulance arrived on a wave of blue light and sound. More could be heard from miles away.

Evans spotted an elderly man in tattered torn clothing wandering in a haze covered with blood, bruises and scratches. They helped him away from the danger area and sat him with others on the floor waiting for attention...

"What the hell next?"

Evans looked lost. Rachel arrived supporting another injured man; helping him to sit beside Evans.....he was coherent, just. Evans gave him some water from a bottle being handed out by the fire brigade; he sipped it before speaking...

"They bombed us, God they bombed us."

William gazed up, across the road he saw Natasha beckoning him over. Evans had his arm around Rachel trying to help her come to terms with the shock of the last 45 mins, people shot, a bomb explosion and carnage... Not a normal day in a sleepy Welsh town.

The cries of others and their sense of duty forced Rachel and Evans back into a role in which they forgot about their own troubles. During the heroic salvation Evans had been speaking to more people as they were being rescued. He was starting to build a picture of what had happened.

Across the road Natasha moved out of Evans sight and continued to call William over. He made his way through the debris towards her.

As soon as he was near she moved swiftly to his side and pulled him by the hand down an alley; "Come on William, quickly…"

William followed; "What is it Nats, what's happening?"

Natasha was in agent mode; "We need to get out of here, things are not what they seem."

William had recovered a little composure; "Well that's good news, because from where I am standing they look pretty dire!"

-58-

Cardiff Airport
3rd August 2009

Natasha had whipped William back to their lodgings, stashed their things and now they were on their way to Cardiff Airport.

William was playing catch up; "We are going where exactly Nats?"

She was driving her Porsche as if their life depended on it. "And we are going to the airport because?"

William's face was a blank canvas, Natasha decided to write on it; "I took the mobile phone from the pocket of Robin Bryant, you know the MI5 agent that we thought saved our life by shooting it out with the gunman……the link to MI5 via the phone was still active. I hacked the operations computer."

William's eyebrows crept over the top of his head as she continued; "In short I discovered a report trail to Evans and Helen Daniels, it confirms that although Evans is Interpol he is working with MI5 on this and so was Helen Daniels."

William was confused; "I thought Helen Daniels was working for the BBC as a Producer?"

Natasha nodded; "Yes, but MI5 recruit people from all over the place for all sorts of reasons."

William was not quite up to speed; "Including you?"

Natasha ignored the comment so William tried a different tack; "So what about Helen being Evans daughter and Interpol laying him off the case?"

Natasha brushed a wayward strand of blonde hair out of her eyes before going on; "All geared to getting in with Rachel and with us to see what info we had."

It was getting clearer to William; "Is Rachel safe?"

Natasha nodded as she changed gear and negotiated a U turn; "I think so, safer than Everson, I think he's been kidnapped…the B and B people saw him being bundled into a people carrier."

William felt terrible; "Christ Nats, Roger shot, Everson kidnapped, it's not going to stop until we are all dead, is it?!"

Natasha was solemn. "Yes, you are right William, information has leaked, some people want it and some people rather it be hidden, I am afraid we are in the middle. I don't know if there is a way out ...but, we have to try... From my hack of the MI5 operations frame it does look like there is something else though, they are calling it Project Meurig."

William was trying to put the thought of Roger falling dead into the raspberry jelly on the breakfast table and whatever Everson must be going through out of his mind;

"Nats, I think I've worked out a little of what's going on!"

Natasha's response was matter of fact; "I knew you would William, you are not just a handsome face, please tell me later, we've arrived at Cardiff airport and I have a plan..."

It was 4pm as the Embraer Legacy 600 private jet drifted into a perfect touchdown in the slight head wind.

Natasha and William had been watching as the graceful dragon circled once before making its approach to the runway.

The short balding man in his 60's who was standing a short distance from them had his binoculars pressed against the window of the first floor lounge straining to see every detail.

He turned to William and smiled."She's lovely isn't she?"

Mildly embarrassed and not a little uncomfortable William looked Natasha up and down; "Now you come to mention it she does scrub up pretty well."

The man looked puzzled but then laughed heartily; "No, no, I mean the airplane looks lovely, it's based on the shortened ERJ 135 model, but includes extra range with extra fuel tanks and added winglets, similar to those on the ERJ 145XR. Launched in 2000 at the Farnborough Air Show..."

William clearly didn't know what to say but luckily Natasha did; "Yes, truly lovely, just listen how sweet those Rolls-Royce AE 3007/A1P turbofans sound in reverse thrust..."

She looked at William as if trying to educate him. As she continued the man looked more impressed;

"She can carry 13 passengers in extreme comfort for 3,250km without a refuel and has a top speed of 518 mph.... Oh and it looks like she has been fitted with a full glass cockpit so she probably has a Honeywell Primus 1000 avionics suite..."

Blown away by her knowledge the man was hastily adjusting his binoculars straining to see.

The man purred as if he was a cat that had the cream; "Wow, your eyesight must be 20-20... did you know there have already been around 100 sold in 19 countries...? They are a real Executives favorite."

Natasha was trying to smile sideways at William but only when the man was glued to his binoculars, she was about to impress him further with her in depth knowledge of aviation.

"Yes, I knew that."

She paused to make sure he was listening whilst observing; "They have a great safety record, shame about the accident in September 2006 when one collided with Gol Transportes Aéreos Flight 1907, a Boeing 737-800, while flying over the northern state of Mato Grosso en route to Manaus from São José dos Campos. The Legacy made an emergency landing at a military airstrip at Cachimbo, Pará, Brazil, with minor damages and with its 5 passengers and 2 crew members uninjured. The Gol 737 crashed in the Amazon forest east of Peixoto de Azevedo, killing all 148 passengers and 6 crew members... I don't think we ever really will know what happened..."

The smart man broke eye contact with his binoculars long enough to offer his hand on the end of a long arm covered with a pinstripe suit; "You are very knowledgeable Miss, miss..."

The man fished for a name. Natasha was used to such situations; "Please call me Sylvi" she said coyly, knowing who the man was and not wishing to give anything away.

"You look fit, do you fly?"

William couldn't resist the temptation; "Only on a broom-stick at midnight!"

The man gave William a look that knocked him sideways...

"Come along my dear, let me buy you a coffee it will be a few minutes before my meeting."

Natasha gave William a get lost look; "Oh, umm, sorry to be rude I have some calls to make and I can't get a signal in here... I'll be back soon."

William disappeared and as the coffees arrived the man in the pin striped suit moved a little further around the table towards Natasha.

William had taken up a position out of their sight but was still able to watch as the ladder from the glossy jet was put into position.

He also noticed quite a bit of movement around the perimeter fencing in the distance. It seemed as if the airport was surrounded with military vehicles and three Black Hawks had landed in different positions. To the left two shiny large black cars approached the plane and parked as near to the bottom of the disembarkation ladder as they could. Six very smartly dressed men in black suits with white shirts and black ties emerged and took up positions around the fuselage.

Back in the coffee lounge Natasha and the man were getting on well, perhaps too well. The stream of one way information, in Natasha's direction was a testament to her considerable skill and charm.

"So this chap is a top dog from South Africa, he must be loaded to have jet like that!"

The man eased his right hand under the table to Natasha's black stockinged leg, she didn't flinch, she never did;

"Does that turn you on? Being loaded I mean."

Natasha was pretty sure she knew where this was going and she wasn't sure she liked it.

"Well money always helps", she said, "and power, I love men with money and power."

He smiled knowingly. She just hoped that he hadn't sussed her. In reality she hated men with power and money, she had spent years being used and abused by them but this wasn't reality, maybe, just maybe this was payback time.

The man slipped his hand under the table and along between her legs until he felt the flesh above her suspender belt, it was soft and warm. She opened her legs a little and his fingers reached her crotch where they prodded and stroked. She could see the stiffness in his lap and the concentration in his eyes.

She smiled; "Don't get yourself all worked up before your meeting Mr? The man had managed to move part of Natasha's G string to one side and could feel the warmth between her legs... he gazed across to her with a triumphant smile...

"Philip Greenaway, Sir Philip Greenaway, lots of money, lots of power."

Suddenly a thick set man in a long dark coat appeared and his probing hand recoiled as if it had been bitten by a snake.

"It's time to meet Mr Luyt" said the new actor on the stage. The man turned to Natasha who invisibly and inwardly breathed a sigh of relief. Unconsciously he brought his fingers to his nose and sniffed, closing his eyes as he did so.

"Please ring me, let's continue, our, umm conversation, in private, I am staying at the Maids Head Hotel in the city... do you know it?" The man hurriedly scribbled a number and gave it to her on a business card.

Natasha tried to smile through gritted teeth... hoping that the man's piercing eyes would avert.

"I'll find you, don't worry, I'll find you."

Natasha just caught a glimpse of William waving in the distance, she stood up, adjusted her short dress that had been thrust higher by the probing and walked over to him.

She was by William's side just in time to see a man almost as broad as he was tall venturing onto the stairway. To the front and back were two large men in blue jeans and black sweaters, each one carried a weapon. They looked around as if their lives depended on their observation.

Natasha squinted but didn't need to look long. "They are Russian secret service elite squad. There'll be more on the plane."

William looked at her. "How do you know that? A wild guess? Women's intuition?"

Natasha was deadly serious, "I'm good at maths William."

William looked lost as she continued. "You know, I can add things up. I found out from my new "best friend", Sir Phillip, that this guy is called Ralph Luyt he's a real big wig in South African mining circles but more than likely working in cahoots with a Russian fuel and mining company because that's where the big money is nowadays. Mind you it cost me a slippery fumble, oh and because the guys have Kalashnikov AK-103's which are modern Russian-built versions of the famous AK-47 assault rifle. It combines the developments made in the AK-74 and AK-101 with a use of plastics to replace metal or wooden components wherever possible to reduce overall weight. The AK-103 can be fitted with a tactical light, laser sight, telescopic sight, suppressor, and the GP-30 grenade launcher. The AK-103 is in limited service with selected units in the Russian army, which means the elite special service."

Yet again William was dumfounded; "Bloody hell Natasha, I'm worried about you, are you sure there is something you are not telling me? Can't we just go back to our nice cozy computer company and forget all this crap. What do you mean it cost you a slippery fumble?"

Natasha wasn't proud of what she'd done. "I mean he stuck his fingers up my crotch and made it clear he wants to screw the arse off me."

Natasha looked upset and pensive, for the first time in her life she had been happy in a normal life and a normal job, what's more she had really fallen for William and part of her wished that he'd just throw his arms around her and fall deeply in love with her for ever and ever. Sadly, in her heart she knew that could never be.

William was horrified; "What a bastard, what a creep... I'm going to give him such a kicking."

This was about as angry as she had ever seen William.

"You look so cute when you are angry William, anyway you are not going to get anywhere near to him to give him a kicking, he's the Home Secretary!"

William stood leaning his nose against the window until his face contorted and he wanted to be sick.

The big South African scuttled like a frightened rabbit down the stairs and into one of the waiting cars, she already knew who this man was and she had a 5 inch scar across her left breast to prove it.

She didn't know how long she could keep William in the dark; she knew that every day that went by was making it more and more dangerous. How she wished she hadn't fallen for him, it was making everything more difficult. Was this really love? Maybe for the first time she knew what it felt like. Something around her icy heart melted and for once she had no answers.

-59-

Margham Abbey, Wales
3rd August 2009

Sitting just off junction 39 of the M4 from Cardiff, Margam was an ancient Welsh community, formerly part of the Cwmwd of Tir Iarll; initially it was dominated by Margam Abbey, a wealthy house of the Cistercians founded in 1147. Some say it was originally the site of an Iron Age stronghold named after Morgan, a son of King Arthur.

There had once been a wonderful castle, abbey and buildings in the grounds but the ravishes of fire and time meant that substantial renovations were ongoing. The grounds of Margam Country Park, the orangery and other buildings are sometimes open to the general public. Today though was different, the secure area within the precinct of the castle and accommodation had been sealed off to everyone, except HM government and its guests.

The place of the meeting had been decided at the last moment for maximum security. Only a handful of important people had been told that Ralph Luyt was an informal envoy for the South African Government and that the representatives of Her Majesties Government were going to meet him. The stone building was criss crossed with some original but mainly replaced oak beams and decorated with reproduction tapestry and painting. The first residence is said to have been built on the site as part of the stronghold system of outposts and forts leading up to Mount Baedon, the site of Arthur's definitive battle with the Saxons which nestled in a valley a few miles away.

It was an ideal secret meeting place with a front of normality. To the outside world it was an important building being renovated. The truth was quite different. A handful of people at the house were employed by the government to keep it secure and in good order. High ranking and important people visited from time to time and this was such a time. There were eight special guest bedrooms with en suite facilities and a superb kitchen and dining room.

In the gardens there was a team of SAS special forces dressed as gardeners to keep an eye on security, an armored jeep and a well made shingled road across to a hidden helipad in case of dire emergencies.

An extravagantly stocked and protected Panic Room had been built below ground at enormous expense. In the process they found skeletons of babies and some young girls, goodness knows what went on there in the mists of time, but it was easy to guess. It was a beautiful building full of secrets from the day it was completed.

The meeting hall was light and airy. There were large mullioned and partly stained glass windows overlooking the lawn. Long red velvet curtains framed the whole of that side of the wall. A very large walk in inglenook fireplace took up almost another wall whilst over and around the fireplace painted on to the blue and red walls were the arms and motives of Henry VIII embellished with scenes of hunting.

In the middle of the room was a large single circular oak table, its patina blackened by age. Austere chairs with wooden arms surrounded it. The seats were softened by red leather cushions which were very necessary in case meetings dragged on and on, as they often did.

Sir Phillip Greenaway politely ushered Ralph Luyt to his chair and sat by his side. A large muscular man, said to be Ralph Luyt's assistant but obviously a body guard sat the other side of him. Vanessa Grey, head of MI5 walked into the room and sat with them.

For an uncomfortable moment or two everybody looked at each other. Vanessa Grey spoke; "Gentlemen, welcome to Wales. Mr Luyt, we understand that you wish to assert your claim that our ex Prime Minsiter Mr Callaghan granted your government rights to open cast mines at certain sites in South Wales, in return for an influx of money to this country during the difficulties of apartheid. Could you please explain your allegations and your formal approach to Her Majesty's Government at this particular time? Ralph Luyt looked around the table, he wasn't going to stand up and speak out of respect for this rabble. So far as he was concerned there was an agreement and the UK Government had reneged on it. There was arrogance in his demeanor from the start;

"I am flattered that your government takes this matter so seriously that the head of MI5 is present. I find it incredible that you have no record of the agreement that was quite clearly reached by my father and Mr Callaghan when he was prime minister in 1978"

Vanessa Grey eyed him with considerable suspicion; she had a feeling about this man over and above her professional observations;

"Why have you left it until years after the death of Mr Callaghan to put forward this claim, why now?"

Luyt pushed some photocopies across the table for Grey and Greenaway to look at;

"You will see that item one is a transcript of a tape recording between your Mr James Callaghan and my father, they clearly had an intimate business relationship, in short your country has received a lot of money in return for this deal but whilst he was alive my father had no wish to fall out with Great Britain, I on the other hand do not have that problem."

Phillip Greenaway had only read through part of this text but his bushy grey eyebrows had risen on more than one occasion;

"I take it that this recording was taken covertly?"

Luyt knew what was coming next, that it might well not be admissible in a court of law.

"Did it ever cross your mind how some businesses in South Africa kept trading with certain companies during the period when we were black balled for apartheid? Did you ever wonder where certain UK very high profile people's fortunes came from? Vanessa Grey was looking at some of the other photocopies, clearly letters and agreements had been made that neither she nor the government of today knew anything about. The meeting was getting increasingly uncomfortable. Luyt continued;

"I think the international press would have a field day with these, don't you? And then, of course, there are the naughty little things you are up to in Wales that people would just love to know about, you know, your little Meurig Project"

Phillip Greenaway went white, how could he know about one of the most secret experiments in the UK, he cleared his throat before answering. Greenaway was on the defensive; "What is it you really want from us?"

Luyt was sure of his position and was not afraid to state it. "We believe that under the agreements we have the rights to mine the whole mountain area at Mynnyd Y Gaer, the ownership of the church, the metal cross found there and everything else buried there but yet to be found. We might be persuaded to let go for £5 billion in a Swiss bank account though."

Grey remained calm; "So, do you have the original cross found at St Peters then?"

Luyt was annoyed; "I didn't say that, we thought you had it!"

Greenaway looked confused; "Well if you don't have it and neither do we how can you demand £5 billion."

Luyt stalled; "Well, I wouldn't expect you to say you had it tucked away in the PM's trophy cabinet, anyway the open cast coal mining rights and, shall we say, its little extras are worth at least that on their own."

Grey wondered how much Luyt knew, surely he could have no idea about the rich seams of gold and the rare metal hidden deep in the quartz all across the area he'd mentioned...was this just one hell of a try on? Greenaway felt the same;

"You have wasted your time Luyt. You can tell your government there is no contract and no proof of any such deal and that the UK is not a charity, we suggest you stay here with us as planned and leave tomorrow."

In the very awkward following silence it was clear that Luyt was not pleased at all. He stood up, pushing his chair violently backwards across the floor and motioned to his bodyguard to leave with him;

"I will report back to my government, I cannot imagine they will be amused... But, I really must decline your offer of accommodation. I want to get out and try some of your Welsh women, I understand they are fiery and beautiful."

Greenaway stood and offered an outstretched hand; "Diplomatic immunity only goes so far Mr Luyt."

Luyt ignored him.The man and his minder left the room and were escorted to their shiny black bullet and blast proof car.As they left Greenaway and Grey looked at each other for a moment or two. Greenaway broke the silence.

"Shit, that didn't go too well, if the proverbial hits the fan then all the top brass and some of the royalty are going to have very large eggs on their face."

Grey concurred; "Do you think it's true that Callaghan did these deals without telling anyone?"

Greenaway shrugged; "God only knows, you can't seem to trust anyone these days!"

Grey managed a grin, she had good reason to; "Hope your dossier of Parliamentary claims is squeaky clean Greenaway, they are about to be published!"

He also smiled but was not sure why; "I cleaned my moat myself."

The reference to an MP who had been too extravagant with his expenses was irresistible.Grey dialed a number on her mobile; a rather large eye had to be kept on Mr Luyt and his band of merry men. After the conversation with the surveillance team she turned to Greenaway;

"You know we don't even have enough resources to staff counter terrorism properly, don't you?"

Greenaway made a gesture as if to play a violin. Suddenly he stopped fiddling and spoke to Grey in a hushed voice; "I read your briefing report on Luyt, you made a mistake, 6 tell me that he is not really an official visitor from the South African Government?"

Grey looked pale, maybe he was not so green as his name indicated Greenaway looked thoughtful; "We have to neutralise him, we don't have a choice. He seems to know rather too much about everything."

Grey looked thoughtful; "If that is true we have a leak feeding us bad intel and we need to plug it."

"You mean your department cannot be trusted, very careless Grey, very."

Grey took an awaited call from her head of communications, nodded into thin air and ended the mobile call, relaying the information to Greenaway; "The plane Luyt arrived on belongs to a private Russian operative. It was hired in Russia by Cygnus Engineering and booked for a scientific research trip to the UK."

Greenaway looked at Grey; "I know, I checked with MI6. So, we let a group in to the UK thinking they are a delegation from South Africa but they turn out to be a band of armed heavies. Now we have let them loose."

Grey was open mouthed, her negligence was obvious; "I delegated the security check on this... is it possible that they really do know about Meurig and that they have come in about the stuff with Callaghan as a Trojan Horse?"

Greenaway was charistically definitive; "Well it's your job to know and your job to tell me what's happening Grey, unless, that is, you don't want your job anymore, sort it – understand?"

Grey looked sideways; "Harsh. Wasn't me that hadn't bargained for them making their own accommodation arrangements... you better call in the SAS. If it's going to be a shoot out at the OK Corale I'd rather be tooled up and the odds stacked in our favour...oh and treble the guards at the sites."

Actually, Greenaway had already done just that and more, he no longer trusted Grey, something was badly wrong somewhere. He took a call from MI6 and shared some of the information.

"It gets worse for you Grey. What the fuck is happening at Caerleon? Dr Felix has apparently been assassinated, the conference on King Arthur has been blown up and our partners in the CIA seem to have disappeared."

Grey looked shaken but not stirred; "We have to work on the basis that the more shadowy side of the church has joined forces with the CIA to try to secure this Arthurian Cross thing and make sure no body of Jesus Christ is found..."

Greenaway looked confused; "But that's what we want as well isn't it?"

Grey agreed; "Yes, but for different reasons. They want to safeguard the stories and religious dogma of the church but we also want the metal for our 'secret' experiments. What if the Americans are using the church as cover to find out about the Meurig stuff and the 'delegation' from South Africa are really an elite force after the Meurig secrets?"

Greenaway and Grey had learned things about each other they did not like or understand.

-60-

Cardiff
3rd August 2009

Natasha and William booked into the Celtic Hotel on the outskirts of the city using Williams credit card. They stripped William's mobile phone of all important information and left it in the room before walking out never to return. This was a decoy they hoped would buy valuable time.

They ended up at the Blue Dragon, a basic but comfortable establishment not too far from the city centre. Natasha was wrapped in a towel drying herself following a much needed shower;

"Mr and Mrs Brown again, not very original William..."

William was sitting on the bed with his head in his hands, he couldn't even raise a smile; "Sorry Nats, finding it a bit hard to cope with all this."

Natasha sat on his lap and pulled his head into her chest. He immediately felt much safer and warm. Her towel fell from her body and she didn't bother reclaiming it. She cupped William's head in her hands and kissed him deeply. Something in him stirred, surely this was wrong, but it felt so right. He allowed his hands to explore her body, she was firm and fit but soft and warm in all the right places. Tactfully he ignored the many scars that criss crossed her torso.

There was something wonderful and magical about her. William felt he could give in there and then, the worries of the last few days evaporated by the feelings he had for her. She was the perfect antidote. Then as suddenly as the intimate moment started it stopped. Natasha looked at her watch, there was something on her mind;

"William, there is something I have to do, please save this for later, I have to go out for a while. Please stay here you'll be safer."

William looked bemused; "But, but I thought you wanted to ..."

Natasha smiled; "Of course I want to William."

He didn't know what to say; "Well, at least let me come with you....unless you hadn't noticed we are in the middle of a battle."

Natasha was all too aware of that; "I'm sorry William, there are some things that are best done alone."

William had never really questioned Natasha; she had been a good faithful friend and a great business partner. Now, just for a moment he felt there could be more but things were on his mind;

"Nats, did you really leave all your past, you know all that secret service stuff, behind when you came here?"

Natasha regained her composure and po face; "Oh, William, William, William, it's a question I've hoped you'd never ask….I cannot lie to you but I cannot tell you the truth either… you'd just hate me."

William was a little shocked. Inside he knew there was something he was not allowed to know and he was scared, very scared.Tears formed in his eyes.

"Try me Nats, over the last few days I thought I'd seen the real you, I, I've fallen in love with you….let me come with you".

Natasha was in tears as she pulled on the little red dress over her skimpy underwear and suspenders; "William, dear William, I so wish I could tell you, but it's impossible."

- 61 -

Cardiff
3rd August 2009

Natasha didn't like dressing up to play the part of a money grabbing tart, but, in this case she had no choice. Having called earlier, following her meeting with the randy man at Cardiff airport, she had accepted the Home Secretary's invitation to drinks at his hotel. Soon she was standing close to the reception area so that she could see people coming in and out. No-one would dream of looking for his two guards, easily sedated with a dart gun, in the underground parking lot and tucked up cosily snoring in wheelie bins.

It wasn't long before Greenaway appeared from the lift and gave her a hug as if they had know each other all their lives; "You look ravishing."

Natasha resisted kicking him in the nuts, preferring to keep to her subtler more original plan. "No guards Mr Greenaway... tut, tut."

Greenaway put his arm around her shoulder escorting her towards the lift door; "They are around somewhere, those sort of guys melt into the background and turn up at the most inconvenient moment."

The lift ride made Natasha feel uncomfortable. In the short elevation he had undressed her mentally four or five times.

The Home Secretary swiped his card in the socket, the door to his room opened and he dragged her in.

It was dim but the sidelights were on. In one swoop Greenaway swung Natasha against the wall, winding her, thrusting himself upon her, squashing her body against the cold shiny surface. He kissed her passionately, his hands all over her body.

She recovered her composure quickly; "I've heard of being frisked for a weapon but this is ridiculous."

Greenaway stopped foraging for a moment to smile; "I'm the only one tooled up and ready to go."

His hard on was obvious. Natasha tried to keep cool.

"Haven't you ever heard of foreplay?"

Greenaway was panting in expectation, he was not going to be put off lightly, again he was upon her pushing, squeezing, thrusting, his face redder and redder with every moment that passed. He pushed her on the bed landing on top of her. She gasped again as the air was knocked out of her lungs. He was pulling and ripping. His hand went up her red skirt, over her suspenders and prodding and probing her most private parts. For a moment she couldn't breathe, let alone respond, where had all her training and fitness gone? For an older man he was powerful and strong.

As he fumbled she felt the warmth of his erect member on her leg then her lower stomach.

Placing her arms around his neck she slid her hands under his collar and removed his tie. With a spirited thrust she flipped the man over and landed on top of him. Keeping up the pretence she held down his arms and rubbed her softest area over his hardest. He was panting and aching.

Moving his neck tie across to the other hand she tied one of his wrists to the bedpost ... Greenaway laughed;

"How did you know I love bondage?"

Many things were going through her mind but none more so than the fact that she had found the Home Secretary's internet IP as a paying guest on Nicole's sexy server. He was logged on the day she died.

With another swift movement she had removed Greenaway's leather belt and tied his other wrist to the opposite bedpost.

Then, slowly, very slowly Natasha stood up and undulated in front of Greenaway's eyes, all the time his panting was getting more and urgent. She removed her skimpy G-string and waved her shapely bottom towards his face, he strained to get to it as he sensed her sex but she was just out of reach.

Climbing back on top of him she ripped open his shirt and rubbed her G string across his chest and shoulders. Then, teasing his lips open with the fingers of her left hand she stuffed her G string knickers into his mouth. Immediately the man tried to kick out and scream but Natasha had already wrapped his trousers around his ankles and secured him to the end of the bed.

Natasha sat beside him and spoke softly; "Now, Mr Home Secretary, you randy little monster, time to answer a few questions." She pulled a flick knife from her slim hand bag and pressed the switch...the blade glinted in the bedside lights as it jerked open.

Her eyes had turned cold and menacing, his glinted with fear.

"You know the game Greenaway, you get a South African hit man and you send him to a young lady. He ties her up and then slits her throat so you can watch it on the internet with your perve friends, right? Only in my case I am not South African and not a man, but you get the gist."

Greenaway was squirming in disbelief as Natasha went on; "I swear I had nothing to do with that, I just thought it was play acting."

Natasha looked dismissive and disbelieving; "Let's see, how does this go?

oh yes I ask a few questions which, of course, you cannot answer because you'd sacrifice your life for your country and then I kill you."

She set up her mobile phone so that Greenaway could be seen tied to the bed. She hit a link button and the connections went live.

The screen came up on in various places such as the desk of Grey at MI5, Williams and Evan's mobile phone.

Natasha leaned close to Greenaway's ear, covering her face to ensure she was not on camera;

"Phillip I want you to record a little message, you have to tell the truth or I cut your balls off, understand?"

Greenaway wasn't sure what to do... Natasha put her hand between his legs cupping his still erect penis and his balls then she squeezed and twisted...and twisted. She didn't give in until Greenaway was sweating and near to losing consciousness, his erect penis flaccid and his balls black and blue;

"You going to talk to me Greenaway?"

Greenaway was nodding furiously so she removed her knickers from his mouth.

"Don't even try shouting out Greenaway..."

He shook his head in terror.

"What's the Meurig Project Greenaway?"

The Home Secretary looked like death; "No, no, I'll talk about anything else but not that, I am sure we can come to some arrangement, how much money do you want?"

Natasha slid the sharp blade towards his balls which she was holding tightly in the other hand. "Wrong answer, I am not interested in your money."

Greenaway flipped; "Christ, alright, alright, it's a secret weapons research unit in the Welsh mountains."

At MI5 HQ Grey was almost having a baby. She was standing beside her top IT guy.

"You have to shut down this feed, now!"

The geeky man shrugged as if he was trying his best;

"This has been set up by a real pro; the feed is signal hopping making it look as if it is from 1000's of different places at once."

Natasha went to wipe Greenaway's sweating brow and suddenly she pulled out a small syringe; "It'll soon be all over Phillip, don't fret so much, you'll only feel a little prick, seems only fair that since you made me feel yours, I let you feel mine!"

The struggle was useless, the sedating truth drug started to work immediately.

"Phillip, tell me all about Project Meurig, I'd love to know..."

Grey was tearing her hair out, Evans and William sat glued but for different reasons and in different places.

"Where is he?... can't be... call his hotel and find out if he is in his room... I'll get the local armed response unit on standby, where the hell are his security people."

Greenaway gazed into Natasha's eyes; "You do have lovely eyes my dear, nice tits as well, I love you."

Natasha knew the drug had worked; "Yeah, yeah, I love you too, now you were saying about this Meurig Project thing."

He laughed; "Oh yes, where was I? Oh, I know... the Mad Scientist of Mynydd y Gaer, real name Mathews.

He worked with Tesla to develop a new kind of teleforce weapon, in fact, a scalar electromagnetic weapon. Tesla claimed that the weapon could send concentrated beams of particles through the free air of such tremendous energy that they would bring down 10,000 enemy planes at a distance of 200 miles and would cause armies to drop dead in their tracks. We've been working on it for years since. We knew that Tesla and Mathews used a strange metal they found in small quantities in the Welsh mountains but we had a jolly exciting breakthrough when Roger Felix discovered that the St Peters cross was partly made from a large piece of this metal which apparently came to earth in a multiple comet strike in the 6th century....you can read all about it if you like, the briefings all on my pen drive... just give me a blow job, that's a good girl."

Natasha foraged for the drive from his trouser pocket whilst Greenaway had his eyes closed in expectation of euphoria. Why, she wondered would he be walking around with a pen drive of secrets in his pocket?...it made no sense. Unless he wanted the information found, that is.

She tucked the storage device into her cleavage.

Suddenly turning back to Greenaway she twisted his balls again, he winced and his eyes watered; "Why did you have Helen Daniels, Morgan and Pender, Nicole and Roger all killed?"

Greenaway half choaked; "Well that's just it ole sausage I didn't have anything to do with it, you'll have to blame the church and the PM for that, in fact you might like to know that Grey may be playing the field she's already double crossed the church and Valetti, a dangerous game I have to say."

"Grey, tell me about her."

Greenaway wriggled, desperately wanting to pee.

Natasha waited patiently; "Well I have had my suspicions about her for some time, she's a cold fish you know, I think she may be trying to make a fortune out of trading secrets, probably playing off the Russians and the Americans against each other."

Natasha looked him in the eye; "But she is head of MI5."

Greenaway had the answer; "Can you think of any better position to be in to make a profit?"

Greenaway paused for breath then continued; "The government have been researching weapons and fuels of all sorts under the cover of coal mining for years. One of the first experimental nuclear bomb explosions was underground in Wales back in the 1940's. It was all hushed up and locals thought the area was suffering natural earth tremors. It was all going so well, then Morgan and Pender started drawing attention to an area we wanted to use for open cast mining. They deduced that King Arthur might be buried there. Somehow they had discovered that, according to the church there are ancient records to suggest that Jesus Christ may be buried somewhere in the same region.

Natasha eased off a little but remained focused; she knew this may be the hub of the matter; "So, why is it that the UK wanted to mine in that exact area?"

Greenaway needed no further encouragement; "Several reasons, there's a mass of gold and that rare comet metal that's thought to be there in tiny amounts. The derivative from the comet metal has to be refined from the quartz and gold layer under the coal in that very specific area and mining is the perfect cover, not to mention profitable, especially as we can now also use the coal to make liquid hydrogen, another alternative fuel source. The whole thing is worth an absolute fortune in coal, gold and the new technology that can be developed from the comet metal. It would be enough to lift this country out of recession and into orbit.

I believed that, Robin Bryant, Helen Daniels, Nicole and Evans were all working as a team for MI5 trying to find out exactly what Morgan and Pender had discovered. Morgan and Pender's research was turning up things nobody had realized before. Most particularly where precisely Jesus Christ might be buried and whether the cross found at St Peter's was genuine. Legend says that Merlin made the cross from various sacred objects including two nails from the crucifixion and most importantly a huge fragment of the comet material we need so badly to develop new technology."

Natasha interrupted; "You mean new weapons of mass destruction I take it."

Greenaway didn't need to reply. Natasha wasn't convinced but knew she had limited time to get information and escape.

"So who killed them? I'm losing patience."

He started to quiver and release urine as Natasha pulled the blade of her knife playfully across his throat;

"Soon Helen Daniels and Nicole felt that the information Morgan and Pender had discovered was so important that the BBC ought to really make the documentaries accurately and not just crucify Morgan and Pender as planned. They wanted out of the MI5 connection but they had information that was sensitive and vital...we thought they may have been accessed as double agents by MOSSAD or an Islamic fundamentalist group. As you know so far as the Jews are concerned the Messiah hasn't been yet and Islam believes Jesus was just an ordinary physical being. Either case could lead to a shift in the moral and religious high ground of the UK, some of Europe and the USA."

Natasha understood; "Ok, so you ordered that they all be taken out?"

"No, no, really, I didn't authorize all this, the orders came from above...not God, of course, but from the next best thing, the PM and the church, they are working with the CIA because of the American link, Botha is just a henchman working for the church, he is a hired assassin"

Natasha knew all too well who he was and what he did. It was now making sense to her; she even started to feel sorry for the Home Secretary. It wouldn't be the first time a government minister had been hung out to dry, but this was serious, very serious.

She saw no reason to disbelieve him; she had relied on the effectiveness of the drug so many times in the past;

"This new weapon Greenaway, tell me all about it"

Greenaway gulped but continued; "Tesla claimed that from their base in the Preseli hills he and Mathews had used a low frequency radio beam to create a blast in the area of the Tunguska River in Central Siberia. The explosion flattened 500,000 acres of pine forest and was heard for 620 miles. Everyone thought a 100,000 pound comet caused the explosion but no one ever saw the comet coming in and fragments of the comet were never found.

The two had stumbled upon the early invention and use of scalar electromagnetic weapons. Mathews had been inspired to use a tiny slither of rare metal he found in the Welsh hills.

Publicly, at least Tesla and Matthews backed off in favour of more domestic applications for their work. Privately we know that their research continued underground in old coal pit workings around Mynnyd Y Gaer, where that damn St Peter's church is.

In the autumn of 1941, Mathews suddenly collapsed and died whilst perfecting his system of defence against air attacks. Within hours of his death his laboratory on the Welsh mountain was stripped of its secrets by Government Officials and agents from Military Intelligence. Two years later Tesla died and his papers suffered a similar fate. Albert Einstein was assigned the job of trying to make sense of the research of both Tesla and Matthews and it was he that set up the current research area in Wales.

The official line was that Tesla had a photographic memory and never wrote anything down. In reality the papers did a disappearing act. This weapon, known as Tesla's Teleforce weapon would be devastating.

The Soviets gained access to Tesla's last living assistant and some of his papers. They started their own research program. It failed because they didn't have the key ingredient needed, that strange and special metal that had been deposited in the Mynnyd Y Gaer region by the impact comets that obliterated the area in the 6th century, the very same deposits that open cast mining would reveal and the very same metal that was apparently used by Merlin when making the St Peters cross.

Tesla and Matthews only had a tiny piece of the comet metal and look what they achieved with that! The fear, of course, was that the first to develop and perfect this weapon could take out intercontinental ballistic missiles, melt and stop engines and much much worse. Research has continued in secret in the Preseli underground bunker. The Americans are livid we won't share this with them but they are undertaking their own similar research at DARPA. Natasha stroked his face and mopped his brow, a touch of humanity in a cruel world.

"DARPA?" she enquired.

"Dastardly thing, a hi power acoustic transducer which can beam sound that will only be heard by a target individual or group of people at a great range making them hear and see things."

William's behavior immediately came to mind, but why would anyone target him?

"Is this thing real and usable?"

The man nodded; "They even have a patent for it!"

Natasha wondered why she hadn't heard of it, could she be so out of touch?

She helped Greenaway to a drink of water from the bedside table, his throat was parched, he looked grateful as he continued. There was something of the look of a last confession about him, an unburdening of information too debilitating to keep secret.

"If you put the DARPA and HAARP research together they make the nuclear bomb look like a child's toy. With the right concentration of the comet material, say the amount said by Dr Felix to be in the St Peters cross, a weapon could be focused on any area around the world from anywhere else and cause the same destruction as 100 nuclear explosions... but much more than that. Scientists working on the small amount of the strange metal available found out that it could also be used to create human brain frequency bands over vast areas.

The human brain code has 44 digits or less, and the brain employs 22 frequency bands across nearly the whole Electro Magnetic spectrum. Scientists say that if 11 or more correct frequency channels can be "phase-locked" into the human brain, then it should be possible to drastically influence the thoughts, vision, physical functioning, emotions, and conscious state of the individual, even from a great distance. Apparently, amplifying unique rays from the imploded supernova in the constellations Cygnus and Casseopia interact somehow with the comet metal to facilitate this process.

A 10-Hz signal has been demonstrated to "phase-lock" the human brain, which could induce death and disease. This could truly lead to weapons of Armageddon."

Natasha was gobsmacked, she had been vaguely aware of the work of

HAARP, the sub artic Alaskan research facility working under the cloak of a weather research station but this in conjunction with DARPA was something else. Evans and William, who were watching on their respective mobiles were speechless.

Grey at MI5 was horrified that Greenaway knew so much. She also knew the implications for her personally. Now Natasha would deduce that she was selling information, and that there was a crack Russian unit somewhere on British soil headed up by the South African Luyt who had come for one purpose, to complete the deal for the secrets of the Meurig project and to take the St Peters cross for its unique metal content. She suddenly felt vulnerable, this was not the way she had planned it.

Natasha opened the bedroom window wide as she heard the rush of footsteps up the hall. A heavy shoulder thrust against the door and it gave way allowing two large men to gush into the room. One rushed over to the window and looked out; the other leveled his gun at the Home Secretary and fired a single shot through his forehead. Greenaway died without a whisper.

In one flash of action Natasha threw herself from inside the wardrobe and in a bound was upon the man at the window. With a drop kick she sent him flying through the air. She didn't wait to hear the sick thud as his head hit the ground or to see the messy shape he had made on the floor below, she was too busy diving to miss a well aimed shot by the other man. As she fell to one side in a forward roll she managed to release her flick knife in the man's direction. It struck him through the heart and he slumped forward looking down at the wound in disbelief.

She quickly checked their clothing, nothing much to give them away, just the call sign code on their watch bands. Their guns were standard Russian secret service issue but these were not Russians, these were CIA. She knew the video link would flush them out. She took a long look at Greenaway and felt some remorse; after all, he too had been played like a pawn in a game. How convenient that the Russian team were in the country and how convenient Russian service revolvers were used by the gunmen. Now the blame could fall squarely on a terrorist hit squad. Yet another cover up. Natasha ripped off the long wig and threw it in the bin, then tied her own hair back. She could hear reinforcements rushing along the corridor, so, tidying her clothing she walked calmly past the onrushing personnel. She had moments before they realized, but moments were all she needed.

Natasha flew down the concrete fire escape and ran down the cobbled ally to the rear of the building. She could hear shouting and footsteps way behind. She blessed her fitness regime for her effortless escape. As she turned a corner and spilled out onto the riverside she could see William sitting in the Porsche, where she had left him, staring blankly at the image on his mobile phone.

He jumped as she opened the door, leapt in, started the car and accelerated off in one slick movement. Neither of them noticed the large black raven carefully watching from what remained of the old city wall.

Natasha took a moment to recover her breath. William had seen most of her escapade via his mobile.

"Thank God you are OK!" William looked unmoved; stunned may have been a better way to describe it. Natasha didn't respond. The car's engine screamed with rapid gear changes as she looked across to him. She could almost hear the wheels turning in his head as he studied a photograph of the markings on the Brynna disc.

"You never cease to amaze me Nats any chance of explaining what you are up to?"

She wore a look that said no chance, she was in escape mode and that was serious.

William pinched himself to check he was awake and then slipped into a day dream whilst Natasha sped away from the scene. Was it only two hours ago that they had kissed and nearly made love? He recalled the warmth of her smile, her touch, her soul. Now he had no idea who she really was, what was happening or what she was capable of next.

The strange hiatus of time, hard driving and bizarre silence passed until Natasha pulled into a Wild Bean cafe and petrol stop. William instinctively handed her £50.00 cash to top up the tank and buy strong coffee. She returned looking more comfortable after a visit to the rest room and a change of clothing, his vacant frozen look thawed in anticipation of the beverage. William's comment was almost a plea.

"Jesus that weapon thing Greenaway was describing sounds horrendous."

Natasha didn't respond, she took a slurp of her strong coffee. He straightened out the crumpled pieces of paper across his lap and cleared his throat;

"I've been chewing over the stuff from Morgan and Pender and what Roger and Father Everson have been telling us. It's been staring us in the face. Let's assume that the history taught in schools up to the time of the Hanoverians was correct and that there was an invasion of some of Britain by Albyne in around 1650BC.

It's been suggested that these people were possibly of the lost tribes of Egypt who settled in Wales and collectively became known as the Khymry, they didn't know they were lost, of course. There was certainly a tribe in South Wales called the Silures who seemed to cling to some Eastern traditions."

Composure almost regained, Natasha smiled, took a sip of coffee and spoke with a terrible impression of a Welsh accent; "With you so far, boyo."

William shrugged off the attempt at humour, pleased, at least that Natasha seemed to have recovered from her adventure. Inside he was still shaking, still wondering what on earth would happen next.

"Let's agree that Joseph of Arimathea was indeed used to trading tin along the West Coast of Britain and Cornwall as all the old traditions say, in which case he'd know the area and the people very well."

"For Christ sake William, get to the point."

Brushing her impatience aside he took another thoughtful sip.

"Suppose Joseph of Arimathea really did bribe Pilate so that he could remove JC from the cross before he was dead and let's say that the Roman soldier who grazed JC with the tip of a spear, Longinus, was in on the act."

Natasha was a little confused; "Why would Joseph do that?"

William thought for a couple of seconds; "Because he loved Jesus, he was a good man and he didn't want to see him die like that."

Natasha nodded; "Who would love someone enough to risk such a thing?"

William smiled; "His real father?"

The air was heavy with anticipation. "Remember what Everson told us, that the ancient texts say that Mary worked in the Royal household in Nazareth at the time of Herod and that Joseph was a trader and master builder. What if Joseph was Joseph of Arimathea?.. What if Mary and Joseph were really married but Herod raped or had an affair with Mary and made her pregnant, that's something they'd want to keep quiet."

Natasha went along with the hypothesis; "And, if Herod got to hear about the pregnancy, that would be a dam good reason for Mary and Joseph to do a runner to Bethlehem and for Herod to send out orders to kill all male infants born in a certain time frame, he wouldn't want any potential unplanned heirs lurking around."

"Ok, let's suppose Father Everson is right and that Joseph is JC's "father" or stepfather and Mary's husband, not her uncle, and that he bribed Pilot. Having saved him he had to get him away from harm and that is why he left the scene with Mary, Mary Magdalen and some of the disciples of Jesus to come to Britain, specifically to the area in which his and Mary's forefathers came, that is, the land of the Khymry.

Some texts say that Longinus, the soldier that stabbed Jesus came to, which would make sense, if he'd gone against his Roman bosses; he'd also need to escape."

Natasha was on the same thought train; "Makes sense, the Romans hadn't penetrated Britain then and so it would have been a safe place to go, especially if they had family there."

William stroked his chin; "and if the Romans discovered that Jesus survived and had taken refuge amongst his own people, then it makes sense that in AD59 Suetonius Paulinus was ordered to massacre the thousands of men women and children of the highest Khymry Druid families on Anglesey, no doubt they hoped they'd get him and his family second time around and murder the morale of the people."

Natasha looked intent; "Much like Herod did to try to eliminate Jesus as a baby."

William agreed; "They didn't get Jesus, the ancient texts tell us he was living in the Preseli area, probably in a hidden cave. The slaughter was a terrible mistake. The Romans, at best, only had fragile alliances with the Brits but this act brought the many tribes together including the Silures, Iceni, Triobantes and the Coraniad under King Arviragus and Queen Boudica. Together, between AD60 and AD62 they ripped the Romans to shreds."

William stopped for another slurp of coffee before continuing; "There's something very special about that whole Preseli area, we know that the special blue stones at the centre of Stonehenge have a petrochemical match to those at the top of Carn Ingli (Angel Mountain) and that the shape they make in Stonehenge mirrors the place on the Preselis known as Bedd Arthur (Arthur's Grave) So, let's skip on a bit. Jesus was a great guy full of wisdom gained from the early years in the learning establishments of Britain, Egypt and India, as a chief Druid his knowledge and use of energy and herbs to heal was renowned. If he was just a man, albeit a pretty special one, as opposed to a divine being that floated up to heaven then he must have died and been buried somewhere."

"So where would you bury such a person?"

"The Druids tradition was to hand down stories and histories by word of mouth, much like the Aborigines of Australia. They had a particular poem called the Songs of the Graves and these were actually sung descriptions of how to find the graves of the rich and famous so that they did not get lost or forgotten. In some of the translations Morgan and Pender found a description of the place of burial of Ner Eli Ner, which, translated, means son of the Holy Lord and, incidentally the description of Arthur's burial place, amongst others is also given. Part of the description, roughly translated reads;

The king of life, Ner Eli Ner lays in the magic place of his ancestors marked above and below by the cross of heaven and earth

Natasha looked aghast; "Christ!"

"Exactly, now we know from the Druids stories that Joseph of Arimathea, who the Welsh called Ilid, which means man of Israel, together with the Holy family landed at Dinas point in what is now west Wales. The name apparently means City of the Cross. They travelled a very short distance to a hill fort and settlement around the base of a mountain range in Pembrokeshire. This Druid village was a well known place of wisdom and knowledge being built over and around the strange and wonderful blue energy stones of the Preseli Mountains, famous for providing the ancient inner key stones of Stonehenge, Avebury and other places. Clearly the area was thought to be one of magic since time began."

Something rang a bell. She fired up the laptop that hardly ever left her side.

"Oh William, be a love, we are out of sight of the forecourt cameras, please change the number plates."

Recalling the wheeze when they left Angela's house he obliged.

Natasha didn't look up as William climbed back into the passenger's seat. She tapped a few keys on her laptop to bring up the image of the painting of the Shepherds of Arcadia which had been wrapped in the wax apple that the girl in the red dress had given to William.

"Using the number sequence from Michael's suicide note she ran the picture through a pixel decoder to see if she was right about a message being embedded. She was, in fact it revealed five co-ordinates, all in the Preseli Mountains".

William's eyes lit up;

"Do you have Stellarium Night Sky software on that thing, Nats?"

Natasha nodded, in a few moments the program appeared on screen.

"Here, take a look at this."

William showed her the sketch he'd made of the star and planet patterns from the Brynna disc.

Natasha looked at the diagram whilst downloading the software updates, then entering the co-ordinates and plotting the planet and star positions. After a while she had managed to match the stars in the sky above with the diagrams on the ground below. On the western horizon as you look out to sea from Carn Ingli stars made a clear pattern of a cross with its lower extremity in the water and its top in the sky. William looked at the disc and then at the screen it was as if the cross was planted in the horizon making a perfect shape in the sky.

"Wow, perfect match, you're brilliant Nats."

She resisted any obvious retort.

"The constellation that forms the cross, it's Cygnus, the Swan, the date AD68."

Suddenly William realised; "The girl in the red dress, she was dancing the dying swan from Swan Lake. All this business with swans, that's the constellation Cygnus, the symbol of enlightenment, wisdom and knowledge. Of course, in the ancient Welsh tales Helen, the mother of Constantine the Great has always been associated with the Swan and the cross, having gone to Jerusalem to find and bring it back to Constantinople , not the one in Turkey but to her palace near Nevern which bore the same name. Remember the cave we were told about?"

Natasha was only half listening; "Look William, anyone standing on the mountain range then would have seen the upright cross on the horizon."

William was impressed; "AD 68, the year that Peter was supposedly crucified in Rome. Could that also have been the year of the death and burial of Jesus on the mountain; is this what the Brynna disc is telling us?"

Nats was looking on the large scale map of the area playing with the co-ordinates; "The name of the mountain range is Carn Ingli, an odd name."

William moved to view the screen closer; "It means Angel Mountain."

Natasha nodded, she already knew of course.

He looked at the surrounding names and translated them with the aid of his Welsh-English dictionary; some were evocative, for example, Crown of Thorns, Cradle of God, Eye of Light.

William followed the grid references that Natasha gave him and discovered that they co-ordinated with ancient monuments in the immediate area. His finger moved from one to another;

"Look, they form a cross on the ground that mirrors the cross in the sky."

Nats looked thoughtfully. She brought up some random information that had survived from Michael's hard drive, she explained to William that it was under a section of quotes from William of Malmesbury…it was the first time the Latin had made any sense to her so she read it to William;

"*Iesus christus secreto ad montem angelorum in regione lapidum vivorum conditus.*"

William wore something of a puzzled expression; Latin translation wasn't his strongest trait. Natasha saved his blushes;

"It means approximately that Jesus Christ was buried in secret at Angel Mountain in the land of the living stones."

She paused before continuing; "As above so below, you thinking what I am thinking?"

William nodded; "I think we have found the burial place of JC. Come on, we can be there in one and a half hours".

Natasha pulled out her phone and sent a text to Evans; William looked enquiringly at her; "Just making sure Evans tries to help out Father Everson."

William nodded, "Thank you."

-63-

Nevern, Pembrokeshire

They pulled off the B4582 and into the car park of the Trewern Arms at Nevern around lunch time. It seemed a shame not to soak up the atmosphere of the flagstone floors, the ancient beams and the stone walls. What tales this 16th century place could tell.

They strolled across the road to stretch their legs and stood watching the river rush under the ancient bridge. It was so lovely to feel the sun on their faces and to hear the constant babbling of the waters, almost as if it was trying to tell them secrets from times gone by.

Natasha sat on a stone step and did that cute thing where she pushed both hands through her long hair and tossed her head back. William sat beside her and found himself staring at her;

"Want another photo?"

William smiled; "Now you're talking, strike a pose!"

Natasha made a long suffering tutting noise. William pretended to be holding a camera in his hand and snapped a few shots in a kind of bizarre paparazzi way. The silly moment passed.

"Roger thought I was being haunted by Brigit, a ghost swan."

Natasha cocked her head on one side waiting; "Care to elaborate?"

He thought she'd laugh but she was serious.

"He says his research had led him to believe that ancient peoples built their monuments to align, north south to track and predict the position of the constellation of Cygnus and a star in it called Deneb, he says that they believed God lived in the north and that Cygnus represented an ancient shape shifting female deity called Asherah who has had many names over millennia."

Natasha nodded; "Well I don't know about being haunted but I do know that the shamans of Russia used to say they communicated with the constellation Cygnus because that is where the soul comes from when we are born and where it goes back to when we die…they thought of the shape of the constellation as a goose or swan flying through the universe, taking the soul back over the river of the Milky Way from whence it came. In fact the belief was apparently universal amongst the ancient peoples…"

William smiled; "Are you being serious?" She was. "OK Nats, why did Roger tell me that?, I think there is something more to all this and I think he knew what it was."

Natasha prodded and woke up the computer that seemed surgically attached to her; "I agree, I think he wanted to tell you something but couldn't... there, I thought I'd seen something about Cygnus recently."

William looked over her shoulder as she brought up an article on her screen.

Scientists say that they have discovered a neutron star that rotates 41 times per second in the constellation Cygnus, which is 9,000 light-years away and is a symbiotic binary containing a compact white dwarf and a red giant star about 500 times the size of the sun.

Two days ago, a dramatic change in the brightness of V407 Cyg was observed which they attribute to a new high-energy gamma-ray source.

A NASA scientist commented, "In human terms, this was an immensely powerful eruption, equivalent to about 1,000 times the energy emitted by the sun every year," The blast created a hot, dense expanding shell called a shock front, composed of high-speed particles, ionized gas and magnetic fields. According to an early spectrum the nova's shock wave expanded at 7 million miles per hour.

William was trying to compute the information and failing miserably; "I'm lost Nats, I mean it's not as if Cygnus is going to get on the phone and chat to us is it?"

Natasha was tapping on her computer. Suddenly something struck her; "What if Cygnus has been talking to us for thousands of years? what if we just don't realize or listen?"

"What if it is the heartbeat of the solar system?"

William laughed out loud but Natasha had raked out a bit of information from a web site reference she had found on the phantom history browser cache of Michael's computer.

Together they read the contents. Minutes of silence passed with only the mutual nods signaling that each had finished a page and were ready for the next.

"Is this saying what I think it is?"

Natasha confirmed his thoughts. In essence scientists have found very high levels of a substance called Beryllium-10 in the Antarctic and Greenland ice cores every two thousand years from around 35,000bc. They argue that this appeared to facilitate sudden developments in human behaviour patterns. Based on calculations the scientists put the source of the cosmic rays as the Cygnus Veil, or Cygnus Loop.

Located in the right wing of the celestial swan, the shock waves of this cosmic event were believed to have ripped open the Earth's protective layer of ozone, causing cosmic rays and ultraviolet radiation from the sun to rain down on the unsuspecting world beneath. For many years the exploding star would have been brighter than the full moon, making it a blinding light source that turned night into day appearing as an extra moon in the sky.

William was fascinated; "Wow!, two moons, a male and a female maybe? No wonder they venerated that part of the sky.If they witnessed this event, you can see how this would have melted into folklore and passed down over centuries, but they wouldn't have known about how it was changing them or helping them to evolve, would they?"

Natasha wasn't so sure;

"We sit here in our modern world thinking we are the best examples of evolution and yet what if we have lost skills and abilities we once had? What if in some way the ancients could tune into what was happening, what if that part of the sky was in essence acting as a telephone to them from the universe."

William was open-minded. Natasha was still researching on the net. "Look at this."

"Deep underground scientists have registered anomalous incoming cosmic rays unlike any detected before. They bore a 'fingerprint' periodicity of 4.8 hours, which they believe comes from a binary star system named Cygnus X-3, located some 30,000 lights years away on the other side of the galaxy.

Visually speaking, Cygnus X-3 is located at the very centre of Cygnus's cross design, next to the star Sadr.

The exact nature of the cosmic rays from Cygnus X-3 are extraordinary. They are tens of thousands of times stronger than anything produced by particle accelerators, and since they are neutral (in that they have no charge) and arrive directly from Cygnus (as opposed to their route being distorted by the galactic gravitational field), it indicates that they travel here very close to the speed of light."

William shuffled closer to Natasha, feeling the warmth of her body next to his.

"This has to be more than co-incidence, doesn't it? I mean all this activity and stuff going on around Cygnus and ancient people's obsession with it."

There was more, much more.

"The strange particles from Cygnus X-3 are uniquely able to penetrate hundreds of meters of solid rock before finally crashing into atomic nuclei to form secondary particles, detected by deep underground facilities around the world. No other point source cosmic ray, besides neutrinos - which are caused

by nuclear fusion reactions in the sun and supernovae, can pass through matter with almost no interaction.

Cygnus X-3's cosmic rays keep coming in waves, the next huge wave being predicted between the end of 2015 and summer 2016".

Natasha's brain was analysing the information.

"Was there something special about the quality of caves which might have enabled supernatural communication?"

William was on a roll; "What if our dear old ancestors didn't actually have to be deep underground, what if they could just build chambers that acted in the same way?"

Natasha was hooked; "Of course, it makes perfect sense, look at the chambers like Newgrange could they have been built to capture the messages from Cygnus?"

William smiled, "You mean we may have misunderstood burial mounds, they may in fact be telephones to the Gods? If that's true then what was being said?"

Natasha looked serious; "I think you are being too literal, Will, we known that Shamans used psychedelic substances inside caves to aid supernatural communications in trance like states... here, look at this."

"At Creswell Crags, on the borders between Derbyshire and Nottinghamshire in Northern England, we see in a cave called Church Hole. Swan-like birds are drawn on its walls as well as an ibis head and egg close to the entrance.

Coincidentally, a person standing in the mouth of the cave in 10,500 BC, when the rock art was created, would have been able to see the stars of Cygnus framed above a south-facing cliff on the opposite side of the valley. It is very likely that as Dr Paul Pettit, lecturer on human origins at Sheffield University, has intimated, the north-facing side of the valley where Church Hole is situated was reserved for cultic practices associated with the realm of the dead".

It seemed to fit nicely, the link with Cygnus and the souls of the living and the dead was inescapable. Maybe the pair were getting a little carried away, the references a little more esoteric;

"Francis Crick, the Nobel-prize winning discoverer of the structure of DNA, heavily supported the concept of what he called Direct Panspermia, in which he proposed that life on earth was deliberately seeded by an advanced civilization, a concept first intimated in the writings of Anaxagoras, a Greek philosopher who thrived c. 450 BC.

It is interesting to note that Crick admitted secretly not only to taking small quantities of LSD, but also to first seeing the famous DNA double helix structure *when high on the drug. If this is true were shamanic journeys during Palaeolithic times, where the initiate would travel to the stars using the sky-rope, vine or ladder, reflective in some way of his belief that life originated elsewhere, and that after death we would return from whence we came?*

All over the world there was once a belief that life came from deep space. The Mandaeans of Iraq and Iran believed that at death the human soul passed beyond the North Star, identified here as Deneb in Cygnus, where it would join a sky-boat that would take it across the celestial river, arguably the Milky Way, to one of the countless 'worlds of light', home to their dead kinsmen. In these blissful realms, governed by 'great spirits of light', they would encounter their purified souls as well as their own 'dmutha, or over-soul'."

William felt a shiver run down his spine and he shuddered visibly. Natasha hugged him spontaneously;
"It's ok Will; you can't wake up yet."
He looked down at his body, his hands, his feet, they all seemed present and correct. He looked strangely at her;
"O, very funny, do I look asleep?"
Natasha looked oddly back at him; "What are you talking about?"
You just said "It's ok Will, you can't wake up yet."
Natasha looked bemused; "Why would I say that?, anyway you always look a bit dozy to me!"
William didn't laugh. She thought for a second before continuing; "The double helix, two connected strands, right? What else bombards the earth?"
Will thought for a bit; "Solar flares, Michael was always going on about them."
Natasha looked thoughtful; "What was Michael's name, I mean his Shamanic name?"
Tears came to his eyes as he recalled the giant of a man he was proud to call his friend; "Grandfather Michael."
Natasha nodded; "Of course, like the Hopi Indian elders." She typed some key words into the search engine.
William was gobsmacked; "How the hell do you know about so much?"
Natasha smiled; "Jealous? I read a lot and I have a photographic memory, well most of the time."
She had ended up on "You Tube" and there before their eyes was a reference to Michael, it was a video he had recorded and posted two days after he had died.
"How the hell?"
Natasha had already noticed, but, unlike William she wasn't seeing any images or hearing any sound. William was just lost in grief, hanging on every

word. Michael came very close to the camera and tapped the lens, William jumped.

"William, are you listening? This is for you."

The bearded giant grinned from ear to ear as he continued; "Don't question how and why you are seeing this. You are on your soul path Will and I have been proud to have been your guide through some of your life. You know you can walk through the forest squeaking like a mouse or roaring like a lion... your choice Will"

Natasha was looking at the screen. She passed her hand up and down between the image and William's face, he was glued. She was not seeing or hearing anything.

"Will, Will! What are you looking at?"

He was glued to Michael's face; "She can't see me Will."

William's mouth dropped as he looked around. Natasha went to turn the computer off but he held up his finger and just pointed...

"It's Michael. He's talking to me."

Natasha had no idea what was going on but was wise enough to sit and observe as he repeated the words Michael said; after all, she had seen Will behave like this in the hospital when he was talking about swans. She so wished she could cure his brain tumour but all she could do was to humour him and care, that was, after all, why she was there, wasn't it?

Michael continued; "Remember the Mayan calendar Will, it ends on December 31, 2012. I'm certain nothing major is going to happen then but I am sure it has some significance, something linked to Cygnus and the sun. Morgan and Pender's research had led them to monuments on the ground that linked to the constellations. They linked Cygnus to Jesus and early Christianity through Helen the mother of Constantine. The vital thing is not where Jesus is buried but why he was buried there and where the metal cross found at St Peters is. You see, it's very likely that soon there will be massive solar flares, they happen every two thousand years or so and they will co-incide with the highest density waves from Cygnus the earth will ever see. The ancient ones knew this; they sat quietly and listened in their trance state travels. The two waves, one from Cygnus and one from the sun will weave around each other in a double helix like DNA; this should herald a brave new world of greater spirituality. It is, if you like, a change to our genetic code, or, if you prefer, instructions from our creator to change the DNA of every living thing for the better, an update to our software, a second coming if you like to see it that way.

Evidence points to an ancient race of space travellers hiding spheres of a unique derivative of Platinum 190 in various parts of the world to form a network. Tiny fragments of this metal have been found in the comet craters of West Wales and have been used in experiments. Roger Felix found a large amount of it in the St Peter's cross but tried to keep it secret. We know these networks around the globe as magnetic fields or ley lines. The largest sphere was apparently placed under what is now known as Angel Mountain in the Preseli range because of the unique quality of the stones in that area to reverse polarity and to act as transmitters of infra sound.

This sphere acts as an earthing mechanism and receiver for the new genetic code, much like a software update for a computer, which will then be transmitted as the double helix spiral around the world to mankind using infra sound and magnetic field or ley lines. This new code automatically connects to each living being using low frequency vibrations and changes DNA which will then manifest in new generations. These rush of energy spirals and wave forms were visualised and meditated upon by shamans in trance states long ago. They were recorded as art of the time, first on stone then in jewellery.

In the 6th century comet strike across West Wales this key sphere was damaged and fragmented across a large crater. A lump of the substance was discovered by King Arthur and Merthyn or Merlin as he later became known. He was drawn to the place by a vision. He thought that the comet had brought it to earth and that it was sacred material from the creator, which in a sense it was. When Arthur died he discovered that the metal could be melted at a high temperature and mixed with other metals. He formed the St Peter's cross to the memory of Arthur out of it. What he didn't realise was that by moving it from its special resting place under the blue stones of the Preseli range he was causing potential future disaster. Without all of the metal from the special sphere in place the new code double helix due in or around 2016 would not be drawn to the right place and would therefore not be transmitted on the magnetic ley lines for the benefit of mankind. As I have said our space fathers chose to place the sphere under the Preseli blue stones because they naturally reverse polarity which is needed to maintain the swirl of energy and propel it into the ley line or magnetic field network around the earth in the same way a transmitter sends sound and vision.

By moving such a relatively large piece of the special metal from the Preselis, from its exact resting place, the waves from Cygnus and the sun have no-where to focus and thus cannot fulfill the destiny of the people. The result would mean that instead of genetically developing the DNA heralding a new dawn or spirituality and peace for mankind the waves could mix randomly above the earth causing high altitude electromagnetic pulses instead, or to be more exact, atomic like explosions and massive worldwide destruction, in short, Armageddon... so your job has to be to find the cross, or more accurately the metal it is made from and return it to its proper resting place... so no pressure there... oh, and don't worry about me Will, I'm safe and sound."

William sunk to the ground holding his head crying pitifully; "Oh Nats, it hurts so much, I'm going mad, I am sure I am going mad, my head hurts so much."

She was at his side holding him tightly and rocking him gently; a very rare tear fell from the corner of her eye and ran down her cheek. How much longer did he have, there couldn't possibly be anything in these mad ramblings, could there? God what if he was right?... the whole computer system, the whole dam infrastructure depends on magnetism and electricity, if this was sent haywire it would almost certainly be a massive dark age. No computers, no mobile phones, no heat and light the end of the world as we know it.

It took William several minutes to recover enough for the focus to return to his eyes. Slowly they made their way back to the inn.

The landlord noticed that William was as white as a sheet and was shaking from head to toe.

A little later the after effects of the attack left William. He even managed a smile as Natasha enjoyed her salmon salad and home baked bread. William was looking around to see if they were being observed, they weren't;

"So how do you like being Mrs Brown?"William smiled. Natasha winced a little; "So unoriginal, fancy telling the chap it's our honeymoon!"

William smirked just a little but nothing took his mind from the problems they were facing for long.

"Just how many languages, apart from Latin do you speak?"

Natasha was coy; "Does it matter? Language is only a code that people use to communicate, if you know the code you know the language."

William felt rebuked, only the glint in her eyes told him she was teasing. He resolved never to play her at poker.

-63-

Preselis, West Wales
3rd August 2009

Faithfully following the co-ordinates calculated from cracking the code on the photo from the la wan they soon discovered the first target. It led them to a narrow lane not far from Newport where they parked. As soon as they entered the field through the iron devils gate they could see the triangle shaped dolmen of Pentre Ifan. It was indeed impressive and obviously the core of a much larger, possibly even communal place of burial. From the information on the thoughtfully placed sign it was clear that the chamber had first been constructed around 3500 years ago. The monument had acquired the local nickname of Arthur's Quoit in the mists of time. Natasha made her way under the giant leaning cap stone and William followed. There were all sorts of markings scraped into the surfaces, mostly recent and connected to the youth of several generations. The views from the chamber were stunning. One thing in particular caught William's attention. Roughly at eye level was a small hole perfectly drilled in antiquity through one of the thick stones facing the peak of Carn Ingli. Natasha came over to examine the find.

Taking her mobile gps out of her pocket she attached it to her camera and captured a picture and the position. It exactly matched one of the five co-ordinates from the code on the map from the la wan. William pointed to the large scale map of the area that the very friendly pub landlord had loaned to him. It clearly showed three more standing stone sites which Nats had seen on Google Earth. William observed how the slant of the main cap stone mirrored the slope of the mountain in the distance.

Natasha punched in the second co-ordinate into her GPS and they set off following the invisible voice.

52.01817 -4 828341 proved to be a monument carefully and strangely located on the edge of a holiday park and labeled by CADW as being Carrag Coetan Arthur dolman.

To them it looked like another burial chamber and possibly an altar, smaller than Pentre Ifan but similar in the way all the earth had been removed to leave a curious stone skeleton. Natasha was first to notice the same cup marked patterns in the shape of Cygnus on the inside of the large upright stones. There was also a sight hole. Taking photographs and making notes they continued their tour. This time the co-ordinate led them to a squat collapsed version of the monument they had just seen. This one was not marked with information, it was tucked away on a private farm. The map revealed the name as Trelyffant and someone had carefully written underneath, "The place of the toads!" There was no time to seek permission so they parked the car and proceeded, somewhat gingerly and furtively, through a gap in the hedge, but not before William had noticed the name on a village sign; Gethsemane.

There was a stiff breeze and an overpowering smell of slurry. The green grass field was uneven and little muddy from the hooves of cattle, some of which looked towards them with alarm in their large eyes.

William observed that there had been a concentrated effort to dig out around the pile of stones, which, it had to be said, did indeed look like a giant toad.

Natasha pulled her hair to the back of her head and slipped on a band to stop it falling across her face. She was standing beside and running her hands across the stony surfaces.

William smiled; "If you rub it too much a genie will pop out!"

The quip was immediately filed under inappropriate behaviour.

The view from this remote spot across to the Holy Mountain of the Angels (Cairn Ingli) was stunning. There and then it was easy to half close your eyes and imagine how the most ancient of monuments combined to construct the shape of the cross on the landscape.

Natasha sketched out Williams thoughts on paper. At what appeared to be the foot of the cross shape there was Pentre Ifan, to the south there was Carreg Coetan Arthur Dolmen. She attempted a bit of geometry to test her theory that the ancient markers traced out a cross on the ground.

There was one co-ordinate that didn't seem to fit in with the cross pattern. 51.999864 -4.82332 seemed to be at or near to the summit of Cairn Ingli.

In no time at all they had re-parked the car in the nearest safest place and were following the map and gps to the summit of the mount.

Even in the warmth of the afternoon the wind was keen. They walked in as much of a straight line as the plethora of stones large and small would allow. After around 25 minutes they came across what looked like a walled enclosure with two large stones forming a gateway. These appeared to be on a direct alignment with the "Place of the Toads". Passing through the decayed ancient gates it was easy, even 2000 years or more later, to make out the remains of a street and stone houses of various sizes. Was this the village that once flourished under the protection of the great Hill Fort, a village renowned for its spiritual and commercial wisdom?

They continued climbing for a further 15 minutes. It was only 350 feet above sea level but the slope made it seem much more. William suddenly felt light headed and out of breath. He became aware of a pure white horse standing watching him from 100 yards or so away. He pointed to it but Natasha saw nothing. As he leaned against a rocky outcrop he started to sway, he could hear voices, lots of voices, all chanting and crying. As he gazed upwards he was consumed by a mass of white light.Out of the corner of his eye he saw the white horse running full tilt towards him. Above him blinding forms moved around him. He cowered under the shadow of beating wings. He sunk quickly to the floor as Natasha tried to steady him. They were swooping on him, screeching, flying right up close to his face and laughing. His arms and hands were flaying trying to beat them off. He was crying, shouting, screaming in delirium.

Natasha moved closer, holding him tighter and tighter.

"William, William, don't do this to me, William, come on I need you."

Something in Natasha's plea shook him out of the vision and he sighed as he calmed down.

"Christ Nats did you see that, did you see the angels?"

Natasha hadn't seen anything but she held him close, warm and protected.

"It's ok Will, they've gone, you are safe now"

It seemed to take William a while to regain some sort of composure. He opened his eyes and looked around, all was quiet and still apart from the sound of the wind across the small purple flowers which created a moving sea of heavenly colour. As they slowly continued William remembered reading an article about how the area had once been used as a training ground for the troops in the second world war but had been abandoned because so many of the men complained of illusions and electric malfunction. Scientists had put it down to a remarkable property of the blue stone which had the capacity to reverse polarity and emit infra sound. Had this or something allied to it made this spot unique and sacred in the past? Could it possibly have been linked to the metal sphere and the comet that Michael had mentioned before?. Just a minute though, that wasn't real was it? How about the angels, the horse, the wings, the swan, the girl, even himself; just what was real and what was illusion.Panic came quickly over him.

"Nats, Nats, are you there?"

Natasha grabbed Williams arm and held him tight again;

"It's ok Will, I'm here, I'll always be here."

His eyes refocused slowly as she pointed. Before them was a large mound of stones. She knew from the co-ordinates that they were almost upon the spot which she had identified from one of Michael's coded clues. The spot that did not seem to fit with the cross shape.

She held out her arm and helped him up the steep incline of loose boulders. After they had climbed a few feet braced against the wind their heart sunk.

From the brow they could see that there was a great dip in the middle where many stones had been moved and stacked around the edge.

Natasha looked sad; "Looks like we are too late."

William looked thoughtful as he carefully examined the site; "I'm no archaeologist but I know enough to say that these stones haven't been moved for hundreds of years".

Natasha's eye was caught by a standing stone partially covered by the smaller ones. William saw where she was looking and, instinctively they made their way over.

Very carefully they started removing the small stones. After 15 minutes William poured the rest of his bottle of water over the indentations. As it dried they could just make out a rudimentary carving. There were three crosses and a man walking. Beside one of the crosses was what appeared to be a ladder and a flower. Natasha looked at it from all angles; "It's a poppy."

William placed his hand upon the marker, for a split second a man's bearded face leapt out at him sending him falling backwards. Natasha wondered what had happened. At that moment he was filled with divine inspiration almost as if the stone was talking to him.

"Three crosses, that ties in with the crucifixion story, the ladder was used by Joseph and Longinus to take Jesus down from the cross and the poppy represents heroine, which can, when used by an expert induce a state that presents just as if the person has died".

He looked at Natasha; "I feel certain that this was the place where the body of Jesus was buried, but someone long ago has taken it, this must also have been near to the place where the sphere Michael mentioned was once buried"

Natasha wasn't convinced by the sphere theory.

"Maybe there was a resurrection?"

The long silent and thoughtful walk back to the car was shattered by William's assertion;

"Amazing isn't it? We have seen the actual burial place of Jesus."

Natasha shrugged unconvincingly; "If you say so."

-64-

Newport, West Wales
3rd August 2009

The sky was darkening and the breeze was turning to short gusts across the harbour at Newport. William and Natasha concentrated on eating their soft Mr Whippy ice creams with chocolate dip followed by a drink of fizzy cola.

William was restless, he just couldn't settle. One moment his head was in his hands, the next he was gazing around at the many distractions. His head hurt as if it was being drilled, for a few seconds the vibration seemed unbearable.

Natasha noticed how odd he looked as he made staccato movements; "Are you ok William?"

"What's happening to me Nats?"

Her eyes held a terrible sadness; she knew he was trying to ignore what the doctors had told him

"You'll be ok Will, I'm here, what more could you need?"

She almost smiled.

It was a brave face. Trying to change the mood she plucked a snippet of information from the dog eared local guide book borrowed from the Inn.

"Did you know that there was a special Holy route through Pembrokeshire to St Davids until the middle ages? The path went along a ridge above Nevern, across to Carn Ingli and to Dinas Head where the saints and others would travel to Ireland then on to Rome or Jerusalem. A pilgrimage to Nevern and Carn Ingli was worth two to Rome!"

William was miles away but suddenly spoke; "If what we have just seen was the burial place of JC in the first century AD then why is this Stone Age, older site relevant? Why are the monuments in the shape of a cross when a cross wasn't relevant until after the crucifixion of Jesus?"

William was back in the real world and he was talking sense. The point was well made, Natasha had been thinking along similar lines;

"Maybe burying him there was the highest honour they could give, maybe there was a race memory of powerful energy, maybe energy in the form of spirals, maybe this story about the sphere of a strange metal is real, not fantasy?"

William shrugged his shoulders;

"Who knows, you could be right, there must have been something very special about the Preseli blue stones to make people 3500 years ago move them huge distances from here to Avebury and Stonehenge."

Natasha seemed inspired; Or maybe the ancients somehow knew about the keystone sphere hidden in the earth, about the creation of mankind?"

William looked at her side ways; "You starting to believe there may be something other worldly going on?"

Natasha was slowly and unconvincingly shaking her head.

The thought hung in the air.

Just then two very large ladies with obscenely tight swimming costumes wobbled past arm in arm. Natasha's eyes followed them carefully;

"My God, every picture tells a story!"

A few moments passed before William raised his head;

"What did you say?"

"Keep up; I said, every picture tells a story!"

William fumbled in his pocket for his compact camera;

"That's it!"

He placed an arm around the unsuspecting girl and hugged her. "You're a genius."

Natasha laughed; "Tell me something I don't know."

William turned on the camera and started flicking through the pictures until he came to the ones he had taken in the ancient church of St Illtyd on Caldey Island...

"Look Natasha."

Natasha snuggled up closer to William in order to see the small images on the camera screen. For a moment she felt normal, cosy and warm. William started with one image and zoomed in. It showed two winged angels either side of a sphere in which sat a grail cup. The angels were placing the sun with rays coming out into the grail vessel itself. Above the scene more rays, from a second sun, rained down upon the scene.

Natasha caught on quickly; "Could this be the sphere the extra terrestrials placed in the ground?"

William looked at her; "You said I was hallucinating, that you didn't see Michael on screen."

She smiled and motioned for William to flick to the next photograph which depicted a small sailing boat but the condition of the plaster and the wall made it impossible to see much more.

The third showed a sphere with eight rays emitting from it. In the centre was the key of St Peter. (the key to Heaven).

William gathered his thoughts; "Every picture tells a story! In this case I believe that the first represents the sun entering a grail vessel, and the angels give this act a holy over tone."

Natasha smiled; "You mean it represents Jesus impregnating Mary Magdalen with a child, the sun of God in this context substituting the son of God."

William nodded; "Yes, that's exactly what I was thinking; don't forget that the sun is the key to all life and that Jesus was aligned with it. The Vatican boasts a wonderful mosaic of Apollo, as Jesus riding a chariot out of the sun, although they keep it well hidden. Before Christianity as we know it people worshipped the death of the sun and its rebirth three days later at Xmas. Not many people realize that Constantine changed Xmas from 1st march to 25th December to celebrate Sol Invictus. Because he was an early British Christian he believed that God lived in the sun. Now look what it has become. It's my guess that there are several descendants of Jesus and the Holy family out there."

Natasha was gazing out at the sails in the bay; "And what of the small boat?"

William was confident he knew; "OK, it could be symbolic. The early Christians used an upright cross in a half moon as a symbol for Jesus. This represented a boat and was a clue to the escape of Jesus. The sign later became an anchor. However, it could be more literal. We know that Arthur was a strong invincible and powerful leader. He would have known who his family was and would also have known of his direct link to the Holy family. He would also know the whereabouts of the burial place of Jesus, as would Merthyn and his closest advisors. If Michael was right then the comet strike could have revealed the fragments of the sphere and the body of Jesus... Or maybe after Arthur's death there were grave concerns about pagan raids on the coast and the safety of the resting place of Jesus, no pun intended. I think this boat is evidence that JC's body was moved after Arthur died"

Natasha was now enthralled; "It's the long bow, isn't it?"

William disagreed; "No, I think it is perfectly logical and possible. In his own writings the monk Nennius tells us that the embalmed body of a very very Holy man with an altar above him held up by the will of God arrived by boat down the Ewenney river and was taken to a secret cave in which Illtyd, Arthur's cousin, had dug a grave out of the rock. There he was interred and the cave sealed. This must be the same cave that Morgan and Pender found with the inscription above the empty grave cut, "here lies the highest ruler". Illtyd was a cousin of Arthur and the same person as lived on Caldey Island. The old church bears his name. The pictures on the wall are just too much of a co-incidence, the monks there wanted to make a record of the story, of that I am sure. I bet that's how Nennius knew about it; he was one of the monks on Caldey which is a great stopping off point between Dinas Head and the Ewenney River."

Natasha couldn't fault the assertion; "But why hide the body in the cave? Why take it there?"

William was on a roll; "Let's look at the third picture, the one of the key of St Peter in the sphere radiating light. That cave is near to the church of St Peters on Caer Caradoc. I think it was the intention to rebury JC at the church of St Peters when the threat of invasion died down and when the church could be rebuilt after the comet damage. Don't forget that St Peters church on Cornhill was the very first Christian church in Europe which was built by King Lucius in around AD160 on the site of a beehive hermitage that may once have been used by Joseph of Arimathea, Jesus and Peter themselves. In AD156 this king issued a Royal decree at Winchester stating that Christianity was the national faith of Britain, now the church lays ruined and sad, the victim of stone looters and night hawks, God knows what has been lost that can never be found."

Natasha stood up stretched, wiggled and yawned;

William was flicking through the photos on his digital camera and Natasha was watching.

"Hang on Will; just go back a bit... stop!"

The photograph showed Everson sitting at his desk with the Book of Life but to the side Natasha had spotted something. She took the camera from William and zoomed in on the image, it was a handwritten text in Latin. It was upside down and a little too blurry to read properly so she took the memory card out of the camera and loaded it into her laptop.

William looked on curiously.

Soon she had opened the image in special software. William was gesturing, asking for a commentary;

"It's a piece of software used by forensics, it's called Genuine Fractals; it enables small images to be blown up clearer with less pixilation."

Soon Natasha had the Latin text on screen;

"Timentes ne pagani sepulchrum Christi profanerint Illtyd et fraters sui corpus sancti effoderunt et eum in renone involverant ; inde ad insulam muttorum nave deinde ad cavernam occultam in silva arcana in terra locatum portaverund"

William was a bit lost but Natasha studied the words carefully.

"Ok, it's a bit convoluted but I think it means something along the lines of:

Afraid that the heathens would desecrate the grave of Christ, Illtyd and his brothers exhumed the body of the holy one and wrapped him in deerskins thence by boat to the island of many and then to the secret cave in the forest of mystery."

William's look implied that she was joking, especially after what he had just been saying. Natasha didn't believe in co-incidence or fate. She was sure that

Everson had left it in exactly the correct position for it to appear in Williams photograph.

"So Morgan and Pender found the grave in the cave in the forest of mystery but it was empty. In that case the body must have been moved again, but who moved it and to where, St Peter's church?"

William seemed inspired, almost as if he inherently knew the story all along; "I think the whole burial place of Jesus was forgotten in the wake of the invasions and slaughters of the 6th century. Only the head Monks and Druids probably had some idea of the stories. The great city of Caer Caradoc on Mynnyd y Gaer that had been such a stronghold for Caradoc and his family and later for Arthur was destroyed by the comet strike. I don't think it ever returned to its former glory.

After the Norman invasion the land fell into the hands of the de Clare family. William the Marshall, originally William Fitzherbert, the greatest knight in the land, married Isabel de Clare, a daughter of Richard Strongbow de Clare, Earl of Pembroke. Thereafter he inherited the title and the land. Nevern, the cave and the whole area of Caer Caradoc belonged to him. William was also head of the Templar's and as such would have had a great thirst for the old stories and knowledge. He would have a good idea about the whereabouts of JC from the old family records. I think William Marshall had an extension to St Peters built to accommodate a special chamber and crypt to hold Jesus and possibly Mary Magdalen who legend has originally buried at Ewenney Priory"

Natasha didn't quite know what to say; "Who do you think you are, William Marshall, knight reincarnated? After all you have the same name and a pretty accurate insight into what is happening?"

William blushed for the first time in years. Natasha had been trying to be funny but William took her seriously; "Maybe, I don't know. I remember my mum talking about the designs and colours of shields and heraldic devices when I was a boy. Just lately I have discovered that they fit with the arms of both Arthur and the knight William Marshall... that can't be co-incidence, can it?

I recall looking at some of the rushes that were on the DVD in Nicole's briefcase, rushes taken by the BBC at the St Peters dig in 1990. Father Everson told me that they reached a layer to the right hand of the altar which had two large stone slabs with nothing on them. He said that he turned one over and it had the letters I and E on it... tempting to think Isus and Esus both names given to Jesus."

Natasha was stretching into another yoga pose as she remembered the recent visit to Shugborough Hall, the Poussin paintings and the relief in the gardens; "The inscription on the carving of the Poussin painting as deciphered by Morgan and Pender, according to them it reads, "I am in the land of Caradoc;" if what you are saying is right, the land of Caradoc is the whole area around St Peters church "

William observed the position she put herself in with some wonder as she continued;

"Do you really think that Jesus is buried at St Peters then?"

William moved his head to mirror hers; "Personally, from what we've seen, I think it's very likely and I think that the church and others also have a good idea, that's why they will never let the site be dug again. They must have cried halleluiah when the storm washed the dig off the mountain never to return and also why they made such a fuss when Roger wanted to re-open the dig, they must have had a hissy fit."

Natasha resumed a normal posture and looked at William; "I guess that the church wanted to hush this all up. They seem to be letting Valetti and his cronies do whatever they have to in order to get the body and the St Peters cross. They are turning their backs on truth and reality pretending to be blind, or Christian!"

They both sat in thought but Natasha was first to break the silence; "What about the St Peter's cross, what do you think Morgan and Pender would have done with that?"

William was not sure; "Maybe Everson never actually gave them the original in the first place?"

Natasha saw the flaw straightaway.

"Hang on, we know that Felix tested something that confirmed its authenticity and it's strange metal content because he told CADW and he ran the tests for Morgan and Pender when they supposedly sold the original St Peter's cross to the antiquities dealer who was no doubt fronting the church"

It all made sense to William. "And Valetti says it wasn't the original St Peter's cross.. no wonder he is going ape, maybe Felix forged the analysis for a back hander from Morgan and Pender?"

They gazed at each other, it was one thing to think they may have solved a riddle but quite another to know what to do next. Natasha sat close to William and kissed him on the cheek, she had just noticed something she didn't like;

"Don't make it obvious, just stroll back to the car with me."

Perhaps they should have been more careful but they could have had no way of knowing that every word was being recorded with the very latest HH1 directional microphones usually reserved only for the top CIA operations and that within five minutes the information had been relayed to Valetti.

Back in the car Natasha fired up her laptop and attached a gizmo that looked like an octopus with long tentacles;

"What the hell is that?"

She put her hands to her lips but wrote a note on a Post-It; "We might be bugged."

The spider sweeper soon picked up the bug inserted just under the skin behind Williams's right ear and motioned to him, reinforcing the message with a note;

"Bug is under your skin behind your right ear... must have been put in at the hospital in Haverfordwest."

William just stopped himself from speaking, opting instead to write his own note; "You mean all of our conversation since has been recorded?"

Nats nodded. William wrote SHIT on the pad and for some reason they both laughed.

Natasha pulled a scalpel out of a small roll of tools and was passing the blade through a purifying flame from a pocket lighter.

William gulped as she moved towards him; "This might sting just a little but I'll be as quick as I can."

William gathered courage from somewhere; He felt a sharp scratch to one side of his ear but tried to make light of it; "Hell of a time to play doctors and nurses!"

-C65-

Caerleon
3rd August 2009

Rachel and Evans had been helping at the disastrous explosion site. Time had just slipped abstractly by. They stank of acrid smoke and singed hair. Their clothes were covered with grey and white ash.

Evans suddenly wondered what had happened to William and Natasha. He asked Rachel to call but, at Natasha's request William had turned off his phone and left it at the decoy hotel.

After turning on his mobile Evans received the message from Natasha. He gathered Rachel and took her back to his aunt's house where they had been staying. There was unwelcome confirmation that Everson may well have been kidnapped. His aunt's carer had called the police but after several hours they still hadn't turned up. Rachel looked forlorn;

"Who has kidnapped him? Will they kill him, how the hell did Natasha know?"

Evans couldn't find it in his heart to lie; neither could he answer all her questions;

"Pretty sure it's someone working for the church. If they kidnapped him rather than murdered him that means they must want to question him. In the long run they probably will kill him to protect their identities."

Rachel was terribly upset. Evans held her close to him, wiping the tears from her eyes. In a moment of madness he held her face softly and kissed her on the lips. He had grown fond of her, perhaps too fond. She didn't pull away; she didn't know how to respond. She felt like a rabbit in headlights. The moment passed uncomfortably without comment.

"We must be able to help him; we can't just ignore what's happened. At least the police know."

Evans looked defeated;

"Not sure if that will do any good they are not exactly quick off the mark are they?"

Rachel was trying to think things through;

"Everson seemed to know a hell of a lot about the subject; do you think he might actually have kept the original cross found at the dig at St Peters and handed Morgan and Pender a copy? If William is right he certainly kept that ancient book he found at the dig, what did he call it, oh yes, the Book of Life."

Evans decided to come clean; "Rachel, there's something you need to know. I haven't been entirely honest with you."

She looked at him wondering what was coming next;

"I have worked for Interpol but in this case I have been on secondment to MI5. Pulling me off the case was a ruse. Helen wasn't my daughter she was a co-operative. We have been trying to work undercover to see if you, William and Natasha will lead us to the cross, I, I am so sorry Rachel, I have genuinely fallen for you."

Although she wasn't entirely surprised she couldn't stop herself pounding his chest with her fists and then slapping him several times across the face. Evans let her carry on, he knew he deserved it. When the tirade had finished Rachel just stood exhausted.

There was a tear in Evans eye, he looked genuinely hurt.

"Rachel, I, I..."

She pulled away but stopped herself from running. Her gaze into Evans eyes was steady, demanding and expectant,

"How the hell can I trust you? MI5? Nicole, Robin Bryant and I suppose Natsaha as well?"

Evans didn't disappoint.

"No, not Natasha. I am truly sorry Rachel, I know you won't ever trust me again. The fact is that we've been chasing shadows for years but about 11 months ago we heard that a secret project which was very near to being tested might have been infiltrated; clearly there was a huge leak somewhere. This was something being cooked up by the UK who had been keeping the research quiet. The USA sniffed a leak out and wanted to know all about it. They threatened to pull the plug on the so called "special relationship" between the two countries, huh, more like they nod and we have to jump. Anyway, we suspected foul play, something was rotten to the core and it involved an organisation which kept coming up in connection with Project Meurig, an organisation loosely called Common Purpose. Their intention was to place people in top positions to gain control and help create a New World Order, we suspected Sylvia Clarke at CADW and Grey, the head of MI5 were involved so this was an operation within an operation to weed out the double agents."

Rachel was flabbergasted; "But what has it got to do with Arthur, Jesus, the cross and all that?"

Evans took a long sigh; "Not obvious at the start, Rachel, but thanks to the help you and your friends have unwittingly given us I think it is much clearer. We knew from Robin Bryant who was at the meeting that Roger had with CADW that there was a chance of another dig at St Peters church and Robin reported how twitchy CADW were about the whole thing. We discovered that Sylvia Clarke, the head of CADW was reporting back directly to the Home Secretary in more ways than one, they were having an affair. In fact she was quite a girl and it seems that she might have been feeding information to others as well. She was or should I say is in cahoots with the church who had been trying to get their hands on the St Peter's cross for years. Back in 1980 Morgan and Pender started publishing material about King Arthur which was challenging the very bedrock of history in the UK. The big problem was that the content could inflame nationalistic and religious tendencies and cause unrest. In order to try to retain the status quo MI5 were involved in trying to diminish their characters by attributing false criminal and other records to them. In some ways they were their own worst enemies as they would rise to any bait laid for them. Somehow they limped along and gained a following on the internet and for the books they were self publishing. It was time consuming keeping an eye on them and when we discovered from a publisher they use that they intended to launch a book with proof that Jesus did not die on the cross and that he was related to King Arthur and worse, that Princess Diana was a direct descendent from the Holy family we had to take this much more seriously. We managed to delay things and get the self publisher they used to say they had lost the manuscript. In the end we appealed to Morgan and Pender's vanity and convinced them that via the BBC a series about their work would be made, of course it was a ruse to get as much inside information about them and the project as possible."

Rachel was trying to absorb the words being spoken;

"So you knew all along what Morgan and Pender were up to?"

Evans shook his head; "No, no, not even close, we were as puzzled as ever about what kept them going, about what their motivation really was. They seemed to be systematically trying to unpick established history and religious dogma. We were tipped off in 1995 by the work of a journalist called Serge Monast that they may be part of something called Project Bluebeam, which was, in essence a NASA mind control experiment using new technology that supposedly had the aims of destabilising all religions by planting seeds in the mind to prove what had been taught over the centuries was false. Its long term aim was to re-establish a new world religion and a new world order with the UK and USA at its head. This project, known in the UK as Project Meurig, was mega top secret."

Rachel's face was a picture of disbelief; "Sounds very X files, the baddies rule the world and all that. So, based on very little you had Morgan and Pender murdered."

Evans shook his head; "That's just it Rachel, we didn't. Our investigatons showed that Morgan and Pender had just stumbled on things that were extremely sensitive, like finding the cross partly made of the metal that was required to make machines for the Bluebeam project and the whereabouts of the body of Jesus which made certain that the Church police took an interest in what was going on. It is a right old mess. I shouldn't be telling you all this but you might as well also know that it is more than likely that the Prime Minister ordered all actions; was he working alone? Doubtful, with the church and the USA, more than likely."

Rachel looked puzzled; "So what about this Bruce Botha who looks like he killed Helen Daniels, Nicole and Roger?"

Evans gaze was steady; "An assassin and a good one.Probably hired by the church. Grey at MI5 spread the gossip that Helen, Nicole and Roger were seeking to sell the cross to a non Christian organistaion and the church probably took the bait and had them killed as rivals.It solved Greys problem of having double agents to get rid of.However it didn't flush out Grey who some believed was trying to do the same thing with the Russians."

Rachel's head was spinning like a top but Evans hadn't finished; "Roger Felix was shot at the café with a high power rifle. Robin Bryant only had an MI5 issue gun when we found him and we think he was trying to stop Botha and protect Roger Felix.However, Robin was shot at point blank range with a CIA pistol which had to belong to Brad Obrien who was working with him. This means that either he is a rogue agent or the CIA are working in cahoots with the church. Obrien has disappeared and the CIA swears blind they are on our side."

I think that Robin tumbled what was going on and they didn't like that."

Rachel looked puzzled; "But, he must have told his boss at MI5 what he had discovered."

Evans thought the point was well made, he did wonder in his own mind exactly how bent Grey was, especially after Greenaways fatal disclosure under the truth drug.

Rachel thought she had almost grasped it; "So, let me get this right, the church want control of the St Peter's cross, the body of Jesus and any other evidence in order to make them "disappear" and protect their version of Christianity whilst the Common Purpose lot, with possibly the PM and his American counterpart want the same evidence just to eradicate it so that it does not get in the way of a one world non religion global community ruled by an elite and to use the special comet metal for priceless experiments.

"Nice try Rachel but these sacred sites sit in areas where the mind control experiments are undertaken. Underneath there is masses of coal which can only be effectively mined by open cast methods. They want to mine the coal and quartz seam to search for the specs of gold and the special metal left exclusively and in tiny quantities by the comet debris which hit Wales in the 6th century. This metal, is known as a derivative of Platinum 190 and has not been found anywhere else in the world. Its value is beyond conception. The attraction with the cross found at St Peters is that Roger Felix discovered that it contained a huge concentrated quantity of this unique material in one place. Even a tiny amount of the metal has been shown to facilitate the production of a beam formed by a combination of ultrasound waves which causes targeted groups of people to hear sounds inside their head. Such a perception could easily provoke mental illness, or seem as if a God like figure is giving instructions. A large mass of the metal might be able to produce strong enough wave beams to affect a whole area, maybe a whole country.

Rachel was curious; "But open cast coal mining in such a sensitive area of beauty and history; surely they cannot get away with that?"

Evans had the answer; "Exactly so, but if the history of the areas are debunked then that side of the protection has gone. Add to that the cover story of wanting to use the coal for the production of a new hydrogen fuel that would be a green alternative and suddenly you have a great reason for the research establishments, the mining and the machinery to be there."

Rachel was on board; "And no reason for the planning department who represent the people to object?"

Evans went deeper; "Back in 1999 the Russians found out that something was going on and in an attempt to head off the reality the European Parliament passed a resolution calling for an international convention introducing a global ban on all developments and deployments of weapons which might enable any form of manipulation of human beings. As a result an addendum to article 6 of the Russian Federation law On Weapons was passed in July, 2001 prohibiting weapons and other objects which are based on the use of electromagnetic, light, thermal, infra-sonic or ultra-sonic radiations. Having done this there was an uneasy truce but clearly no-one really stopped experimenting."

Rachel looked like a rabbit transfixed by car headlights, it was an impression she had perfected over the last few days.

"So they aim to replace the words of God with their own words, in effect they become God."

Evans thought that was a great way of putting it but she hadn't finished. She was recalling Morgan and Penders translation of some of Taliesins words from the ancient Welsh.

"In the year of Eli Ner 530 after the arrival of the dragons from space and after the pestilence had passed I took a fragment of the sacred sphere of that heavenly metal sent from God and fashioned a special cross which would change the minds and souls of men forever and make Arthur a once and future king."

Evans seemed impressed venturing a hypothesis of his own; "What if the metal from the sphere or the comet acts as a kind of receiver as well as a transmitter? Maybe in some way it could be used to tune into the accumulated wisdom of the universe?"

The idea resonated with Rachel; "A universal harmony, the genetic code, the combined energy thought fields of all those in the universe that have lived and died."

Even Evans was getting excited; "So anyone that could understand how to use the metal or the St Peter's cross could in effect tap into that wisdom and knowledge for good or for bad."

Rachel nodded, "So, Merlin or Arthur, if indeed they ever had contact with the metal may well have the aura of wisdom and knowledge. No wonder everyone and their dog wants that cross."

Suddenly Evans made a calming gesture; "I think we might be getting carried away here Rachel, its all speculation and a bit science fiction isn't it?"

Rachel sighed; "Is it?"

There was one thing that Evans was in no doubt about;

"If somehow Everson really had kept the original cross from the St Peters dig and in some way had fobbed off Morgan and Pender with a copy, we have to find it, and quickly. Can you think of anything at all he said to you that might help?"

Rachel was trying to think back to the meeting with Everson; "I do recall one thing; he said that the real cross had to be put back where it belonged."

"You mean he might have reburied it in the church at St Peters where it was found in 1990."

"No, no, not at the church, he said were it belonged, not where it was found I think it could be two different places. I think it belongs with the body of Arthur or Jesus, or, more likely, a strategic place where the metal from it was originally."

Evans though for a while; "Great, but where on earth are we talking about? What do Morgan and Pender have to say about the burial places?"

"Originally they thought Arthur might be buried in St Peter's church but then they had second thoughts, oh, what did they say now? I know, they said that in many of the ancient histories Arthur's Grave is said to be at Caer Caradoc, the castle of Caradoc, so that it is important to correctly locate Caer Caradoc which they place in South East Wales. They said that there was a topographical description of how to get to the place in the Perlesvaux Tales and in the Songs of the Graves".

Evans mobile phone rang and he jumped, it was a text from Natasha; "Evans, picked up Eversons beacon, he's at Llandaff Cathedral, you owe me one."

He explained the text to Rachel; "Natasha?! I thought you said she wasn't working for MI5 as well!"

He shook his head; "No, certainly not, she's a cut above anything they have."

"Meaning?"

"Sorry, classified!"

Evans made a call and grabbed Rachel's arm; "Let's go and rescue Everson before it's too late."

-66-

Llandaff Cathedral, Cardiff
3rd August 2009

Evans pulled his car into the Llandaff Cathedral car park. Unusually, the building itself was down a slope near to the river. Three cars along he spotted two men, Grey's reinforcements, one of whom waved as he arrived. He left Rachel in the car and went to chat to them.

After a few minutes he returned and told Rachel to stay put. She rebelled but Evans was having none of it;

"This could get very nasty; you have been through enough already."

She sat on her hands as the three men walked down the tarmac slope to the wooden cathedral door.

Evans looked for an alternative way in. Round the side near to the old well there was a simple single door He pushed quietly and it opened easily. The three of them pulled their hand guns and gingerly made their way into the main church area, it was empty. Evans looked back to see the huge window depicting the descent from Jesse in the Old Testament. The colourful tree of life was vibrant and stunning. As they moved carefully through the church Evans noticed the stained glass windows of King Arthur and his grandfather Tewdrig amongst many others. Clearly those that had built the cathedral had known much about the history of the region from the time that the original land and building was granted to the church by Arthur's father Meurig.

Evans kept close to one side of the church where he soon came across a dark alcove with a spooky partial skeleton carved in stone, the classic symbol of resurrection. It was the tomb of Dyfrig, the person who crowned Arthur king at Caerleon centuries ago. In the same alcove, visible only from the floor looking up, there was a shield with a cross upon it, a ladder, some tools and a poppy. It was much the same, but a more sophisticated image than Natasha and William had found on the memorial stone at Carn Ingli. This array of tools around the cross was known to those enlightened ones as an indication that the buried person was of the line of Joseph of Arimathea and that Jesus had been rescued alive by him from the crucifixion cross.

Suddenly one of the two men that had been sent to help Evans passed wind which echoed around the Cathedral; Evans rolled his eyes and hoped they wouldn't be noticed.

They found themselves in front of a corridor that led away from the main church. They walked slowly along it as Everson had done earlier.

They jumped as they passed the gargoyle figures on the left. Soon they found the door to the crypt; a light was visible through the keyhole. Evans nudged the door and it gave way with a squeak. Slowly the three men made their way down the winding spiral staircase and along a dank damp corridor. The electric lights hung dangerously from wires and water oozed from some parts of the walls and onto the floor. Suddenly they heard voices in the distance. Evans pushed a side door which opened with a slight groan. They seemed to be creeping along the passageway for ages but the voices were getting louder.

Evans was trying to weigh up how many people where in the room and their relative positions. He heard an older man with a broken Italian accent and Everson's voice, frail and weak. The man with the Italian accent was talking to others, there were at least three of them and Everson, but were they armed?

Evans nodded and in one sweep they launched themselves into the room, Evans and one of the men dived low and to the right and the other low and to the left. There was an immediate exchange of gunfire and Evans threw himself behind a stone sarcophagus as the semi automatic weapon that was aimed at him sprayed a round of bullets raising dust and fragments of marble into the air. Evans cursed as his foot caught awkwardly in a space between two rough floor stones. The co-operative that had followed him stayed low but the other one who had gone to the left was hit by a hail of lead, dying instantly. Everson could just see into the room through a crack in a plinth, his foot and ankle throbbing with pain. In the lull he saw Everson through a settling layer of debris. He was tied to the chair, blood coming from his eyes, nose and mouth. In front of him Cardinal Valetti stood hunched and sneering. To the side were four guards with semi automatic pistols trained in his direction.

Valetti knew instantly who had barged in unannounced, the recognition was mutual;

"How nice of you to drop in to our little trap Evans."

Evans realised they were outgunned and outplayed. He kicked himself for being so stupidly impulsive in his aging years. He was desperately computing the chances of survival. It didn't look good. How could he have miscounted the number of people in the room? How did Valetti know he was coming? What did he mean welcome to his little trap? Natasha?! No surely she wouldn't have dropped him in it.

Evans tried to tough it out; "There's more coming Valetti, the game is up. All I want is the St Peter's cross, tell me where it is and we can all walk away from this."

Valetti laughed; "Seems we all want to know the same thing but Father Everson is being a little obstinate."

Everson rallied a little from his abuse; "You will all know by now that the St Peter's cross is a very special thing in its own right, not something to be fought over or toyed with. Merlin made it from the crucifixion nails, gold, silver and the sacred sphere fragment gleaned from the crater of the comet shower that destroyed so many people in the early 6th century. It was a symbol and reminder not only to remember the soul of Arthur but to encapsulate and embrace with the energies of the Jesus and the Arthurian bloodline. Within the mix of metals is a most precious crystal which, thanks to the magic of Merlin, holds the vibration of their souls and in some circumstances acts as a direct connection to creation itself."

From behind a gap in the sarcophagus Evans recognized the success he and Rachel had in deducing some of what was going on. He could see Everson's sad old face, frail and white in pain but never giving in. It reminded him of the determination of Jacques de Molay the head of the Templars as he was being burnt alive in the square of Notre Dame in Paris. Evans was not surprised at all to see the figure of Brad Obrien in the group.

Valetti was persistent; "You must tell us where the St Peter's cross is father, there has been too much bloodshed over it already."

Everson could just see through watering eyes; "Why, why must I tell you where the cross is, what do you care about bloodshed?"

Valetti jumped in front of the monk and slapped him again hard across the face, Evans winced, helpless. Everson's head judded back from the blow.

"Because my dear father you will die if you don't."

Everson seemed to have the mental strength of 10 men; "I will die if I tell you and I will die if I don't. We sit here in the shadow of the tomb of Joseph of Arimathea a most holy man, so your lies are as transparent as those of whom you serve. You will kill me as surely as the church has murdered the true words of wisdom from wise men over thousands of years. When you kill me you kill part of the lineage that has been passed down, I am a descendent of Jesus, is this how you would treat him? Of course it is!"

Valetti laughed nervously; "Then you must ask God to come and help you, or is he going to desert you like he deserted Jesus at his crucifixion."

Everson managed to laugh loudly, it unnerved those present; "You don't have the faintest idea Valetti, do you?"

Valetti's phone rang shattering the suspense, his men kept their guns trained on their targets.

He listened intently to the information, "Thank you Natasha, you have played your part well."

He switched off his phone with an arrogant flip. His smile spread from ear to ear as he turned to Everson.

"Seems as if our Russian friend has worked out where the St Peter's cross is, so, we won't be needing your help any longer."

Evans grimaced, Natasha, he knew she was special, was she really working for the church? Had she tipped him off about Everson's kidnap to lead him to Valetti and into the trap?

He looked around trying to plan a way out. His colleague slipped him a yellow canister, good old SAS issue, colloquially called a 'big burger' because it combined smoke, cs gas and a stun grenade. It was only small but in the confined space, the result might be devastating enough to buy them some time. He had to take the risk.

Evans pulled and pulled at his foot, it was stuck fast. This was last chance saloon.

Tugging the cord with a sudden movement he rolled the device along the floor. It detonated almost immediately to one side of Valetti but almost in front of Everson. There were heavy footfalls accompanied by frenzied shots ringing out in all directions. Valetti and his men minus one who had been killed in the exchange of fire headed up some stairs at the far end of the chamber and out of an emergency hidden passageway that led to the nearby ruins of St Mary's church which once stood on an island. Now it is hidden in an overgrown copse not far from the cathedral walls. It was the ancient burial place of Joseph of Arimathea, so often confused with Glastonbury in Somerset. The ancient records specifically advise that Edward the first, second and third knew of the site and that it was holy and venerated, now it lays unknown and unkempt.

Valetti, shaken by the impact of the blast staggered out behind his coughing heavies, he just managed to shout;

"See you in hell Evans..."

The heavy door slammed shut which added to the ringing in his ears. Evans eyes were running, and his head pulsating. He recovered slowly from the cs gas, adjusting his vision to the dimly lit space. It was an ancient reservoir chamber and judging from the green slime above his head he was below water level. Christ, there was no apparent way out and his foot was stuck solid. In what seemed like moments he heard a trickle of water that turned to a gush. Water from the nearby steam was seeping in as it did at every high tide, soon, very soon, they would be in a watery grave. As usual Valetti had timed things to perfection.

Evans shouted to Everson; "Are you ok father?"

There was no response.

Evans felt such a fraud, he cursed his impetuous stupidity, after all he should have been rescuing Everson not putting his life at risk. This incompetence would never have occurred in his youth.

He lit his small flashlight. The stench of the CS smoke was still in his eyes and on his chest. His colleague was coughing blood as he fell forward beside him. He had been fatally injured in a blind exchange that followed the blast.

In the melee he heard a small female voice from the top of the stairwell…

"Evans, Evans are you in there, are you ok?"

Evans responded; "Rachel, thank God, I'm trapped and father Everson is bound up, the others have gone."

As soon as she heard Evans voice she pushed the door open further and rushed into the room, much as Evans and his men had done a while back, this time without the fatal consequences. In the faint sporadic blinking lighting she saw Father Everson tied to the chair, his head slumped on to his chest. The water level rose quickly up his legs.

She hurried to him, stumbling, wading water as she went.

"Father, father, are you ok? What have they done to you?"

She reached him and took a tissue from her pocket trying to clean his blood stained face. She was only too aware of the water spiraling up around her feet and legs.

Slowly Everson opened his eyes and managed a smile;

"Ah, Rachel my love, is this heaven?"

Rachel hugged him so hard it hurt; "Rachel, my lamb, there is something I must tell you. I knew as soon as I saw the mark on William's heel the other day, he, he is my son. My real name is Marshall and I am of the bloodline of the Holy family, now, I totally recall… The cross, tell William, the cross on the wall."

Rachel stepped back, she thought that Everson must be delirious but he was insistent; "Rachel, please, if I don't make it please tell him that I always loved him, they, they said he and his sister had died in the car accident…I don't know how he is still alive, it's a miracle…I have told Natasha, I have told Natasha…. the cross, the cross on the wall."

The monks head sunk to his chest. The information wasn't really sinking in. Rachel made short work of untying the ropes that held the monk tightly and he instinctively rubbed his hands together to try to get the feeling back. He tried to get up and collapsed as the water reached Rachel's knees.

"It's ok, father, just relax I'll get you out of here and to a hospital, you're going to be ok." She was talking to herself.

Rachel placed his limp arm around her shoulder and dragged him slowly through the water to the safety of the stone staircase where she left him whilst she waded across to help Evans. The water was almost up to her hips. On his side with his foot trapped Evans was trying urgently to keep his mouth and nose above water so that he could breath.

He was failing, swallowing large gulps of quickly rising water. His speech was staccato and spluttering; "Rachel, my foot, my foot is stuck fast I can't feel it."

Rachel pulled and pulled splashing and falling with no luck whatsoever.

Inspired, she held her breath and dived down. Suddenly she came face to face with one of Evans dead colleagues, his eyes open and staring, blood still ouzing into the water from his mouth. She tried to scream but just gulped water. Trying to focus she felt Evans leg and followed it down to his trapped foot. With difficulty she managed to undo the tight boot strap of his trapped footwear. As she flayed about like a fish in shallow water her lungs felt close to bursting. Evans head was now right under and he was fading fast. In a last ditch attempt she wiggled and wiggled his foot, loosening the stiff leather bit by bit. Now with his head underwater and his eyes closed with bubbles racing from his mouth and nose, Evans was in the last thropes of drowning. For him time had stopped, he was floating away. All was quiet and serene. If this was death then a large part of him welcomed it.

Rachel changed position, came up for a second gulp of air, then maneuvered herself behind him lodging her arms under his solid form. She pulled and pulled levering herself against the cold damp wall. Suddenly, like the climax of a birth Evans socked foot slid out of the boot and he was free, his head above water.

Instinctively he breathed in air feeling a searing pain across his chest as he vomited water. Exhausted, she waded with him, gasping for air, through the flooding chamber and across to the steps and safety. He coughed and spluttered looking blue and white in the half light.

For a few moments they sat on the stones just looking at each other wondering if they really were alive, Everson's chest was very slowly rising and falling. This time, they had escaped.

-67-

Nevern, Wales
3rd August 2009

The place behind his ear certainly stung but Natasha had been as gentle as a surgeon with the scalpel could be.

Fully aware that they were being listened to Natasha looked straight at William; "We have to get back to help Evans and Rachel, like you I am sure that the St Peter's cross and the body of JC are at or near St Peter's church... I found a further Latin text amongst the things we found on Michael's hard drive which seemed to confirm this."

William was looking but Natasha was not showing him any text she was just putting her finger to her mouth and swaying her head as if to say, "Play along."

William caught on quickly; "Ummm, what does it say exactly?"

Natasha recited a few words from memory; "Let's see, something along the lines of William the Marshall, Robert de Spencer and Joseph Berkerolls located the burial by virtue of the sacred texts held at the castle of the chalice and with due reverence exhumed the body of the Christ and buried him with glory in a chamber next to the grave of the king Arthur son of Meurig at the church built by St Peter in the city of Caradoc."

William let the words sink in for a moment; "Well, that's it, that's what we thought....hadn't we better hurry?"

Natasha was caught up in the drama; "Yes, yes of course but how is your headache? Do you want to rest a while first?"

Natasha was nodding furiously giving him a clue to the answer.

"Now you mention it I could do with a bit of a rest."

Natasha started the car and nursed it back to the inn where they left the bug under the pillow and quietly sneaked out. Natasha thought William's attempted falling off to sleep snore might be a little over the top but didn't say anything.

A little way down the road Natasha stopped and turned around...

William looked at her quizzically; "It's ok William, we are not going back to

St Peters. If I am right neither JC or the cross are there. I think there has been a double bluff to hide the real location. They are nearer than you think."

In no time at all they were walking beside the little rippling stream along an avenue of ancient yew trees and into the church of St Brynach.

"Exactly what is it we are looking for Nats?"

She looked at him bringing her finger to her lips to indicate silence. Pulling his head to her she whispered; "Window sills"

William was no wiser.

Natasha had soon made her way down the aisle and to the right. When William caught up with her he could see what she was looking at. Two stones had been used as sills one had an inscription in Latin and the other a shape, rather like a stylised fish. Natasha was running her fingers along the edge of one of the stones;

"Look Will, it's made to look like Ogham, but I think it's a code."

William had heard the name but had no idea what it meant. "Not another code?"

Natasha waved William away; "Do something useful and go and keep a lookout."

By the time William had made it outside into the sunshine Natasha had already set up her laptop and was hard at work.

Near to the entrance was an impressive and ornate thirteen foot Celtic style cross set up for Higuel Rex also known as Hwell Dda who died AD 948.

He was attracted to it like a moth to a flame. He must have been staring at the intricate designs for some time when he was suddenly aware of a familiar scent by his side. He couldn't look up or around, all he saw was her pretty naked feet, the bottom part of a white robe and the ends of long golden red hair tossing gently in the breeze.

He wanted to move, to look, to reach out, to stare, but he couldn't.

He felt a small but warm hand in his; "Don't despair, William, you are between worlds, one foot either side of the veil."

He should have felt afraid but instead an overwhelming peace descended as he found the courage to speak; "Who are you?"

She spoke almost as if her voice was the breeze itself; "You know who I am dearest. I have many names, as have you....I am Isis, Brigit, Guinevere, and Demeter.... but your spirit knows me as Maria Magdalena, your soul my loved one has slipped out of time."

William felt happy and secure just standing holding hands; somehow he knew if he looked up she would disappear; "Are you real Maria?"

There was a little laugh; "I am as real as you want me to be, as is everything we see, hear and touch. Do you remember saying once; when you were Jesus, whatsoever your heart desires, believe it and so will it be?

It rang a far and distant bell somewhere in Williams mind.

"Jesus? I was Jesus? How could that be? But you, you were the nun at Canterbury, Sister Herbert at the hospital, the woman in white at St Govans and the ghost in the church on Caldey island."

Maria put her other arm around his soul; "and the swan and many many more, I am the female of creation just as you are the male. We are all made of matter some of which dies and is reborn, some which never dies; we are in everything and everywhere at every time, the matrix of matter and creation, worlds with no end."

William went to return the hug and was surprised that he felt solid warm flesh and blood; she seemed to snuggle closer; "I have missed you. I have had your child dear one; he is being cared for by the monks on Caldey."

William was stunned; "We have a son, but, how?"

The woman chuckled; "The same way that babies are always made. Do you recall way back in time, we met by a stream, and made passionate love under the sparkling sun, the disciples used to get angry when you kissed me on the lips?"

William was struggling with his memory; "How fair you were, I loved you well……But, but that was just a dream of two thousand years ago… wasn't it?"

She smiled; "Was it? When nothing is permanent and we are all particles of nothing vibrating into something for indeterminate periods of time, how do we know what reality is, if it exists at all?"

He was stunned. As he looked up he saw the most beautiful pale white face surrounded by thick long red hair dancing in the breeze. He felt her hand let go and heard a noise behind him. It was Natasha;

"You must stop talking to yourself, Will. Just had a text from Rachel, they have rescued Everson but he is in a bad way and Evans is also hurt, she said Everson wants to tell you, the cross on the wall and he is proud you are his son."

William thought; "The cross on the wall? His son? Is that all he said?" William pinched himself to make sure this was really happening. "Am I going mad Nats?"

Natasha nodded; "Probably, you certainly behave like it sometimes… oh, by the way, I think I've cracked it."

William looked around everywhere but Maria was nowhere to be seen. "Remember the co-ordinates we used to find what might be the original grave of JC?"

Re-focusing William nodded.

"Well, if you extend the main line from the head, it stretches inland."

William was still looking around for Maria, to Natasha he looked distracted. She was a little annoyed.

"William, listen, this is important!"

He listened; "The Latin on top of one of the sills describes the stone as the memorial of Maglacunous dated 580ad.. Well, the Ogham doesn't appear to say that, it seems to be indicating distances. Three distances match exactly to the top bit of the cross and the last bit by extension indicates a place not far from here, in fact just up the hill and into the forest."

William wanted to backtrack a little and just remind them both of the gist of some of Morgan and Pender's research.

They sat together on the ancient little bridge over the steam next to the church and read some of the notes from Morgan and Pender's dialogue that Rachel had given them.

They believed that one of the best know stories of the early Christian Era in Wales was that of the Empress Helen and the true cross upon which Jesus Christ was meant to have been crucified. In Britain this story is virtually unknown.

Contrary to popular taught dogma the original Christianity arrived in the UK in AD 36 ("the last year of Tiberius") when it became the religion of many of the royal and noble families.

Christianity had spread from Britain to Rome, not the other way around, when Caradoc 1, son of Arch was forced to spend seven years there after being captured by the Romans in Wales. (AD 51-58)

The Caradoc events led to a series of royal alliances by marriage with the Roman Imperial families. As a result of these ongoing liaisons Princess Helen (daughter of King Coel) married Constantius Chlorus the Emperor of Rome.

The Empress Helen is said to have been born in AD 265 and to have lived to 71, dying in AD 336. She was the mother of Constantine the Great who became the ruler of the entire Roman world in AD 324. (He re-established Christianity in Rome allowing it to be practised as an official religion).

The story goes that the Empress Helen went on a pilgrimage to Sinai and Jerusalem with a large bodyguard of soldiers. She visited the site of the Exodus and the Red Sea. She supposedly had a vision in which she was told to light a fire and follow the smoke until it reached the earth. There she would find the True Crucifixion Cross. This event led her to Jerusalem where she demanded the city elders hand over to her the true cross upon which Jesus had been crucified. After an exchange of threats and excuses the cross and the crosses of the two men crucified with Jesus were produced. The correct cross presented itself when a woman who had been sick touched it and was healed.

She immediately had two of the nails in the wood made into a bridle bit for her son's horse and sent it on to him. She had the cross member of the wooden cross encased in silver, gold and jewels and placed in a silver casket which she took to the nearest port from which she sailed with her knights back to Britain.

The result is that the true crucifixion cross was said to have ended up in Britain in AD 325. This story and the resting place of the relic are clearly recorded in the Black Book of Carmarthen.

After bringing the cross back to Britain the Empress Helen is said to have spent her last ten years in Constantinople. The crux is, which Constantinople?

In Western Dyfed in mid Wales there is a strangely named collection of small villages and places. These include Nanhyfer, (the stream of the sanctuary), Gethsemane, Bethlehem, Dinas Cross (city of the cross) and Constantinople. Nanhyfer is now Nevern and running into the stream there is Afon Bannon (the River of the Empress).

Around this area of Wales there are roadways called Sarn Helen (the causeway of Helen) we know that Helen did not build these roadways. What is significant though is that in following these roads from East to West and North to South there is a route marked by cross names.

There are continuously, the Pass of the Cross, the Mountain of the Cross, the Valley of the Cross, the Ford of the Cross, the Vales of the Cross, the Fields of the Cross and so on. It appears that Helen paraded the crucifixion cross around the area on a grand tour before depositing it in a safe place.

In the Black Book of Carmanthen (written approx AD 920 – AD 1100) it states that the cross (at that time of writing) was still where Helen had placed it.

The place name is given as Lodiernum which appears to be a corruption of Lodes (lady or damsel) and Ermyn (Ermine or Ermine clad lady).

This adds significance to the cluster of names around Nevern and there can be no argument at all that the church at Nevern was the most celebrated in Wales before the building of St David's cathedral. The Bishop Cuhylyn (a brother of King Meurig, Arthur's dad) was at Nevern singing its praises two generations before St Brynach the re founder of the church.

Equally, at the church site there is the Vitaliani Emerito Stone which is most likely to be the memorial stone of Utherpendragon Gwythelyn whom as the Cattigern (Battle Sovereign) or Vortimer was killed in crushing the Saxons around AD 456.

Also at this place is the Maglocunos Stone (now used as a window sill which Natasha had just seen) He was undisputedly King Maelgwn Gwynedd who was elected king in the north of Wales in AD 580 after the death of Arthur in AD 579.

A thirteen foot cross was set up at Nevern by Higuel Rex aka Hwell Dda who died AD 948.

The importance of this place was underlined by the fact that the castle there was defended down to the slaughter of the last man. Only the ramparts now remain hidden in a wooded copse.

In 1284 Edward 1 of England held a massive tournament of knights at this seemingly insignificant place.

As Nanhyfer means the stream of the sanctuary it would be only logical that there was a sanctuary somewhere there. Indeed there is such a place, a double walled up cave along the old Pilgrims Route which was hidden until relatively recent times. Morgan and Pender found it.

According to them on the front of the cave is a carved cross acting as a kind of seal. The outer wall does not seem to have been disturbed since the cross was carved and it is likely therefore that whatever was noted as in there in the Black Book of Carmarthen is still there.

We also know from an old Anglo Saxon poem (The Dream of the Rood) that kneeling at this place praying often brought a vision of the cross.

The region was incredibly important to the Knights of the Temple.

There is nearby Temple Bar and Temple Gate. A safe harbour and landing place with easy access to the area.

Above the cave is a ruined castle. Could this be the lost Templar fort of Troed Yr Aur (Steps of Gold).

There are records of such a station re-inforced by Gilbert de Clare in 1156. A Templar presence here may well have guaranteed that the cave survived intact and then after the Templars dissolution in 1308 and the ravages of Wales by the English the cave most likely was simply overgrown and forgotten.

There is a rider to this story in that it is possible that some Templar treasure may have been brought to this place after leaving in ships from Paris following the persecution and slaughter of the Templars by the church in France.

The clincher, they believed was that until fairly modern times the OS maps of the region showed the ancient name of the fort as Castell Elainfawr (The Castle of the great Helen) and an ancient farmstead nearby is shown as Constantinople.

The choice of where to put the Crucifixion Cross would have been a matter for great consideration.

The answer almost certainly lays in the fact that the Khumry-Welsh nation migrated from Assyria around BC 740 – BC 690. They received Christianity in AD 36 or prior. The original Christianity was sometimes referred to as Cathars ("chanters") or "Gnostics" (knowledge).

As a daughter of Coel, Helen would have been a Cathar-Gnostic or original Christian.

This early original Christianity was much more aligned to the heavens and it is no coincidence that this area of Wales is littered with carns, dolmens and cromlechs laid out to mirror the major stars and constellations.As above, so below.

Cygnus, the great cross in the heavens is mirrored on the ground around Nevern and it's pretty safe to assume that the cave with the crucifixion cross is at its very centre.

Archbishop Usher lists no less than 25 sources for this story.

Melanchthon in his "Epistola" states, "Helen was unquestionably a British Princess."

The coins of the Empress Helen read "Flavia Helena Augusta" (Vatican and British Museums).

Giovani Batista de Conegliano painted his "Helena" in 1459 depicting Helen with the cross.

The Roman Matyrologies tell her story.

The Anglo Saxon Vercelli MS records the story and Welsh references to Helen are everywhere!

One thing continued to bug the Normans (and probably still does) and that was the almost suicidal way in which the British/Welsh continued to fight and reinforce Nanhyfer castle at Nevern. Thousands died and would not surrender. The quiet wooded area is all there is left now but this hides the fields of slaughter.

We know now that Nanhyfer means "River of the Sanctuary" other field names relate to treasure, god and religion. What was so special that people would gladly give their lives trying to defend it, was it the crucifixion cross that Helen brought back from Jerusalem covered in jewels, was it the Templar treasure or was it something else? Something like the body of Jesus Christ?"

-68-

Llandaff, Cardiff, Wales
3rd August 2009

The ambulance arrived quickly at Llandaff Cathedral and Everson was soon wrapped in silver foil and given oxygen. He was still unconscious as the vehicle left for the University Hospital.

One of the paramedics indicated that the monk's condition was serious, very serious. Evans didn't need to be a medical man to spot that but he was grateful to the ambulance crew for binding his sprained ankle. He had refused the offer of a trip to have it x rayed, he wanted to stay with Rachel and try to keep her safe. His movement was slow and restricted but at least he could move.

Rachel was shivering and cold, more with nerves than from her soaking clothes. Damp and drained the two bedraggled campaigners booked into a nearby hotel. They told the receptionist that Evans had fallen into the nearby river and that Rachel was his daughter who had dived in to save him. It was as near to the truth as they dared go.

The room was comfortable and following a small bribe the porter quickly arranged for their clothes to be dried.

Whilst they were waiting Rachel's beauty in a skimpy hotel dressing gown was obvious but Evans was agitated with other things on his mind. It wasn't often that he'd been seen crying but today was an exception.

Rachel went to sit next to him on the bed and put her arm around him. The gesture seemed to make it worse and he sobbed and sobbed.

Minutes passed before he could speak;

"I'm past it Rachel, I should never have led those men into that, that death chamber. It was so stupid and I didn't even get to Everson before he was so badly hurt."

Rachel was sympathetic; "You did what you thought was right Bryn, you did your best, no-one can work miracles…"

Evans was not to be consoled; "If we had gone straight to Nicoles instead of having a pizza she'd still be alive…if we had met somewhere other than the café at Caerleon Roger Felix would still be alive, if I had kept closer in contact with Helen Daniels she'd still be alive and if I had worked out what was going on with Morgan and Pender they would still be with us..."

Rachel knew what depression was, after all she had suffered enough during her life, but this was major. She held his face so that he had to look into her eyes much as he had done to her earlier;

"Bryn, come on Bryn you can't give up now, if you do it will all have been in vain, none of this is your fault, you are not the criminal here, you are a good man... you can sort this, you have to!"

She placed a kiss on his lips and he held her tightly as if he never wanted to let go.

At the hospital a South African with breath that smelt of cigars had all too easily sneaked into the hospital ward to which father Everson had been taken, changed into a male nurses uniform, walked brazenly into the ward and smothered the ageing monk behind closed curtains. His secret of where the body of Jesus and the St Peter's cross had been hidden died with him, only Valetti, Natasha and the church thought they knew now.

They seemed to have been curled up together napping for ages when a loud knock hit the door of the hotel room.

"Room service, your clothes are dry."

Rachel peered through the safety spy hole and saw the porter from earlier with the clothing folded neatly over his arm. She re-tied her dressing gown to preserve modesty, opened the door and took the clothes. The man nodded and smiled as she gave him £10.00.

Evans mobile buzzed impatiently, it was a text from Grey. "Everson has been murdered in hospital, where are you?"

Evans put his head in his hand. This had to be the end of the career trail for him. He had to retire before he made any more fatal mistakes.

Rachel looked at him and just knew what had happened.

-69-

Nevern, West Wales
3rd August 2009

Now in the church porch William and Natasha were still discussing possibilities. She balanced her laptop and a large scale map of the area loaned to them by the Inn keeper. Google maps didn't show the area in high enough resolution and what it did show was mostly covered by forest in the very area they wanted to see. The old fashioned map was more helpful and they could see that there was a minor road and then a footpath called 'The Pilgrims Way' that led them to a place along the line of the extended cross member drawn on the coded map they had been following. They picked up their bits and pieces and headed off.

There was something in the sun, blue sky and fluffy clouds that instilled an air of wellbeing. All around the church yard there were ancient Yew trees, a tell tale sign of the significance of the area to the ancient druids, shaman and elders long before Christianity was ever dreamt up.

They were just about to leave the hallowed ground by the main gate when William spotted something next to one of the trees. Moving towards it he could see what looked like blood dripping from a branch. For a moment he was transfixed by the shadow in the sun. There, swinging by the neck, he saw a girl, her neck slashed and bleeding.

"Christ Nats, look at this..."

William was quite pale, transfixed by the hypnotic movement of the branches in the wind. Natasha ran across as fast as she could, she saw how distressed William looked. She smiled, stuck her finger in the goo and put it to her nose and mouth. It's ok Will, it's only sap, there must be something in the earth here that colours it like blood.

"But, but, the body Nats..."

There was no body. William's mind was playing tricks again. There was silence as Natasha took Williams arm and led him up the path away from the church.

He wondered just how he could have been so stupid. They had been walking up hill for 15 minutes or so when they came to a right hand bend in the narrow lane, it had been quite a steep climb between the trees. The left hand fork had an old wooden sign almost hidden in the hedge, "The Pilgrims Way". The two explorers took the guided path. On the left there was a steep slope lined with bracken and other foliage which fell sharply down to a rushing river, on the right was a rocky formation overgrown with vegetation. The height varied from around 20 feet to 50 feet.

After a few moments Natasha consulted her GPS;

"If our deductions are correct the cave should be here on the right."

The stratified rock face was covered by thick undergrowth and creeping ivy. They started pulling at the foliage clearing their line of vision. The place did not seem to have been disturbed for some time. Slowly they revealed the natural rock and what looked like an ancient man made wall. The remaining undergrowth soon gave way to their manic pruning. They stood back looking at what they had revealed. William had no doubt that it was an old cave that had been bricked up.

On the front of the stone was a cross hewn into the surface mainly over the man made part but partly over the natural rock. Someone had turned the light on;

"Remember the message from Father Everson, the cross on the wall, this is it I just know it!"

Natasha had the same feeling. From her calculations using Michael's code, GPS and triangulation it was bang on target. Where the wall met the ground there was a plinth, he moved over to it and stepped up. As he reached he could just touch the base of the carved cross and felt a tingle wiz through him. Natasha came alongside him. He fell to the ground as if struck by lightning. Natasha was by his side instantly; "God Nats did you see that flash, did you see it?"

Natasha had seen and heard nothing. William looked pitifully at her, gaining her attention and sympathy;

"This is the place Nats, I just know it. I bet the real crucifixion cross is in this cave, maybe even the body of JC as well...do you think that Everson hid the original St Peter's cross here?"

Natasha looked pensive; "How could he? This wall hasn't been disturbed for centuries."

William nodded; "There must be another way in."

William was jiggling uncomfortably. The experience had affected him on many levels; "Must have a wee."

Natasha exhaled a long suffering sigh; "God you know how to pick your moments..." She waved him off; "Go on, I won't look."

For a child of the 60'S William was far too shy. He walked off into the undergrowth.

"Won't be long."

Natasha heard the bushes rattling, how far had he gone, men, honestly.

She stood looking at the rock face, off guard for vital seconds. Suddenly she felt a searing pain around her neck. Only the speed of her reaction stopped the wire from cutting deep into her flesh. In one movement she had two thumbs between her skin and the metal. Someone was behind her thrusting a knee into her back and pulling hard on the wire around her throat.

Why hadn't she heard her attacker creep up?

Instinctively her training kicked in. She moved suddenly backwards going with the energy rather than fight against it, the back of her head met the nose of her assailant with a crack and at the same time she stamped as hard as she could on the bridge of his foot. The man had instinctively loosened his grip buying Natasha the luxury of a delicate self defence manoeuver.

She rolled down to one side and around to face him, blood seeping from lacerations around her neck. Immediately she used the momentum to rise quickly and nut the man again on the bridge of the nose. She felt it crack again and his grip eased. In one movement she slid from under the killer wire. She had thought as much from the acrid smell of bad teeth and cigars, the stocky man in front of her with the bleeding nose was Bruce Botha. She sprang backwards to give herself time to think.

Slightly dazed he wiped his sleeve across his face taking a smear of blood with it. It wasn't the first time his nose had been broken in a fight.

His smile was spooky and sadistic.

"So nice to meet you Natasha. The last time we met you were just a little girl and I raped your mother, you just ran then, no doubt you will now."

Natasha's breathing was recovering. There were deep scratches on her neck oozing blood and deep lacerations on her thumbs, but the wounds were much more than physical, she knew one day this moment would come;

"Why didn't you just shoot me Botha?"

"My dear girl I want to fuck you first!"

That threw Natasha just a bit but her mind returned quickly when the man pulled a beefy looking knife from a sheath on his leg;

"How unprofessional, you make me sick Botha."

"I intend making you much more than that, you have been my fantasy for years."

"And you have been my nightmare."

The two circled each other like wild animals Botha thrusting his knife towards her and she deftly moving. It was like a deadly dance. She could see that he had a pistol in a holder around his waist. She knew he was just toying with her. Was he really hell bent on using her for his sexual pleasure or was he scared of something?

From whichever way she looked at it the picture wasn't exactly rosy. Where the hell was William?

No, it wasn't fair to involve him in this, it was far too personal. Now she hoped upon hope he wouldn't turn up, this was her problem, not his. One way or another it ended right here, right now.

-70-

Caer Caradoc, South Wales

The wind was keen on the mountain, even at this time of the year, it always was. They could still hear the constant rhythmic hum of the giant land based wind turbines that ran up to the highest point near to the grave mound of Caradoc.

Evans and Rachel made their way slowly over a rickety style, along the narrow single earth pathway and the 200 yards or so to the ruined church of St Peters. Evans was nursing his sore ankle but the movement wasn't too bad thanks to the tight binding and the pain killers. So much had been said about the place but the reality was a little disappointing. The outline of the church could be seen from the ruined crumbling walls that varied between four and five feet in height. Rachel felt some trepidation; the bullocks lose in the field mingling through the ruins made her feel uneasy. They wandered around the ecclesiastical skeleton. There was no sense of time and place for either of them. No loud bells, no flashing lights, just flint and stone. It felt as if the heart had been ripped out of the place eons ago. They both went and sat on the stone slab in what remained of the porch. Evans looked over Rachel's shoulder as she tapped in the co-ordinates to Google Earth on her laptop.

She located the church on screen easily enough. The mountain range was above Brynna and very near to Llanharan. Using the satellite feature she zoomed in to appreciate the topography.

The two of them huddled together to re evaluate Morgan and Pender's notes about the death and burial of Arthur.

Morgan and Pender believed that although few people know about it there is a preserved record of the earliest voyages. They think that there is clear evidence of the assassination of Arthur in the USA and that the body was embalmed, wrapped in deerskin and stored through the winter under a cliff overhang then taken to an embarkation point in Yarmouth Bay, Nova Scotia, USA.

They believed that by looking at the most ancient texts some of the stories of Arthur make sense. The notion of an aged, dead king sailing away across an unknown sea accompanied by three queens in a mysterious boat has firm roots.

Three ladies of the Court embalmed ("dry withered") the body of the king and wrapped it in leather deerskin.

Again in the Incantation of the Druids (Gwarchan Maelderw) there is much information about the happenings in America.

The texts clearly say that Arthur was struck down by a dark skinned man after removing his golden armour. Lines 85 – 102 tell how the Native Americans sought to raid the growing crops and fighting broke out. After the skirmish the troops returned to camp to rest. Arthur removed his golden armour and a dark skinned assassin is said to have crept around the thickets without causing alarm and with one well aimed thrust of his lance murdered Arthur then ran away.

It describes the embalming and says that it was directed that Arthur's body be brought back to St Illtyd in Glamorgan, Wales.

There was apparently a temporary burial in a cave and then the funeral close to the field of Drunken Helplessness, near to the fields of the Mayers and in the field of the highest ruler. They had found these fields and they all adjoin.

The Incantation tells of 300 gold wearing Mayors (rulers) gathering for Arthur's funeral (the field of the Mayers is therefore evocative).

At the time of his burial Arthur is said to have been wearing his suit of golden armour with a gold face mask and fine bracelets etc.

St Peter's church is in a field/area known as Llanbad Fawr (meaning Great Ships Boat) again evoking part of the story. There is a giant boat shape ellipse to the East of the church where Arthur's father Meurig is said to be buried. It is more than likely that this area was once the shrine of a water deity and the creator god, Yahweh. Over the years the ancient boat shaped burials which echoed the coming of Christianity with Jesus and his family in a boat became incorporated into the building of a church in what we now know as the Nave, an Italian word for ship.

Morgan and Pender excavated this church and discovered that buildings on the site date back to the 1st Cent AD. They also found the Arthurian St Peter's cross, a plate with a M or W on it, a dagger and an axe which was used to engrave coelbran writing.

However due to lack of funds and the fact that a tremendous gale blew the team off the mountain the dig was prematurely ended; but, it is clear that there is still work to be done there and the evidence points to something very interesting yet to be unearthed.

Apparently two main texts surviving from around AD 670- AD 822 tell of Arthur's body being brought back to Britain.

The texts are, The Life of St Illtyd (a cousin of Arthur) and Nennius's "Historia Britonrum" they have the same story:

"There is another wonderful thing in Guyr (now Ogwyr); an altar is in the

place called Loyngarth (Llwyngarth) which is held up by the will of God. The story of that altar, it seems better to me to tell than be silent. It happened when St Illtyd was praying in a cave which is by the sea which washes the land above the said place; the mouth of the cave is towards the sea-that behold a ship sailed towards the saint form the sea, and two men sailing in it. And the body of a holy man was with them in the ship and an altar above his face was held up by the will of god. And the man of god (St Illtyd) went forth to meet them and the body of the holy man and the altar was continuing inseparably above the face of the holy body. And they said to St Illtyd "This man of god entrusted it to us that we should conduct him to thee, and that we should bury him with thee and that thou should not reveal his name to any man, so that men shall not swear by him... and they buried him and after the burial the two men returned to the ship and set sail... but that St Illtyd founded a church about the body of the holy man and about the altar and the altar held up by the will of god remains to this day."

The place referred to as Loyngarth is Llyfngarth or Llwyngarth and it means smooth ridges or sand dunes. The description matches the area around the Ewenny River estuary.

Other episodes in the ancient texts give the location of St Illtyd's cave in the Coed y Mwstyr woods (the woods of mystery) above the Ewenney River in Ogwyr, Wales.

The location of this cave was found by Morgan and Pender from these and other stories in 1990. One story from the Life of St Gildas tells how Gildas cast a bell for St David who was at Menevia and the monks from Llancarfan Abbey who were carrying the bell along the old road were heard by Illtyd in his cave who came out to speak with them.

Another story records St Illtyd fleeing from attackers and making it back to his cave.

These accounts match those in the authentic Gwarchan Maelderw (Incantation of the Druids) The Courtesy of Taliesin and the epic poem Preiddeu Annwn (The Migration to the Other World).

In the cave they found a large grave pit cut into the hard rock in an east west direction, around 9 feet long, three feet wide and 4 feet deep. It was empty. Above the top of the grave there was a cross. There was also an inscription that read in coelbran. "This is the place of the Bier (or crib) where the dry withered (the embalmed) Highest Ruler who was impotent was placed."

Clearly this was the place mentioned in the old records. The records also stated that the body was buried at this place temporarily and then reburied nearby.

The big question is whether this history refers to Arthur or to a possible relocation of the body of Jesus.

This cave was sealed until modern times. A Cardiff man into fossils and prehistory started making visits in 1887 and with the aid of a friend partly opened this up until his health failed.

Mr Leyshon, in his 90's in 1990 said that some local people were aware of its importance. When Morgan and Pender visited the site they cleared the entrance enough to enter, and some 15 yards or so in the opening widened out to reveal the grave pit. Clearly the rectangular shape had been hewn out of the rock by hand as was evidenced by the right angles.

Although Morgan and Pender erected a metal gate and tried to preserve the cave for future enquiry it was vandalised. When Helen Daniels and the BBC went to try to film there the entrance had been dynamited and there is now no way in.

Near to this place, by way of further confirmation is a church dedicated to St Illtyd. Also there is a gravestone there of St Pawl, a brother of Arthur.

Following these and other notes she had taken from Morgan and Pender's guide she carefully examined the area. The obvious landmark was the ruins of St Peters church in which they now sat. It was clearly built on the summit of a raised earthwork which they thought may have been a learning establishment founded by Ambrosius Aurelianus, whose name in Welsh is *Emrys Wledig*. There was a rock jutting out and towering over the churchyard area towards Gilfach Goch. Typically such rocks had been used in very ancient times as oratories. On the satellite image Evans pointed out the feint marks along the ground which may illustrate long large walls that ran beside the ancient rocky track way over the mountain.

To the East was a boat shaped burial mound and a smaller but similar area to the North West. In the first century AD it was the fashion to build burial mounds in the shape of a boat as homage to the fact that JC and his family came in such a vessel to bring Christianity to the UK in AD35, maybe even earlier. Morgan and Pender's notes indicated that Arthur's father Meurig was buried in the giant boat shaped burial area; they called it the Giant Circle. Interestingly the name of the field in which the feature sits is still called Llan Bad Fawr or "The Church of the great boat."

To some this might seem strange as Meurig almost certainly helped to fund the building of the original Llandaff Cathedral in nearby Cardiff and so, logically, he ought to be buried there. However, as evidence now proves the whole area was devastated by the impact of a meteorite shower so that burial in the cathedral would have been impossible at the time of his death.

Not far from the church and to the North East the track intersects a Pass leading into a hollow. The names on the old sketch maps amongst Morgan and Pender's notes were provocative. The Pass is still called the Pass of the Soldier. It leads to a virtual dead end and a hollow which is the home to the source of the Nant Ilid, meaning, the River of Joseph of Arimathea. Above the hollow to the north are the signs of the ancient remains of beehive hermitages. To the East, according to Morgan and Pender sits the great lost city of Caradoc, another beehive hermitage and what could be a small funerary chapel. To the west are the remains of standing stones know to this day as the Grave Monument of the Soldiers. Was this where Joseph of Arimathea made his first home in Britain? Historically it fits; the area is near to the village of Llanillid, which actually means the holy estate of Joseph of Arimathea. If this area really was the site of the mystical lost fabled city of Caer Caradoc aka the Castle fortress of Caradoc then it would be logical for Joseph to be there. The reason is simple, King Caradoc, known to the Romans as Caractacus, is said to be buried at the highest part of the mountain. It is a well know historical fact that he actually took the original Christianity to Rome and that he or his true Christian successors would have welcomed Joseph with open arms.

Rachel shuffled her notes a little and Evans picked out details of the Perlesvaux manuscript; "Morgan was convinced that these stories of French knights coming to pay their respects at Arthur's grave acted as a topographical map."

Rachel nodded as she looked at the text Evans was pushing under her nose.

The description mentioned a landing place marked by two distinct landscape features, the first being a castle ruin and the second, Hen Eglwys, meaning, Old church, the burial place of Ceri ap Caid who died in AD80. Morgan believed that there was only one possible place that fitted the description, a natural harbor at Nash Point. Evans carefully read out the route that the knights took. Rachel was following as best she could on the satellite map. The ancient way did indeed lead up from the landing point, between the castle and the burial place, along a track to a ruined monastery, where knights and other travellers often stayed for a while on their pilgrimage to Arthur's grave. It then wound along the ridge of Llantrisant Forest, above Llanharan, through a small forded stream that comes down from the mountain of Mynydd y Gaer and on to the ancient highway to Caer Caradoc itself! The tale mentions three beehive hermitages, two of which were in a field called, The Field of the Highest Ruler. One of the hermitages had once supposedly belonged to Joseph of Arimathea. They tell of visiting Arthur's "hidden" grave then giving thanks and prayers at the funerary chapel beside it.

"Woo, just a minute, it doesn't say that Arthur was buried at St Peter's church though does it."

Rachel agreed. She zoomed in on the satellite image, manipulating it from different angles. It was clear where most of the walls of the old city had stood, it must have been quite a sight.

"Look at this."

Evans strained his eyes as Rachel ran her mouse pointer around an unusual area near the source of the Nant Ilid. The river of Joseph of Arimathea actually led down to a village called Llanllid, meaning the 'Holy estate of Joseph of Arimathea'.

"The Welsh tale Culhwch and Olwen tells of Arthur's search for the Cauldron of Di-wrnach, and in another Welsh story, the Spoils of Annwn, Arthur recovers the cauldron from the mystical isle of Annwn. In each case the cauldron which is said to carry the treasures of Britain is said to be hidden in Caradocs cave in middle earth. Both tales appear to have been composed before the first Arthurian Romance, perhaps as early as 900AD. The themes of Avalon and the quest for the Holy Grail were probably based on these early legends and firmly rooted in this part of Wales, not Glastonbury in Somerset."

"Can you recall what Morgan and Pender said about the description of Arthur's resting place from the ancient texts "The Songs of the Graves"?

Rachel flipped through her notes. "They said that the burial of Arthur was one of the best recorded Dark Age events. They said it was mentioned in many ancient manuscripts, including, The Life of St Illtyd, the Marvels of Britain No 9 by the monk Nennius, in the Brut Tyssilio and many others."

Evans looked skeptical; "So why is there so much mystery and doubt about whether an Arthur even existed?"

Rachel thought for a moment; "Ummm, Morgan wasn't very complimentary about a guy called Rev Robert Williams who was employed by Skene to translate the ancient texts way back when. Morgan believes he could have deliberately mis translated the Songs of the Graves to hide Welsh connections in favour of the prevailing church movement."

Evans was tapping his feet; "Did they come up with the right wording then?"

Rachel nodded and turned the screen; "Go on you can read it you are Welsh aren't you?"

Evans tried his best;

> *"Bet y march, bet y guythur*
> *Bet y gugawn cletfrut*
> *A noeth bid bed y Arthur*
> *Bet elchuyth yn gulich glaw*
> *Maes Mavetauc y Danaw*
> *Dyliei Cynon yno cunaw...*

Let me see, bet I think means grave...some of it is unfamiliar, it must be a very ancient version of Welsh."

Rachel put him out of his misery; "Morgan and Pender say it means: The grave of the knight, the grave of the wrathful one (Arthur). The grave of the angry red sword, a bare/exposed place, so be it, the grave of Arthur. A grave extremely windy in a narrow wet place, the field of helpless error the reproach. The duty of the chiefs to bear him hither."

They say that the great thing about Wales is that the old field names were mostly not affected or changed by the Norman invasion. They say it is vital to find the right Caer Cardoc, apparently there are several contenders. They are convinced this is the right one because they have found reference to events at this place which name it as Caer Caradoc. For example, the grave mound of the great Carodoc is said to occupy highest point on the mountain and there is a burial mound in the right place called Twyn Caradoc. There is an ancient grave monument of the soldiers there, the ambassadors of Vortigen-Gwrtheyrn met Myrddyn Em-Rhys and his mother there and also there was a great massacre at a peace conference with the Saxons at this place. The old field names, such as Field of the Quarrel, Field of Beer tent and Field of drunkenness all point the way. In effect, the Marwnad Uthyrpendragon (Grave elegy of the Uthyr Pendragon) from the Songs of the Graves gives the actual name of a field in which Arthur was buried and the field still bears the same name!

Interestingly there are a couple of other field names that are pretty evocative as well. Por Tref, for example, means high or supreme place and another translates to, the field of the highest ruler.

The highest ruler being?

"Arr, thereby hangs a tale, could be Jesus or the highest ruler at the time, maybe Arthur?"

Rachel accessed a video clip from the several on the DVD of rushes for the proposed program. One showed a man using a large, rather unusual metal detector. It was about four feet square. The enthusiastic man was saying that he'd never seen anything like this in his life...she looked at the screen and the topography and thought she knew where it was.

She beckoned for Evans to follow her and this he did slowly and painfully, still cursing his carelessness in trapping his foot and ankle in the debacle in the cistern at Llandaff Cathedral.

They made their way slowly back out across the field and onto the ancient track way. Although this was clearly still a bridleway it had been unkempt for many years. The uneven stone and earth surface interspersed with deep puddles and crossed by springs and rivulets made the going tough.

Heading back towards the wind turbines they saw the sun glint on a surface of smaller rocks to the right up on a hill. Rachel pointed.

"I am sure that's the place where the guy was detecting."

The climb wasn't easy, especially for Evans nursing a sore appendage but it was not long before they sat next to a large shield shaped area of stones. Part of the side had been scrapped away by sheep to reveal what appeared to be a stone wall, perhaps even a walled up cave.

Rachel sighed; "Yes, this is definitely the place where that guy was using that odd metal detector."

In the distance Rachel heard the low drone of an engine making its way across the undulating approach to the mountain. The speck looked like an armoured vehicle of some description. It was followed by another from a different angle and yet another from behind. Closer inspection revealed soldiers. They were heading towards them and the church and there was nowhere to run.

As the vehicles moved closer men jumped off and seemed to deploy making a circle or cordon around the area. At this stage they looked like ants but soon they would be much bigger shapes to contend with.

The feeling of disappointment was mutual even if Evans and Rachel had found the sites there was no way they could excavate them or do anything about it now, they couldn't exactly shovel earth with their bare hands.Slowly they retreated down the hill, across the marshy source of the River Ilid and up on to a promontory where they hoped they could observe without being seen. Could it just be a co-incidence or had their movements somehow been tracked?

-71-

Nevern Cave, West Wales
3rd August 2009

William had slid and fallen through a crevice formed by the recent torrent of rain. He seemed to fall for ever until he landed with a thud on his back. He lay still on the damp earth for a few moments, winded, just aware of the light streaming through the hole through which he had tumbled. Slowly, very slowly, he was able to move, he stood up rubbing his elbows and his head, oh, his head, it felt so sore.

Near to the front of the cave Botha had resorted to grunting and thrusting his knife in Natasha's direction with movements indicating a sexual perversion;

"What's happened to you Botha, I thought you were a pro?"

Botha seemed genuinely moved in some little way;

"We are both the same Natasha, we are both assassins and dam good ones."

Natasha sensed the smallest chink; "Then why does it have to be like this? I'd have thought working for the church would have taught you some morals."

Botha smiled; "It's just a job my dear Natasha, some days I love it some days I hate it but it pays the bills and gives me a life style my parents could never have dreamed of, so why do you do it?"

Natasha thought for a moment; "Because I had no choice, Botha, what's your real excuse?"

He looked at her; "Maybe I have no choice either."

They both stood and starred at each other both trying to keep alert but both deep in thought. Why **did** they really do it?

Botha was the first to break the eerie stand off looking as if he had experienced an epithany; "Why don't we just go our separate ways Natasha, call it two professionals making an arrangement, all I want is the St Peter's cross. Thanks to the wonderful listening devices of the CIA and MI5 I know you have traced it here… So, why don't you just walk away?"

Natasha was thinking about the proposition as they stared at each other. They both knew if they continued the fight one of them would have to die.

"I'd need safe passage for William and I."

Botha nodded;"Who are you working for, Natasha?"

"I thought you knew everything."

"No-one knows everything."

Natasha didn't allow herself to be side tracked; "Maybe I want a nice quiet life and was dragged into this accidently."

Botha laughed heartily; "You'll be telling me next that you have fallen in love and just want to settle down and have kids."

Something about his manner hurt her; "What's so wrong about being loved and being happy, it's something you know nothing about?"

Botha sensed a little chink; "The great Erin Svetlana, marrying and settling down with 2.4 kids, are you going soft?"

Natasha had to get off the psychological back foot; "Bet you've never been loved then Botha, bet your mother used to beat you up all the time"

The laugh turned to anger; "Leave my mother out of this."

Natasha had found a trigger; "Knew I was right, your mother never wanted you, never cared about you, never loved you."

The man covered his ears, something snapped as he lunged at the woman making slashing motions with his knife.

Natasha was more than prepared. She jumped high, like a startled cat from a standing position, managing to miss the lunges at the same time connecting a boot with the hard man's head.

He stumbled backwards furious, out of control, just the way she wanted him to be. The lithe athlete cart wheeled towards him but he recovered enough composure to jink out of her way and his fist came into contact with Natasha's stomach, knocking the wind out of her sails. She fell like a stone and stayed down holding her stomach whilst the big man came closer. Surely his punch had immobilised her, after all she was only a woman. Big mistake, Natasha was no ordinary woman. Suddenly she moved into a squat and flashed a perfectly timed leg and boot out catching him squarely in the groin. Rolling to one side then flipping to her feet she turned and exhaled loudly as she sent her clenched fist towards his neck. The man reacted too quickly for the blow to land correctly and grabbed a handful of her hair. He smashed her face down against a tree trunk but almost simultaneously she sent a stiff fingered jab into his penis and balls making him yelp and let go of her hair. Without thinking she automatically flipped backwards twice putting some distance between them.

His neck and his balls throbbed painfully, he was breathing heavily, there was no trace of a smile this time;

"What a shame we can't be friends Natasha."

Her face was focused on one thing only; "I'd rather shake hands with a scorpion."

In desperation Botha reached for his gun, playtime was over; at least he had given her a chance to play fair. Finally his anger had consumed his logic.

He was quick but she was quicker, much quicker. Before his hand even touched the handle the throwing knife had been released from her boot and was imbedded in his chest. He looked down in disbelief but still trying to pull the gun. Natasha was upon him in the whirl of a Catherine wheel, her kick hitting him squarely in the stomach sending him over the precipice adjacent to the Pilgrims footpath and into the river way below, how appropriate that it is called the river of heaven but how unlikely he'd end up there, she mused to herself.

She sat hurt, panting, bleeding, crying, trying to recover. Her will to live, to breath, to be a better person had shone through.

-72-

Caer Caradoc, Wales
3rd August 2009

In the sky over south Wales an Erickson Aircrane helicopter CH-54B, with two Pratt and Whitney JFTD-12-5A engines was lifting a BagerHitachi ZX250LCN-3 excavator with pulveriser attachment across the sky towards the mountain of Mynyyd y Gaer not far from the ruin of St Peters Church on Caer Caradoc. A further convoy of soldiers moved along the A473 to Llanharan with the idea of a rendezvous with the sky crane and its crew on the mountain ridge at Brynna. Valetti was typically impatient with the slow moving local traffic.

The advanced detachment of soldiers had cordoned off the area around the base of the mountain and its environs on the pretence that there had been earth movement and large sink holes that had emerged following heavy rain, well, at least that was partly true.

From their vantage point hidden in the rocks that overlooked the Pass of the Soldier, Rachel and Evans could see the soldiers all around the area some way off, what were they waiting for?

As Valetti's cavalcade arrived in the distance a small gaggle of curious locals were gathered around the entrance to the main track way that led across the mountain. It wouldn't be long before the media arrived but releases had been well prepared and rehearsed in advance. The spontaneous manifestations of large sink holes in this once heavily mined area was common enough and the furore would soon die down.

The aim was to land the heavy duty helicopters, use the machinery to gouge out the earth in the two sites that Rachel and Co had unwittingly led them to, scrape up anything of interest or importance and take it to a secret location for examination.

Evans looked at Rachel. They were on an exposed mountainside surrounded in the distance by soldiers. Had they been seen? If they had he was guessing they were not about to just let them walk away.

"I'm sorry Rachel we've been played like pieces in a bizarre chess game."

All she could do was bite her lip and nod as she tried to stop the tears welling up in her eyes.

Evans reached for his gun, just to make sure it was still there, if he had to go down he'd make sure it was in a blaze of glory.

Rachel stared at him; "Are you mad?"

Evans shrugged; "Years of work for Interpol, several with MI5. I am sick of other people using me and calling the tune. They don't give a shit if we live or die, we are just pawns in a game to them. Maybe it's time to make a stand for what is right, to have something to really believe in."

Rachel admired his spirit and felt maternal towards him, perhaps the feeling was a little more than that;

"Don't lose it now Bryn, you are a good man, why not just try to sit this one out and try to find some peace and happiness with a good woman."

The idea made him smile; "I can't think of a woman alive who'd want an old fart like me, can you?"

The loaded question hung in the air like a ripe apple.

-73-

Nevern, Wales
3rd August 2009

Natasha was feeling battered and bruised. It had been a close call, one she didn't wish to repeat. She should have felt pleased and proud to have killed the beast that mutilated her mother; after all, she had trained and lived for this moment. She knew she would flush him out by being involved in this case, leaving clues for him and his cronies to find. Sadly, all she felt was numb. Shouldn't revenge feel better than this?

The realisation that she too was only an assassin hadn't really sunk in before. Was she really no better than Botha? As if to reassure herself she had to look over the ridge. She could see the ogre's large frame face down in the water below surrounded by seeping red being taking on the flow to another place and time.

Is this what justice looked like, why couldn't he have suffered more for what he had done? Would something just like this be her untimely end as well?

There was no time to dwell on him or the past, there were things to do, important things. Where the hell had William gone and just how long did he need for a wee?

Luyt and his Russian task force had melted away into the Welsh hills like ghosts in the fog.

Natasha was sure they were near because she had laid GPS beacons for them. She had known for a while that the secret UK research lab was far under the Hills but it had taken some time to gather details of the old 19th century coal mine vent shaft system that should take them to the very heart of the facility undisturbed. She knew she was playing with fire and just hoped that Valetti and his men would be held at bay long enough for her to complete her task in the Preselis.

Luyt was in a copse with twelve men and lots of firepower less than half a mile away. Could he trust Natasha? He was paying her a fortune for her services. She was the best there was, no doubt of that, but, the two of them had issues from the past and that was always going to make him a little nervous. So far what she had said stacked up. There were indeed plenty of undercover guards in and around the main pit entrances towards Newport but not many people around on the barren windswept hillside where they found the vents she had located and prepared. There was no real way of knowing though if the walkers, people on horseback or four wheel mini off road quad bikes were part of the defence system. There always seemed to be plenty around.

Occasionally a micro light passed over.

-74-

Caer Caradoc, Wales
3rd August 2009

Rachel had an odd idea, convinced that Valetti and his men had not yet seen them amongst the outcrops on the mountain she was pulling and tugging at bracken and twigs from the hedgerow.

Evans couldn't help smiling as he observed Rachel covering herself as if she was building a nest and then disappearing into it. She caught him looking at her strangely;

"Any better ideas, Evans?"

He didn't like to dishearten her and tell her that they could easily be spotted by a heat seeking scanner. Oddly the invaders didn't seem to care about their presence.

Soon they were lying almost next to one another doing their finest impressions of scrubland amongst the rocky outcrops.

Evans couldn't help but see the funny side; "Never thought I'd be re-incarnated as a bush."

Rachel smiled nervously.

Two large helicopters passed so closely above that the downdraft threatened to de twig them. Evans adjusted his position so that he could observe with binoculars. The sky ships gently lowered the machinery into place next to the shield like mass of stones that appeared to be concealing a large cave. Another two metal birds came from the other direction and were hovering over the level ground next to St Peter's church with the intention of landing appropriate machinery there. The whirlwind scooped up any loose grass, weeds and rubbish and hurled it around much as the tornado had done on the day the dig ended all those years ago. The whole exercise came together with military precision. On the site which Morgan and Pender thought might contain the body of Arthur the excavator was already taking large hod fulls away from the front which may have been a concealed entrance. The cranes were depositing the spoil far enough away so that it did not destabilize the effort.

It only seemed a matter of minutes before someone shouted for the digger to stop. In the sunlight that played through the smoke of the panting diesel engines Evans could see something gleaming golden. He was relaying each movement via the binoculars to Rachel.

Suddenly Evans let out a loud gasp and Rachel moved over grabbing the field glasses and pushing Evans to one side. He grunted but she was transfixed. It was indeed a walled up cave but the diggers had revealed something extraordinary. The large heavy gates glistened like gold. This was car crash archeology at its worst. The speed at which the dig was occurring was criminal. CADW would have apoplexy had they seen this. Evans wrestled back the glasses just in time to see the machinery pull down the golden gates. Someone was filming every move they made; it was Sylvia Clarke, the head of CADW! Evans recognized her from a previous encounter, so even she was in on the act, was there anyone that wasn't?

Four men had arrived in a black four by four with blackened windows and two of them were being ushered by the other two into the cave. It was frustratingly difficult to see what was happening; Evans was transfixed, trying to get a better focus on the subject through the field glasses. No, it couldn't be, could it?

When the men were in the cave Evans lowered the binoculars and just stared into nothingness, his face as white as a sheet.

"Bryn, what's wrong?" Rachel shook him back to sense; "Bryn, what's wrong?"

Somehow he felt it impossible to accept what his eyes had seen; "It's Morgan and Pender, I, I've just seen them go into the cave."

Rachel looked at him; "Don't be daft, that's impossible."

She grabbed the glasses and waited patiently. The two "dead" men emerged. Lowering the field glasses all she could do was to shake her head in disbelief.

Not far from the grave cave site Evans and Rachel could see heavy machinery starting work on St Peter's church. They felt so helpless as the mechanical instruments moved into place and pulled and gnawed at what remained of the sacred site. The diggers looked like aliens rising and falling against the backdrop of the sky and hills. They were concentrating their annihilation of the earliest church in Europe at the near end where Everson had found the grave stones with "I and E" hidden under a tiled floor next to the altar at the "right hand of God" in 1990.

Back at the first site away from the church it seemed like an age before a tall wrapped figure was brought out and placed carefully on the grass. Four figures knelt over it and gently unwrapped the deerskin. Bit by bit the armoured figure was revealed, it shone like a beacon of pure gold across the mountain. On his face, as the ancient texts had described was a golden mask. Two of the men stood and raised up their handcuffed hands to the heavens, it was indeed Morgan and Pender.

Rachel engaged Evans; they looked strangely surreal dressed as bushes.

"You were right Bryn; it's definitely Morgan and Pender."

Bryn was seething; "Everyone from the PM, the church, through to MI5, the CIA and CADW seem to have been in on this from the start."

Rachel looked down; "Not forgetting your lot, someone at Interpol knows, are you sure you didn't know exactly what this was all about?"

Evans looked perplexed; "I thought I did Rachel, but obviously I don't, seems like Morgan and Pender may have been in on this all along, all I have done is create a bumbling diversion!"

They looked totally defeated with nowhere to go but one thing was clear, there were many more questions than answers. Right now they were completely dispensable.

Two other wrapped bodies were brought out in rapid succession and laid alongside the giant gold clad figure

Barrow after barrow of what appeared to be grave goods where being brought from the depths and piled together. Occasionally the glint from the sun on the goods confirmed that they were made of gold. This sort of find in the British Isles was unique but they both knew that the chance of them seeing the light of day was impossible.

Evans turned to Rachel; "So Morgan and Pender were right, this is Arthur's burial site and it is in a "city of gold."

Rachel nodded; "We came so close, now the church has won and the truth will never be told."

Evans winced; "It's ok for the church and the government to move in and rape sites like this but you try getting legitimate permission for a dig in Wales!"

Rachel recalled Roger's experience; "Do you think Felix was part of all this?"

Evans looked downbeat;"I don't know what to believe any more."

Rachel still looked puzzled; "Do you think that Morgan and Pender were in on this all along or that maybe they were kidnapped and held hostage? Why go to so much trouble to fake their deaths? Why kill Helen, Nicole, Roger and dear old father Everson, was it just for the sake of it or was it really as you said because they were double agents playing the field?"

There were genuine tears in the hard man's eyes. He looked at her as if to say, "I don't have any answers any more."

This time she believed him.

Over at St Peter's church the digger had made short work of dismantling the remaining walling around the right side of the altar and was excavating down. Three men lifted the heavy slabs with no writing and turned them over on the spoil heap. There indeed were the letters "I and E" that had caused father Everson so much angst. On closer inspection there was a drilled hole in one of the slabs at around about the place where a spear might penetrate a side. It was a very Templar thing to do.

Under the slabs, where Everson had found the pottery container with the Book of Life at the dig in 1990 there was sand. Everson had noticed at the time how odd this was given that sand didn't occur naturally on the mountain and that the nearest was on the beach some miles away.

The smaller digger moved in place of the larger one and started scooping out the heavy damp sand.

At the Arthur burial site there was now a large crate almost full with the artifacts and the bodies. The diggers were replacing the earth and the stones. The finds would be whisked away and probably never seen again.

Back at the ancient church ruins the sand had been scooped out of the area to the left of the altar. It was clear that there were stone steps leading down to a crypt. Valletti had made his way across from the adjacent Arthur burial site to be present for the final scoop, the body of JC and the St Peter's cross.

Valetti barged past the workers on the stairway to the crypt grabbing a jemmy from a soldier of the Royal Engineers. He was manically prising at the remains of the old metal door cursing in Italian as he went. Red faced he gave in and handed the tool back with a huff. It took something a bit stronger to budge the impasse but eventually it gave way and an accelerating torrent and putrid hiss of air ripped past their faces knocking them back with a salvo of unseen power as if something had escaped that was meant to be locked in forever.

-75-

Nevern, Wales
3rd August 2009

Listening very carefully Natasha thought she heard William's voice calling her in the far distance. Trying to triangulate she honed in on the hole down which he had slipped. He looked up pitifully as she looked down the fifteen feet or so to where he was illuminated by a shaft of sunlight. He was on his feet rubbing his head.

All William could think of saying was "sorry".

Natasha smiled; as heros go he was hopeless.

She pulled a longish piece of orange thin nylon rope from her backpack and secured one end around an old but firm looking tree stump tossing the other end down to William. He held on to it and looked confused;

"I'm never going to shimmy up that thing Nats"

In her heart she knew he was right.

"Can you see any other light chinks down there Will?"

The lost man gazed around, he could see a few faint shafts of daylight but he didn't know how far away they were or where the tunnel led.

Natasha pulled up the rope and lowered her torch down to William. He looked around carefully and curiously. As his eyes got used to the torch light he could see that the walls looked as if they had been hewn out of the rock. On the ground to the front and behind where he had fallen were flag stones and marks along the walls;

"I think it's a tunnel Nats."

She had thought it might be. She slid down the rope like a monkey and half tripped into William's arms.

In the light he could see her bruised face and bleeding neck.

"Hey, what the hell happened to you, are you ok?"

Typically Natasha brushed the whole episode to one side and laughed; "Wrong time of the month!"

William looked steadily at her demanding to know. Uncharacteristically she broke down in tears, throwing herself at him.

She sobbed and sobbed in his arms for what seemed like an eternity.

"Oh William, how can you ever forgive me?"

She was inconsolable in the half light, just as if all the sins of the world had landed on her shoulder.

After a while the sobbing died down a little and William held her face gently in the shaft of sunlight streaming in from the sky above the tunnel they found themselves in. She still looked pretty but it was as if she had aged two thousand years. He fished a vaguely used tissue from his pocket and dabbed it carefully across her face and neck;

"What really happened up there Nats?"

She knew that years of hatred and anger had left her as she stood in the light in William's arms. It was the nearest thing she had ever had to a religious experience.

It was time to unburden her soul and slowly she explained how she had been forced to be an assassin for money and how she had first seen Botha and how little remourse she felt for killing him.

William didn't seem surprised or judgmental.

"Can you ever forgive me Will?"

William looked deeply into her wet and reddening eyes; "Oh Nats, my dearest soul, don't you know that all around you is forgiveness and light, it is in the nature of the universe to forgive you and not for me to ... by showing this compassion and heartfelt regret for your actions your soul is free."

Natasha stuttered for a moment; "You, you don't think I am a bad person then?"

William smiled; "I don't think I'd ever find a more loving, kinder person than you if I searched the world over".

"Why are you so wise Will?"

He laughed; "Why I am so soft" he replied.

They both smiled but deep down happiness would take longer. A raw nerve had been uncovered and that would take time to heal in this lifetime or the next.

Deep under the Preseli hills

Learning from the problems that had arisen with the recent terrorist attack on the Hadron Collider, which had closed down the experiment, delaying it indefinitely, the hush hush research establishment deep under the Preseli hills had been locked down temporarily. In one sense it was too late, Natasha had already been into the main frame computer and the two back up servers. So far her plan was working.

It didn't take Luyt and his men long to locate the disguised breather vent that surfaced at the top of the old stone lined moat of the Castle of the

Empress, less than a quarter of a mile as the crow flies from where William and Natasha were finding their way along an ancient tunnel.

William was puzzled; "This is all a bit clean and well maintained for an ancient tunnel Nats."

His female companion was listening carefully into a very sensitive device which behaved a bit like a bat to seek out fissures, hollows and tunnels.

"Well observed Will, I'm sure this was originally a tunnel connecting the cave with the cross carved on it to the castle. The Templar knights that lived and worked here would have regularly used it to check on the cave contents and make sure they were safe…"

Will was no clearer; "OK, so, if something valuable is hidden down here shouldn't it be in the direction of the walled up cave and not the castle?"

Natasha didn't really want to be that forthcoming. She rested for a moment taking off her back pack and leaning it against the tunnel wall. To Will's utter amazement she started fishing out strange looking grenades and fixing them to her belt. In the torch light he counted ten. Following that she took three compact stubby looking guns and magazines and placed them on the ground.

She loaded the magazines with breathtaking efficiency. She took a moment to look at Will; "They are the latest Uzzi models."

William raised his hands; "OK, OK spare me the technical details…just tell me what the hell is happening?"

-76-

St Peters, Caer Caradoc
3rd August 2009

The odd stench that had come fizzing out of the sealed crypt died away on the wind. Using a strong searchlight Valetti made his way gingerly into the room that had been sealed for centuries. It was still in remarkably good condition. The thick cobwebs and dust from the disturbance played in the beam like mist across a lake.

Morgan followed him into the room his eyes searching with Valetti's torch light;

"You better be right about all this Morgan".

The historian rubbed his wrists, they still hurt from the binds Valetti and his henchmen had applied when they had stormed their house and taken them after Rachel had left them in Newcastle;

"I'm right, give me the torch"

Morgan was looking slowly and methodically around the chamber. There was no natural light whatsoever. To one side there was an archway over a tomb. Laid on the top was a skeleton in stone with a shield on its chest and a sword in its hand. The colours had faded but at one time it had been red with silver chevrons, the mark of Arthur's family. The short inscription revealed to Morgan that this was the last resting place of Arthur's father Meurig. He sighed as if acknowledging what had happened and how close their deductions were to the truth. In the middle was a double tomb, very much like the one in Pousin's painting The Shepherds' of Arcadia. The walls had been plastered and painted but there was not much left to see. Green mold and flaking plaster had made sure of that. On the side of the tomb Morgan could just make out the remains of what looked like the very same artwork that William had seen in the church wall on Caldey Island.

Three beefy looking men with torches came into the room and Valetti motioned to them to move the lid of the double tomb and gazed steadily at Morgan;

"Are you sure the body of Jesus is here?"

Morgan nodded, "As sure as I am about anything"

Inside Morgan was hoping upon hope that the clues to what really laid beneath the stone floor would remain hidden… if this treatment was what co-operating with the authorities was like he wanted no part of it.

Another two men were called, the tomb was not about to give up its secrets that easily.

-77-

Nevern, West Wales
3rd August 2009

Thanks to Natasha's computer hacking skills running false bypasses the alarm didn't go off as Luyt's men removed the one way valve cover from the breather vent. Soon the long rope they had brought was secured at one end and lowered down. Luyt and 12 heavily armed men followed until they stood in the metallic shaft. Nearby a seconded helicopter was waiting to help them escape.

In the ancient tunnel Natasha was moving ahead slowly and carefully. With almost every step she stopped to listen for ultra-sound feedback.

William was following cautiously with one of the Uzzis on a strap around his neck.

"Tell me again Nats, what the hell I am supposed to do with this?"

The special agent stopped and tutted; "Simples, look, this is called a safety catch, you flip it up then you aim and fire. The harder you hit the trigger the faster the bullets fly out…it's got a kick so aim low to score high."

William was not at all happy with the situation; this was not him at all; "Ok, but don't expect me to kill anyone".

Natasha nodded; "Ok Will, whatever, just look mean".

-78-

St Peter's church crypt,
Caer Caradoc, South Wales
3rd August 2009

Five muscle men were now trying to shift the heavy slab from the top of the double tomb.

Overhead they heard the sound of the helicopter from the King Arthur burial site lifting the precious finds and taking off to a secret destination. After a few moments it all seemed eerily quiet way down in the cold stone room.

Suddenly there was a crack as the seal gave way and bit by bit the top moved to one side then toppled, fell and smashed on the flagstone floor.

Valetti pushed his way in to be the first to see, the tomb was empty.

Morgan peered over the top following the scan of Valetti's torch beam.

Without warning Valetti screamed and punched Morgan who crumpled up and fell to the floor where the irate man continued to kick and punch him. Falling to his knees he grabbed Morgan's shoulders and shook him;

"The body of Jesus, you promised me Jesus, you promised me the real St Peter's cross, you bastard, you bastard, where is it, and where is Edward's treasure?"

Morgan was putting his hands up to stop the blows raining down on him and mumbling trying to respond but Valetti wasn't listening. One of the soldiers tried to step in and stop the onslaught but was hit across the face with the heavy duty torch. Alerted by the commotion the burly commanding officer bounced down the steps and flung himself into the room. In an instant he was holding Valetti's arm restraining his outburst and staring into his eyes:

"I'm in charge here Valetti and my brief is to return Morgan and Pender to MI5 unharmed, do you hear me?"

The unexpected physical intervention and the verbal warning was enough to bring Valetti back to the time and place."

No-one had talked to him like that and got away with it, but he knew he had to bide his time.

Morgan looked grateful as he managed to speak; "It must be the cave at

Nevern, the cave of the cross. Jesus must be buried there, yes, of course, a double bluff, that would be a perfect way to keep the secret and if Everson had the original St Peter's cross I bet he has hidden it near there as well."

On the one hand Morgan seemed pleased and yet on the other he was kicking himself for not working the whole truth out before.

-79-

Nevern, West Wales
3rd August 2009

Luyt and his men were following the plan of the underground vent system that Natasha had given them. In the security nerve centre of the research establishment the unit commander for the SAS was following their progress with the tracking device that Luyt had unwittingly downloaded when Natasha had sent the plans to him. How was he to know that she had invented an untraceable stealth virus, a variant of Zeus, which would load on a mobile computer and act as a GPS signal for the SAS.

Natasha felt bad about luring Luyt and his men into the trap, after all he had transferred two million pounds to her Swiss bank account in payment for the information to locate and seize the St Peter's cross and for details of the Meurig project. She made a pact with herself to give the money away to charity if she survived the ordeal, maybe she would keep just a little back to live on. After the things he had done to her in the past it seemed like justice.

-80-

St Peter's Caer Caradoc,
3rd August 2009

The Royal Engineers laid explosives at both the Arthur Grave and St Peter's church sites. There could be no trace left of what may or may not have been there and what may or may not have occurred.

Morgan and Pender's wrists were rebound as they were bundled back into the black Range Rover 4 x 4. As they left they saw the other helicopter lift off and disappear in the blue sky interspersed with fluffy white clouds.

The explosions were simultaneous. Now there was nothing left on the mountain to suggest that King Arthur had ever lived at all.

-81-

Nevern, West Wales
3rd August 2009

It was all going so well. Luyt and his men followed the ventilation shaft plan closely until they became aware of a light at the end of the metal tunnel just as Natasha had predicted. One operative scouted forward and reported that the vent grating was above a corridor. Luyt and two of his men worked on the grill with portable oxy acetylene lamps and soon it came off. One by one the men dropped into the corridor below and pulled their chemical breather mask apparatus in place. When the last man hit the floor they started off slowly eastwards.

Natasha looked at her clock. If all had gone to plan Luyt and his men were in for quite a shock.

The raiding party progressed through two metal lined corridors and into what looked like a main entrance chamber. The heavily armed group removed explosives from their kit bags and set about laying charges to break in to the main research area. Behind the last man a tough metal sliding door sprang across the corridor sealing off a retreat from the direction they had come. In front of them a grill fell protecting the entrance. It was the perfect trap.

Blue and yellow smoke puffed out from nozzles along the ceiling and the men grabbed at their throats.

Luyt tried to cover his nose and mouth over the top of his mask but there was no defence against the deadly fumes. His last thought as he stumbled forward onto a pile of dying men was to curse Natasha for double crossing him, she had, after all deliberately provided anti chemical masks that were useless.

On the other side of the complex Natasha and William were creeping slowly down the tunnel they had found themselves in. This was a very different way in to that which Natasha had originally planned; at least she hoped it was a way in.

William suddenly stopped; "This is ridiculous Nats, what the hell are we doing?"

The girl stopped for a moment and looked in the half light at Will; "Ok, you want to know the truth? Here's the score, this is an allegory of your future. Your real physical body is in hospital suffering from a brain tumor. You are having a major operation right now and you may or may not pull through. We are living as projected characters of a game in your mind trying to locate the real St Peter's cross in order to put it back where it really belongs and ensure that in early 2016 ish when the God code dna rays from Cygnus and the massive solar flares combine they can earth and be transmitted around the world on the ley lines to ensure a new era of enlightenment and not armageddon. You have slipped out of time and out of reality so what seems jointed and normal to you would seem disjointed and unnatural to others. I am a scientist who has been able to project into your mind by hypnosis to try to help you survive but like all the other characters I only exist whilst you think of me or them. I am trying to rescue and help you because you have been identified as special by the spirit world of the future."

William shrugged his shoulders; "Christ Nats, I may be nuts but come on!"

Natasha smiled; "Well you did ask!"

William didn't know how to take her; "Sometimes I just don't get your sense of humour!" She smiled.

Suddenly Natasha heard a large explosion at the opposite end of the tunnel to which they were heading. She instinctively knew what had happened;

"Valetti!, I bet they haven't found the real metal cross at St Peters and have worked out the 6th century and medieval double bluffs which confirm that JC must be in the Cave of the Cross, just like I did. William looked thoughtful;

"You knew all along?"

Natasha smiled; "The Cave of the Cross is a bit of a giveaway, it's the perfect double bluff."

William was not so sure; "Yes but it has always been thought to be a hermit's cave not a receptacle for valuable goodies, only Morgan and Pender had worked that out"

There was a silence as if Natasha had just realized what he had said; "Christ, what if Morgan and Pender are still alive and have been forced to help Valetti and that's the only way he could know, I mean, if Morgan told him."

William was getting lost; "But you knew, err didn't you? And all this ear wigging or eavesdropping or whatever you call it that odd people have been doing to us, surely they'd work out what was going on as easily as we have!?"

Natasha nodded; "Oh yes but that is because we worked it out from Morgan and Pender's research."

William was not following; Duh, if you worked it out then why couldn't Valetti?"

Natasha was trying to weigh things up in her mind; "Because that is not the way it was supposed to happen."

Above them they heard a helicopter. They were not to know but it was the air ship bringing the crate of finds from King Arthur's burial site to be examined and kept at the secure facility a mile below the surface at Nevern.

Natasha checked her bat antenna listening device;

"Look Will, you head towards the explosion and I'll catch you up, just keep out of sight...there is just something I have to do and it is not fair for you to risk your life doing it".

Initially William's look said "in your dreams" but one look at the serious expression on Natasha's face said it all, he didn't argue. He watched her move cautiously away from him and reluctantly he headed back towards the Cave of the Cross.

At the cliff face Valetti and a handful of men had blown open the outer wall of the sealed cave and were planting explosives against the second.

Natasha meanwhile was moving swiftly through the tunnel without William, clearly there was something on her mind. She entered the uniquely generated pass code into her ultra sound receptor and part of the brick wall slid to one side revealing a black metal door. She pressed her body against it and it scanned everything from her brain to her toes. The door opened with a hiss and let her in to a holding chamber. A few seconds passed and a second door gave way. There waiting for her was Grey from MI5.

"Youv'e done a great job Natasha, Luyt, his men and a huge terrorist threat has been neutralized. Someone has rubbed out our security leak, the Late Home Secretary. I don't suppose you know anything about that? And the body of King Arthur has been found where Morgan and Pender believed it was and is on its way here for examination and storage. Soon we will have the St Peter's cross which apparently was right under our noses and all will be well."

Natasha smiled; "All very convenient, why didn't you tell me that Morgan and Pender hadn't been killed in the smart incendiary bomb at Newcastle?"

Grey looked stern, the flyer she took was correct.

"Because you didn't need to know. You may have been hired by MI6 but you don't have a right to know everything"

Natasha persisted; "And Valetti, why are you working alongside him and the CIA and why did you hire Botha and have Helen and the others killed?"

Grey was losing patience.

"I don't have to answer to you Natasha or whatever your real name is; you have fulfilled your roll now, you can go out to grass."

Natasha had worked out exactly what Grey was up to;

"So how come you didn't mention that Valetti and his men have just blasted the front off the Cave of the Cross and are planning to plunder it. So much priceless treasure including the Templar hoard, King Edward's stash and the Crucifixion cross encased in gold, silver and jewels!... a little bit more than 30 pieces of silver isn't it?"

Grey was not pleased; "I don't know what you are talking about."

Natasha was livid; "Yes, yes you do. How ironic that Father Everson knew of a secret way into the cave, a way known only to the descendents of some of the top Templar Knights and thought it was the safest place to hide the real St Peter's Cross. You must have a nice cosy arrangement with Valetti. Using the work of Morgan and Pender was a great elaborate scheme to make it appear that someone just blew up the cave and stole all the goodies including the St Peter's cross which was under your nose all along. That must make you feel very stupid. When did you find out it was here?"

Grey looked triumphant; "For some time, Everson and I knew each other very well, he was my brother."

Even Natasha had to swallow hard; "You know Valetti and Botha killed him"

Grey was matter of fact; "Collateral damage I think they call it."

Natasha couldn't believe how cold she was; "So how much will you pocket for all this, Judas, two million pounds, four million, seven million?"

Grey scowled; "I think you know a little too much, you have done your job, you have been paid. You know I cannot just let you go now."

Natasha was in no mood to play games; "What will you do, have me killed like you did Helen Daniels and the others?

Grey smiled; "No need, I think your friend Mr Botha is looking for you, he is hoping you will both be good friends."

Natasha spat on the floor; "I've already met him, he did this to me, but you should see him, what's left of him."

The very worst of Natasha had surfaced.

Grey had her arms crossed against her chest, Natasha was vaguely aware that her rather larger than normal watch was pointing in her direction. The shot seemed to come from no-where. It hit Natasha just above the heart.The impact threw her backwards. Her Kevla vest took the strain and, as she flew backwards she let fly from two Uzzis. Grey hit the floor quickly, landing in a contorted mess. One of the real traitors had been found and dealt with, her creator would be very pleased indeed. But, how would she explain that to the guards, she couldn't.

The shockwaves from the shots set off the alarm. She dragged Grey's body across close enough to scan her fingerprint and swipe her ID card. Mercifully the doors opened and she made a bolt for the tunnel before the guards had a chance to follow. Stopping momentarily she set sleeping gas grenades on a short timer and ran.

William was at the other end of the tunnel near to the cave of the crucifixion cross trying carefully to pick his way through the half light using a fading torch, whatever happened to long life batteries he mused as he felt something sharp dig into his back and a hand whip the gun from his grip;

"William Marshall I presume, how nice of you to come to the party."

The smell of the foul breath from Valetti's brown and white teeth permeated William's soul. He felt he had been captured by the devil himself, maybe he wasn't far wrong.

William was led at gunpoint into the cave. The dust had been stirred up by the explosives and his men were placing light bulbs all around and firing up a generator.

"You have been very clever Mr Marshall but you don't fool me. I know that you and Natasha want the St Peter's cross and the body of JC to sell to the highest bidder, why do I know? Because I want that as well... shame you have failed".

William was surprisingly calm. He cleared his throat;

"That's not why I want the cross Valetti, I want to replace it from whence the sacred metal used to make it originally came so that when the next massive wave of energy is expelled from Cygnus at the date foretold there will be an enlightenment and not a destruction of mankind."

Valetti laughed; "What a load of bollocks,I didn't have you down for a superstitious idiot; the metal this cross is made from is priceless in the hands of those who wish to make the weapons it is so suited for..."

William tried to appeal to the man's better nature but he had none; "But if everything is in place as the creator planned then the energy from Cygnus will combine with the earth energies to create a world of peace, harmony and compassion, it will herald a new world where all can be free and happy."

Valetti scowled; "Who on earth would want that?"

William was overcome by a great sadness. He could feel tears running down his cheeks; "You mustn't cry for your friend Natasha William, she'll be dead by now."

William looked him straight in the eyes; "I am not, I weep for you."

Valetti struck William across the face and he fell to the ground.

Natasha was listening from a niche in the tunnel. She knew from the acoustics and the transmission from William's minute camera built seamlessly and invisibly into his glasses that there were five people and Valetti in the room. She assumed their weapons were cocked and ready. Taking two small canisters from the rear of her belt she set up a frequency that slowed reactions just a little whilst wearing ear defender plugs herself. She released the canisters into the cave, and primed both guns she was touting, one in each hand. Screaming at the top of her voice to add further disorientation she athletically cart wheeled into the chamber. In the commotion William cowered near the wall making himself as small as possible. Natasha squeezed the triggers hard showering the whole area with a hail of bullets. He had never seen anything like it before in his life. She managed to take out most of the men before they could return fire. Disastrously though, Valetti, seemed unmoved by the sonic blast and had time to aim and shoot and that was deadly.

Natasha staggered backwards from the force. Two bullets from the automatic weapon had hit her Kevla vest knocking her off her feet and slamming her against the wall. Much more vital were the two holes through her legs and the deep ravine of red that appeared across the top of her head splitting the flesh at the roots of her blonde hair. As she dropped to the floor she managed to squeeze her triggers and let rip another salvo of bullets. All the pent up anger and hate of centuries were released in that moment. At close range the lead had blown great chunks out of Valetti and even from across the room his blood splattered across her face as they both sunk to the floor. Her legs twitched involuntarily as if still trying to move and fight, the first reaction of a professional right to the end. The pool of her blood grew like the sea covering the land. Her head laid down almost in a kind of slow motion. The sonic bomb she had thrown into the cave suddenly stopped screeching.

For a while William heard it still ringing in his ears. Then there was an eerie silence. He looked down at his white shirt and blue jeans, around him there was the arid smell of cordite and blood. Dust moved in disturbed swells like mini tornados illuminated by the cascade of temporary generator powered lights that clung to the cave walls like spiders to a web.

Valetti lay dead in one corner, the look of the devil upon him defying the power of goodness to the very end. His five henchmen were horribly splayed across the cave leaving the stench of guts hanging in the air like an abattoir.

Miraculously there was not a mark on him. For a moment he thought that he must be dead, he felt numb, his ears still intermittently ringing from the sonic waves and the savage and constant burst of machine gun fire. Somewhere in the distance he thought he heard his name being called.

It suddenly sunk in, Natasha, the woman he thought was so strong and invincible lay injured, dying. He rushed over to her damaged body, only now he realised that she was the most important thing in his world and now, too late what she really meant to him…… All that time grieving for his ex wife had left him blind to the happiness he could have recaptured. He put his face next to her pale cold skin, she was breathing, just. He steadied her head on his arm and held her; "Natasha, Nats, come on, come on, don't leave me Nats, I love you."

At last, he had said it, the words he had wanted to say for months and had never been able to, now in these last moments of her life he had managed to say them and she hadn't even heard him.

Her bare legs were still twitching and blood seeped from them as he rocked her in his arms. He ripped off his shirt and tied it tightly around her head trying to stem the flow of blood. He removed his socks and belt making tourniquets for her legs. He found himself sobbing and muttering to himself; "Oh God, why have you forsaken me, why me, why this, why do this to her…she was a good woman, an angel, one of your own." William pulled out his spare mobile, there was no signal. There hadn't been all day. He knew that Nats life was draining out of her in front of his eyes in that remote cave, the cave of the cross, and there was nothing he could do.

He sobbed and sobbed but suddenly stopped when Natasha's head rolled towards him, for a moment her big brown eyes shone out to his, he thought he detected a faint smile...she was trying to speak...she whispered something he couldn't quite hear.

He moved his ear closer to her mouth and held her clammy hand, she managed to squeeze it as she painfully spoke...

"I did hear you William, I did hear you...I love you too... Take me with you God man, don't leave me here."

Her head rolled back, the grip of her hand relaxed. It took William a few moments to realise she'd stopped breathing...what on earth did she mean; "take me with you God man?"

He kneeled, just holding her for what seemed like an eternity in the warmth of her blood that was quickly congealing and growing cold...

He cried out loud for no-one to hear.

"It can't end like this, please don't let it end like this."

There was a glint of light in his eyes. Something very bright was shining forcing his gaze upwards.

It was a bright golden colour, the colour of the sun.

William rubbed his eyes covering his face with blood but the glint was still there.

He stood up and moved across to a hole that had been made by the hail of Natasha's bullets...it was only a small hole in the rock face but as he touched the sides he realised that it was a false wall. The stones had been laid one on top of the other then covered in some sort of cement and dirt to conceal a chamber behind.

Almost in frenzy William scrabbled at the hole making it wider and wider....At first he saw a body covered with a white sheet lying on a stone plinth. It seemed to glow with an unearthly light. As he looked closer he realised two things, that the chest was moving very slowly up and down and secondly that the body was his!. The vision was unsettling and disturbing, he rubbed his eyes but it was still there. How could he be looking at his own body in a cave that had been sealed for centuries? Shaking slightly he looked around. He could see what was glinting. It was a gold and silver case about six feet long. He reached and pulled it towards him. It was heavy but with some effort it spilled out onto the floor. Gingerly he rubbed his hands along removing the centuries of dust. Part of the crucifixion cross, it had to be. Bit by bit he ran his fingers along the front of the case trying to find a clasp. Slowly the top lifted to reveal an ancient looking wooden cross member made of dark crumbling wood. William felt a buzz like an electric shock. He thought he heard a female voice calling his name. Sandra, no, no it couldn't possibly be Sandra?

William peered further into the hiding place, his eyes getting used to what little light there was. It was stacked with glinting gold, silver and bronze objects speckled with sparkling jewels of differing colours. This must be it, he thought, this must be the place of the treasure.

Something caught his eye more than anything else. Two discs on chains seemed to be glowing. They were very much like the design of the Brynna disc and the ones Rachel had described as being in the painting on the walls of the Mynde in Caerleon. One was a deep reddy gold colour and the other bronze and silver. He placed the red one around his neck and felt a warm glow.

Natasha's body twitched and he moved quickly to her side cradling her in his arms. Almost instinctively he placed the bronze and silver disc around her neck as he swayed backwards and forwards. He took some of the crumbling wood from the cross and placed it on her wounds.

"Of course I'm taking you with me Nats."

He looked around frantically, the St Peter's Cross, it was no-where to be seen. Again he looked across to the breathing body that looked like him. He was drawn to it as if it was a magnet, floating headlong towards it. He couldn't stop. Somehow he and the body that looked like him were becoming one.

Something very odd was happening before his eyes. The whole scene seemed to be dissolving around him and swirling like a whirlwind. There was a rumbling as if time itself was moving and changing. The walls and floor started to rock and crumble. William hid his eyes, unable to move. He gazed across at Natasha she was dead still. Suddenly the cave walls started crumbling and boulders came crashing down.He heard a great sound like the exhalation of air and felt a massive force on the top of his head as if he was being sucked powerfully through a long white tunnel...

-82-

London, 7th July 2005

...down and down through the tunnel, further, deeper, then, all he could see was the most brilliant white light. It was blinding, biblical and life changing.

Slowly oh so slowly a face was manifesting before his eyes, it was Sandra's!

He blinked and blinked, it hurt to keep his eyes open for long at a time... yes, it really was Sandra;

"William, oh William, I thought I had lost you."

Sandra turned and shouted down the hospital ward;

"Nurse, nurse, he's opened his eyes."

William tentatively held out his hand, expecting a ghost, but Sandra's warm flesh was real enough.

"Sandra? Sandra, it's impossible, you're dead."

Sandra smiled at nurse Herbert as she came to the bed side and spoke; "Nothing is impossible, you know that William."

He felt odd, displaced, between worlds. The nurse's smile was angelic; "Welcome back to the land of the living William, I have been with you all the time, just as I promised you as a young boy."

William was entirely discombobulated. His mind shot back to the times when as a lad he had heard his name called and had looked out of the window to see the girl in the black robes... yes, yes it was sister Herbert... the red head, Maria Magdalena, the swan they were all her. His head was throbbing but his numb limbs started to tingle and then ache before slowly wiggling. His life force was returning.

"Sandra? Sandra, is that really you?"

Sandra leaned over him and kissed him on the cheek; "It's OK love, everything is OK, you are safe now. They let you wear the talisman I brought you from Michael."

Sister Herbert moved to William's side, looked at the talisman that he had put around his neck in the cave and smiled. She removed a canular from his arm before whispering in his ear; "Now you know who you really are William. Thank you for setting the truth free, for helping to save humanity, this is your time to rest, your job is not yet finished, but for now, this is your reward, your second coming, make the future count, I'll be waiting for you."

The nurse's smiling eyes and ambience were truly beautiful and peaceful. He looked around the ward. For a moment it looked oddly like the one in Canterbury.

"What's happening? Where, where am I?"

Sandra moved her hand over his brow to soothe him; most of his hair had been shaved for the operation on his brain.

"We're in London, near Tavistock Square William, it's a special unit, you remember? You had an operation, it's been touch and go for a week or so, but the doc says you are going to be OK". Sandra paused for a moment. She heard a bit of a commotion in the entrance far away. An attractive blonde haired girl with a slight Russian accent was trying to get on to the ward;

"How many times do I have to tell you, I must see William urgently, he has to return the cross to its true place!!?"

The nurse gave her an odd look but made the mistake of trying to ignore her.

Sandra was gently stroking the back of William's hand;

"Your mum and your sister Rachel send their love; they are looking forward to seeing you again..."

William was still dazed, his mum still alive? Rachel; his sister; Michael?

Sandra saw the bemused look on his face. She put her arm gently around his shoulder;

"There's great news Will. The Welsh Tourist Board love the game you developed for them, you know, the one where the gun slinging female Russian agent has to find the artefacts, the body of Jesus and King Arthur... in order to save mankind."

William was struggling to recall anything at all. Sandra continued; "I was so frightened I was going to lose you William... everything is going to be ok now."

He just managed a faint smile as she continued; "I brought the book in you were reading, just in case you feel like it".

Sandra put the copy of Artorius Rex by Wilson and Blacket on the bedside table.

"I have to get off to work luvvy but I'll be back later, I'm so happy you made it, we have so much to catch up on".

She kissed William on the mouth and turned to leave.

William managed to stretch out a hand that meant, "come back!"

Feebly he held on to the disc talisman on his neck and looked at it closely. It was exactly like the Brynna disc. The one he'd found in the cave. Yes, that's right, the cave, Natasha, he hadn't saved Natasha.

Sandra read his troubled brow. She turned around and sat down by his side holding his hand again, work would have to wait for once.

In the distance Natasha had forced her way on to the ward by grabbing the nurse's neck nerve and putting her quietly and temporarily to sleep. Unseen by William she was strutting towards his wing, the disc on her neck bouncing from side to side.

William was truly confused, had he really been unconscious for days, weeks? He just didn't understand.

He looked in Sandra's eyes: "What is the date?"

"7th July 2005."

"And the time?"

"9.43am."

Will was shaking, he was recalling from his dream the terrorist attack in which Sandra had died.

He held Sandra's hand so tightly that she felt a little uncomfortable, then it happened, the huge bomb blast in Tavistock Square.

There were tears in William's eyes; "It's the bus you should have been on which Terrorists have blown up."

The rumble passed, Sandra's eyes were glazed; "Terrorists?... don't be silly!"

He pressed his emergency button and a young nurse came to see him; "Where is Sister Herbert?"

The nurse looked at him oddly; "Sister Herbert? There is a no sister Herbert here luv."

Natasha had hidden behind screens a few beds along waiting for Sandra to go; she had to tell William what was really going on. The St Peter's cross and the body of JC, they hadn't taken them back to where they belonged, but that was only the start.

The game was not over.

-83-

Caldey Isand,
12th August 2009

From a comfortable manger on Caldey Island a gentle monk picked up a crying baby. In a secret compartment at the base of the cot, the St Peter's cross that Father Everson promised to keep safe for Morgan and Pender glowed lovingly, protecting the infant foretold by Illtyd so many centuries ago.

Looking out to sea across the bay he offered up a prayer for his son William and the two researchers. He knew they would never tell anyone the truth about their findings. He feared the worse but he hoped upon hope that their wisdom and foresight would be suitably rewarded in this life or the next.

Lightning Source UK Ltd.
Milton Keynes UK
UKOW05f0804280814

237657UK00001B/1/P